Buried in the Sand

Celia Raynor

Copyright © 2025 by Celia Raynor

All rights reserved.

No portion of this book may be reproduced in any form without written permission from the publisher or author, except as permitted by U.S. copyright law.

contents

CHAPTER 1

"He's dead," I declared with a huff when the last pack entered the clearing.

I could practically hear my mother roll her eyes next to me as she flicked me behind the ear, "Be quiet Tate."

I grumbled under my breath as I watched all the unmated wolves run into the arms of their newly discovered mates.

Honestly, my mate was as good as dead.

As everyone gathered around in their own little groups, my mother finally turned to me with a sad smile.

"He's not dead... he's just not here yet," She suggested as she shrugged.

"Mom, I love you, but you and I both know you're wrong."

Today's our annual Mate Meet-Up. Wolves usually meet their mates at sixteen and most of the time their mate is in the same pack. The others usually find their mates in neighbouring packs. Therefore, the Alphas of the four closest pack to our territory all meet up with their unmated wolves so they'll be able to find their match.

Most of the time, everyone who had yet to find their mate does. However, there were a few that didn't.

I, of course, landed in that niche as I have not found my mate yet. This leads me to believe that my non-existent mate is either dead, a rogue wolf, or simply does not exist.

I'm going with the first since I was a few weeks shy of being eighteen and Mr. Mate still had not shown up.

"Listen to me," My mom grabbed my shoulder and looked me in the eye, "mates are nice...sure. But you're Tate Blackwood, Alpha's daughter, and warrior extraordinaire. To be honest, I don't know any wolf that'll be able to balance you out."

"So cheesy," I said as I wiggled my nose, but she just flicked my ear again.

My mom, Anne, could always make me smile, no matter what.

"Let me rephrase," I smiled as her eyes narrowed on me. "Very wise words mom. Thank you for being my Yoda."

That made her laugh because she loathed Star Wars. Giving me a warm embrace, she made me feel a lot better.

Mom's hugs were the best. I don't know what I'd do without them.

"How about you go mingle with your friends while I go help Emery with Luna duties," She suggested, and I nodded as she walked away.

As I stood looking around the clearing, I watched as my friends and fellow pack members all fawned over their mates and received an equal amount of affection in return.

It's not that I necessarily wanted a mate...I just wanted to know what it felt like. That bond. The connection. The deep emotional connections formed by some magical powers that were bigger than us all.

I was curious about it because it wasn't something I could feel or touch. The only way I could see these strings connecting two souls was through the people around me. My parents and my brother with his mate. Watching them was like watching the most beautiful and most amazing love story unfold before your eyes.

My parents were as much as in love as they were when I was a child. I'd always assumed that because your mate is your one true love, that you'd instantly fall in love. The superficial notion that one would feel that much passion within a second of meeting someone always made me loath the concept.

But that all changed when I witnessed my brother and his mate, Emery. Their story of falling in love was something else entirely. They certainly weren't 'love at first sight' with Emery hating Thane's guts and Thane refusing to tell her his secrets.

They fought for it though. Their love was built by them but strengthened by the mate bond.

That was what I wanted.

Not a superficial fairy-tale but a roaring fire of passion.

To be in love instead of loved.

To experience the thing that was as invisible as air but as necessary as oxygen.

Just as I started marching out of the clearing, as I'm not needed there anymore, Bailey, the Beta's mate, stopped me in my tracks.

"Hey, where are you headed off to?" She questioned.

"To pack on a few pounds in whatever dessert's brewing in the kitchen," I grinned, and she shook her head knowing that was a given.

"Fine, but while you're there make sure and help out the pack in preparing the guest rooms for the other packs."

I saluted her and started to trail off again before she grabbed my hand, "And Tate, don't wander off alone."

Before I could ask, she switched over to her mind link since we were in a field of werewolves, most of who weren't our pack members.

'The Alpha of the Oaks Pack hasn't shown up yet, but his Beta said he's expected to arrive soon, so be careful.'

'Right Alpha Dickhead,' I said in apprehension and she smirked because she created the nickname.

Alpha Dickhead, more formally known as Alpha Aiden Oaks was the ruthless, callous, dangerous, and mate-less Alpha. The one who just so happened to be on a hunt for a Luna.

He usually skips these meetings and sends his Beta, Rick, in his place but this year, the infamous Alpha of the Oaks pack has decided to join in the festivities.

The reason being, he was finally in search of a mate to strengthen his pack.

An Alpha wasn't an Alpha without a Luna to lead by his side. Two figures leading the pack always made them stronger. But with Alpha Aiden being the arrogant narcissist everyone proclaims him to be, I see why wanting a Luna is of use to him.

Not because he wants one, but because it will just give him more power. But he hasn't found his true mate yet at the age of twenty-one.

I mean, sure the Alpha can mate with any other wolf if he doesn't find his mate, but the pack would only be strengthened if the Luna was a true born Luna. This meant that she or he had to be an unmarked mate of an Alpha or an Alpha born male or female. That's the only way he'll be able to reinforce the power and strength of his pack.

And that's where the Luna of my pack comes in.

My brother, Thane, the Alpha of the Blood Moon pack, met his mate Emery a few months back. She's human so they've been moving slow and haven't mated yet nor has Thane marked her. This puts her in the face of danger since Alpha Aiden can challenge my brother for the pack, kill him, and then claim Emery. Or he can simply kidnap her and mark her before my brother does.

Twisted, I know, but apparently, Alpha Dickhead didn't give a flying fuck about who he must kill to get what he wants. His main concern was finding a mate and Emery was the only Luna not marked which made her a prime target. So, until Alpha Aiden showed up and we had eyes on him, all of us were on high alert.

Was I worried? Heck yes.

Alpha Aiden fought dirty, won quickly, and didn't show remorse. I'd be an idiot to not be apprehensive about him, especially since he wanted something that didn't belong to him.

My brother Thane was strong but I'm afraid he didn't have the prerequisite of being a crazy killing bastard. Now that would have worked out in his favour if Alpha Aiden did decide to challenge him.

Worst yet, I feared for his mate Emery.

Since she's human, there's no way she could defend herself against a werewolf, it was physically impossible.

If something went down, the plan was simple. Take Emery and run for the hills as I was one of the fastest wolves in my pack.

As I made my way back to our packhouse, I sighed in frustration at the possible shit show that could go down between now and the next few hours.

But we couldn't do anything until Aiden arrived, so I followed my nose directly to the kitchen. I greeted some of the pack members in there who were preparing a big meal for our guests since they're staying here for the next two days.

Instead of offering help, I grabbed a plate of cookies and a soda to induce a diabetic coma by way of sugary goodness. One hundred percent don't recommend unless you're a werewolf and can't get diabetes.

Just as I plopped myself onto the soft recliner in the living room, snuggled deep into the soft material, popped open my can of soda, and brought a warm cookie to my mouth, my brother's voice echoed through my mind link.

'Where is she?! Where's Emery?'

His Alpha tone made it exceedingly clear what was about to go down.

"Oh shit," I cursed as I scrambled to my feet.

Soda can knocked over, cookie crumbs laying on the floor and my comfy seat long forgotten, I sprinted towards the front door just as Thane busted in.

His enraged expression warned everyone to back up as he fumed.

"What happened?" I questioned.

His eyes were wild as he sniffed the air, "Emery came here looking for you but I can't smell her. Her scent's not here! Where is she, Tate?"

Panic gripped my insides as I shook my head, "She hasn't been to the packhouse."

The fear that overtook his face was one I never thought I'd see on his usually relaxed and controlled features.

Without another word we all rushed outside and tried to find her scent.

But like a ghost, she disappeared without a trail.

CHAPTER 2

A n hour later and we still hadn't found her.

No trail, no scent, no Emery.

According to Thane, she was on her way to the packhouse, but her scent lingered past the house and towards a small trail leading to the forest. It disappeared beyond that point and now everyone was on the hunt for her.

'Tate, go back to the house. If Emery turns up, I want you to take her to the human town. Jane would make sure you get in unnoticed,' Thane mind linked me as and the others ran further into the forest.

The human town of Fairbairn was where Emery used to live but since she's considered a missing person there, it would be dangerous if she turned up. If the humans knew she was still alive, it would risk the secret of werewolves. She couldn't exactly tell them the mythical beast they've been hunting for centuries was a werewolf who's her soulmate. They'd probably lock her up in a mental institute. Hence the reason why my great-aunt, Jane, who lived there would be able to sneak us in.

Heeding my brother's words, I ran back towards the house in my wolf form. The cool evening air brushed through my dark grey fur and my paws sank into the warm earth below me. Running in the woods was an indescribable feeling. A sudden rush of endorphins.

But the fear of the unknown sank its claws into my happy state of mind and left my insides feeling like blocks of ice. This only triggered an undeniable pain in my chest which was an after effect from a wound I sustained a few months back.

I was on the brink of death that day, but Emery saved my life. Which is why I owe her my life and my time to ensure we find her now.

As for my severe chest pains, it happens every once in a while, which was something I have to live with. According to the pack doctor, nothing's wrong per se, but the pain wasn't right either.

Shifting behind the packhouse, I hunched over as I breathed through the pain as it sent ripples of pain through my upper torso. They don't usually last more than five minutes, which I'm grateful for as I pulled on a pair of jeans and a t-shirt stashed in a hollow out tree.

Before I could go inside, however, I heard shouting coming from the clearing where everyone was gathered. My chest eased as I briskly walked in the direction of the drama.

Breaking through the trees and into the clearing, I saw Beta Lucas holding a man to the ground and yelling in his face.

"Where the hell is she? Tell me!" He shouted as he lifted the man's shoulders and slammed him back into the ground.

My eyes picked up the angry wolves from Alpha Aiden's pack who were growling lowly at Lucas. As I neared the men, I realized it was Rick, Aiden's Beta, who was currently being knocked around by Lucas.

"As I told you already, I don't know what you're talking about. Let me up man, before I report you to your Alpha," Rick seethed.

"Whose orders do you think I'm under? You're honestly lucky it isn't Alpha Thane or else you'd be dead by now."

Rick narrowed his eyes at him, "Is this how your pack treats guests? By threatening them after they've been civil?"

"If you answer the question, I won't have to threaten you."

"You're forgetting that I don't know what the hell you're on about."

Lucas attacked the man again, but this time with a fist to his cheek, "Your Alpha kidnapped our Luna. Tell me where they are, now wolf!"

"I told you, we don't know. And trust me you'll know when my Alpha arrives," Rick spat some blood out from his busted lip.

"You little-"

"Wait!" I grabbed Lucas's wrist before he punched Rick.

They both turned to me. While Rick was taken aback by my involvement, Lucas was fuming in anger.

"Tate, what the hell are you doing?" Bailey, Lucas's mate, queried.

"Prevent Lucas from sending us into a war," I grumbled, and they all seemed rather confused. "Geez guys, think about it for a second. Why would Alpha Aiden leave his Beta and pack members here at the mercy of our hands while he kidnaps Emery? It doesn't make sense because he would and should know that we'd kill them for that. Would he really let his Beta die for this?"

When everyone lifted their eyebrows at my contradiction against our Beta, I realized it may not have been as obvious as I assumed.

"Look, I'm not saying they're to be trusted, but I don't think he'd leave his second in command to die just to get a mate." My eyes flickered to Rick, "Would he?"

"He wouldn't," He answered before turning to Lucas. "From one Beta to another, would your Alpha leave you to get murdered by a lesser pack?"

Lucas stole his hand away from my hold and punched Rick again.

"Jesus dude, shut your Jell-O hole would you!" I said exasperated by his stupidity.

He chuckled but held his hands up in surrender, "Okay fine, I concede. But you know she's right. My Alpha doesn't have your precious Luna."

Carson, my father, stepped in and placed his hand on Lucas's shoulder, "Tate is right, I don't think he knows what happened to Emery. Let him up and go help Thane track her down."

He nodded and headed off towards the forest.

I gave Rick my hand and helped him up from the ground as he gave me a thankful smile.

Before he could pull away, I tightened my hold on his hand and lowered my voice to a deadly tone, "If you're lying and take my trust for granted-"

"I'm not and I won't. You have my word."

"It means very little to me," I said as I dropped his hand and backed up as he nodded.

"While we're not going to kill you right now," My dad started, "it doesn't mean your pack is free. I must insist that we keep you in our packhouse until we find our Luna or your Alpha. It's either that or our Crypt."

Rick wiped some blood off the cut of his cheek as he agreed, "My Alpha's innocent but lead the way I guess."

"You're Alpha doesn't exactly have a clean track record," I noted, and he smirked.

"That he does not, which is why I won't kill your Beta for putting his hands on me."

A few of my pack members growled at his words and I cut him a look, "You really need to learn to shut up dude."

"Forgive me..." He trailed off as he waited for my name.

"Tate," I answered.

His brow rose, "You're Alpha Thane's little sister."

I narrowed my eyes at him, "Very strong and fast sister, yes."

Sure, I was Thane's little sister but that shouldn't overshadow the fact that I could kick his ass.

Not Thane's sister or Carson's daughter. Just Tate; destroyer of rogues and master of bad luck.

Has a ring to it doesn't it?

"Come on, I'll show you to the packhouse," I gestured to him and his pack before turning to my father. "I got it over here, you can go help with the search."

Taking orders like a champ, he went off as I escorted Rick and the other wolves of his pack back to the house.

"I must ask," Rick started, "why did you help me?"

"As I said, I was trying to prevent a much bigger problem as I don't believe your Alpha took my Luna just yet," I threw him a questioning look.

"Good call," He nodded approvingly.

"Well, I for one am not in a mood for a war with your pack."

He chuckled, "You're very wise Tate Blackwood and to be honest I don't have the time for a war right now either. As for your brother, he has my sympathies. I don't know what I'd do if she was missing. Frankly, I think she would rip everyone to shreds if she doesn't know where I am for even five minutes."

"What's her name?" I asked and he practically grew heart eyes at the mention of her.

"Calypso," he smiled.

"Like the Goddess," I noted in admiration of her unique name.

He chuckled, "Trust me she definitely makes me treat her as such."

I smirked, "Then she's definitely doing the whole mate thing right."

He nodded before giving me a knowing glance, "You were expecting to find your mate today, weren't you?"

I felt uncomfortable by the question but nodded anyway, "Don't all unmated werewolves expect it? It's a part of our nature like an itch you can't scratch until you find them."

He chuckled as we entered the packhouse, "Yeah, I suppose that is exactly how I'd describe it."

I nodded as I stood before the members of the Oaks pack and announced, "Welcome to the packhouse. Your pack will be staying in the left hall on the second floor and your bags are already there. Until we find our Luna, everyone's required to stay in here. I assure you, if you break our one rule, my Alpha won't take kindly to it."

A few snarled at my threat but Beta Rick snapped them into line with one look before they all nodded and dispersed around the house.

"I hope I can trust that you ensure they stay in the house?" I asked Rick as I watched the foyer clear out.

"Trust me, Aiden would chew them out if they get themselves thrown in your pack's Crypt. Plus, he keeps everyone in line, so they know when to follow rules. Considering how much they've all been working back home they're probably happy to stay indoors for a few days," Rick answered.

"Isn't your pack the largest in the country? Would you all not have shifts that are far between?" I asked with sudden curiosity.

His eyes were shielded, and I knew pack business wasn't something he was about to discuss with an outsider.

"It's complicated," he finally said. "I think I'll go join the others in the game room."

And just like that, the conversation ended abruptly.

"Of course, let me know if your pack needs anything," I said as curiosity burned through me.

He nodded with secrets hidden behind his eyes as he walked away.

Something was up with their pack, that was pretty obvious. But from everything I know they don't have any issues aside from missing a Luna.

But what if the sudden need for a Luna was connected to what's happening behind the scenes?

The only information I know about their pack is that it's settled deep in a forest nestled by thousands of old oak trees, hence their pack name, and there aren't many rogues around, so they don't have issues with wild wolves. I also knew for a fact that their pack had at least a thousand wolves so even if there were rogues, it wouldn't be an issue.

Was it none of my god damn business? Of course.

Was I still going to figure it out? Mhmm.

There's a link with needing a Luna to make their pack stronger and whatever's going on, that's as far as I've got.

Well as far as I've assumed. Unless of course Alpha Dickhead really is a condescending leader and just wants more power. But if they really do plan on taking Emery, this could be vital knowledge.

I may not be a conversationalist, but I am good at observing.

You'll be surprised at how easily anyone will divulge their deepest darkest secrets when they think no one's looking. It could be a jagged breath, a nervous laugh, a moment forgotten to blink, or a hesitated answer. The key was to listen more than you speak. Talkers always tell more than they hide.

If only I could get some blackmail material. Just enough to make a difference to prevent Alpha Aiden from taking Emery.

As I stepped towards the living room where most of the Oaks pack trailed off into, I heard a loud commotion in the backyard. I went on high alert as I took a detour and I stalked down the long hallway.

Halfway to the back door, I caught the scent of sea-washed mahogany and fresh waterfall. The calmness that spread through me felt exceedingly foreign in my body but oddly fitting. It was as if a missing piece of me that was stolen all my life was finally returned.

The scents drove my mind to a picturesque coast with sky blue waters and sugar brown sand. It didn't go unnoticed that I'd never been to a beach before but somehow knew what it would feel like.

My feet moved as my mind entered a hazy, almost opiate state, and I shuffled hurriedly at the door knowing the scent meant one thing.

Mate.

My mate.

My presumably dead mate.

Well, living mate now.

Fumbling with the handle, my palms became sweaty as I felt nerves rushed through my body and caused my heart to thud in my chest like a thunderstorm.

I closed my eyes, sucked in a breath, and count to three before grabbing hold of my distorted mind.

Rubbing my sweaty palms on my jeans, I grabbed the handle one more time and pushed the door open as the scent hit me with its full force.

My eyes fell on the man standing in the backyard with my brother, Emery and Lucas.

His ocean eyes snapped towards me as I nearly stumbled down the steps.

His dirty blonde hair, however, was a dead giveaway of who he was.

Alpha Dickhead.

Alpha Dickhead is my mate.

CHAPTER 3

I felt my breath catch in my throat. My mind was definitely play-ing tricks on me as it showed me the man who was supposedly my mate.

Pounding my chest and letting out a sound that could only be described as a squawk from a dying duck, I gaped at him.

"Mate," He whispered, and I caught the deep timbre of his voice.

Aiden.

Alpha Aiden.

The Alpha of the Oaks Pack.

He's my mate.

The Alpha who's known for killing people if they hover around him too long. The fricking Alpha who planned on kidnapping my brother's mate if he didn't find his own.

Who wanted a mate? I did. Who got a mate? I did. Who got an evil mate? Ding-ding-ding ladies and gents... I did.

My title as master of bad luck was certainly showing itself to be true.

Alpha Aiden kept his eyes on me while my brother and his mate's eyes shifted between the pair of us and waited for the scene to playout.

Emery grinned, Thane growled, Alpha Dickhead didn't even blink and Beta Lucas looked rather agitated.

"You're mates with my little sister?" Thane seethed accusingly at Alpha Aiden as my mate slowly blinked before turning to Thane with a hard expression.

Oh, oh... this can't lead to anything good.

"She's my mate, what do you expect me to do?" Alpha Aiden growled through clenched teeth.

I frowned at his tone. I didn't know him, but he sounded almost accusatory. As if he wasn't expecting these turns of events and wasn't too pleased.

Maybe I was being pessimistic?

Don't judge a book and all that...

Alpha Aiden took a step in my direction and while my head said one thing, my legs were saying another as I shifted and mirrored his movements. There was an intense pull between us that screamed at me to go to him and his movements conveyed that he was feeling it as well.

However, my brother, being the dipshit that he is, stepped between us and immediately shoved Aiden back. My instinct to protect my mate was overwhelmingly strong as I growled.

Aiden began to look extremely pissed off and I hurried my strides.

"Thane stop," I seethed at him, but he wasn't even listening.

Emery caught my angry expression as she grabbed Thane's shoulder, "Thane let them be, they're true mates."

"I don't care, he's too damn old for her," Thane growled back.

I snorted behind him. I was two weeks away from eighteen. Only a year and a few months younger than Thane. And certainly not that much younger than a twenty-one-year-old Aiden.

Three years and some difference. Big deal.

Well...unless he turns out to be a psycho killer then my sentiments may change.

"It's the wolf world, Thane, I don't think it matters considering the Moon Goddess paired them together," Emery fought for us.

"He's a killer and I won't allow him to take Tate," Thane was about to push Alpha Aiden back again but Emery wrapped her hands around his arm, and he froze.

"My pack affairs don't concern you and neither does Tate now," Alpha Aiden growled out.

I rolled my eyes so hard I'm not sure how they hadn't fallen out of my head.

"Okay knuckleheads, shut it," I stepped beside them and their eyes animatedly landed on me. "First of all, Alpha," I glared at Aiden, "Tate's actions and everything Tate-like concerns only Tate as Tate does as she pleases."

He opened his mouth to protest but I held my hand up and he forcefully bit his tongue to keep quiet as Thane smirked at him.

"You're already wh-" Thane started but I flicked him on the head, and he grumbled.

"As for you, oh brother of mine, stop being a complete moron. Do you want to start a war over who is mated with who?" He opened his mouth to answer but I glared daggers at him, and he shut up. "Yeah, didn't think so. Now if we can settle this over talking like civilized humans would be amazing. Maybe over cookies?"

What? Emery was safe and I wanted back on that plate I had abandoned earlier.

"I agree with Tate," Emery grinned as she looped her arm around my own. "Thane, he wouldn't hurt her. Trust me if he wanted to kill anyone, he would've killed me in the forest. Plus, Tate's his mate, just as I'm yours and you would never hurt me."

Thane turned away from my mate and looked Emery over before storming off. He headed towards the forest before shifting and running off.

Emery's grip left my hand as she tried to catch Thane, but it was futile because he was already gone.

Alpha Aiden's eyes once again zoned in on me as if he was watching his prey...and frankly, I felt like one.

My heart rate sped up in anxiousness and I heard Lucas say to Emery, "He just needs a little time alone considering he almost thought he lost you and now his sister's mated to the Alpha he despises," He looked over at Aiden, "no offense."

"None taken," Was Aiden's only response as he strutted right up to me. His hands firmly but delicately grabbed my arms as he pulled me flushed against him and sniffed my neck.

I tensed under his touch. Both from fright and the shocking buzz of awareness that blossomed against my skin. It was alarmingly pleasant.

Emery and Lucas left us to own devices before Alpha Aiden lifted his head from my neck and peered down at me.

I gulped as I kicked my brain to respond. What do I do? Shake his hand? Curtsey to Alpha Dickhead?

There wasn't exactly a manual on 'How to greet your rumoured psycho murdering werewolf mate' for dummies lying around.

"Hi," I breathed out and managed a somewhat warm smile.

His eyes narrowed on to my mouth and I felt butterflies in my tummy as his eyes traced over every inch of my face.

"I'm Tate," I continued, and he nodded.

"I know," He finally said before the back door opened and his Beta, Rick, walked out.

"Alpha, I heard you-" He stopped short as he took in the sight of both us and gaped in shock.

A growl rumbled through Alpha Aiden as he pushed me behind him with such force that I stumbled.

Damn Alpha.

My hand grabbed onto his bicep as I caught myself before I fell.

"Be careful," He seethed as his grip on my arms tighten and glared at me.

The butterflies I felt quickly shrivelled up as I stared at him in disbelief.

"If you didn't push me, I wouldn't have tripped," I narrowed my eyes at him.

I could tell from the quick rising of his eyebrows that he was shocked by my firm tone.

"And loosen your grip on me, would you? There's a fine line between manhandling and helping," I shrugged out of his fierce grip and he easily let me go.

"You're my mate," he barked as if it wasn't obvious.

I glared at him, "Exactly. Note the difference."

His jaw clenched as he assessed me with those soul-searching eyes of his but I stood my ground. I don't know why, but he's getting a rise out of me even though I didn't expect our first interaction to go as it was.

Rick chuckled nervously and brought our staring match to an end as we looked his way.

"Uh, mates? You two are mates?" He lifted his eyebrow in surprise and Alpha Aiden snarled at him. Rick quickly threw his hands up in surrender, "I got my own mate dude, relax."

That calmed him a bit as he shifted closer to my side but refrained from touching me again.

"Yes," Alpha Aiden nodded, "Tate's my mate."

My insides warmed at the affirmation and of him saying my name. I peeked at his 6'2" frame and saw his blue eyes staring down at me.

I was about 5'7" so he had quite a few inches on me. He had grown-out wavy dirty blonde hair that was somewhat tied up, sun-kissed skin, cerulean blue eyes, and a drool-worthy scent. A combination to kill.

Rick grinned and gave me a little bow, "Well let me be the first to welcome you to our pack Luna Tate."

The title threw me for a loop as the unexpected realization of what being the mate to an Alpha meant. Not only did I have to lead beside him, but I also had to help him make decisions.

Decisions which I don't know if I'll like considering his reputation for violence.

"Thank you, Rick," I said in appreciation with a smile that I knew was as real as a barbie doll.

Could you blame me? Becoming Luna really wasn't on my bucket list.

"It must have been why you protected me from Beta Lucas, your Luna instincts were already kicking in," Rick commented.

Alpha Aiden looked over at him in question, "What do you mean protected you?"

"Their Beta almost killed me since you took your jolly time to get here but Tate got him to back off and brought us here," He gestured behind him to the packhouse.

"Why?" Alpha Aiden aimed his question to me.

I shrugged, "It was the right thing to do."

It was. Even if it was some weird Luna instinct, I wasn't going to let our pack go to war without knowing for certain that Emery was taken.

I wanted to ask him a question of my own. Several that threatened to bubble out of my mouth, especially why he planned on giving up on searching for his mate. However, I held off as his Beta still stood before us.

His eyes held mine in surprise and once again I was captivated by the mystery of him and his pack. But I knew that figuring him out wasn't going to be easy. Not when there was a metaphorical mile-high brick wall topped with barbed wire that surrounded him.

I wanted nothing more than to take a good ole sledgehammer to it and knock it all down and peek inside at what he was hiding.

Maybe it was his one-worded answers, his lack of smiles, or even the mysterious aura he held. But I had this innate need to know why he ticked the way he did.

Of course, his few words ruined my vision by what he said next.

"Rick, prepare our pack to leave at first light. There's no use staying here any longer."

"Of course," Rick said as he turned to leave.

Once Rick was out of earshot, I shook my head, "We can't leave tomorrow."

His eyebrow slowly lifted, "And why not?"

"One, we just met," I pointed out the obvious. "Two, my brother's getting married in three days and I'm not leaving before that. Not to mention that every pack is meant to stay here for two days to give newly mated wolves time to plan which pack they want to be a part of."

His jaw clenched and I could feel his anger simmering below the surface like a volcano waiting to erupt.

"One, my pack is loyal to me, so I don't have to wait for them to decide." Ahh, he was very narcissistic. "Two, we're mates now so we'll get to know each other soon enough." Condescending as well. "Lastly, your duties no longer lay here, and my pack needs me back." And of course, he was also patronizing.

He swiftly turned on his heels and walked towards the house as I was left glaring at his back.

Standing by the door, he called back, "Are you coming? You need to be briefed on what your role will be."

Briefed? Did he think the job of a Luna could be explained in point two-five seconds?

I closed my eyes briefly as I absorbed his words and lack of emotions. Clearly, he didn't care for my polite request, but I'll be damned if he thinks he could just show up here and leave within five minutes.

"Listen here buddy, I was being polite by asking to stay a little longer. But let me rephrase it for you, I am not leaving until I see my sister-in-law walk down that aisle. We may be mates but you're not about to boss me around like some psycho-"

"Are you calling me crazy?" He accused but I could detect a light lilt to his voice as he found this amusing.

I, however, nodded along because I was ticked off, "That's exactly what I said, didn't I?"

His eyes narrowed in on me warningly, "Tate-"

"Alpha," I replied cheekily with a smirk.

For some reason that soured his mood as he growled deeply, "We're leaving in the morning. There are far more important things than a stupid wedding to get dressed up for."

"It's not about dressing up, it's about family. If you have more important things to do then you can either tell me about the severity of the situation and we can leave or you can leave on your own," I raised a brow and waited for him to tell me.

He didn't as his gaze drifted away from me.

"Fine, if you won't tell me what you need to get back to then you can leave with your pack now and I promise you, I'll make the journey after the wedding," I offered.

He shook his head but didn't look at me, "I'm not leaving you."

"Then don't blame me for keeping you here if you're needed there," I said in frustration. "I know that you have Alpha duties, but you were meant to clear your schedule for this meet-up today. I'm sorry but I'm not leaving with you in the morning. Plus, I'm sure your pack can take care of it until you can get back-"

"Don't be a child Tate. You know leading a pack isn't a game," I can practically see the fumes coming out of his ears and nostrils.

But being called a child struck a nerve, "I may only be seventeen but I'm far wiser than-"

"You're seventeen?" He growled and his volcano of anger finally erupted as his face lit up in shock and fury.

I rolled my eyes, "Obviously old man, keep up."

He didn't seem to like my nickname much more than I liked being called a child, so I guess we're as good as even.

"No wonder you're this immature," He growled in a very harsh tone. "You'll pack your bags because we're leaving in the morning. Do or don't, I'll haul you out of here myself with whatever you've got on you."

The urge to punch his god damn beautiful face spiked in me.

I'd been a complete fool wishing for a mate. Of course, I pulled the short straw.

Alpha Dickhead was an arrogant asshole who certainly lived up to his name.

"You can leave when you please Alpha Aiden, but I won't be leaving this pack until my brother gets married," I didn't bother giving him the satisfaction of seeing my hurt expression before I walked off inside the house without another word.

Seemed fitting right? Storming off like a teenager.
Maybe I should have flipped my hair for added finesse.

CHAPTER 4

I nside the packhouse, my parents were already heading towards the back door but froze when they saw me.

I'm positive that someone had already informed them I found my mate. After all, word spreads like wildfire around here.

They both held worried expressions as I approached, but when I heard Aiden's heavy footsteps walking towards us, I sped up and didn't slow down.

"Tate," My mom called me back, but I didn't stop as I brushed past her and headed straight out the front door.

I paused on the front steps and took in a deep breath as my chest squeezed in protest from whatever underlying condition I had. Or, maybe this time it was caused by my newly found mate.

"Now's really not a good time," I seethed to my heart before sitting down on the steps.

'Tate? Come back here and introduce us to your mate,' My mom mind linked with a scold.

But like the immature child that I was, (Aiden's words, not mine), I didn't respond.

It was one thing to be called immature, but it was another thing to be called that from your soul mate. Maybe I was right in judging him from the start. He probably didn't want the responsibility of having a true mate and only the power that came with it.

What stung the most wasn't his words though; it was everything that came crashing down on me from finding him. I had to leave my family behind. My parents and three brothers. My friends. I didn't even have a choice as to what pack I stayed in, not when my mate was an Alpha. Not unless I rejected him...but even if he is an asshole, I don't think I could it...yet. We barely knew each other and in the span of fifteen minutes, we've already had our first fight.

Things weren't looking so peachy.

Especially since I had to leave my family behind. The place I've been for the past, almost, eighteen years.

What if his pack didn't like me? I've heard stories of that happening to some Lunas. Well only one so far in history, centuries ago. But the possibility wasn't ruled out. They could hate me just for belonging to another pack.

I'm to be the Luna of the Oaks Pack.

Aiden Oak's mate.

No pack has ventured into their territory for a while. They stopped hosting the annual Mate Meet Up several years ago when Aiden's parents died. I did learn that their territory is quite something though, like a fairy tale scene stolen from a novel. So far that was the only thing I looked forward to.

I folded my hands on my knees and watched as birds flew around in the late evening sky. The hues of pink, orange, and blues were all perfectly blended together and radiated warmth and comfort.

The aroma of dinner being served in the kitchen permeated the air and my stomach growled in its usual fashion, but I made no move to get up. One, because I was lazy and two, because I didn't exactly want to sit and get to know my mate over casserole.

I heard the front door open and I tensed, thinking it was Aiden, but I caught my father's familiar scent and relaxed.

"Dinner's ready," He announced to me cheerily.

"Thanks, Dad," I replied but remained in my seat.

His footsteps shuffled over towards me, "My girl doesn't want food? Should I be worried about that mate of yours?"

Sitting beside me, I turned to his worried expression and shook my head to put his mind at ease.

"It's not that," I lied, and he could tell as he frowned.

"Your mother and I spoke to him..." Dad took a pause before continuing, "He's not much of a conversationalist. Very private man. He did tell us that he has important pack matters to attend to which is why he needs to leave soon."

"I know and I understand that he has his pack to run but I can't leave before Thane's wedding..." I trailed off knowing my wants is nothing in comparison to what his pack needs.

He remained quiet before giving me a knowing look, "Is this really about your brother's wedding?"

"Partially," I shrugged as I picked at my shoelace.

He wrapped his arm around my shoulder, "What's wrong Tater-tot?"

A small smile graced my face at his term of endearment.

"I want to be here for Emery and Thane, especially after Em saved my life. But I also don't want to leave yet, Dad. He came out of nowhere and it hadn't exactly occurred to me that I'd have to leave you all behind."

Humming in understanding he said, "I don't want you to leave and I'm not forcing you to go either. You know this is your home," He raised his eyebrow to me in question and I nodded in understanding that he meant it. "But, if you did leave, you won't be leaving us behind or losing us. It's just another chapter of your life. A new adventure with your soul mate... and there's a thing called phones you kids are always glued to-"

"Dad," I playfully nudged him as a smile graced my face before fading away. "I'm scared."

"Of Aiden?"

"No," I answered immediately but then retracted. "Not really, I don't think he'd hurt me." Especially since he kept his hands off me when I told him to let me go. "It's his pack I'm worried about. They're ruthless, that's what you and Thane always say. How am I supposed to show up and become their Luna?"

He looked appalled, "They'd love you. Not just because you'll be their Luna but because of your heart and your head. You're a smart kid Tate, your mother and I did good with you kids. Plus, just look at your mother and Emery, the pack loves them and they're humans. The Oaks Pack will love you. Just trust the process Tater-tot and always hold your head high."

I wrapped my arms around him, "Thanks, Dad."

"Anytime, kiddo. Now, why don't you get something to eat and put that mate of yours at ease. He's going stir crazy in there," Dad dropped his voice, "I think he's checked the window at least twenty times in the past ten minutes. All bark and no bite huh."

I giggled at the knowledge of Alpha Aiden pacing. Dad dropped a kiss on my head as he got up and headed inside.

I followed suit as my back was aching from sitting on the steps, but I didn't go through the front door. Instead, I looked at the window for any sign of Aiden but when I saw that he wasn't there, I rounded the house towards the window to the kitchen. Peering inside, I ensured no one was in there before I slide the windowpane up and climbed in.

My avoidance game was on par, I must admit.

Grabbing a bit of everything laid out, I secured my plate and was about to stealthily climb out and head back to the porch when I heard footsteps approaching and Aiden's scent growing.

Ducking below the counter, I held my breath and my food as I prayed, he took a hint.

But today wasn't my lucky day as he rounded the counter and peered down at me with an unimpressed expression.

"Hiding from someone?" He asked.

I stuck my chin out in defiance, "Clearly, now move along before I'm found."

His expression shifted but I couldn't tell if he was amused or annoyed. Maybe a little of both, I deduced.

"I think your hiding spot has already been compromised, how about you sit at the counter and eat?" He suggested as he held a hand out for me to take.

I shook my head, "I'm good right here."

"On the floor?"

"Yes."

Please leave, I thought to myself.

"Fine, suit yourself," He shrugged as he disappeared from my view but his scent was still in the room, so I didn't breathe easy.

And as if it was the most casual thing on earth, Aiden came back around to where I was seated on the floor and gracefully took a seat beside me with a large piece of chocolate cake on a plate.

As he began eating, he nodded to my own dinner, "You should eat, the food's really good."

"You already ate?" I asked.

"No," He simply said as he continued to dig into his cake.

As confusion swirled around me by our precarious situation, I started to eat.

Aiden didn't say anything more and I focused on my meal. The muted chatter inside was comforting along with the quiet chirps of the crickets in the forest that filtered through the open window. I enjoyed being in a lively room filled with people laughing and talking animatedly but I also savoured moments of peace. Moments like this.

Which was oddly calming with Aiden next to me.

Even though Aiden hadn't eaten the food yet, he was right, the food was good. Compliments to the chef who was anyone but Emery. I loved her but she couldn't cook to save her mate's life.

Standing up, I gestured to the window, "I'm out."

I didn't wait for his reply as I stealthily climbed out and headed for the porch. But just as I planted myself on the porch swing made for two, the front door opened and another none invited person joined my little party of one on the porch.

His scent of sea-washed mahogany and fresh waterfalls was comforting but his presence set me on edge even though I knew he was going to follow me out. But I wasn't in the mood to argue with him nor was I ready to forgive and forget.

I didn't know if we'd stay here for another day and I don't want to leave my home in a sour mood.

I didn't look up at him as he slowly trailed towards me.

Shifted around, I gave his broad frame more space as he took a seat beside. My eyes remain focused on the trees across the front lawn as I felt his thigh brush my own, but he remained quict.

My fingers fidgeted in anxiousness as I waited for him to speak but he didn't.

Instead, a small ceramic dish was held up before my eyes. The smell of chocolaty goodness evaded my senses as I saw the slice of cake.

"It was the last piece," He said softly.

I turned to him and there was a storm brewing behind his irises, but he said nothing more as he waited for me to take the plate.

"I bet it is after you just ate most of it," I quipped, and the corner of his lips lifted in a half-smile but was gone in the blink of an eye and I wondered if I'd dreamt it. Gingerly, I took the dessert from his hand, "Thanks."

One minute he's threatening to drag me away from here and the next he's bringing me cake.

Ugh, why were boys this complicated?

Alpha Aiden was a tough cookie to crack and I wondered if this was him usually or if he was more open around his pack members.

I'd ask but he didn't seem to be into many conversational topics this evening. Especially since he kept his focus on the setting sun behind the mountains in the distance and just brooded.

"Is it poisoned?" I asked jokingly because I wanted him to speak.

"No," he answered in a gruff voice.

My stomach protested from already having eaten a large dinner but as I lifted the fork I was already salivating. No one could resist the best God damn creation that was chocolate cake.

Even though he had just eaten a mountain load of it on the kitchen floor, I offered an olive branch, "Want a piece?"

Well technically it was the branch he offered but I was trying to be nice here.

He gazed at me out of the corner of his eyes and as he shook his head, I felt my smile fall in disappointment.

However, before I could take a bite, Aiden took me by surprise when he grumbled, grabbed the fork and shovelled half of the slice down.

The genuine grin on my face wasn't hard to miss as I realized he did that for me.

His usually dark eyes lightened as he watched my smile and passed me back the fork.

Shrugging he said, "I just really like chocolate cake."

"I could tell," I muttered with humour as I polished off the cake.

He ran his hand through his hair and pulled at the strands before turning to me fully.

"I... I've never had a mate before."

"Most people haven't," I answered as I narrowed my eyes at his angle.

Sighing he nodded, "What I mean is, I don't know how to do this."

"This as in?" I asked curiously.

He opened his mouth to answer but he seemed at a loss for words so he shook his head, "Never mind, it's not important."

I set the empty dessert plate down and tenderly placed my hand on his arm, "Alpha-"

"Aiden, just call me Aiden."

Looks like Mr. Brooding over here had a nice side.

"Aiden," I tested out his name and I heard a content sigh left him. "You can talk to me. Isn't that what mates do? Talk to each other."

He shrugged, "I wouldn't know."

"Neither would I, but there's no formula. We make it up as we go," I offered, and he nodded.

I expected him to go on with whatever he had started with, but he shifted gears faster than a formula one driver.

"I didn't mean to call you a child," He admitted.

I sighed, "Yeah, that was a low blow."

He nodded and took a deep breath before continuing, "If you still want to stay for your brother's wedding, then we'll stay."

"Really? But your pack?" I asked as I clutched to hope.

"They'll be fine without me until then and Rick's heading back tomorrow," He answered.

Guilt clawed at me, "Look I know running a pack isn't easy, I've seen my parents do it and then my brother and his mate. If you need to go back immediately, then I'll go."

His eyes found mine and there must be something in the air because Aiden's eyes were a clear blue as he looked at me tenderly. It was a brief glimpse into him that was concealed within a second, but it gave me hope.

"I need to be back but a few days away will be alright," My eyes widened in excitement.

"So, we're staying until the wedding?" I asked again just to ensure I was hearing correctly.

"Yes, but on two conditions," He finalized.

And there went my hope and excitement sailing away to a foreign land without me.

I nodded for him to go on.

"One, we'll leave immediately the day after. I have a lot of work to get back to," He said, and I nodded.

"Easily done," I complied. "What's the second?"

"You won't get angry at me again."

I blinked at his condition as I processed it, "Aiden, I can't control that. If you do something to make me angry, I'll probably be angry."

He mulled over what I said before agreeing, "Fine... then my second condition is that we'll be friends."

Friends?

"Friends?" He said again as he held his hand out towards me.

I eyed it as my stomach twisted in knots. We're mates. Friends seemed like a very loose term and I briefly wondered if it had to do with my age. Does he mean just friends or Monica and Chandler type of friends? I don't know, but the prospect of being called a friend didn't sit right with me.

"Tate?" He asked again when I hadn't responded, and he was about to retreat his hand, but I grabbed it.

Holding his large hand in my own, I felt my skin tingle from our connection, but I ignored it as I nodded, "Friends."

His piercing eyes held my own as he didn't pull his hand away.

"Good, most of the pack will leave tomorrow with Rick and the rest will go back with us after the wedding."

"Sounds good," I mumbled as our hands came apart and I wondered what our future held. If there was one outside of being 'friends'.

CHAPTER 5

After being completely friend-zoned by my mate, Aiden went back inside to inform his Beta that he's staying here until the wedding. I, of course, had a mini-meltdown from going from Single Tate to Tate with a Mate to Friend-zoned Tate.

Goddamn, was friendship really the best we could do?

Three days later and I still don't have an answer because I've barely seen him. It was as if he was never truly here.

While we had our cake moment, we hadn't made much headway. A 'good morning' here and a 'how was your day' there. It was as if we were just two ships passing in the night.

Anytime I spotted him in the hall, he was always on his phone shouting orders to his pack. But, every time I approached to ask him how I can help, he just shook his head, said he's got it handled, and walked away.

So, I ended up helping Emery as a designated bridesmaid. And by that, I mean I sat tasting samples of wedding cake with her while she stressed out and I nodded along. I can't remember what she was stressing so much about but I can tell you that the champagne cake with strawberry cream was heaven in my mouth.

My brother, on the other hand, was busy brooding over my mate and his absolute dislike towards the guy. So, Emery sent him and Aiden out together to do some tux shopping.

According to Taylor, the tailor of our pack, Thane and Aiden nearly had a brawl in his shop. Apparently, my brother wanted Aiden to wear a burnt orange tie, for no reason whatsoever.

Luckily, they didn't kill each other and there was less glaring and snarls by the time they made it back.

"Your hair looks beautiful Tate," Emery grinned at me from her chair.

I looked at my crown braid that had flowers twisted in.

"I know, it's a God-given gift," I gloated, and she threw a make-up brush at me which I easily dodged.

Our friend Bailey frowned, "Who's going to do my hair when you leave?"

I groaned, "Don't remind me. Seriously, I might lock myself in the Crypt knowing that it's my last day here."

The Crypt is where the pack kept rogues that wandered into our land. It was underground and covered in silver doors and locks. I don't know what sounded like the worst option, moving away with a mate who hardly speaks to me or staying in the chamber of silver.

Emery turned to me with a sad smile, "Your brother and I didn't start off great either, remember? Trust me, he'll come around."

My gaze fell to hands as I anxiously chipped my painted nails, "Yeah, I'm not too sure about that."

"Tate," She got off her chair and stood behind me as she wrapped her arms around my shoulders, "you two just need time. Trust me, you're going to be calling me a week from now telling me about how in love you are."

I crinkled my nose as I looked her in the reflection of the mirror, "Love does not move that fast."

"Tell that to Romeo and Juliet."

"I would but they're both dead," I deadpanned and she and Bailey both laughed at my cynicism.

After getting ready, I threw on my wine-red bridesmaid dress before we all helped Emery with her wedding dress. Mom cried, my great aunt Jane talked about wanting babies around and soon enough we were lined up to walk down the aisle before the bride.

I was paired up with my two brothers Teddy and Thomas, the troublesome twins. Actually, they weren't that bad, they were honestly adorable but they, of course, had their moments as most eight-year-old boys do.

Thomas seemed annoyed and Teddy frowned as I approached them.

"What's wrong? Did you lose your boutonniere already?" I looked at the lapel of their jackets and realized they both weren't sporting the flower.

"No, mom said we'd probably poke ourselves with the pin," Thomas shrugged and I couldn't help my snort.

"Mom's not wrong," I replied just as Teddy wrapped his arms around my waist.

"I'm going to miss you, Tay," Teddy whispered to me with a frown.

I lowered to his height and wrapped my arms around him, "I'll be back you know. I'll come back for Christmas and your birthday."

"It's not the same," He said as he pulled back. "I don't want you to leave with Alpha Aiden."

"Dude, you weren't supposed to tell her that. Remember what mom said? Tate would feel sad," Thomas said as he walked up beside his twin.

Teddy's frown deepened as he looked at me, "Sorry Tate, I didn't mean to make you sad."

I placed my bouquet on the forest floor and pulled them both towards me, "Hey, you didn't, and you don't need to be worried about Aiden either, okay? I'll be fine."

"But he's evil," Thomas whispered to me with a grimace.

"Thomy's right, what if he tries to kill you?" Teddy asked as he waved his arms above his head frantically.

"But if he does, we'll beat him up," Thomas shrugged.

"What he said," Teddy nodded in delight.

I let my smile consume my face as I ruffled their hair, "As sweet as you two are, Aiden isn't going to hurt me, so you have nothing to worry about. And even if he did, you guys know I can fight better than Thane." I made my hands into fists which they gleamed at. "Now give me a smile because, after the ceremony, we get cake!"

They both grinned and I breathe easy knowing they weren't going to punch Aiden with their little chubby fists. Who knew how he'd react or if he even likes kids?

Thomas hesitated before he gave me a quick hug, "I'll miss yah too Tate."

"Not as much as I'll miss you both," Choked up with emotions, I picked up the flowers and held onto their little hands as Teddy stood to my right and Thomas to my left.

The violin started to play a soft tune as two of Emery's friends walked down the aisle with their mates before I stepped out with my brothers at my side.

Lights were strung up from tree to tree above us with a canopy of flowers. We were in the middle of a clearing in the forest with everyone from the pack sitting on log benches.

The full moon was illuminating brightly above us and my brother's wolf stood at the end of the aisle as he waited for his mate.

As my eyes scanned the guests, out of all eight hundred, my eyes immediately went to one person.

His penetrating gaze held mine as I walked closer to where he stood in the front row. The black fabric of his suit was moulded around his broad shoulders and trim waist and boy was he drool-worthy out of jeans.

In jeans too, if I'm being totally honest.

His gaze landed on my brothers and I saw his lips twitch into something that resembled a very small smile. As I approached where he was seated up front beside my mother, I caught his beachy scent.

It was heady and seemed to always make me feel as if I was breathing in fresh air after being stuck in a windowless room all day.

Thomas and Teddy ran off towards the groom's side as I took my spot where the bridesmaids stood.

As the ceremony unfolded, I kept sneaking glances at him and wondered how his pack will react when I get there.

He hasn't told me anything about them or much about anything else. Not a single detail and my curiosity was starting to get the better of me.

If his lack of communication wasn't enough, he also refused to take our cargo plane out of here and to the human city. Instead, he said that we'd run in our wolf form to the city and we'd take a car from there.

That was odd for a guy who only days ago was in a rush to get back to his pack. However, after my mom told him it would be wiser to take the plane since it would be easier to move some of my personal belongings, he caved and agreed.

As I turned around again to look his way, he was already staring at me. The word 'friends' echoed in my head and I watched as Aiden frowned at my annoyed expression.

Rejection was a hard thing to swallow, even if it wasn't an official 'I reject you.'

After the ceremony, the clearingwas transformed into a reception area and along the way, Aiden managed todisappear once again.

I searched the crowd for him, but he was a no show and before I could start towards the trail between the clearing and the packhouse, Bailey stopped me.

"No running off now, it's time for the speeches," She said as she looped her arm through my own and led us back.

"But-"

"No, if I have to sit through it, then so do you," She smirked, and I turned back wondering where he snuck off to.

The speeches were the snooze fest of the day but luckily Lucas, as best man, saved everyone from falling asleep with his slew of innuendos during his toast.

And like a ninja, Aiden suddenly reappeared as he took his seat when the newlyweds began to cut their cake.

"Hey, where'd you go?" I asked coyly.

"Phone call," Was his only response as he continued tapping away at the thing.

I crinkled my nose at him, "You're worse than a teenager."

"Like yourself?" He smirked as he looked up at me.

Flipping him off I grumbled, "I rather do anything else but take pictures of my salad and put it on the internet."

A low chuckle emanated from him and I watched in surprise as he set his phone down, unbuttoned his jacket, and gave me his undivided attention.

"You know Tate, you're lucky," He commented as his gaze flittered around the clearing.

"Why? Because I'm not glued to my phone?" I prodded.

"No," He sighed heavily. "You have a family."

Right, his parents died when he was young. Of course, at an event like this, he'd feel singled out.

"Aiden I-"

"Don't say it," He stopped me as he looked my way. "I know what it's like to have a family, but some people don't. So again, I say you're lucky."

"I am," I nodded because it was true. Three siblings, parents, and everyone else. Aiden lost his parents when he was fourteen, it couldn't have been easy for him to lead a pack so young, let alone do it without a family behind him.

Before I could say anything else, his phone buzzed on the table and as he looked at the name, he gave me a regretful look, "Sorry, but I've got to take this."

As he strolled away, I decided to get another piece of cake but a member of the pack, Hayden, stopped me with a smile.

"Care for a dance?" Hayden gave me a charming smile as he held his hand out for me.

I rather ask my mate but when I looked back at our table, Aiden still wasn't back, so I shrugged and accepted.

"Lead the way," I placed my hand in his.

Hayden laid on the charm as he spun me around the dance floor and I briefly wondered if he knew I had a mate.

He spun me out of his arms and with my stroke of bad luck, I landed straight against someone's chest.

I stumbled back and rubbed my nose but tensed when I smelt him.

A low growl rumbled from Aiden as he stared daggers at Hayden.

"Be careful with her," He seethed in anger.

Turning to Hayden, I saw him go pale as he gulped before slowly backing away.

"My apologies Alpha," He whispered before taking off.

Holding my aching nose, I turned back to him.

"I think you scared him," I snickered.

Aiden didn't laugh and his glare wasn't gone as he peered down at me, "If you wanted to dance, you should have just asked."

I raised an unimpressed brow at him, "Isn't it a more gentlemanly thing to do for a guy to ask a girl?"

"Maybe, but I doubt you're one to follow social rules."

His eyes held irritation as he hit the nail right on its head.

"Fine, then would you like to dance with me Alpha?" I asked with my hand stretched out for his.

He eyed me cautiously, "Will you step on my toes?"

"Will you step on mine?" I countered.

I could see the anger in him slowly trickled away as he laced his fingers with my own.

The upbeat music stopped as the live band started up again and a slow song played.

Aiden pulled me closer and I placed my other hand on his shoulder while he kept one on my waist. Even though we were close, there was still a large gap between our bodies. If I didn't know any better, I'd think this was a cotillion.

It must have been at least a few inches, but it represented an entire ocean between us. Physically close yet mentally miles apart.

"Remember, I asked you, therefore I lead," I winked up at him and he shook his head with a small laugh.

As we started dancing, I was shocked to see that Aiden could dance.

"Huh, who knew Alpha Dickhead could dance," I mumbled without thinking.

"What did you just call me?" He stopped our movements as he peered down at me with a shocked expression.

I chuckled nervously, "Who me? I didn't say a word."

"Oh, but I think you did."

"Weird, because I definitely didn't say something," I feigned innocence.

His eyes narrowed on me, "Alright... just one question though."

"Yes?" I asked quickly to change the subject.

"Was Dickhead the best you could have come up with?"

I stared up at him in shock as he continued to sway us around the dance floor, "You're not angry?"

"I'm deciding if I should be," He mused.

"Well, you definitely shouldn't be," I said firmly.

"I'll take it into consideration," Was all he said, and I felt my tension dissipate.

Hopefully, he won't chew my head off.

"How'd you learn to dance?" I asked to steer him away from being angry.

A rare light flickered in his eyes as his expression softened, "From the internet, because my dance partner back home insisted that I learned."

Jealousy was an ugly thing. And call me the ugliest being to ever exist because I was jealous over someone I didn't know. But also, who the heck is she?

"Well, she must be lucky if you learned just for her," Maybe I should have just continued our discussion on badly chosen nicknames. I'd much rather have him be pissed than me jealous.

Aiden shook his head, "She isn't. She's been dealt a hard card in life, so I try my best for her."

My eyes met his briefly, but I couldn't decipher his expression, so I quickly averted my gaze.

Way to make a girl feel good about herself Alpha Dickhead, I thought.

You know what? His name suited him just perfectly.

"Well I can't wait to meet her," My voice came out more strained than I wanted it to.

Out of my peripheral vision, I saw his face contorted into concern as he saw my expression, "Why are you-"

"Let's just enjoy the music," I cut him off as I closed the gap between our bodies and hid my face against his chest.

His body was rigid against my own from the sudden contact, but he managed to keep his steps light as the song continued.

Don't start a pity party, you idiot! I yelled at myself.

Of course, he had someone else back home. He certainly didn't expect to find his mate so his life back home was still there. And I was just the friend. The friend that was tasked to become the Luna, make the pack stronger, and then live life with a mate who doesn't want a mate.

Doable. Totally and completely doable.

As the song faded to the end, Aiden kept swaying, but I cleared my throat and stepped back.

I kept my eyes focused on the ground as I excused myself, "Thank you for the dance. Now if you'll excuse me, I have to check on... the cake."

"Tate...?" His hand reached for my wrist, but he held himself back as if I would burn him.

He let me go without another word and I realized how transparent I was. And such a bad liar.

Really the cake? It was already cut and served.

I struggled with my breathing as my chest felt that familiar pinch of pain from my healed heart.

Pulling off my stupid heels, I noticed the bride and groom were long gone and I took that as a cue that I could leave as well.

CHAPTER 6

I scold at Aiden's back as he thanked my dad for letting him and his pack stay a day longer on our territory.

We haven't spoken since last night and honestly, I never imagined that when I met my mate, I'd be friend-zoned and jealous.

"And thanks again for the book, Mr. Blackwood," Aiden said gratefully to my father as he gestured to the book in his hands.

"No problem at all, son. Just be sure to bring it back next time you visit," My dad patted him on the back.

Son?

When they even get time to bond? I haven't even been able to have more than two proper conversations with him.

"I will," Aiden assured him before heading towards the plane.

My parents' attention landed on me and I could see the tears welling up in my mom's eyes as she pulled me into her arms, "Make sure and call and let us know you got there safely."

Dad joined in and squished me between them both, "And call every day after that. Also, don't forget to come back home for Christmas."

I bit back my laugh and revelled in their warm embrace one last time until who knows when.

"I'll try my best," I said as I pulled away and gave them a watery smile. "Tell everyone I'll miss them," I squeezed my mom's hand and she nodded as she brushed away some tears.

I hadn't gotten the chance to say goodbye to Emery and Thane since they snuck off to start their honeymoon early and it was ten in the morning. I'm pretty sure they weren't leaving their new house anytime soon anyways.

"You take care of yourself okay and remember if your chest-"

"I know mom, I got it handled," I assured her before giving her a kiss on the cheek and turning away before I ran back into the car and floored it back to the packhouse to hide from Aiden.

His eyes followed my every movement as I walked to the plane.

"Are you alright?" He asked in a gruff tone.

I nodded, "Just peachy."

He narrowed his eyes at me but didn't say much else as he stepped aside for me to walk up the ramp to the plane.

Inside I noted three other pack members from Aiden's pack sitting in the designated passenger seats that ran across both sides of the plane. Two other wolves from my own pack were upfront in the cockpit.

The three from Aiden's pack was sitting to the left, so I opted to sit across from. Unluckily for me, Aiden took the seat beside me.

As I buckled in, I realized that Aiden hadn't taken the opportunity to introduce me to his pack, so I shot them all a smile.

"Hey, I'm Tate, sorry I haven't introduced myself yet."

From the three of them, there were two guys and a girl. One of the guys had a sharp edge to him as if he was ready to bite off the head of anyone who breathed too close to him.

And of course, he was the first to address me as he assessed me with calculating eyes, "Oh, we know exactly who you are Luna."

He might as well have held up a sign saying 'I don't like you' because judging by his tone and expression, he certainly didn't.

When he turned away, Aiden growled at him, "Paul, shut up before I kick you off the plan and make you run back home."

Paul shrunk back in his seat after Aiden made his threat crystal clear.

"It's okay," I shrugged but neither of them looked at me.

"It isn't," Aiden persisted as he started fastening his belt. "Tate is to be treated with respect as Luna. Is that clear?"

The three of them nodded and I shifted awkwardly in my seat from embarrassment. It felt like a teacher calling out your bullies in front of the entire class and you know deep down it's only going to get worst.

I reluctantly looked back up at them and while Paul was simmering in his seat, the woman and the other guy, both gave me welcoming smiles.

Relief flooded through me knowing that at least these two liked me. Unlike Paul and his Alpha.

As the plane ascended into the sky and levelled out, I turned to Aiden and saw his nose deep in the book he borrowed from my pack's library.

He didn't look up as he concentrated intently at what he was reading, and I took the moment to study him.

You can't tell from far, but he had tiny freckles littered across his cheeks. His smooth skin was pulled against high cheekbones and then dipped into cheeks that held dimples. Eyebrows furrowed and lips pulled thin, he looked about ready to go enter the gates of Olympus or wage a war.

Catastrophically beautiful but carrying the wrath of a thousand men. A potent combination.

"Luna," Someone called, and my head snapped to the other side of the plane just as Aiden looked up from his pages.

A blush coated my cheeks as I felt Aiden's eyes on me, but I ignored him as I nodded at the other guy from Aiden's pack.

"Please, call me Tate," I told him.

"Well, Tate, it's nice to officially meet you. Name's Kai," He grinned as he unbuckled himself and got up to shake my hand.

I shook Kai's hand grateful for his kindness.

Aiden growled lowly as he looked at our handshake, "Hands Kai."

"Don't worry Alpha, you know you're more my type than she is," He winked at me as Aiden let out a grumble and kept quiet.

"I won't let Matt hear you say that if I were you," The girl said as Kai took his seat again. "Hey, I'm Loly."

"Nice to meet you both," I said as a genuine smile graced my face. "But who's Matt?"

"My mate, who's back home," Kai informed me. "He's been excited about meeting our Luna ever since I told him Aiden found you."

I chuckled nervously as I wiped my sweaty palms on my jeans, "To be honest, I'm quite nervous to meet the pack."

"What? Don't be," Loly waved. "They'll love you. And Alpha Aiden who will probably kill anyone who crosses you," She threw in with a mischievous wink.

"Loly," Aiden warned.

She simply shrugged as she and Kai started talking about their pack back home.

But then Kai said something that threw me off.

"You'll love the sand-"

"The what?" I looked at him in confusion. "Do you have a sand-pit in the middle of the Oaks Forest?" I joked.

He gave me a baffled expression and even Paul turned around with a dumbfounded look.

"What are you on about?" Paul asked.

I raised a brow, "Kai said sand but you all live in the forest..."

"You haven't told her?" Paul turned to Aiden whose knuckles were white from the tight grip he had on the book in his hands.

"Haven't gotten around to it," He muttered under his breath.

"Tell me what? Aiden?"

When he didn't answer Paul spoke up, "You need to-"

"Leave it," Aiden growled at him.

"But Alpha-"

"I said leave it, Paul," Aiden snapped at him.

"No, no, you go on Paul. I'd like to know what's going on," I urged.

Aiden shook his head at me as his eyes flickered to the two members of my pack flying the plane, "It's not up for debate."

I narrowed my eyes at him, "The hell it is. I want to know."

He turned back to his back and simply said, "Not now Tate."

Everyone went deadly silent as I fumed at his dismissive behaviour. What the hell was he playing at and why did Kai say 'sand'.

Most importantly, why was Aiden's reaction hostile? As far as I'm aware a pack doesn't leave their ancestral land and marked territory on a whim. And even if they did, why was it a secret?

My eyes shifted between Loly and Kai, but they didn't offer up anything more.

I briefly wondered if when I became Luna, if they'd still keep me out. Like an outsider.

Roughly five hours later we landed on the airstrip and everyone helped me haul my luggage into the boot of the rented car. I could only pack up so much of my life into a few suitcases but most of it was pictures and memorabilia. Hopefully, wherever this pack was located, I could get new clothes.

When we were loaded up, Aiden got into the driver's seat with Paul riding shotgun while Kai, Loly, and I sat in the backseat. No one had spoken since Aiden made it clear that his pack's location was an almighty secret.

Well, no one spoke verbally or to me, but I could sense them mind linking each other. If it's going to be like this back at their pack, I might end up talking to the trees just to keep myself entertained.

We were about a few hours into our drive when dusk began to consume the daylight outside of the car. Wherever their pack was, it was too far away as the overwhelmingly long day began to catch up to me.

"It won't be much longer," Aiden said as his eyes found mine in the rear-view mirror.

I nodded before closing my eyes and laying my head back. I really should have brought snacks for this journey. Maybe some chocolate cake to bribe Aiden with?

I don't know how long I was out for, but I was startled awake to the sound of something very heavy landing on the roof of our car.

I rubbed the sleep out of my eyes just as Aiden hit the brake. The tires of the car squealed to a stop as we were all hurled forward and something rolled off the car and onto the road.

"What the hell was that?" I sat upright.

But no one answered as the streetlight illuminated the object rising from the ground.

Ice filled my veins as I stared at the person standing before the car as if they didn't just get launched off a vehicle.

Everyone began opening their doors and I caught the most gut-wrenching and pungent scent of rotting flesh.

It was as if death was bottled up and sprayed in the air.

Aiden flung open his door but turned to me with rock-solid expression, "Stay in the car Tate, I mean it."

I didn't have time to ask any more or say anything because he got out and everyone closed their doors behind them.

"What the hell guys?" I yelled as I tried opening the door. It didn't budge and I moved to the opposite door, only to realize they engaged the child lock.

My eyes shifted to the front of the car as two wolves attacked the person. It easily defended itself as shifted abnormally fast.

What the actual flying...

It leaped unto the hood of the car gracefully as its eyes lifted to stare straight at me. Gleaming silver eyes illuminated against the dead features of the man who slowly smirked my way.

It wasn't a wolf.

It wasn't a demon.

It wasn't some crazed superhuman.

It was a vampire.

Horror gripped me as I saw the tell-tale sign of fangs protruding from its mouth right before a wolf gripped its head from behind.

I felt my heart lurch from my chest as it began beating one hundred miles per hour. A sickening slam rocked the back of the car and I turned in time to see a wolf grip a human body in its jaws and hurled it against the trunk of the car.

Hurrying, I crawled over the centre console and onto the front seat.

And my first struck of luck blessed me as the door opened and I leaped out of the car and straight into wolf form.

Just I tried to catch my bearings, the vampire from the back of the car ran straight towards me, faster than I imagined it would.

It took about as long as a hummingbird takes to flap its wing once for the vampire to get to me knock me to asphalt with its porcelain hands.

I growled in anger as I wrapped my tail around its leg and pulled it down before I leaped up and grabbed its foot in my jaw.

It was like biting into an ice block. When I got a firm grip, I felt its hand curl around the fur on my head and yanked me off.

My body hit the car and as it sneered at me, I realized just how much I underestimated their power.

Not like I had any knowledge to go off of since they were supposedly extinct.

The filthy bloodsucker smirked at me as a rumble escaped me. I pounced on him and used all my force to push him flat on his back.

I sunk my canines into his neck as his hand grabbed my fur and started to yank harshly. Suppressing a whimper, I tried to tear into him, but he moved his hand from fur and towards my front paw.

With a shift shove, on my paw, he dislocated my shoulder.

A whine escaped me as I backed off and heard the angry growl of an Alpha in front of the door.

I didn't dare turn away to watch where Aiden was as the vampire stood back up and sniffed the air.

"I smell O negative. My favourite," He smirked.

He was too cocky because before he could touch me, a wolf grabbed onto his head. Kai ran towards the vampire in human form and drove a wooden stake through its heart.

I watched in amazement as the body disintegrated into ashes.

Holy shit.

Aiden and Paul rounded the front of the car in shorts and splattered in blood. My mate didn't look too pleased to see me on the ground as he rushed to my aid.

"Tate," He scolded. "When I said stay in the car, I meant stay in the damn car."

I bared my canines to him in anger as the pain of my shoulder made my entire arm feel as if it was on fire.

"I think she dislocated her shoulder," Kai said just as Loly returned, dressed.

"Guys move. Once she shifts, we can pop her arm back," Loly said and they cleared out as she handed me a t-shirt and shorts.

I howled in agonizing pain as my bones shifted back into my human form which only aggravated the pain in my arm.

"Just breathe," Loly instructed as she helped me pull on the shorts and laid the t-shirt over my torso since I couldn't pull my hand the arms.

As I was covered, the boys returned, and Aiden wasted no time as he knelt beside me and I noticed a jagged slash running from the top of his shoulder blade to his elbow.

"You're hurt," I grumbled through clenched teeth.

"You don't look so good yourself, Cupcake," He said as he took my hand in his. "Now you need to relax your arm, you're too tense for me to help."

"How am I supposed to relax when my arm is literally on fire?"

"Well you won't need to if you stayed in the car," He seethed.

"Not to rush or anything Alpha, but we need to get out of here soon," Paul cut in.

Aiden nodded before taking my other hand and placing it on his chest.

"Ugh, I don't think now's a good time to feel you up," I coughed out as he rolled his eyes.

"Just feel my skin and breath in the scent of the t-shirt you're wearing," He instructed.

I reluctantly did as he asked, and I realized the t-shirt was his. The warmth of his skin combined with his heady scent worked it magic as I felt the tension in my arm relax.

And with a shift of my arm, Aiden popped my shoulder back into its socket.

"Mother fudging applesauce!" I cursed as the other all looked at me oddly.

"Did you just say-"

"No time guys, get her in the car," Kai rushed us.

Aiden scooped me up in his arms, despite his injury, and crawled into the backseat.

Paul got in behind the wheel with Kai upfront with him and Loly and Aiden at my sides.

"Floor it," Aiden growled from the backseat.

Paul didn't waste a second as he stepped on the gas and we step down the asphalt.

I shimmered into the t-shirt and realized that my shoulder was sore but thankfully not in any more pain.

I turned to Loly and noticed an already healing cut on her neck. "Are you alright?"

"I'm fine, Luna," She smiled appreciatively.

"Do you have any more extra t-shirts?" I asked her and she passed me one from a duffel bad without question.

I began tearing it to shreds before turning to Aiden's gnarly cut that would take longer to heal because of its depth.

"So, when exactly were you going to tell me that vampires exist?" I questioned.

"You should've already known that they exist."

I glared at him, "Aiden-"

"I'll explain everything later," He sighed.

"Yeah well I'm not holding my breath on that one, now give me your arm," I held out my hand and he looked to me with confusion swirling in his eyes. "You're bleeding over the car, which I'm pretty sure you can't return now anyways. Honestly, why'd you even get a fancy electric car if you knew something like this was going to happen?"

He begrudgingly placed his arm in my open palms as I looked at the deep wound.

"I didn't know it was going to happen."

"Clearly you did, seeing as you locked me in the car."

"For good reason to seeing as you almost got yourself killed," He snapped at me.

"As if you're better off," I pointed out by tying the cloth on his wound tight enough to stop the bleeding.

"That's not the point."

"I'd say it is."

"You're not trained to fight them. They aren't your regular rogue wolves Tate, they're stronger, faster and bloodier. So, when I say you're safer in the car, I mean it. You can't take one down on your own, not without training," He enunciated.

"Maybe if you'd told me that before, I wouldn't have jumped out of the car," I said sighed as I let go of his arm and turned to Kai was had a gash on arm.

As I began helping Kai, who gave me a grateful smile, I heard Aiden sigh behind me.

"I know they haven't been around for centuries," He started. "But they've always been around, just in hiding. Werewolves aren't the only species that managed to survive this long, we've just maintained a decent population because of our pack mentality."

As I finished patching Kai up, I sat and turned to Aiden, "You're not making this up, are you?"

"He isn't," Kai said from the front seat. "Did you catch any scent when they attacked?"

"Death," I whispered.

"That something to be mindful of to know when they're close. Besides that, they sneak up pretty easily and quickly," Kai informed.

This was huge, massive, exponential. Vampires and werewolves have coexisted in the past according to my history lessons. But about a century ago they started dying out and in turn, they started attacking wolves to diminish our species. From all the text that I read, they had all died. One by one they dropped off the face of the earth.

"If the vampires are back then why haven't you informing the other packs? Why didn't you tell me this prior to jumping on a god damn plane?" I asked my mate.

"I didn't because they aren't going to attack any other pack. They don't want to kill wolves," His voice took on a dangerously low tone but kept his answer vague.

"And how exactly do you know what they want?"

"Because if they try to attack a pack, they risk wiping out their already small population," He said matter of fact.

Before I could rebut, Paul cleared his throat, "Alpha, we're here."

I watched out the window as we continued driving and Aiden sighed next to me.

"Here where?" I asked suspiciously.

"The thing is," Aiden started. "We don't live in the Oaks forest. We live on the beach."

As he said that, we broached through the thick trees lining the sides of the road and I saw a lighthouse in the distance casting its light beam to navigate sailors and show me the crashing waves rolling in.

And right next to it, sat a magnificent castle perched on the cliff.

"Holy..." I whispered as I perched across Aiden's lap and pressed my face up against the car window.

CHapter 7

"This can't be real..." I trailed off as I continued to marvel at the castle.

"You've just been attacked by vampires and you don't think we can own a castle?" Paul asked from behind the wheel.

I rolled my eyes even though he couldn't see me.

"No offence but it's hard to believe a pack of wolves can live in a fancy castle without someone breaking something every second," I replied.

Kai snorted, "Trust me, it happens."

Aiden shifted beside me with a grunt before he lowered his voice, "Could you sit back?"

It was only then that I realised just how much I was pressed up against him from leaning to peer out the window.

I scrambled back quickly into my seat because that was certainly too close for friends to sit.

We continued down a narrow stretch of road until the car slowed to a stop before large gates. I watched as it opened onto a stretch of road lined with palm trees.

"Gee Aiden, did you forget to mention you were a prince or something?" I questioned as I gave him a sideways glance.

"Or something," Was his only cryptic response as we pulled up to the front of the castle.

We sure weren't in Kansas anymore if you know what I mean.

"I'll add the beach to the list of things you didn't bother to tell me before it happened," I muttered to him as everyone started to file out of the car. "Just wait to hear about the other thing," He quipped.

I narrowed my eyes at his back as I got out of the car, "What other thing?" When he didn't answer, I pressed, "Aiden, what other thing?"

His lips twitched in amusement, but he didn't say another word as a guy equipped with wooden daggers stepped closer us.

"Luna," He smiled with a bow, "welcome to the Oaks Pack."

I held my hand out for his, "Nice to meet you..."

"Dylan," He introduced himself as he grabbed my hand and brought it to his lips, but Aiden was quick to slap his hand away.

"Don't Dylan," Aiden growled at him but Dylan simply sniggered in amusement.

"Fine," He rolled his eyes before turning to me. "It's also Gamma Dylan, the best of the best in the pack."

"More like the cockiest," Aiden tapped him over the head.

"That is what she said," Dylan shrugged and I could see the pained expression on Aiden's face from the bad joke. " Anyway, catch you later Luna, I've got patrol."

As he ran off, I heard Aiden grumbling under his breath.

I took the chance to look around at the expansive front yard. There were a few members of Aiden's pack situated around the building with either their weapons drawn or in wolf form.

And by weapons, I mean wooden daggers, spears, and arrows. I'm pretty sure if I looked harder, I'd see Buffy the vampire slayer around here somewhere.

They bowed their heads at my presence, and I nodded back as I took in the scent of the fresh ocean. It was laced with the saltwater and the fresh air. The cool breeze grazed my cheeks as I itched to go down to the coast but I'm guessing standing outside in the night wasn't a possibility with the vampires around.

It was no wonder that Aiden smelt like sea-washed mahogany and fresh waterfall. He was a part of this tropical paradise.

I was now a part of this paradise.

I rounded the car to the trunk for my bags, but Aiden placed his hand on my back and steered me inside, "They'll bring it in for you."

Following his lead, I let my eyes travel along the expanse of the stone castle walls as we trudged up the staircase, "I still can't believe you own a castle, I mean, you don't exactly peg me as a prince type."

He snorted, "Whatever the opposite of royalty is, is where you'll find me."

My lips tilted up at that because even if I didn't know him, I knew that was true.

Kai and Loly entered the large doors before us and my state of disarray planted a seed of self-consciousness in me as we entered the large foyer.

Luckily there were only three people standing inside and I recognized one of them. Beta Rick, who I presume to be his mate and another male.

As my eyes glided across the room, I felt nerves spike by its elegant charm. It was no dark gothic castle. It was light, airy, and coastal with touches of royal gems like the large chandelier hanging on the high ceiling and the priceless painting of the sea on the left wall.

The walls were white with seafoam green moulding, the tiled floors had an intricate shell design, and there was a large double staircase that was made for gods and goddesses to grace.

Beta Rick and the beautiful woman at his side, beamed at me.

"Tate, let me introduce you to my mate Calypso," Rick looked at the dark-skinned woman with the light of a thousand stars in his eyes as he introduced us.

I held my hand out for hers, "It's great to finally meet you Calypso, Rick here couldn't shut up about you."

She laughed slowly as she looked at the dried blood on my hands before pulling me into her arms, "What can I say? I've trained him well."

I returned her warm gesture and was immediately relaxed I beamed at her jest towards Rick.

As she pulled back, she gave Aiden a once over before tsking, "Only a few days in and she's already beaten you up? I like her already."

Aiden's lips thinned, "Bloodsuckers."

"How many?" Rick asked in concern.

"Three, they got us at the end of the interstate. The rental's done for, you'll need to send a cheque to the company," He informed his Beta.

"I'll get on that and make sure the guards are prepared in case they retaliate," He headed off past the double staircase and to the left.

As fast as Rick had stepped away, the other guy saddled up before me with a large grin, "Luna Tate, I've been waiting to meet you."

Kai trudged over and wrapped his arm around the waist of the man, "This is Matt, my mate."

"Kai told me you play the guitar?" I recalled our conversation on the plane as I gave him a hug.

Matt blushed and elbowed his mate, "It's more of a hobby."

"He's being modest, he plays for us down on the beach whenever we manage to have a bonfire going," Kai shared.

Bonfires? I think I might just start falling in love with the beach already.

"We should have a bonfire tomorrow," Calypso suggested. "It'll be a great way to introduce you to the pack."

"What do you think Alpha?" Kai asked but Aiden was already halfway across the room as he approached a woman with brunette hair that had bright green edges.

She had just stepped out of the doorway to the right and I felt my stomach drop to my feet as I wondered if she was the dance partner Aiden learned his moves for.

If that wasn't bad enough, she was stunning and looked about his age.

Call me Jealous Judy because that was how I felt.

I faintly listened to Matt, Calypso and Kai discuss the bonfire tomorrow as I focused my attention on my mate.

"Where's Tourmaline?" Aiden quietly asked.

But before the woman could answer, a little girl no more than five years old with pastel pink hair started running down the staircase.

As she landed on the ground floor, her little legs took her directly to Aiden as he instinctively lowered himself and scooped her up.

"Dad! You're back!" She cheered ecstatically and wrapped her arms around his neck.

CHAPTER 8

Dad?

The twilight zone was less confusing than my life right now.

Aiden's eyes locked onto my own for a split second and the guilt on his face was unmistakable.

But instead of offering up an explanation, he focused his attention back on the girl, Tourmaline.

Goddamn it, was this why he didn't want a mate? Because he's already got someone and a kid?

"Were you up no good again?" He asked her with a smile. A genuine, face splitting, eye crinkling, dimple showing smile. Something I'm seeing for the first time on Aiden's face.

"Maybe..." Tourmaline grinned mischievously and grabbed Aiden's cheeks. "But you've been gone forever. You said only one day, and it's been a whole year!"

"It's been four days Tourm," He answered but his smile didn't waver.

"Well, it's been sooo boring here! Jenny wouldn't let me do anything," She slumped and sighed as a kid does.

"I'll-"

"Alpha," Rick appeared from the hallway he'd just been through, "north coast spotted a vamp sneaking around in the marsh."

"Go eat your dinner, I'll see you later," Aiden ruffled Tourmaline's hair before setting her down and disappearing with Rick.

Uhm, hello Alpha Dickhead, I'd really love an explanation right now.

I watched as Tourmaline looked me over before approaching me with a shy smile.

I love kids, they're adorable. But right now, I was particularly wary of this kid and the impact she was about to make on my life.

As she skipped closer towards me, I couldn't look away from her mesmerizing features. Her odd pink hair, her striking blue eyes, and the similarity between her and Aiden. It wasn't obvious but you could tell they were related.

"Hi, I'm Tourmaline."

My knees were wobbly by the impact of this secret but I lowered myself none the less. I also couldn't help the authenticity of my sudden fondness for this child.

"It's nice to meet you Tourmaline, my name's Tate," I was about to shake her hand but remembered that there were specks of blood from helping Aiden with his wound and hid them behind my back. "And I love your hair by the way."

She beamed at me, "I really like yours," she reached into my messy hair and twirled her finger through a loose curl. "Will you be joining us for dinner?"

I spluttered, unsure of how to answer her because I was hungry, but I wanted nothing more than to take a shower and hit the sack.

Calypso luckily answered for me, "How about we let Tate go rest after her long trip and in the morning we can all have breakfast?"

She frowned but it was quickly turned upside down as she beamed at me, "Okay but you have to promise to go swimming with me tomorrow."

"It'll be my honour," I grinned.

The woman, who Aiden had spoken to before, strutted over and grabbed Tourmaline's hand, a bit too roughly if you asked me. But from what I could assume, she could be Tourmaline's mother.

They didn't share any noticeable features except her hair was also dyed a peculiar shade of green as Tourmaline's was pink, so I won't count it out. She also hadn't addressed me directly either so maybe she was ignoring the presence of her child's father's mate?

"Come on Tourmaline, you have to eat your dinner before Aiden gets back," The woman said.

"But-"

"Now Tourmaline," She cut off the little girl firmly and I couldn't help but scold.

"Fine," Tourmaline grumbled. "Goodnight Tate."

"See you in the morning," I waved.

The woman spared me a glare before leading Tourmaline through the large doors to the right.

Suddenly my teenage years didn't seem so rough. Aiden must have had at her sixteen after losing his parents and becoming an Alpha at fourteen.

"Jenny could be a bitch sometimes," Calypso said beside me.

Kai snickered, "I think you mean all the time."

I turned just in time to see Matt elbowing him again.

"Calypso's right, she's been pinning for Aiden for a while. If I were you, I'd keep an eye out for her," Matt said with a frown.

Calypso nodded, "The girl can't think a hint, poor thing. You'd think now that you're here that she'll back off, but she seems relentless."

So, was she not the dance partner?

"She's Tourmaline's mom?" I asked slyly and they all immediately shook their head.

"She could never be half as amazing as Tourm's mom," Matt shook his head.

"Didn't Aiden tell you?" Calypso asked.

"He hasn't told me a thing before it happened," I muttered.

"He's better at fighting and baking than talking to girls," Kai smirked. "Don't worry he'll come around."

I nodded, unconvinced, before looking at Calypso as dread filled my veins, "What did you mean when you asked if he didn't tell me?"

She bit her lip unsure as she exchanged glances with the guys, "I think it will better if Aiden explains it himself. He can be a dickhead sometimes with his secrets."

I felt my eyes light with humour at the word she used, "In the few days that I've known him, I know just how much of a dickhead he can be."

She smirked, "I'm really glad you're here Tate."

"So am I," Matt agreed.

Kai patted my dishevelled hair as he gave me a wink, "And trust me, it isn't what you think."

Oh, so it isn't Aiden a total shit by having a kid and not telling me?

It's what I wanted to say but instead, I nodded, "Thanks, guys."

"Now, come on, I'll show you to your room," Calypso said as she began leading me off and I stifled a yawn. "I think the day's finally catching up to you."

I nodded as my eyes felt droopy, "It's been longer than expected."

"So, Aiden didn't tell you anything?" She asked in shock.

"Not a word," I shook my head. "Imagine how shocked I was when a vampire told me I was his favourite blood type."

Her eyes widened, "You fought with them?"

"I couldn't exactly sit back and watch everyone be attacked."

"Why am I not surprised that you're a Luna. I can't believe you made it out without a scratch, my first vampire attack left me with a bloody leg."

"No scratches but there was a dislocated shoulder."

"Oh, if you were on the beach, we would have given you a green whistle for that."

"Green whistle?" I asked confused as we walked up the staircase.

"It's methoxyflurane, an inhalation anaesthetic which helps numb the pain so we can help pop the shoulder back in place. It happens all the time here on the beach, the boys say it's like a drug," She shook her head.

"Whatever it is, it sounds better than having to breathe through that pain," I winced as I remembered the pain.

"If your shoulder gets soar, let me know I'll bring up a heated pad," She said before giving me a rundown of the castle.

There were over a thousand rooms, four floors, a giant court-yard set in the middle, and towers at each corner to monitor vampires.

As we walked down a long corridor, one wall was made entirely of glass and I could see the brightly lit courtyard outside with a few patrolling wolves around.

I was way out of my league in this place.

My room was on the top floor, east wing. Meaning I had a view of the ocean.

"Alpha Aiden's room is the last down the hall," She pointed as we stopped at the last door on the left, "this is your room."

I watched as she opened the door to a room that looked as if it was made for a princess, "Wait, am I not staying with Aiden?"

"I was told this is your room, I thought you two decided on this?" She looked as confused as I felt.

Shaking my head, I turned away from her in embarrassment. I mean of course, we weren't sharing a room. Friends didn't do that, did they?

"I'm sure it's just until you turn eighteen," She said in a comforting tone and I knew she was only trying to make me feel better. "Rick told me you were still seventeen."

I plastered on a smile and turned to her, "Yeah, you're right. I'm sure my brother probably threatened him before we left."

Or so I thought to make myself feel better.

She pulled me into her arms and said, "If you need anything, I'm in the north wing, first door to the right."

"Thanks, Calypso," I smiled gratefully just as my phone started to buzz in my pocket.

Pulling it out I saw my mom's caller id show up.

"I'll let you take that, goodnight Luna."

"Night," I waved at her as she stepped out of the room and closed the door behind her.

As I answered the call, I looked over the expansive room.

"Hello?" My mom's voice came over the line.

"Hey mom, sorry I hadn't called earlier. We only arrived about fifteen minutes ago," I informed her.

Even though I trusted my mother with anything and everything, I felt as if I would be betraying my new pack if I told her I was by the ocean instead of the forest.

So, I chose to omit my location, my enemy, and Tourmaline for now.

"That's alright honey, it must have been a long journey," She mused, and I could hear her voice waver.

"It was. Is everything okay?" I asked as I walked over to an armed chair sitting near a vanity table.

"Everything's fine," Her voice cracked, and I went on high alert because I knew she was fibbing.

"Mom, tell me. What happened?" I questioned anxiously.

She sighed, "Nothing's wrong, I promise. I'm just missing you already is all."

I still felt uneasy as if she was keeping something from me, "Are you sure that's all?"

"Yes Tate, can't a mother worry?" She scolded.

"Not if she's keeping something from me," I retaliated.

"It's fine, I'm fine and everything is just fine."

"Mom, if you're lying-"

"I'm not. Now tell me about your new pack," Her tone made it clear that she was finished with the discussion and I had to believe that if anything was seriously wrong, she'd tell me.

We spoke for a few more minutes before she let me go with one last assurance that everything was okay.

Setting my phone aside, I finally took in my room. The room was a stark white with a muted blue tone on the fringes. A large bed sat against the wall opposite the door with large windows flanking each side of the bed and the vanity sat on the right of the room. Opposite the bed and near the door held a very comfortable look-ing chaise, an armchair and a bookcase filled with books about the ocean and random sea-themed trinkets placed for aesthetic purposes. The left of the room held two doors to which I figured were a closet and the bathroom. There was also a chest of draws, a large painting of a shipwreck, and a decor piece of a fishing net with seashells tangled in.

Having not much else to do and the weight of the day pressing me into the marble floor, I found my bags already laying at the feet of the bed and pulled out a pair of pyjamas.

Unpacking will undeniably be done tomorrow.

The bathroom followed the marine theme going on and was already fitted for a guest with soaps, towels, and a toothbrush.

I headed straight into the shower and let the warm water relax my aching shoulder.

Vampires. A daughter. A castle. The possible mom of said daughter.

And the kicker was that we were on the beach and I couldn't even swim. The irony didn't go past me.

After my shower, I got dressed in my pyjamas and braided my hair before heading straight to bed.

But before I could call it a night, I caught Aiden's scent outside.

I could leave it be until tomorrow, but I had to know.

I had to know why he kept Tourmaline a secret.

Opening the door, I stopped short when I saw him with Tourmaline in his arms and Jenny following closely behind him.

Tourmaline sleepily smiled at me from her rested position on Aiden's shoulder, "Goodnight Tate."

Aiden's eyes assessed me, and my gaze flickered to a very pissed off Jenny.

If she wasn't the mom, then what the hell was her deal?

Maybe she was an aunt? Jesus, I need to stop making assumptions.

But the picture of a family stood before me and I couldn't help the unease I felt.

Nervously I waved at them, "Goodnight."

Stepping back and shutting my door I felt the embarrassment creep up my neck. You'd swear I would have done some bad things in my past for karma to be such a bitch today.

Rubbing my eyes in frustration and shame, I slowly stepped away from my door as I heard the door across the hall open.

What really had me curious was that I had not picked up Tourmaline or Jenny's scents. It must be the saltwater affecting my scenes because their scents were very muted and indistinguishable.

Not five minutes later and I heard two footsteps exit the room.

"Goodnight Aiden," Was the only thing said followed by a gruff reply as the lighter footstep faded down the hall to the right, which was the opposite direction of Aiden's room.

I couldn't help the small smirk on my face or the relief in my bones in knowing that at least she wasn't his bed buddy.

But it was short-lived as Aiden's scent approached my door and I could see his shadow at the crease below the door.

A light knock sounded, and I gulped as I got up and slowly opened the door to reveal his tired yet ruggedly beautiful features.

"I..." He started before trailing off.

I nodded for him to go on. He paused as his eyes flickered down the hallway.

I took the time to see that the cloth which was wrapped around his arm was gone and the wound was healed perfectly.

"It's just that Tourmaline said something when we arrived," He said as his eyes found its way back to mine, "and I didn't get to say anything, nor did anyone correct it."

I raised an eyebrow, "Yeah, I would have appreciated knowing that you're a dad before I met your daughter."

The corner of his lip quirked up as he bit his lip to cover up a smile. His eyes twinkled against the light that escaped my open room door and I was caught off guard.

I braced myself for what I did to deserve this response. What could possibly be so amusing about this situation?

"The thing is, that's where everything got twisted and you've been misinformed," He said.

"Which part?" I faltered as I asked.

He tucked his hands in the pockets of his jeans as he shrugged nonchalantly, "Tourmaline isn't my daughter, she's my niece."

I gaped like a fish swimming in the ocean outside as I blinked slowly at him.

"Sh-she's your what now?" I asked for confirmation.

"Tourmaline's my niece," He repeated.

"Niece?"

"Yes, my brother's daughter."

"You have a brother?" I asked in confusion.

"Had," His tone faltered.

Goodness gracious.

"But she called you dad..." I trailed off in question.

He nodded as he rubbed the back of his neck, "She does that sometimes and I honestly don't have the heart to correct her. But she knows who her parents are."

"Aiden..." Words failed me from this news and the fact that his brother was gone. "What about her mom?"

His expression turned cold as his eyes hit the floor, "My brother and his wife died when Tourmaline was born."

I felt a pinch in my heart and didn't question my instincts as I wrapped my arms around him. He was tense but relaxed and wrapped his arms around me.

"I'm sorry," I whispered softly into his chest.

"It's alright, wasn't your fault," He said in a gruff tone.

I waited for him to pull back before I asked my question.

"How did they die?" I hesitantly asked.

"Vampire attack," His voice had an edge to it. "Tourmaline never got to meet them."

When he said that, it all made sense. Tourmaline's his dance partner. She doesn't have a family, but she has Aiden, who I'm sure would do anything for her. Even learn to dance.

"She already likes you," Aiden gave me a small smile. "She only just met you and she's already excited to spend time with you."

I shrugged, "What can I say? The kids love me."

"Just be careful with her. She gets attached easily and I can't see her hurt," The seriousness in his eyes didn't surprise me.

"I don't plan on leaving or putting her in danger, that you can be sure of," I vowed.

"Good, because she's the only family I've got."

CHAPTER 9

That night I twist and turned in my new bed with pictures of thirsty bloodsuckers crawling in my mind. Even though my encounter was brief with one, it felt like they've intercepted my mind and now my skin crawled from being touched by the dead.

A projected image of his silver eyes, cold skin, and bloodthirsty fangs kept my eyes open and my body on high alert.

Nothing about this situation felt real. Nothing made enough sense for it to click together.

Why were the vampires only after his pack?

How did they manage to get into the castle and kill his brother and sister-in-law?

Unless it happened in their old territory... but then that would mean they vampires followed them here to the coast. That suggested that they wanted something.

Because that was always the question; what do they want?

One thing I could count on was their lack of ability to walk in the sunlight. Nope, they didn't shimmer and shine like Edward, they burnt to ashes.

But what really chilled my bones was when Aiden said that Tourmaline was his only family.

They both had each other and a big pack, but they didn't have a family like me. They didn't have the luxury of receiving the love of a parent and the laugh of a sibling.

And that pained me the most. I'd be damned if I didn't make them see that I was here for them now...both of them.

Aiden can have friendship all he wants but I'm still going to be here for him, as family. That he can count on. No matter how hard he tries to be distant, I'll weasel myself in.

Especially now that he revealed Tourmaline was his niece and not his daughter. To think Aiden was more zaddy and less daddy.

Goddamn, his fatherly instincts should be the least of my concerns, but when the man looked as he did, it was hard to not want what I can't truly have...

The following morning, I was groggy, grouchy, and hungry after skipping dinner and lacking sleep.

Worst of all, as I got ready for the day, I realized my entire wardrobe was mountain chic and not beach goddess. Which meant I was about to sweat buckets in sweaters and jeans if I didn't buy myself new clothes soon.

At least I had a few t-shirts.

After getting ready for the day I made my way to the dining hall or what I thought was the dining hall. I apparently took the wrong turn as I ended up in a hallway without windows and only one door at the end. As I stalked closer to the giant double doors, I realised that there was some sort of crystalized mineral embedded on the surface.

The crystals were pale yellow and covered every square inch of the doors, including the handles. To the right of the door, there was a black screen that looked oddly like a hand-scanner.

And what exactly was behind the door? Hell, if I knew.

Maybe vampires? Or maybe where Aiden keeps all his words and emotions?

Option two seemed more likely since there weren't any guards posted outside the door.

Before I could turn around and go in search of food, the door cracked open and Jenny stepped out.

Her expression went from shock to seething with rage. While I know her name, I had yet to learn of her relation to Tourmaline.

Maybe an aunt?

As my eyes moved over her and to the door, it closed before I could see what was in there.

"You shouldn't be down here," She snapped at me. "It's off-limits to you and I'm sure Aiden would be very mad once he knows you were snooping."

Calypso was right, she certainly had a thing for Aiden.

"You and I must have different definitions of snooping," I raised a brow, unimpressed by her anger.

She smirked haughtily, "I know you're only a teenager Tatelyn but as an adult I know my terms."

I felt my fists clench at my side, and I had to say a prayer to hold me back from punching this chic. Tatelyn? And she's calling me out on my age when she's name-calling?

"Does being that old come with severe memory loss along with those wrinkles," I waved my fingers at her eyes. "And it's Luna Tate."

"You're not my Luna, wolf. As for you, this area is restricted, so if I were you, I'd stay away before I report you to your Alpha," She sneered.

"Funny, Aiden didn't mention any part of the castle being restricted to me before bed last night," I said.

Smoke was spewing out of her ears and watched in amusement at her reaction.

Stepping closer to me, she dropped her voice deadly low, "What's funny is the fact that he put you in a separate room. And what's even more amusing is that when I went to his room this morning, you certainly weren't there. Aiden doesn't need another child to babysit, he needs a woman and you're just not that."

Heat crept up my neck as I tried not to let her words get to me, "He needs a mate and that's what I am. Unlike you, I don't tear another woman down by going after her mate. And your games don't bother me because at the end of the day you won't be the one at his side leading this pack, I'll be."

I didn't wait for her reply as I turned away and walked out of the dark hallway. As I strolled around, looking for the right way to the kitchen, I thought about just how much her words really did affect me.

She was in Aiden's room this morning. Why? Were they really something a bit more friendly or was she simply lying?

I'd never given much thought to wanting to be older than I am. To me, being older was trivial. But now, not so much. Now I wondered if being eighteen would have brought me more respect.

Though I was only a week and a half away from eighteen and that clearly didn't matter.

I felt the pinch of pain in my chest and cursed as I keeled over from the immediate piercing my heart felt.

Pressing my hand into my chest, I prayed no one walked down this corridor to see my awkward position on the floor, but of course, I was the master of bad luck.

"Tate?" I heard behind me and immediately stiffened as I tried to sit up.

First my age and now add an unfixable wound and the whole pack's going to think I'm more of a liability than an asset.

"Shit, Tate, are you alright?" Gamma Dylan appeared above me and I nodded.

"I'm good," I squeaked in pain.

Jesus, it's never been this bad before. I was definitely not good.

"You don't look alright, should I call Aiden?" He asked as his eyes took in my position.

I shook my head furiously, "Don't you dare."

"Alright, alright. Let me help you up."

I allowed him to pull me into a sitting position on the floor as I pressed my palm harder where the pounding pain sliced through me.

Damn, Moon Goddess. Couldn't she have made Emery's powers a bit more fool proof? You know, so when she brought me back from the brink of death, I'd be as healthy as a werewolf should be.

"Are you having a heart attack?" Dylan asked in a panic.

I managed a chuckle, "Werewolves don't have heart attacks."

"Right...I knew that," He said awkwardly before going quiet while the pain in my chest ebbed away.

Embarrassment ate away at me at my moment of weakness and I can only hope Dylan doesn't repeat this moment to anyone else. Especially Aiden.

As the pain slowly faded, he helped me to my feet.

"I'm all good now," I said patting his arm and he let me go.

"What was that?" He asked curiously.

"If I tell you, you can't tell anyone about this," I gestured to the grown.

He narrowed his eyes suspiciously but nodded, "Alright, I promise."

"A while back I was attacked by some rogues and it took a while for my heart to recover. It left me with a pain in my chest that only happens sometimes," I said.

His eyebrows were drawn together at my vague description, but I left out the part of Emery healing me for a reason. No one outside of the Blood Moon pack knew the human Lunas had powers and I'm not about to divulge that information to Dylan.

Gamma or not, it could be dangerous if that information fell into the wrong hands.

"Have you seen a doctor?"

"Multiple times, but my heart is all healed up. The pain is just a symptom I have to live with."

"Does Aiden know?"

"No, and you can't tell him," He looked at me suspiciously and I continued, "yet. You can't tell him yet because I haven't gotten the chance to let him know."

"Well you better tell him soon before you drop to the ground again," He said.

"Yeah...I will."

"Where were you heading anyway?" He asked

"Kitchen."

"You're going the wrong way," He chuckled as he started steering us the right way. "So does it happen often?"

"No, it comes and goes," I shrugged.

"Hmm..." He mused before starting to talk about the bonfire tonight.

I almost forgot about that. Tonight, I had to meet the pack and goddamn was I nervous.

As we approached the dining hall, I caught Aiden's scent and my stomach turned remembering what Jenny said.

"This is the main dining room," Dylan said as we stepped into a crowded room with rambunctious laughter and light-hearted conversations.

There wasn't one big table but about forty or more round tables set up throughout the large room. I guess if you own a castle and a large pack it's bound to look like a kingdom at feast every day.

"Wow...it's-"

"Huge, I know," Dylan nodded. "Usually everyone sits wherever they wish but the Alpha likes to sit near the window over there," I followed his pointed finger to the table that was near a large window that looked out at the coast and was situated at the head of the room.

Aiden, Tourmaline, Calypso, Rick, Matt and Kai were already seated.

Aiden's eyes immediately found me when we stepped into the room and I watched as his gaze hardened on Dylan.

"It's the best view in the room," Dylan continued, "you can see the water."

The entire room was magnificent, and I honestly think it was meant to be the ballroom, but I could be wrong. I'm not that well acquainted with castles.

"Tate!" Tourmaline squealed happily as she spotted me near the table.

"Hey Tourmaline," I greeted her as she rounded the table and gave me a hug.

"I've been asking Uncle Aiden to wake you up for breakfast, but he wouldn't listen," She frowned as she went back to her seat to the left of Aiden and I took the seat at his right since Dylan filled the only other available seat.

I didn't miss Tourmaline saying 'uncle' instead of 'dad' and I wondered if Aiden had something to do with that. I didn't want him to correct Tourmaline because I was okay with it. It didn't bother me and I won't do that to little Tourm.

"I was awake, but I got lost," I laughed as I looked over the various breakfast dishes laid before me.

"Good morning Tate," Aiden said from beside me but I didn't turn to him as I still felt my anger simmering from what Jenny said.

"Aiden," I replied good mannerly before grabbing some toast.

"Are you okay?" He asked.

"Fine," I shrugged.

"Tate, you should try the seaweed pancakes," Tourm said as she passed me a tray of pancakes that had some brown bits in it.

Aiden stopped the plate from sliding any closer to me, "Tourm, I don't think Tate would like those."

I watch Tourm frown and grabbed the plate out from his hold and pulled it closer, "It won't hurt to try."

Her frown turned upside down as I took a pancake.

"You're not going to like it," Aiden leaned closer to me and whispered.

I narrowed my eyes at him, "You don't know that."

"Yeah Alpha, let her try it," Dylan said with a mischievous lilt in his voice as everyone at the table looked at me expectantly.

Bottoms up, I guess.

Cutting a piece, I brought it to my mouth, but the smell psyched me out and I almost gagged. Aiden coughed next to me and as I looked over at him, he was staring intently at me with an expectant brow.

Wanting to prove him wrong, I held my breath and shovelled that piece of pancake into my mouth and chewed.

Chewing was where everything went wrong because this was single-handedly the most disgusting thing that I've ever eaten.

I placed my fist over my mouth as I gagged again.

Oh crap, what did I get myself into?

Looking around the table, I realized I hadn't poured myself anything to drink so I reached over for Aiden's glass of orange juice, gulped the contents, and washed the horrid chunks down.

My fingers were firmly placed over my lips as I set the glass down and tried not to bring up what just went down.

"So, how was it?" Tourm asked.

I nodded at her with a thumbs up, "Terrific."

At that point, everyone at the table, except Aiden, burst out laughing. I mean full out, teeth bared, stomach hurting, eye-watering laughter.

Even little Tourm giggled at my demise.

"You should have listened," Aiden whispered to me and I all but growled at him.

"I don't exactly trust you," I tossed his way.

"Sorry Tate, I make everyone try it but not everyone likes the taste of seaweed," Tourm shrugged before going back to her meal.

"Was it really seaweed?" I asked hesitantly to the table.

"Sargassum seaweed," Calypso informed me. "A more...pungent type."

Tourm gave me an innocent smile.

"Sorry Tate, I make everyone try it," She giggled in amusement.

"It's alright, though I think I need some lobster to wash that taste down," I joked as I looked over the table and saw that there wasn't any seafood around. Surprising seeing as they lived on the coast.

Everyone's eyes looked at me as if I just said something wildly inappropriate. My smile dropped as the uncomfortable silence swept through the room.

Calypso broke the tension by laughing as if I had just told a joke, "You're a funny one Tate, I must admit."

I laughed nervously, "Right, of course, I was only kidding..."

Aiden chuckled next to me and I turned to him with a glare, "We don't eat seafood."

So, seafood was off the menu. Duly noted.

"Maybe if you'd told me..." I trailed off.

"Are you angry with me?" He asked bluntly.

"Not at all."

"Then why are you being so weird?"

"Am I?"

"Tate..." He trailed off before shifting closer to me and lowering his voice. "Why was Dylan with you?"

My eyes sparkled with humour at his tone, "Jealous?"

He instantly shook his head, "No."

"He helped me find my way here," I said as his 'no' poked a hole in my already wittering confidence. "Why..."

"Why what?" He asked.

I turned to him about to ask about Jenny but changed my mind last minute, "Nothing."

I could tell he didn't believe me one bit, but he didn't push, "Okay. The bonfire will start at four, that way we can have enough time before the sun sets, and we'll come back to the courtyard."

"Sounds good to me," I nodded as I pushed around the eggs on my plate. "When do I start training?"

"Tomorrow, if you want. Tourmaline asked if you'd spend today with her."

I smiled, "That would be great."

"Good. Jenny will join you."

My expression immediately fell because no way in hell do I want to spend the day with Jenny. I think I might accidentally murder her...

If anyone asked, plausible deniability.

"Is something wrong?" He asked.

"Nope."

Both of us went quiet as we ate our breakfast without another word. I wanted to ask him about what Jenny said but I'm not sure that I want the truth.

Not if the truth was going to crush me.

And certainly, didn't want my heart to start acting up again. I'm beginning to think it ached mostly from emotional distress rather than physical.

"Are you joining us in the water later?" Kai asked from across the table.

Dylan smirked, "You have to. I'm sure we can get you a smoking biki-"

"Complete that sentence and I'll..." Aiden started but trailed off as his eyes flickered to Tourmaline who was happily enjoying her breakfast.

"Yes, Alpha?" Dylan prodded and Aiden growled at him.

"You're running patrol today, leave now," Aiden said instead.

Dylan shook his head and remained seated, "I'm not on the schedule."

Aiden seethed in anger at his Gamma, "Don't make me repeat myself, Dylan."

The entire hall was silent as Aiden's anger echoed against the marble walls of the ancient castle. No one dared to make so much as a squeak as Dylan left the room.

"Uncle Aiden?" Tourm questioned the brooding man.

"I have some work to do Princess, I'll see you later," He said as his demeanor towards her softened considerably before turning to me. "Tate."

I only managed a nod as he began walking away.

"Duty calls," Rick sighed as he hurriedly grabbed another slice of toast before kissing Calypso goodbye.

As the men left, the room reclaimed its life as the conversation picked up once more.

"Someone's certainly jealous," Calypso smirked.

"Tate?" Tourm asked.

"Yeah?"

"Are you Uncle Aiden's girlfriend?" She asked innocently.

I stuttered, unsure of what the answer is.

"Uhh, we're friends," I settled.

"Oh... but he really likes you," She shrugged as she went back to her pancakes.

I turned back to the others and they gave me a questioning look. "What?"

"You're more than a friend to him," Matt said.

"Definitely more," Calypso agreed.

CHAPTER 10

"I have important things I need to take care of, so you and Tourmaline can run along," Jenny said as we stood outside the dining hall.

I looked down at Tourmaline who was gripping my hand and she simply shrugged, unfazed. From what I'd gathered so far, Jenny took care of Tourmaline. Yet, she didn't seem keen on sticking around today when Tourmaline was with me...a practical stranger. That wasn't something I would have done with my little brothers.

Tourmaline didn't seem as if she minded either as she tugged on my hand.

"Come on Tate, I want to show you the entire castle."

"Not the..." Jenny started but narrowed her eyes on me before she continued, "pool. You can't take Tate in there."

"But I-"

"Tourmaline!" Jenny said sternly. "Listen to your elders without throwing a tantrum."

The child reeled back hurt as her eyes went to the floor, her joyful mood deflated, and her lower lip quivered.

"Yelling at her isn't going to make her learn any better," I said with an edge to my voice.

Jenny's eyes glinted with anger as she sneered, "I've been taking care of her for two years, I know just how to speak to her to get her to learn. Isn't that right Tourmaline?"

The little girl nodded without looking up and I wanted to drag Jenny by the tips of her green hair outside and smack some sense into her.

"Don't give your uncle any trouble," Was the last thing she said as she sauntered out the door.

I lowered to Tourm's height and tilted her chin up, "Do you know what my grand aunt Jane always says?"

She shook her head as a tear escaped her eyes and I brushed it away.

"She said that adults were a bunch of knuckles heads who forgot what it was like to be a kid. Jane said to never be like them. Never grow up too fast because when we do, we become a bunch of cranky old people who throw worst tantrums than any kid."

I saw her lip curled up as she rubbed her eyes, "Is Jane a cranky old lady?"

I laugh as I bopped her nose, "Jane may be old but she'll never admit it. And she most certainly isn't cranky because she's a kid at heart."

"Can I meet her?" She asked with hopeful eyes.

"Definitely," I promised. "Maybe we can take a trip back to my old pack."

She beamed at the idea, "Yay! Uncle Aiden never lets me go anywhere."

Unease settled over me at the prospect of not keeping my promise to her knowing that Aiden may not let her go. But if there's a will, there's a way, right?

"Maybe we can convince him, if not, I'll ask if Jane can visit," I stood to my full height and held my hand out for hers. "Now come one, you said you were going to show me the castle."

Tourmaline happily grabbed my hand and when we turned around, I saw Calypso and Matt both sending grateful smiles my way before scurrying back to the dining hall.

"First I need to show you the courtyard. Come on Tate!" She said happily once again as she pulled me along.

We walked beyond the grand staircase and down a long, broad hallway, towards a thick glass door. Outside, was a giant courtyard that was boxed in by each side of the castle.

Bright green grass covered most of the ground only to be broken up by a pebbled walkway. Off to the right was a pergola swing with yellow Lady Banks' roses growing off the wooden panels and cascading off the sides like wild vines. A few palm trees lined the sides, with a very comfortable looking hammock tied between two. There was also a swing set, monkey bars, and a slide to one corner and I knew from the shade of pink that it was put there for Tourmaline.

What was the most distinctive feature of the set-up, though, was the manicured hedge in the middle of the courtyard that was trimmed to represent a trident.

"Is that-"

"It's my mom's family crest," Tourm said. "Uncle Aiden said it represents my family."

A trident?

My thoughts were muddled as I wondered what it represents or why her mom's family had a crest. Were they royals?

It would explain the castle.

Tourmaline led me to the pergola swing as she began telling me about the beach and I noticed that her hair was unitedly thrown into a ponytail.

"Do you want me to braid your hair?" I asked her and from her reaction, I could tell that she doesn't have her hair braided often.

"Yes, please," She said as she turned around for me to have access to her pastel pink hair.

"Tourm...is Jenny your aunt?" I asked nonchalantly as I loosen her hair.

She shook her head, "No."

Huh, had I known that Jenny wasn't family, I would have given her a piece of my mind. Or a memorable bite from a wolf.

But I also didn't want to put my two cents where it didn't belong and if Aiden trusted her to take care of Tourmaline, then I had to respect that because he's her uncle. I didn't have a place in saying what I thought about Jenny's scolding of Tourmaline, but I also wasn't going to let this sweet girl be subject to her awful manner of teaching.

Patience was key here. I just also had to ensure I was around Tourm and Jenny more to make a solid case. That is of course, if he believed me against the word of Jenny.

Tourm continued, "Jenny was mommy's helper and started taking care of me after..."

My hands briefly froze in the middle of braiding her hair at the tone she used. Her voice dripped with the pain no five-year-old should carry as her shoulders sagged.

I tread cautiously and gently as I asked, "After what?"

"After Anvi was taken by the vampires. She was my mom's best friend."

Taken?

A million questions surfaced in my head as I considered what Tourmaline disclosed. But none that I could truly ask her.

Deciding that changing the topic is the wise decision, I asked if she usually braids her hair.

"Not really. Jenny never wants to do, Uncle Aiden tried, and he was horrible," she exaggerated by throwing up her hands and giggling.

"Well, we're just going to have to teach him," I decided.

She agreed as she started firing off questions at me. Everything from how many siblings I had to the colour of my wolf.

I could tell she loved the way I braided her hair as she delicately placed it over her slender shoulder. As we made our way through the castle after, she stopped and showed it off to everyone and even though I've known her for less than a day, she's already eating away at my heart.

It was no wonder Aiden was wrapped around her little finger.

We ran around the castle for most of the day. Through the kitchen stealing sweets from the pantry, up to the north watch-tower where we nearly set off an alarm before the guard kicked us out with a laugh, to a playroom where Tourm showed me her favourite doll, it was a mermaid with blue hair. And lastly, we ended up in the library.

It was much bigger than the one back at my old pack. It was no Beauty and Beast grand palace library, but it was spacious, and books lined every wall and then some.

A spiral staircase led up to a second story, two windows were set along one wall and there was gold filigree wrapped around the bookcases, staircase and onto the painted ceiling.

The ceiling depicted what could only be described as a rumbling storm of clouds above the rocky waves of the ocean crashing into a cliff side.

And at the wall between the two large windows, sat an immaculate mahogany desk that seemed to belong in the office of an old English professor.

But it wasn't empty, oh no. Occupying the seat behind the desk was Aiden sat perched over a book, in deep concentration.

As Tourmaline skipped over to him, he looked up and seemed surprised to see us both.

"Hey princess," He greeted Tourmaline as she rounded the desk and crawled into his lap.

The nickname for his niece pulled at my memory as I couldn't help but recall what he'd called me yesterday during our bout of slaying vampires.

Cupcake.

I hadn't given it much thought after, seeing as I was still reeling from vampires, castles, a niece and a dislocated shoulder, but now that I did remember, I don't think I'll forget it anytime soon.

I also couldn't help but wonder why that name specifically. Maybe the vampire attack made him delirious? I'd place by bet on that against the other option that I didn't want to think off.

"Alpha," I greeted and saw his jaw tick.

"Luna," He retorted, and I felt my eyes widen.

Well, he definitely best me on that one.

"I knew we'd find you in here," Tourm said.

"I just finished ran patrol and I assumed you were enjoying your day with Tate and didn't bother you. So, did you?" He asked as I strolled towards them and took a seat in the armchair opposite to him.

"Of course, I did!" Tate said with a 'duh' tone. "We had so much fun."

"That's right, I heard just how much fun you've been stirring around the castle," He said while shaking his head. "Stolen cookies and bothering my guards."

"All in a day's work," I winked conspiratively at Tourm who giggled along.

Aiden shook his but I caught the small trace of a smile pulling at his lips.

"And might I ask where's Jenny?" He questioned as his eyes went to the empty doorway.

I couldn't deny the unwelcome bite of jealousy I felt as he asked for her. I was half human after all.

"Dunno," Tourm shrugged indifferently.

His eyes gleamed with a sizzling anger as it landed on me next, "Where is she?"

"Dunno," I repeated what Tourm said and added. "She just left us."

"But we had fun without her," My little accomplice grinned.

Aiden nodded but I could tell from his expression alone that he didn't like Jenny leaving us alone one bit. That and I was pretty sure she was in for a scolding from him.

I wasn't sure if Aiden had good graces, but I would rather stay on that side of him any day than face his wrath.

"And Tate braided my hair, just like how mommy's hair looks in the pictures," She held her hair out for Aiden to inspect.

And for the briefest of moments, I watched as his otherwise stoic expression softened into something akin to vulnerability. Something that I knew he wore hidden under layers upon layers of armour and never revealed to anyone. It was something I knew he would never share with anyone because it was something I did.

As long as I could hide my chest pains, I will. It was a weakness that placed pushed me back further in the eyes of anyone. Sympathy was always handed out where it wasn't needed and as such, I hide it. I made it a mission of mine not to tell anyone unless I couldn't help it, like what happened with Dylan today.

"It looks beautiful," He commented on Tourm's hair before mouthing a 'thank you' to me. Aiden closed his book and stood up with Tourm in his arms as he said, "I think it's about time we started getting ready for the bonfire."

"Can we go swimming?" Tourm asked.

"Not today," Aiden shook his head sternly.

"But Da- Uncle Aiden," She whined.

"Soon, I promise."

"Fine."

He pinched her nose between his thumb and forefinger and gave it a wiggle to make her frown turn upside down.

As she smiled at his antics and batted his hand away, he put her on her feet, "Why don't you find Calypso to help you get ready?" He suggested.

"Would you fix my hair after Tate?" She asked.

"Of course," I agreed and went to follow her outside, but Aiden's hand caught my elbow.

"Tate..." He whispered as Tourm left, leaving us standing alone.

I turned to back to face his burning blue eyes that assessed me cautiously, as if I was about to snap at him.

"Hmm?" I whispered, unable to find words.

"Are you still angry with me?"

"No," I answered too quickly.

He narrowed his eyes, "You seem unsure of your answer."

"Do I?" I asked with a nervous chuckle.

"I wouldn't have said so if I didn't think it."

"Well, I'm not," I tried again.

"Is it about Tourmaline?" He asked and I shook my head furiously.

"Of course not! She's a sweet kid, Aiden. You've done a great job raising her and I'm definitely not angry at her," I said because it was absurd to think anyone could be angry because of Tourmaline.

"So, you are angry," He noted with a raised brow.

"Does it matter?"

"Doesn't it matter?" He countered.

"You're being annoying," I scrunched my nose up.

"Good," He said, and I gaped at him.

"Good?"

"Yes," He confirmed with a devilish smirk. "If you're angry at me and won't say why, I'll just create a reason for you to be. Can't make you a liar now, can I?"

"Or maybe you just need an excuse to annoy me."

"Maybe..." He said as he studied me like the book he was just preoccupied with.

He still had a hold of my elbow and the sizzling warmth from the mere contact burned through my body. It left me feeling dopy and Aiden's intense blue eyes wasn't helping the situation.

But as he was just stood there and gazed at me, I began to squirm.

Clearing my throat, I broke the silence, "I meant to ask-"

"Ask." He nodded for me to go on.

"Well, yesterday Tourm had called you Dad but today she's been calling you Uncle Aiden. Did you tell her not to call you that?" I asked hesitantly.

He nodded as he released me elbow, "I thought that it may make you uncomfortable-"

"It doesn't," I declared with a small smile. "Please, don't stop her. Not for me. You said she's all you have, and I suspect you're all she has as well, so don't deny her that."

I felt his demeanour shift. As if a layer of the brick wall that surrounded him cracked. A piece of himself shining through in all its bright glory, just for me. And what a wonderful feeling it was, to know that one day I might be able to know Aiden.

Not the tough Alpha or the vampire slayer. But the boy who raised Tourmaline, survived losing his family and who sat in a library reading.

"Thank you, Tate," He said earnestly as his features softened and relief filled his eyes.

I reached out and squeezed his hand, "I'll see you down at the beach."

As I turned to leave, I saw the barest smile on his lips. But small or large, it was there, and it was an unknown but welcomed victory.

Calypso and Beta Rick both led me down to the beach as it neared time for the early bonfire.

We trailed through the courtyard and across the backyard before we came to a long cobblestone staircase that was built into the side of the cliff and ended on the sandy shore.

As we trailed down the staircase, the saltwater invaded my heightened senses, the wind bristled against my hair and blew lightly against my dress and the sound of seagulls and the wave crashing was oddly comforting.

It was foreign but homely.

Crystal blue water went on for miles and miles along the coastline and pushed all the way out as far as my eyes can see into the Atlantic Ocean.

But as we neared the beach, I heard the laughs and chatter of Aiden's pack down below and felt nervous at the prospect of being officially introduced to the pack.

My age may be a hindrance, but I'll try my hardest to win them over. That began by throwing on my best but most suitable dress. A simple sundress but one that screamed warmth and friendlessness. I did however forgo Calypso's offer at a swimsuit because I won't be heading into the water until I knew how to swim.

When we landed at the bottom of the staircase, I kicked off my sandals and sunk my bare feet into the warm sand and marvelled at the feeling. My toes sunk in and the fine grains immediately coated the skin on my feet like sugar.

"First time on a beach?" Aiden's voice drifted towards me as he neared, and I nodded with a grin.

"Living in the middle of the forest doesn't offer much of an opportunity to get to the coast," I answered.

He hummed in agreement, "I hadn't been to the beach either until the pack moved. Just wait until you get in the water."

My eyes shifted from the sand to him and I took in the sight before me. He was dressed in a plain white cotton shirt and pair of knee-length dark green cargo pants.

"You're going to have to teach me to swim before I get anywhere near the water," I said offhandedly as my eyes continued to roam over Aiden's muscular form.

"You can't swim?" He asked in surprise and I suddenly felt embarrass.

I shook my head as I waited for him to comment about my age being the key factor for my lack of skills. But I was happily surprised when he simply shrugged.

"I'll teach you," He said like it was no big deal as he held his hand out for me to take. "But first I need to introduce you to your new pack."

My hand, with a slight tremble, stretched out and gladly took Aiden's. He caught the shake of my hand and gave it a gentle squeeze.

"It's the vampires that bite, not the wolves," He winked as he led me towards the crowd.

"Did you just make a joke?" I asked in feign surprise.

"I make jokes," He said accusatory.

I smiled up at him, "Huh, look at that, you just made another joke."

He shook his head as everyone turned towards us.

"Oaks Pack," He called to attention.

"Alpha," They responded.

"This pack hasn't had a Luna in a few years. We still mourn the lost of my mother and the late Luna Amethyst, both of who were taken away from us too soon. Just as when my father past and then my brother, Will, the pack needed an Alpha. It's always hard to adjust, especially when we cherished our leaders and lost them without warning." I detected the smallest trace of pain in Aiden's voice. It was undetectable if you weren't listening closely, but I was. And so, I squeezed his hand, as he had done mine, in an offer of comfort.

His thumb brushed the back of my hand as he continued his speech, "But as you've stood by side and helped me lead our pack, I wish you do the same for your new Luna. A Luna who I'll protect will my life and who I wish you all can make the same vow to as you come to know her. Everyone, I would like to introduce Tate Blackwood. Your Luna."

My heart stuttered at what he said. The promise he made. He'd protect me with his life.

I watched as everyone dipped into a synchronized bow and collectively said, "Luna."

"Welcome to the Oaks Pack," Aiden said beside me.

And just like that, I was being introduced to almost everyone in the pack one by one as they approached me.

The bonfire was lit, music began playing quietly and some of the pack members were out in the water on their surfboards albeit there not being big enough waves.

What took me by surprise was Aiden standing beside me throughout the entire introduction to everyone in his pack. He greeted everyone by name and spoke proudly of their place in the pack.

As for everyone, most of them seemed happy that I was finally here. A few others looked a bit weary and even questioned my fighting skills.

I, of course, happily told them I was a trained and seasoned warrior. While I may not know the technique to successfully take down a blood sucker, there was nothing a little training won't help.

When the questioning was over, however, Aiden was backed to his reserved self as he left me be and went over to Rick and Dylan.

I suppose his company can only be kept for so long.

But as he left, I was happily preoccupied with a few of the members who wanted to continue chatting until Tourmaline popped up with a mischievous smile on her face.

"Tate, come on, I want to show you something," She pulled on my arm as I hurriedly excused myself from the group I was talking to.

"What's that?" I asked as we walked closer to the water's edge.

"You'll have to wait and see," She giggled as she let go of my hand and approached the water.

"But Aiden said-"

But before I could finish my sentence, I heard Aiden growl behind me and yelled, "Tourmaline!"

The little girl paid him no heed as she dashed into the water and disappeared below the crashing waves.

I watched and waited for her to pop up and I heard Aiden approaching but as the second ticked by, she wasn't coming up.

Just as I took a step into the water, a strong arm wrapped around my waist and pulled me back.

"You can't swim, remember?" Aiden said in an extremely pissed of tone.

He let me go and I turned to him with wild eyes, "She disappeared under the water!"

"I know," He simply said but there wasn't a trace of concern on his face.

Only anger and frustration.

"Fucking h-" I began but was cut off.

"Tate said a bad word," A little voice chimed, and I turned to see Tourmaline happily in the water.

"Thank the Moon Goddess," I muttered quietly as I rubbed at my chest which had started to pinch in that familiar pain.

"She can swim," Aiden said beside me.

"Really?" I said sarcastically. "I didn't expect her to disappear for so long underwater."

"Tourmaline, what did I tell you?" Aiden questioned his niece.

She grinned, "Not to go in the water."

"And what else?" He asked.

"Not to tell Tate."

"Not to tell Tate what?" I asked with narrowed eyes, but they ignored me.

"And what's this?" Aiden asked.

"This is me showing Tate," Tourmaline enunciated as she dipped back under the water and kicked her legs up behind her.

Except...it wasn't legs.

I rubbed my eyes to make sure I was seeing this clearly as Tourmaline continued to swim around the ocean.

"I guess now you know our secret," Aiden whispered in contempt.

My jaw was on the sand as I gaped at what was before me.

"She's a..." I trailed off.

"Yup," He answered.

"And she just grew a..."

"She did indeed."

Well shit.

First vampires and now...

"Mermaid," I struggled to process this. "Tourmaline's a mermaid."

It was no tail of a dolphin or a trick of my eyes. Tourmaline was swimming around with a very real pink mermaid tail.

But before I could strangle Aiden for keeping yet another secret, one of the surfer's yelled something that filled my veins with ice and caused goosepimples to rise on my skin.

"Vampire!" He yelled.

CHAPTER 11

Aiden didn't miss a beat as he rushed into the water as Tourmaline, with a panicked expression, started swimming towards the shore.

Uselessness and helplessness weren't feelings that were familiar to me, but in that moment, they sunk their claws into every inch of my skin and left holes for fear to creep in. As the darkness clung to my pores and left my fractured heart screaming in anguish, I chanted to the Moon Goddess to protect Tourmaline.

To protect the only good thing left in Aiden's already shattered life. The last string holding him together.

Aiden was hard to read but the one and only thing anyone could read on his face was how much Tourmaline means to him.

Swim. Swim. Swim Tourmaline.

Loud sirens blared an ominous but alarming shrill across the coast and everyone set into motion. If I guessed right, it was an alarm to signal a vampire in the water, like those used for sharks.

As I ventured knee deep into the blue water, I watched in relief as Tourm swam right into Aiden's arms. He quickly pulled his soaked t-shirt over her pink hair before making quick work of getting them back to shore.

Further out in the ocean, five of the pack members, including Kai, floated on their surfboards and created a circle around a still part of the water. There was no vampire breaching the surface and there won't be anytime soon either. Not when the glorious sun was out and threatening to burn any blood sucker alive.

But that didn't provide much comfort because the water was a playground for these vamps. One that werewolves had no place in because unlike the vampires, we need oxygen. They're already dead so they can swim in the deep blue for the rest of their existence.

"Go back to castle!" Aiden commanded to the crowd behind me as he passed a frightened Tourmaline into my arms. "Tate, take her back, please."

The desperation in his voice cracked my already aching heart and I didn't fight him on it. This was a battle I couldn't fight. Not without knowing how to swim or take down a vampire. Ensuring his niece's safety was the one thing that I could do.

"Uncle Ai-" Tourmaline protested.

"Go!" He rushed sternly as he dove back into the water just as Tourmaline's small hand reached out for him.

I staggered my way back onto the shore with a human Tourmaline in my arms. Sometime between reaching Aiden in the water and being placed in my arms, she'd shifted back to her legs.

"Tate," She sobbed quietly into my neck as I tried my best to calm her and get her back to the castle, unscathed.

Calypso and another wolf, Pete, reached out to me and pushed me forward and further away from the water. As I hurried my way up the grand staircase on the cliffside, I peered down and saw Rick, Dylan and Matt all heading out into the water on jet skis. But I was too far up to see where Aiden was in the water.

Oh, Moon Goddess, please keep this stubborn, secret keeping, dickhead alive.

Tourmaline's arms were wrapped securely around my neck as I led her into the castle and straight to her room.

Her room was made for a princess. The walls were painted in shades of pastel blues, pinks and purples arranged in a scale pattern. Her bed head was cut into a clam shell shape with a crown canopy that draped dusty pink curtains down. The entire room was fashioned with mermaid themed bits and bobs but what caught my attention was the picture hanging above her dresser.

A man who was the spitting image of Aiden stood with his arms wrapped around a beautiful woman with striking blue hair on the beach. Tourmaline looked just like the woman and I could see the similarities she took from the man. So, this was Will and Amethyst Oaks, Tourmaline's parents.

Both of whom I'd only learn their names of during Aiden's speech earlier.

From what I could deduce, mermaids all seemed to have one peculiar trait, and it wasn't their fins. They had coloured hair which didn't fall into the basic browns, blondes, blacks and reds. But that also meant one thing, Jenny was also a mermaid, a fact I didn't know how I felt about.

"How about we get you something dry to change into?" I said soothingly to Tourmaline and she nodded her head but didn't release her hold, so I didn't dare set her down.

With one hand holding her to me and another rummaging through her clothes, I grabbed a pair of pyjamas and helped her dry off and change before wiping away her tears.

"He'll be alright," I whispered to her as I set her down on her bed and grabbed a hairbrush.

"You promise?" She asked as her sniffles persevered.

I held out my pinkie and she wrapped her much tinier one around my one, "Promise. Now why don't you tell me about your parents?"

That distracted her long enough as I finished braiding her hair and she laid back in her pillow with wild but tired eyes. I threw the t-shirt Aiden threw on her into the laundry basket before taking a seat on the armchair beside her bed.

"Tate?"

"Yes Tourm."

"You're not going to leave like anyone else...are you?"

Her innocent blue eyes stared up at me with so much hope that right there and then, I made a vow. I may not know what my future of friendship may hold with Aiden but neither him not anyone else would make me leave this little angel if she doesn't me to go. I'd protect her alongside Aiden, and she could count on that.

I took her hand in my own, "As long as you want me here, I'd be here. That's something you never have to worry about, alright? You don't ever need to question it because I'm certainly not going anywhere."

I was rewarded with a smile before she was lulled to sleep after facing the harrowing threat of a vampire attack.

Placing my head in my hands, I felt the ache in my chest lingering as my concern for the pack members in the water grew.

And I was still processing the very big elephant in the room which was that mermaids existed.

First vampires and now mermaids. I felt like I was living under a rock before coming to this pack. How did my family not know that mermaids were still around?

Frankly speaking, the only mention of mermaids in our supernatural library were from the ancient texts. The mer-people haven't been mentioned for over five-hundred years and to any wolf today, we'd believed they were a myth. An old legend created to make us believe that there were protectors of the sea as werewolves were the protectors of the land.

Unlike vampires, who've only disappeared a hundred years ago. The vampires were mentioned more often, they existed longer and was why we knew they roamed the earth once. But the mermaids were hidden and buried through the passage of time, only being mentioned in the stories of sailors. A mere fairy-tale.

But both species survived. They survived the evolving world and kept themselves hidden, even from the likes of wolves. As for why they're all entangled into the lives of the Oaks Pack still has me bewildered.

Also not forgetting the fact that Aiden kept the mermaid secret from me.

A light knock on the door pulled me from my reverie but as it opened, I was slightly disappointed to see that it wasn't Aiden but Calypso.

"Hey, is she asleep?"

I nodded as my eyes went to the little mermaid, "Yeah, I think her worrying over Aiden lulled her to sleep. Are the others back yet?"

"No," She shook her head and I could see the worry in her eyes, after all her mate was also out there. "They're all good at what they do, but I always worry when they're in the water. We're not as resilient as the mermaids or the vampires under there."

As she sat on the arm of the chair next to me and wrapped her arm around my shoulder, I appreciated the comfort of her company.

"How many are there?" I asked in a soft voice.

"Rick said one that they spotted, but Loly is checking our underwater motion sensors."

"The what?"

"Aiden had the pack install motion sensors in the water creating a perimeter safe enough for the mermaids to swim. It detects any big movement and send an alarm to us, but today we didn't get an alert. There are cameras there to, to help us ascertain whether it's a just marine life or a blood thirsty dead piece of poop," She crinkled at her nose at the mention of the vamps and her sentiments were mutually felt.

"I hadn't realised how serious the vampire situation was," I commented, still feeling in the dark about what was truly happening.

"Oh, it's bad. I suppose that's why we call it Alpha Aiden's Protection Program, because he has everything figured out to make sure the vampires are slayed, and the princess is kept safe."

"Protection program," I repeated dazed.

She gave me a small smile, "Yeah, because he makes sure the pack is in line to ensure Tourmaline's and the rest of the mermaid's safety. A protection program for the mermaids."

Clarity broached me as I nodded impressed, "It does have a ring to it."

She agreed with a laugh and as silence fell between us, she shook her head, looking a bit disgruntled.

"He didn't tell you about her, did he?"

My eyes shifted to the carpeted floor, "He didn't."

"Ugh, Aiden can be very obtuse at time, I swear...just give him a chance to relax around you. He just has a time trusting anyone new," She assured. "Soon, though, he'll be blabbering everything to you. Trust me, Rick was the same."

"I've never given him a reason to trust me."

"So then give him a reason to trust you."

I watched her dark, coffee brown eyes shine with wisdom and I nodded as the door quietly swung open.

A drenched Aiden stepped into the room and I was on my feet at once as he came closer to the bed.

"Are you okay?" I asked with a hush voice.

"I'm fine," He responded as his eyes went to Tourmaline. "Is she alright?"

"Yeah, just tired and worried about you. But I tried to calm her down."

"Good," He said as he walked over to his niece and brushed her hair back. "I told her not to go in the water."

I didn't respond because his voice was very low, as if scolding himself for not keeping her out of the sea.

Aiden placed a kiss on Tourm's forehead before turning to me, "We should talk."

"Are you sure you're able to? Because from what I've seen so far, talking seems like an impossible task for you," I murmured with an edge to my voice.

His eyes hardened but he ignored me as turned to Calypso, "Can you stay here with Tourmaline?"

She nodded her head before Aiden was storming out the door without turning back to see if I was following.

As I closed the door quietly behind me, Aiden headed to his bedroom.

"I'm going to change, I'll meet you in the library," He said and I glowered at his back.

It didn't went over my head that he didn't want me in his room. Not that is was important, but I'm guessing if my room was as grand as it was with a seating area, Aiden's room would be just as large or bigger. A perfect spot to talk.

But I shrugged off that notion as I swiftly made my way to the library. We had bigger issues to discuss.

Upon entering the room, I breathed in the scent of old pages and dusty spines as I ventured closer to Aiden's desk.

The book he was reading earlier sat closed on his desk: Mythical Properties of Supernatural Beings.

Interesting title.

I rounded the desk and plopped down in Aiden's chair as I bristled my fingers along the sharp edges of the pages. I turned to the bookmarked chapter, The Theory of Blood.

My eyes scanned the pages as I tried to ascertain what Aiden was researching. As I came upon the 'mermaid' section, I read the ancient words of the researchers from a hundred years ago.

According to the book, they theorized that mermaids' blood held a compound property that could heal any wounds or infliction, no matter the age or origin. But from what I was reading, the researches only went so far as to hypothesis since they weren't able to get their hands on a willing mermaid before they supposedly went extinct.

I highly doubt these scientist were actually waiting around for mermaids to willingly let themselves be treated as lab rats. I think that it was just hard to track down a mermaid who can breath underwater easily.

The hypothesis, on the other hand, was peculiar. While I'd never thought mermaids were actually real, it was more mind boggling to learn that their blood may be some super antibody for...well everything.

When I heard Aiden approaching, I shut the book and went to my feet as he entered the room with a troubled expression.

"Is everyone else alright?" I asked and his eyes snapped to mine as if he was pulled out of a deep thought.

"Yeah, luckily Kai's our best swimmer and subdued the blood sucker before taking him out," He explained as he gestures to the couches near one of the large windows over looking the coast.

I nodded before taking a seat across from him as the light rays of the setting run dazzled through the room. The warm orange haze set Aiden's blue eyes ablaze and glowing. I shifted nervously in my seat at his piercing gaze and looked towards the horizon.

"I'm so mad at you," I said, defeated as I picked a lose tread on my dress.

He snorted, "Tell me something I don't know. Since we've met you've hated me."

"Hate's a strong word."

"But isn't it true?"

"No," I pinned him with my eyes as I said it and watched as his frame relaxed slightly.

"Then why are you always mad at me?" He queried with a raised brow.

I shrugged, "Because you always do something to make me angry."

"Yeah?" His tone had a challenging lithe to it as he continued, "What exactly did I do this morning to make you angry?"

Heat rushed up my neck, turned my cheeks pink and the tips of ears hot as recalled being jealous over Jenny.

But discussing the green monster wasn't what we were here for.

"Never mind that," I quickly shifted gears and his eyes narrowed. "Just explain to me what's happening."

I could tell he didn't want to drop the subject but by some stroke of luck, he didn't push.

"Where do I even start," He sighed as he scrubbed a hand down his face.

"How about why you kept Tourm being a mermaid a secret?" I suggested.

A dark shadow crossed his features then, "I don't trust people easily."

I folded my arms and tucked myself further back into the armchair, "I'm not just 'people', Aiden."

"I know that," He groaned.

"Then why'd you not tell me?" I asked again, but with a gentler tone.

He shut his eyes and bent his head with his hands interlocked behind his neck before he answered, "Because it's hard. It's hard to trust anyone when you've already lost so much... I've lost everyone I've loved and I can't lose Tourmaline. And letting her identity be exposed is a sure fire way of losing her."

My hands itched to reach out and comfort him but I held back and tighten my folded arms.

"Why?" I asked, though I had a sinking feeling that it had something to do with what I read in that book minutes ago.

"If you're going to understand this, I should start with my brother," Aiden said in conviction as he raised his head and straightened his back. "You know my parents died when I was fourteen?"

"Yeah, but I had no idea you had a brother. I don't even think my father or brother knew," I clarified.

Aiden nodded, "William, my brother, was ten years older than me. When I was born, even though he was young, he knew he didn't want to be Alpha. One summer, he came to the coast to visit my grandma, who at the time was living not far from here. She'd moved when her mate had passed and Will wanted to visit so he did. He was about twelve when he told my parents he wanted to stay on the beach.

"No matter how much my parents tried to keep him in the Oaks Forest, he said he didn't belong there. So, reluctantly my parents allowed him to move. I guess since then, my dad always introduced me as Alpha so no one really had a chance to know about Will."

"It must have been tough for them to let him move away at such a young age," I said with a heavy heart.

"I was too small to remember or understand, but it did leave hole in our family," The forlorn expression on Aiden's face cut me deep as he shook it away and went on. "Will visited a few times a year, so I still got to spend time with him, but never enough. When I was fourteen, my parents were killed by wild rogues."

This time, I did get up and sat next to a surprised Aiden. I held my hand out, palm facing up and slowly, he placed his giant hand in mine and I gave it a good squeeze. He didn't say anything or acknowledged what I'd done but the appreciation in his eyes were enough for me.

"They died so suddenly that I felt like I couldn't catch my breath. Between their death and becoming Alpha, I was slowly slipping into an unhealthy state of mind. But then, Will showed up like my saviour dressed as my dork of a brother," Aiden shook his head at the memory as a small smile touched his face. "He'd not long ago found his mate, Amethyst. Mom and Dad were excited to meet her, but for one reason or another, they couldn't make it to the pack...not until it was too late.

"But Amethyst wasn't werewolf, nor was she human. And the forty or so other wild hair coloured people with her, weren't either. You see, my brother was drawn to the water at a young age because that's where his mate lived. Amethyst was the Queen of the sea, in every sense of the word."

"Queen?!" I said startled. "Is that why you call Tourmaline Princess?"

"Well, technically she's the Queen now, but yes, she's the princess of all the oceans and seas. The little mermaid."

I stared at him gaping, "I didn't even know two different species could be mates."

"They don't, usually," Aiden confirmed. "When Will told us what Amethyst was, we were all shocked, but she was family from that moment on. Will still didn't want to become Alpha, but after seeing his mate lead her own people, he decided to handle Alpha duties, even though I held the title. And he was great at it, a natural born leader. He helped me deal with our parents death as well, really stepped up as a brother.

"What he didn't tell us though, was why he and Amethyst moved from the coast all the way to the middle of the forest. It couldn't have been a wise decision since her people needed the water. But I guessed since my grandma had died and now my parents, Will didn't need to stay there and knew I needed him here. It wasn't until three months into him and Amethyst being at the pack, did we truly know why they'd come to the pack. Vampires."

The one word was laced so much malice and hatred. A storm brewed in Aiden's eyes as he released my hand and strolled closer to the window. He folded his arms as his eyes stared intently at the sea.

"The vampires were hunting the mermaids. It became exceedingly dangerous for them in the open water, so Will thought they'd be able to hide out here. But he was wrong. Somehow, they tracked them there and attacked the pack in the dead of night. We weren't prepared for it. By some miracle, we pulled through the night. Amethyst lost ten mermaids and our pack lost over a hundred wolves. It was a blood bath mixed with piles of ashes.

Their silver eyes haunted my dreams for the next week as we packed up everything and Will moved us here.

"The forest was too much of a risk because of how dark and enclosed it was because of the oak trees. But here, it's sunny, open and hard for the blood suckers to attack. We bought the castle, fixed it up and created the best defenses against the vampires. Monitors in the water, all night patrol, wooden stakes, sea patrol during the day when the mermaids are out. We'd thought of pretty much everything...

"Then when I was sixteen, Amethyst and Will announced they were having a baby. They were trying for a while as it was much harder to conceive between two species. The chance of Amethyst carrying the baby to full term was low and there was even higher dangers when it came to her giving birth. But they knew the risk and yet they'd done it because they wanted to be parents.

"As a mermaid, Amethyst had to bring the baby into this world in the ocean, it was just how it was done. Will didn't question it though, because I guess we all thought it would happen during daylight. Oh, how wrong we were. Ame went into labour eight in the night. We didn't have a choice but to carry her down to the beach. We had the monitors going, the boats out in the water and patrol everywhere as Amethyst spent two hours in labour on the shore."

My stomach sunk, my chest twisted in breathless pain and I worried. I worried over the past that felt vividly like reality playing out before my eyes.

"It didn't take long before Amethyst brought Tourmaline into the world. A crying little girl with curls of pastel pink hair and blue eyes that I share with my brother. Amethyst held her in her arms as the water lapped over her Tourm's feet," Aiden chuckled and I heard a crack in his voice but he covered it up with a cough. "Like

I said, there were risks when the actual birth came around, and whatever God I believed in, died that day. I watched in horror as the newborn was pushed into Will's arms as Amethyst got a seizure. It was like the ugliest, nastiest nightmare was pulled from our heads and being played in slow motion in front of us.

"The doctor tried. The mermaids tried. But Amethyst died right there in front of our eyes and we couldn't do anything to help her...save her. As if that wasn't enough, the sirens we have for vampires in the water came on like a screaming pulling us from one nightmare to the next. There were over a dozen of them in the water. Everything moved so fast, one minute Will was shouting at Ame to wake up and the next, he was pushing his daughter into my arms and telling me to run. Run, that was his last word to me.

"He died that night, protecting his daughter. Right after losing his mate. His hatred for them and the pain he was in drove him to fight messily, sloppily. Tourmaline lost both her parents and I lost my brother and sister-in-law. But I had Tourm now. I had to protect her because she was all I had. She was my responsibility and I knew I couldn't let down her parents."

Aiden turned to me and I watched as his Adam's apple bobbed up and down and he swallowed his pain. I watched his eyes hold un-shed tears. His shoulders carrying the weight of becoming a father to his niece, being Alpha and mourning the lost of his family.

I watched the man before me who felt the need to walk around with an amour beneath his skin and over his heart because of the pain he endured at such a young age. His stern features, unapologetic eyes and warrior spirit. All the production of his traumatic past.

"I'm sorry Aiden, for everything that you've had to endure," I said sincerely as I brushed away a stray tear for the boy who was forced to grow up.

He shrugged, "It's just life."

"No, life isn't meant to be shit. It's not meant to put one single person through the ringer," I shook my head.

"Life's not all butterflies and hearts, not here anyways. It's rough and hard and if we're lucky enough, we get small moments of happiness. Little bursts of peace that remind us what we're living for," His eyes focused on me then. "Who we're living for."

I fiddled with my fingers as I digested what he said. All my questions were answered except for one very important one.

"Why were the vampires hunting Amethyst?" I finally asked.

"I was wondering when you'd get to that," He said as he came back to sit on the sofa. "The vampires can't go out in the sun. But it isn't just direct sunlight that affect them, it's also heat. Their bodies are dead, once rotting flesh. They need the cold survive. Frigid temperatures."

"Then what the heck are the doing near the beach?" I asked.

"Climate change. Global warming."

I reared back in surprise from his answer but nodded for him to explain.

"The earth's temperature is rising which means the vampires are becoming more susceptible to going extinct. It's not just the polar bears and koalas whose numbers are dwindling, its also the vampires and mermaids. Since the global temperature is becoming hotter by the year, the vampires want a more permanent solution to their heat problem. One that would allow them to live anywhere besides Antarctica and one that would allow them to roam the streets during the day."

I had a strong feeling, I wasn't going to like the ending to this explanation.

"It's been rumoured for centuries that a mermaid's blood can cure just about anything. Including sun issues that vampires face. A fix to cure their problem permanently. It hasn't been proven to be true but they're not going to give up hunting the mermaids until they know."

I blinked in slow procession, "They're hunting the mermaids so that they could survive the sun. So they could become invincible."

"We managed to secure any mermaids who've died during a vampire attack so they won't get the body but three years ago, they managed to kidnap one. Anvi used to help take care of Tourm when she was a baby. But one day, she disappeared from the beach. Just like that, they got her. We haven't seen her since and we haven't come in contact with any daylight walking vamp, but they're still attacking us for mermaids. So I have no idea if it worked or if it failed and they want to try again.

"All I can do is try to find some proof. Some kind of evidence that proves it won't help them. Then and only then would they stop attacking us. Until then, we have to stay on alert and protect the mermaids. Because they're a part of this as much as any wolf," He explained.

"The books," I guessed. "That's where you're hopping to find proof."

"And let's hope we do fast because they're becoming more vicious and unpredictable by the day. More so as Summer begins," He said grimly. "As Queen, Tourmaline would be the first one they target. She has the most powerful blood."

And just like that everything clicked into place. The mermaids and vampires and the werewolves place in all of it.

"What about Tourmaline? Would she shift as well when she comes of age?"

Aiden's concern was visible on his face, "I don't know. There hasn't exactly been a mermaid-werewolf hybrid before, so we're learning as we go. We won't know until she does or doesn't. And Tate?"

"Yeah?"

"You can't tell anyone about this. Not the vampires or mermaids and definitely not Tourmaline," The pleading in his eyes was enough for me.

"I wasn't going to before and I'm not going to now," I swore. "I would never put Tourmaline or you in danger."

CHAPTER 12

As the next few days went by, I began training. The training regiment that was the building blocks for this pack's infamous reputation for being cruel and dangerous was rough, tough and almost blood inducing.

It was the most disciplined system of training that I've experienced. The Blood Moon pack back home trained us well and I knew my way around rogues. But the Oaks Pack trained us for something much worst.

Since the vamps were almost faster and stronger than werewolves, we couldn't simply train as if it was another wolf that would end up at the ends of our canines. First, I had to learn to narrow my target because the vampire's had a smaller shape than a full grown wolf, which made it harder to capture them.

Next, Gamma Dylan had me running patrol during the day. It kept me moving, increasing my agility, speed and reflexes as I trudged through the unfamiliar terrain. It also helped me to adjust to the scents of the ocean's salt water and other unfamiliar scents that may hinder my senses from detecting the scent of rotting flesh, the sign of a vampire nearby.

As my sped and senses picked up, Kai helped me master the art of 'staking'. Fighting in wolf form was easy. Natural. It was a part of us. But fighting in human form was rougher than I expected and Kai wasn't an easy soldier to defeat. My hand-eye coordination had me in shambles when I was first given a wooden stake. It had felt like I was back in a classroom, fiddling with my pens between my fingers as if it was a mini bo staff. Except now, it was real life and I had to master handling the weapon if I wanted a chance at fighting.

A chance at protecting a withering species that meant more to my mate than anything else in his life.

That's why I kept practising with the piece of wood on and off the training grounds.

Beside the physical, I also began learning as much about the vampires as possible. Every detail about their existance, strengths and weaknesses.

Aiden and I were still in the 'friends' territory, but he was warming up to me...well at least I hope he was. Between him having his duties, me training and both of us spending time with Tourmaline, it was hard to deepen a relationship that had been labelled to be surface level from the start.

His inner book nerd, though, was something I didn't see coming. He spent his spear time in the library. At first I thought it was because I was there reading up on vampire and mermaid history but according to Calypso, my mate was an avid reader. Although, the only books he's been reading were to find answers that would suggest the mermaid blood will not help vampires walk in the daylight.

Sort of wishful thinking, but it was the only way to get the vamps to stop. He had to try, even if it meant reading hundreds of ancient texts, some being written in Greek.

And the answer is yes, Aiden learnt Greek in order to translate the text.

It wasn't just all old text filled with the works of supernatural beings that he read...oh no. I caught him reading poetry in between pouring over the archaic texts.

I'm talking Emily Dickinson, Oscar Wilde, Sappho and T.S. Eliot.

The ocean eyed man with locks of blonde hair surprised me every day. If only I didn't have to learn about him from the sidelines. Surfer by morning, Alpha and Uncle by day and secret poetry reader by night.

On the days that he was free, Aiden did show me around his pack. He took me to the controls room where the screens that monitored the water played live footage. Then we went down to the marsh where the vamps usually came through since it was harder to detect them through the swampy water.

It was no romantic picnic, but it was something. I got a first-hand witness to the proud spark in Aiden's eyes and the comfortable steps he took through the terrain of his land. This was home for him.

He also showed me the indoor pool.

It was the large double doors I came across the morning Jenny mouthed off on me. To which I still didn't have a definite answer if she really was in Aiden's room that morning or if she was just a compulsive liar. And I certainly wasn't about to broach that subject with Aiden.

However, I did learn about the weird mineral that coated the outside of the door. It was sulfur crystals, which are the vampires' kryptonite. Apparently, sulfur was the one thing they couldn't touch, like silver was to werewolves.

The oddity of it was that the old myth of using garlic to ward off vampires held some truth to it. Garlic has sulfur compounds and since those blood suckers can't touch sulfur, they hated garlic.

And while hanging garlic outside the mermaids' pool was a viable option, it wasn't feasible for two reasons; one, replenishing the perishable good would be expensive and two, the sulfur in garlic was in small doses. So while the vamps hated it, they could still touch it long enough to remove it from the door before it caused too much harm to their dead fingers. The raw sulphur crystals, however, would burn their hands as if they were to stick it in molten lava.

Inside the indoor pool area, I met all twenty-three of the mermaids. All different hair colours. Mermaids and Mer-men.

I'd come to learn a lot from them in my short time in the pack so far. The first thing I learnt was that they could shift on command. So even if they were in the water, they could remain with their legs. Kinda like werewolves, we shifted when we wanted.

They were also the protectors of the sea. Helping the marine life, nursing the corals back to life from the overheated waters and trying to fight man-kind's destruction of our water systems by cleaning up the water. But it was a battle they were at a disadvantage at. Water pollution was becoming a bigger concern by the day. The seafood industry was destroying the natural balance of the ocean by killing off species that have been around before humans and were vital to the planet's existence.

Cruise ships, cargo boats and poachers with nets were also making the mermaids job harder because it increased their risk of exposing their existence. One that was so far only myth and fairytale. But in a matter of seconds a video could capture their mermaid talc and would be viral all over social media.

It wasn't just the humans that threaten their existence but also the vampires who craved their blood to become daylight walkers. But what was even worst for them was the oil spills that happened across the globe undetected and untreated as no one is held responsible and more animals die.

Seven billion humans against one hundred or so mermaids.

The twenty-three that resided here at the pack was here because of their Queen, Amethyst. And now they stay behind to protect Princess Tourmaline who will one day rule the ocean. The other seventy-six roamed the oceans, helping. Unable to set aside their duties to the ocean because a lack of their population.

What once was thousands, is now a functionally extinct species.

And while they weren't a part of the Oaks Pack, they were under Aiden's protection. Which what Jenny meant when she said I wasn't her Luna. Until the blood suckers back off or Tourmaline is old enough to lead her people, they'll stay here to protect her.

But they still take care of the marine life. Through a magical connection, they can sense when an animal in the ocean needs their help and the animals sense where they are. So a lot of them end up on the shores of the beach here where the mermaids then help them any way they can. Through the indoor pool area they have a sort of infirmary set up for the animals. Then their nursed back to health and set free again.

But no one's been in the water since the vampire attack. Aiden and the pack was still trying to figure out why the motion detectors in the water didn't set off the alarm, despite it working when they tested it afterwards. It was a major concern for everyone, because without it, it left one of their defences open wide for attack. So until then guards were monitoring the screens and patrol on the beach was tightened.

As for Jenny, well she got an earful from Aiden. He wasn't too pleased when he discovered she dropped Tourmaline in my hands to go shopping in the human town. I, of course, didn't hide my smirk when Aiden scolded her for being reckless going out alone.

I also had a strong inkling that Aiden didn't feel anything non platonic towards her.

And as the days went by and I began settling into my life at the Oaks Pack, I was patiently awaiting my eighteenth birthday.

But on the eve of that day, I received a phone call from my mom that tore my heart from my chest and left a bloody cavity that ached.

I had just finished training for the morning and went to my room when my phone rang.

"Tate?" My mom's voice came over the line.

"Hey mom, sorry I haven't been able to call more, I-" I stopped mid sentence as I heard a sob escape from her. "Mom? Is every-thing alright?"

Panic gripped me in its clutches as I waited for her to answer.

"Sweetie, your brother..." She trailed off as her voice wavered into a cry and I felt the pain in my chest crackle to life like a fire.

"Tell me," I rushed. "Is Thane alright?"

God damn my brother was an idiot but he was my brother.

I heard her sniffle before she continued, "Thane is alright, but he almost died."

"What?!" I yelled.

"But Emery...oh sweetheart. Sh-she's not doing too good."

"Mom, tell me. What happened?" I questioned anxiously as I began to pace.

I listened in horror as she explained how the Blood Moon pack had been discovered by the hunters and they'd just fought a war. That was what she hid from me in her last call.

She failed to tell me that any of this was going on. And now...now Emery was laying unconscious after taking a bullet and bringing my brother back from the dead.

And I wasn't there to help.

"I'm coming home," I decided as I grabbed at my chest.

"Honey no-"

"I'll be there by tonight," I cut her off.

She didn't fight me on it as she stayed on the phone a little longer and explained the casualties. My brothers and dad was alright, but Emery was battling for her life.

And Thane...well he wasn't any better without his mate awake and healthy.

When I got off the phone with mom, I went directly to Aiden. He was in his usual spot, the library.

As I opened the door, he immediately looked up and his eyes narrowed on my face as he went to his feet and rounded his desk.

"What's wrong?" He asked with concern laced through his voice before I could say a word.

I didn't have much time to dwell on the fact that he read me easily as I reiterated everything my mom had told me.

"I have to go Aiden. I need to be there for my family," I blinked back the tears that threatened to escape.

I watched as his own features contorted into a painful expression for a brief moment before his eyes dimmed and he nodded.

"I won't stop you," He answered.

Something about his answer didn't sit right with me. But I couldn't decipher what the underlying meaning of his wording meant.

Nodding I asked, "Will you come with me?"

His eyebrows rose slightly in surprise, "You want me to go with you?"

"Yes," I answered having to think about it.

Wasn't it obvious to him that I wanted more than a friendship?

I watched as his eyes went to the polished floor and he leaned back against his desk. As he shook his head, I felt my chest take another stab at me.

I rubbed the spot where my heart laid and Aiden's eyes picked up on the movement. I dropped my hand and forced my hands to clasp behind my back to hold back my habit of rubbing the ache.

Aiden didn't push or question it.

"I won't be able to leave the pack anytime soon. Not with the monitors in the water being unpredictable. I won't be able to leave Tourm behind and we can't take her out of the pack's protection either," He finally said.

"I know," I gulped as I realized that I probably won't be seeing him for a few days.

It was strange, just how much I've grown fond of the pack and the people in it so quickly. Especially brooding Aiden and little Tourmaline.

"Tate-"

"I understand Aiden," I cut him off with a shake of my head. "Just as I need to go back to my family, I know you have to protect yours."

And I did understand and I don't blame him for one second. How could I?

He opened his mouth to say something but snapped it shut as he nodded, "It's best if you leave early. That way you'll make it out of town before nightfall. I'll prepare a car and our plane for you."

I didn't get another chance to say anything more because one minute he was standing before me and the other, he was out the door.

Sighing, I rubbed at my prolonged aching chest and headed back to my room.

As I took a shower and packed a light bag, since I still had some clothing back my old pack, I contemplated just how often my chest pains have been coming on lately.

Usually they didn't appear that often or lasted that long. But lately it felt as if they were being more persistent and the stretch of time was increasing.

I'll definitely have to let the pack doctor give me a check up when I get back.

By the time I made it to the foyer with my bag, Aiden, Tourmaline and the others were standing near the door.

A wave of unease settled in me at the prospect of leaving.

"Kai, Loly and Paul will go with you," Aiden informed gruffly. "Kai's our best warrior so you'll be safe."

I nodded as I looked around at everyone. Dylan's eyes were icy as his eyes focused outside and I briefly questioned if it was because Aiden said Kai was the best warrior.

Of course he probably meant the best after Alpha, Beta and Gamma.

But I didn't ponder about it anymore as I caught Tourmaline's expression that brought me to near tears.

"You promised you wouldn't leave," She pouted.

My bag was forgotten on the floor as I dropped it and picked her up into my arms, "If it's one I don't do is break my promises."

"But you said you'd never leave Tate," Her lower lip started to tremble and my decision started to crumble in my head.

"Maybe...maybe I shouldn't leave," I said as my eyes found Aiden's penetrating stare.

He shook his head, "No, you have to go. For your family."

"But-"

"We'll be fine," He assured as his hand rubbed Tourmaline's back as she clung to my neck. "Tourm will be alright, she's got me."

"But I don't want her to leave," Tourmaline whispered.

I brushed her hair away from her face, "I'll be back little one. I promise."

"And if you don't come back?"

One little question loaded with so many emotions.

"Then you'll tell that Uncle of yours to go find me and bring me back," I said lightheartedly.

Aiden didn't say anything at that but Tourm rewarded me with a small giggle as she lifted her head and hugged me.

"Come back soon Tate," I could detect the sorrow in her voice and I wanted nothing more than to park my butt in this castle and stay. But I had to make sure my family was alright. And then I'd be back, for good.

I lowered her to her feet and grabbed my bag as I said goodbye to everyone; Calypso, Rick, Dylan and Matt.

And then slowly, I turned back to Aiden whose eyes hadn't left me this entire time. But as I stood before him, he didn't say a word and I felt a lump in my throat.

How had I gotten this attached by only spending a week with him?

Finally, he spoke up, "Tell your family that we send our regards and wishes for a fast recover. And let your brother know that I'd be there if I can...and when Emery wakes up, because she will," His words held so much promise to it that I hoped he was right, "tell her that she owes me better advice."

My eyebrows scrunched together in confusion, "Advice for what?"

The corner of his lip lifted in a secret smile as he shook his head, "She'll know."

I didn't mean to be, but I couldn't help but feel jealousy grate at me.

Shaking it off and remembering my dying sister-in-law, I nodded and waited with baited breath for Aiden to say something more.

To ask me to stay.

But he didn't.

"Be safe, Tate," He said with serious eyes.

I nodded, "Of course."

With one last beat of staring at each other, I turned to leave.

But before I could move a step away, I turned back and flung my arms around Aiden's neck.

He grunted in surprise at my action but he wrapped his arms around me and pulled me closer.

Breathing in his sea-washed mahogany and fresh waterfall scent, I whispered, "Goodbye Aiden."

He didn't respond as I pulled back and turned back without looking at him because if I did, I wasn't leaving.

Safely tucked in the car, I held my emotions together as Kai, Loly and Paul began chatting away as we headed to the airport.

During our flight I prayed to the Moon Goddess to protect Emery and the Oaks Pack. I didn't know if she ever listened but according to what my mom said, Thane being alive was nothing short of a miracle.

So I had to hope that if she was real, she was keeping an eye out on her wolf children.

As we descended on the runway of my pack's private landing strip, I couldn't help but wonder back to week ago when we were all here, with the exception of Aiden. Me a week ago had not known about mermaids and vampires.

Now I was slowly learning.

As we stepped out of the plane, we were greeted by my parents.

"Tater-tot!" My dad yelled as he scooped me up and spun me around. I laughed as he set me to my feet. "We missed you kiddo."

"Missed you too Dad," I patted his arm as I approached mom who was sporting a watery smile.

"Mom," I said as my voice cracked and she wrapped me in her arms.

"My girl," She whispered as she squeezed the life out of me.

"Can't breathe here mom," I squeaked and she let go and brushed back her tears.

"Sorry honey, just glad to have you back," She said.

"Feels good to be back," I said as I breathed in the comforting scent of the forest.

But it wasn't the same. It wasn't home anymore.

Turning to the my pack I reintroduced them, "You guys remember Kai, Loly and Paul."

Mom and Dad nodded.

"Of course we do," My mom smiled and pulled them all into a hug as if they were old family friends.

I held back a laugh as I watch Paul squirm in mg mom's arms and looked thoroughly uncomfortable afterwards.

We all pilled into the car and went directly to the pack house. My new pack was getting settled into their rooms as I went to the third floor where Emery was set up in her and Thane's room.

As I made it up to the third floor, I saw my grand aunt Jane snoring away in the living room. Smiling to myself, I crept over and threw a blanket over her before placing a kiss on her head.

No doubt come tomorrow she'll be hounding me about babies now that I have Aiden.

I walked further down the hall until I made it to the room and gave the door a light knock before going in.

Thane blinked sleepily at me from his spot in the chair next to the bed.

I watched Emery's overly pale body laying on the bed, un-moving. It wasn't the lively woman who burnt food and told bad jokes. It was a shell of her laying motionless. And it wasn't for the heart monitor beeping a steady rhythm, I would have assumed the worst.

As I watched as Thane saw it was me and shock and the relief passed his features as he shuffled over towards me and I pulled him into a hug.

I heard him sniffle and in all my years of knowing my brother, I'd never seen him cry.

Okay, that was a slight lie, I made him cry when I was five. He broke my piggy bank and tossed my coins all over the backyard and then I kicked him in the family jewels.

He squealed like a little piggy before sobbing in pain. Served him right back then.

But now, it broke my heart to see my tough older brother looking broken.

"I should have protected her," He growled angrily at himself as I released him. "I should be the one laying there instead of her."

"Thane, don't," I placed my hand on his arm and led him back to his chair. "What Emery did was to protect you as you would her. You can't blame yourself for this. She wanted to protect you and she did."

I sat on the armrest of his chair and threw my arm around his shoulder as he pressed the heels or his palms to his eyes.

"I know but I'm the werewolf. I'm their protector," He said and I gasped at his words.

"Their?" I questioned with wide eyes as he looked up at me and a small smile was on his lips.

"Their. As in my wife and our baby," He answered with pride.

I squealed before blinking at Emery's flat stomach under the duvet.

"But is the baby alright? Did she survive?" I asked as my heart held on by a string.

"He," Thane corrected and nodded. "Yea, by a miracle they both survived, but won't wake up to me."

"They'll be up in no time, you wait and see."

The next day, Emery still hadn't woken up, but I was officially eighteen.

And in no mood to celebrate.

Not with Emery still in a coma and Tourmaline and Aiden hundreds of miles away.

My mom still made me a cake, though. A vanilla one. Not my favourite, but cake was cake.

I spent some time Mom and Jane. Babies were brought up twice, both time by Jane. Once to discuss little Thane and Emery Jr. and the other time was to throw in a suggestion for a Oaks baby.

The topic was immediately shut down when I told them I would castrate Aiden if they didn't quit it. They happily obliged.

Around lunch time, when I sat alone with an old party hat Bailey dug out from somewhere, I couldn't help but check my phone every minute. It definitely begun to feel like a pity party as I expected Aiden to call.

I wasn't even sure if he knew when my birthday was, but he also seemed to know everything about everything. I was pretty sure I mentioned it once when Tourmaline asked me and Aiden was with us.

And yet, no call.

What a good friend he is...

But just as I was about to rip off the stupid hat and chuck my phone across the room, a text chimed in.

Aiden: Happy Birthday Tate!!!

I looked down at the text in surprise, especially at the use of emojis. But before I could respond, another message came in.

Aiden: This is Tourm btw

And then it made much more sense. Tourmaline had Aiden's phone. To think for a minute I had believed he'd actually wish me a happy birthday.

Taking off the hat from my head, only to be stung by the rubber band that held it together, I texted Tourmaline.

Tate: Thanks Tourm. Miss you much! We'll have cake when I get back.

Aiden: (heart)

The heart emoji was the only response I got and I decided to pocket my phone and find something to do. Anything would be better than agonising away behind the screen.

Everyone was busy. Every single person.

Even the trio I traveled with were busy keeping up on their training. I was taking an honorary day of on breaking a sweat.

Birthdays weren't meant for excessive. They were meant for cake...or pie. Depended on the person really.

As I walked aimlessly through the halls of the packhouse, I stopped in front of the infirmary and saw Dr. Adler sitting with a book in his hand.

"Hey Doc," I greeted him and he looked up with a smile.

"Tate, I heard you were back," He smiled warmly as he gave me a pat on the back. "Happy birthday, dear."

"Thanks," I grinned as I grabbed a lollipop from his desk. "I've been meaning to come to you."

"Oh, is everything okay? Is it your chest?" He asked with concern.

I nodded and he gestured to take a seat on one of the cots.

"It is," I confirmed as he grabbed a stethoscope. "The pain's been a bit stronger and has been lasting longer."

"How long?" He asked.

"Well before it lasted for less than three minutes. Now it's about ten minutes or so," I averaged.

He frowned but placed the stethoscope to my chest as he plugged in the ear pieces.

"Deep breath in," He instructed. "Out."

I followed the directions before he stopped and held up his watch as he timed the beats.

As the minute ticked away, the frown lines between his brow deepened.

When he pulled away, I could something was wrong.

"Everything okay with the good ole heart?" I asked and wished he said nothing was wrong.

"The beats are a tad slower than usual," He said as he walked over to his filing cabinet and pulled out a file that I guessed belonged to me. "Before your heartbeats varied between seventy-five to eighty. Now it's sixty-five, which is still good. But it's at the edge of a what's regular."

"And what exactly does that mean?" I questioned hesitantly as I opened my lollipop. I already began feeling sickly uneasy at this.

"Well usually, the heart in an adult beats around sixty to one hundred times a minute. I check your own three times and they all sixty-five. Now you're still in the clear but it can go lower. If it does, it doesn't necessarily mean a bad thing, but it could mean Bradycardia. It's only bad if your heart doesn't pump enough oxygen to your body. As a werewolf, that could be a concern when you're fighting or even training," He explained. "Having you experienced anything besides the chest pains? Dizziness, fatigue, shortness of breath?"

I shook my head, "No. Just the chest pains."

He nodded as he grabbed some other things.

"Okay, hopefully it may just be an odd day for your heart. It's been through enough when Luna Emery healed you. I doubt you have anything to be worried about but I'll take a few blood samples to test your oxygen level. In the mean time, I suggest taking it easy and when you get pack to the Oaks Pack, inform their doctor."

I soured at the idea. There was no way I could let the Oaks Pack know I was a weak link.

Plus, it wasn't as anything was sure yet. Adler still had to run his tests.

At least that's what I told myself as I stuck my arm out for him to get my blood.

When he had his vile, I looked at him.

"Would you not tell anyone about this?" I asked.

He looked disapproving, "Tate..."

"Please?" I asked again with a pout until he sighed.

"Fine, but only because of doctor-patient confidentiality."

"Thanks Doc," I grinned as I skipped away.

But as soon as I cleared the door, my steps faltered as I leaned against the door.

Could something truly be wrong with my heart?

CHAPTER 13

Aiden's POV

"Please, Uncle Aiden?" Tourmaline pouted as she sat next to me in the living room as we watched Frozen.

You'd think she would be obsessed with the Little Mermaid, but nope, she was all for Queen Elsa. I think it may have to do with the fact that Ariel gave up her tale and voice for a 'stinky' boy, her words not mine.

Tourm may be five but she was perceptive about everything, including small details.

Which was why she was now begging me to call Tate for her so that she could wish my mate a happy birthday.

"Tourm, I told you, she's with her family," I explained softly as I wrapped my arm around her tiny shoulders.

Her frown deepened and I almost broke and gave her my phone, but held my resolve.

"But it's her birthday dad," She continued.

It like a sucker punch when I couldn't give her something she wanted but I knew that she knew exactly what she's doing by calling me dad.

"I promise when she gets back we'll bake her a cake. But right now she's with her family who's just been through some tough times, so we should let her spend her time with them, alright?"

She wasn't too pleased with me as she shrugged off my arm, folded her own and turned to the television as the end credits began to roll.

"I'm going to the pool because you're no fun," She huffed as she walked out of the room with her hands still folded and a pout marking her features.

"Tourm?" I called back but she ignored me.

Sighing, I contemplated making her seaweed cupcakes, her favourite, but none of the mermaids have been out in the sea for the week, we were out of the main ingredient.

'Calypso,' I mind linked, 'Tourmaline's headed to the pool, can you keep an eye on her?'

'Of course, Alpha,' Came her response.

I pulled my phone out of my pocket and flipped it over and over above my head as I contemplated what do to. On one hand, what I said to Tourmaline was true.

Tate's family was hurt and I wasn't going to interrupt her time with them. That and Tourmaline would no doubt video call her and spend the rest of the day chatting away.

But as I sat staring up at the ceiling, I couldn't help but think of her. My brown eye girl who intoxicated me with her scent of pink summer berries, bergamot and tropical hibiscus. A perfect slice of summer paradise in a scent.

My mate who I also called my friend. I'm an idiot for doing it.

It hadn't exactly been what I wanted to say but I failed to articulate my words when I sat next to her. Worst yet, I didn't know how to resolve our argument that followed right after we met.

I didn't mean to argue with her but seeing her there, standing in the late evening with the sun gleaming over her brown hair and her eyes searching my soul as if I was an open book... I just couldn't believe I'd found her. And my instinct to protect her drove through me like a tornado as it blew past my senses.

There was no question in my mind that staying back there would be a safety risk because of the vampires, but I couldn't deny her for a few reasons.

One being she was mate and she may not have known it, but as soon as I met her, I knew I'd travel great distances and wage wars for her.

Another reason I didn't deny her was because I knew the value of family and I couldn't make her leave.

But most importantly, I couldn't tell her about the vampires' existance while we were in her pack. One wrong person overhearing our conversation and I'd risk putting Tourmaline and the other mermaids in danger.

Trust was a hard thing that I came by. Especially after losing the ones close to me.

So, I kept everything a secret until we arrived back here to the coast. It may not have been the wisest decision, especially after we were attacked on our journey back, but it was strategic.

If only I'd account for the fact that Tourmaline would have called me 'Dad' right before I was whisked away to deal with a vampire trying to get in. It was comical really, seeing Tate tring to be okay with me having a daughter.

She didn't have a mean bone in her body, but I could tell she wanted to wring my ear and find out who the mom was. And while Tourm was in many way my daughter, I could tell the title of uncle and niece put Tate at ease.

My heart also warmed to see them both getting along. Tourmaline seemed considerable more happy with Tate around and I can't deny that I was as well.

She had an instinctive warmth about her. A ray of sunshine in this considerably bleak part of the coast where we've been fighting for our lives.

And I friend-zoned her.

While my lack of words played a part in it, there was another reason. Her age.

Age didn't play that big of a role in werewolf packs because typically you found your mate at sixteen. Most cases, both partners were the same age or two years apart.

With me being twenty-one though, it hadn't felt right to want anything more while she was just shy of eighteen. And yes, while a week may not be a defining moment in making a teenager become a wise adult, I wasn't going to want her before she was old enough.

Even now, on her eighteenth birthday, it didn't feel right. We still don't know that much about each other. I was hiding myself from her and she... Well, I'm terrified of losing her.

Just as I'd lost my parents, Will and Amethyst.

I couldn't unravel my heart to her only to lose her.

I won't survive it. It was one of the few things that I was sure of.

Yet as I clicked on my phone, I already felt the threads that held my heart close unravelling at it's seams. Waiting for me to open it up again.

Here's to hoping that she won't see as a friend in the future. Because God knows I won't survive it.

I typed out a simple Happy Birthday to her but as my finger hovered over the 'send' button, I thought better of it and backspace the words.

When I laid my phone down next to me, I rubbed my jaw as the need to wish her grew stronger in me.

I really screwed myself by calling her a friend.

Before I could over think it anymore, I picked up my phone, I typed out the message and added a few emojis under the pretence that Tourmaline was sending it.

Aiden: Happy Birthday Tate!!!

As I stared down at the message, anxiety took over my thoughts as I realized that she may not realise it was Tourm.

Aiden: This is Tourm btw

I felt my heart pounding erratically in my chest as I saw that my message was read. Does everyone feel this nervous while texting their crush?

Honestly, if anyone from the pack saw me now, their faith in me being the brooding Alpha will quickly dwindle.

Tate: Thanks Tourm. Miss you much! We'll have cake when I get back.

A smirk slowly crept onto my face as I read her message like a giddy teenager. But it was slowly ripped away when I realised she thought it was Tourm.

And my idiot meter just crept up into dangerous territory.

Aiden: (heart)

I didn't bother holding anymore of her time because I couldn't exactly carryon as a five-year-old or monopolize anymore of her time.

Yet there was so much I wanted to text again. I wanted to press call and hear her voice. I wanted to ask her why she holds her chest when she thinks no one is looking. I wanted to ask her why she agreed to being friends.

But I couldn't because if I told Tourmaline calling was off limits, then it was for me as well.

Tucking my phone away, I turned off the television and made my way to the kitchen. But before I could make it to the door, Jenny popped out with a sinister smile.

Oh shoot me now, I groaned to myself.

I didn't hate the girl but when she kept trying to corner me and get handsy, I get annoyed. Mate or no mate, I didn't like it.

"Aiden, I've been looking for you," She grinned and I narrowed my eyes on her as her manicured fingers reached out to touch my chest.

But before she could make contact, I stepped out of her reach.

"What can I do for you?" I asked her without preamble.

"Oh I think there are many things you can do for me and I for you. If you know what I mean," Her eyelids looked droopy as if she was sleepy and I had an unpleasant feeling standing near here.

Folding my arms, I feigned innocence, "I'm not sure what you mean but I'm not interested either way."

She flipped her green hair as a fire blazed in her eyes, "What I mean, Alpha, is that I can do what that child Tate can't."

My jaw ticked in anger when Tate's name left her lips, "Say anything of that nature again, Jennifer, and I'll throw you back in the sea without protection. Don't test me."

Shock consumed her features as if she wasn't expecting me to say that.

But what did she expect? That I'd fall in bed with her? That I'd allow her to talk about my mate in such a nature?

She's tested my patience since she begun taking care of Tourmaline when Anvi disappeared.

One minute she was quiet and shy, sticking with her people. The next, she was crawling in my bed in the middle of the night.

She lucky I let her off with a warning and a scolding that night. And that was only because I was awake reading when she thought she could just walk into my bedroom.

Since then she stayed out but she kept making advances and my patient was warring thin.

Especially with the way I've seen Tourmaline act around her. Jenny didn't pay attention to taking care of her. No patience was used or the correct teaching.

But she was the only mermaid available to help raise Tourm since the others were still taking care of the ocean and its creatures. I could raise her on my own, but my knowledge of the mermaid world and culture was next to none existent.

She needed a mermaid to take care and spend time with her. Which was Jenny's job. But she's abusing her free time.

Which was why as I looked at the mermaid before me, I made a decision I should have a while ago.

"And while we're talking about your awful behaviour, you're hereby relieved of your position as Tourmaline's caretaker," I enunciated.

Her eyes widen and she gaped at me but I didn't entertain her flabbergasted expression as I walked around her, keeping a wide berth, and went to the kitchen.

One of my many secrets was that I liked to bake. Odd, but I craved chocolate cake too much to wait around for someone to bake for me.

So I learnt from my mom when I was about twelve. As I raided the pantry, I ensured I had all the ingredients needed to make my classic chocolate cake. Because when Tate comes back I was going to mend our mate bond and that started with cake.

I had to admit, there was a part of me that was scared that she may not want to come back.

Maybe she'll realise how much better off she is without me and my slew of problems.

But after she left me with that hug... Well I had an ounce of hope after all.

CHAPTER 14

Two weeks.

It took two weeks for Emery to awake from her coma and ensure us all that she and Thane Jr. was alright.

And its also been two weeks since I've spoken to Aiden.

I didn't expect him to call and chat for hours like some gossiping teen. But I'd hoped he would have at least called and said something, anything.

The phone did work both ways I suppose. I could have called, but I didn't because Aiden did call, just not me.

He was on the phone with Kai every day for the past two weeks. At least, that's what Kai said.

Twice I was in the living room with Kai when he called and when Kai asked if he wanted to speak with me himself, he said no.

No explanation or excuses. Just a simple 'no'.

Which only left my feelings for him even more muddled after Kai explained he wanted to check up on us and ensure I was alright.

Except I didn't know if he was concerned for me or for his Luna. There was a distinct difference being a token of power compared to someone he was actually concerned about.

And while I was mostly fine, my heart was not. Dr. Adler's blood test came back with a healthy amount of oxygen in my blood but we did do a test on my heart rate.

He made me run on a treadmill as he monitored my heart rate to see if it will increase as it should while I doing physical activity.

Results concluded it was a bit behind.

And as we monitored it over and over again, it dropped from sixty-five to sixty-four. Only by one, but it was inching closely to dangerous territory.

I did hold back on telling my family and I trusted Adler to do the same since everyone was still recovering from their losses.

He did, however, right up charts and notes and an entire medical file on my heart condition to take back to the Oaks Pack.

What was my title again? Oh, right, Master of Bad Luck.

A day after Emery woke up, I contemplated asking her to try to heal my heart but she was still worn out and weak. My new pack also made it clear it was time to leave, so we did.

On the plane back, I felt the medical file burning hole in my bag, threatening to make its presence known to everyone.

"You okay?" Kai asked from his seat next to me as his eyes landed on my tight grip on my bag.

I forced my fingers to relax as I nodded with a strained smile, "Fine."

"Luna-"

"Tate," I corrected.

He rolled his eyes playfully, "Tate. If something's wrong you can tell us."

My eyes cut across to Paul who seemed extra moody next to a sleeping Loly. Kai's eyes followed my own.

"You can tell and trust me," He clarified.

I nodded as my eyes looked over his features. A kind smile, dark eyes, hair as straight as needles and complexion sun-kissed from his time on the beach.

I did trust him. Oddly enough we've spent more time this week than anyone else. That was mostly due to him shadowing me through out the day except when I snuck off for my doctors appointment. But his presence was appreciated since it didn't truly feel like home back there. Not anymore.

I got to know more about him and Matt. How they met, his love of surfing and Matt's love of the guitar. But something was missing from his story.

He brushed over how they went from dating to mates. There was a pause while he was talking, brief but noticeable.

I hadn't pushed. It was his story and he'll say when he's ready.

"I do trust you," I grabbed his hand. "It's just something I've been processing lately."

"Nothing bad I hope?" He asked with eyebrows drawn in con-cern.

"Nothing of that sort," I said and hoped I was right.

But Adler's warnings rang through my head. Shortness of breath, tiredness, cardiac arrest, dizziness. All symptoms of a slow heart.

And if I didn't try to get it healed, I may need to get a pace maker.

Except, I didn't want to be a weak link. I couldn't afford for Aiden to see my condition as being a downfall for his pack or something that would weaken his defences to protect Tourma-line.

I saw just how much my age bothered him. What would a heart condition do?

So, the plan was simple. Wait for Emery to recover in a few weeks and then have her make a trip to the beach or go back for a few days to the Blood Moon Pack to see if she can fix me up.

She did bring me back from the brink of death, what was a slow heart compared to her powers? Especially after she literally brought Thane back from the dead.

Kai didn't question me further as we landed on the airstrip with only a few hours to get back to the castle before sunset. It should an easy trip since time will allow us to reach well before darkness came upon us.

Before the vamps crawled out of their hidey holes.

When we exited the plan, I spotted Dylan's smirking face as he leaned against a car and waited for us.

"How was the vacation?" He asked as he grabbed my bag for me.

"It wasn't a vacation," Kai grumbled as he hauled his suitcase into the trunk.

Dylan chuckled but shook his head, "Keep telling yourself that bud."

Paul and Loly looked between the two with narrowed eyes and I felt the atmosphere become tense.

"How about we get going before we lose daylight?" I suggested as I took my bag out of Dylan's hands and stepped between the pair.

Dylan's eyes snapped to me and I saw his step hesitate before he nodded and his easy going smirk returned.

"Of course, Luna," He agreed as he strolled over to the driver's seat while I got my bags into the trunk.

Kai's shoulders were bunched up and he shut the trunk with a little too much force as he glared icely into the car at Gamma Dylan.

"You alright?" I queried.

He nodded his head, "He just gets on my nerves sometimes. Actually all the time."

I cocked an eyebrow at him, "Why?"

Kai shrugged, "Too cocky for his own good."

The explanation didn't go any further as he led me to the backseat and I was again placed in the middle seat in the back. Except instead of having friendly Loly, I was next to brooding Paul.

The man was always in a bad mood. A butterfly will piss him off, I kid you not. He was just an old cranky man in a young man's body.

"Next stop, Castle de Oaks," Dylan announced as he turned the radio up to some funky pop music. "So, Tate, how's your family?"

I explained how Emery was safe and while they lost some wolves, most of the pack was safe with the hunters obliterated. Of course, I left out the bit about Emery being a healer.

The powers of the Lunas of the Blood Moon Pack were a secret from everyone. Especially other packs, since it put her at danger.

Kind of like how Tourmaline and the mermaids are with the vampires.

Information like that can be exploited and it wasn't my secret to tell. Any Alpha would kill to have someone like Emery and my mother in their pack.

A healer to protect their army from dying and an earth manipulator to use the surrounding environment as their weapon.

Therefore, going into details about Thane's survival or explaining how I came about my heart condition wasn't a viable option.

On the drive to the castle, the car begun sputtering until we came to a stop in the middle of a street.

"Shit!" Dylan cursed as he banged his fist on the steering wheel and exited the car.

"What happened?" I asked the others as I watched Dylan lift the hood of the car only to get a face full of fumes.

They seemed as perplexed as I felt as they shrugged.

"This is a new car," Kai commented as he climbed out. "Stay here Luna."

"Oh, no. Not again," I snorted as I swung my leg out to prevent him from closing the door.

He looked at me unimpressed but I shrugged and followed him out of the car.

They left me like a sitting duck once, so there's no way I was going to let that happen to me again.

I put my hand over my eyes to shield it from the blazing brightness of the sun as I looked around.

There were no houses, buildings, farms...nothing. It was miles and miles of nothing but the stretch of road surrounded by grass and open field.

The others were all hovering over the engine of the car and as I approached I noted that it was an electric car. The Oaks Pack was set on protecting the environment but I did see a few gas guzzling vehicles in their garage before, but they mostly had electric and hybrid cars.

"What's wrong with it?" I gestured to the battery with my chin.

Loly sighed, "I can't tell but the battery seems overheated or maybe overcharged."

"This is one of the new ones Alpha brought in a few months back, could it really be overheated?" Paul asked as he stupidly touched the engine and hissed as he pulled his hand back.

Dylan grinned at him, "How exactly did you expect it to feel?"

"Shut up," Paul bit back as he cradled his palm.

"Well whatever the problem is, we need to get back to the castle before the sun sets," Kai said as he looked at his watch.

"And how do you suppose we do that?" Dylan asked as he folded his arms.

"Shift and run back, we'll have a few miles to cover but the sun has about two hours before it sets. We should make it back before then since we're faster than the car anyways."

"You seem to be missing something."

Kai's jaw clenched as he turned to Dylan, "What?"

Dylan spread his arms out to our surroundings, "From here until the beach is all open fields. How exactly are we suppose to run when a car full of humans could be driving along the road and spot us?"

Well he did have a point there. I'm guessing massive wolves would raise a few eyebrows, especially since wolves aren't native around this area. We'd risk exposing ourselves and attracting unwanted human attention.

"You got a better idea, Gamma?" Kai seethe with pure disdain.

Dylan's nostrils flared and I watched as the pair looked ready to break out in a fight.

Pulling out my phone from my pocket, I waved it between them and broke the tense bubble, "I'll call Aiden."

They snapped out of it and nodded as I looked down at my screen.

No signal.

No god damn signal.

"Flapjacks," I groaned as Paul took from my hand and sighed.

"This is just great," He said kicking up a loose pebble. "No signal."

Loly sighed as she tied her dreadlocks up and nodded towards the road, "Get your hiking boots on kids, we've got to get a signal before the sun goes down."

"She's right. Paul help me push the car to the side," Kai instructed.

Dylan rolled his eyes and helped them even though Kai didn't ask. When it was off the road, we grabbed our bags and started walking as I held my phone up for the barest signal.

The evening heat was bearing down on us and turning us to a sweaty mess. I watched as the sun shined off of Paul's bald head, sweat trickle down Loly's dark skin and Dylan patting his forehead dry every two seconds. Kai was the only one not looking like he was about to pass out.

On the other hand, I kept having to draw in large gulps of breath, which was unusual for a werewolf. I did try to disguise it and normalize my breathing as we trailed on.

As Dylan had suspected, there were cars on the road. Three passed us.

The first went by without stopping. The second was a car filled with a family and didn't have space for us. The third was a creepy old man whose eyes lingered too long on my boobs.

They guys scared him off with threats of broken bones.

An hour into walking, I finally got a signal strong enough.

I prayed he'd answer when I called or else we were about to be vampire food when the sun sets over the horizon.

On the second ring, he answered.

"Tate?" He said disbelief.

"Aiden," I answered with an ounce of relief.

"Where the hell are you all? You were suppose to be back by now," The concern in his voice was palpable. "I was calling but-"

"The car broke down," I cut in, "and we couldn't get a signal until now. We're going to need some help here."

There nothing but silence on the other end until I heard a loud shattering before hurried footsteps and shouting.

Finally he said, "Pass the phone to Dylan."

When I did, I could hear the loud baritone of Aiden's voice yelling into the line as Dylan winced and held the device back a few inches.

Dylan rattled off how far we were and our predicament before his eyes looked me over and he said, "She's fine."

I heard Aiden on the other side of the line saying he'll be there as soon as possible before hanging up.

Dylan's expression was sour, no doubt from being yelled at his Alpha, before he turned to us.

"Aiden said we continue walking, fast. As soon as the sun begins to lower we shift. That way the human's won't be able to see us. We have an hour until the sun goes down and the vamps come out to play," He said and we didn't waste another second before picking up our pace.

I'm sure if another car passed by they were going to assume we were bunch of people high off something.

I watched as the sky blended into an array of pinks, oranges and purples and the sun began its decent.

And my heart begun to protest.

I rubbed the aching spot and Dylan caught my movement.

"Again?" He mouthed to me and I nodded.

"I'm fine," I mouthed back and he nodded but Kai turned just then rose a brow at me.

"What?" He asked and everyone turned to me.

I dropped my hand, "Nothing, just skipped out on working out the last week and it apparently wasn't my greatest decision."

I was really beginning to contemplate my karma because all this lying was going to catch up to me. Of course I worked out this week.

A wooden stake was tucked into the pocket of my jeans and while I'm not an expert, I'd like to think I was much better now than three weeks ago.

They nodded and as we moved together with the sun's decent, we trailed off into the grass, away from the road.

When we were sure no cars were headed our way, we all shifted and picked up pace as twilight settled.

The faster running began to take a toll on me as my heart burned up a defying pain in my chest.

What was worst, though, was the chill of fright that crept into my bones as the last bit of sunlight was extinguished. Leaving us at the mercy of the darkness and its creatures.

Like a ticking time bomb, I caught the whiff of rotting flesh.

The dead was among us.

The others could mind link but since I wasn't mated to Aiden, I couldn't mind link with the pack. Hence, I couldn't decipher what was our plan of action.

I think we were all holding on to the hope that Aiden would have reached us by now.

Loly and Paul flanked me as Kai stayed behind me and Dylan to the front as we sped across the grassy field.

But these creatures were fast. And I watched as one jumped out from nowhere and landed on Paul's back.

Dropping my bag, I grabbed the wooden steak from the outside pocket.

As three more vamps charged at us, the others took one each while I shifted.

Paul cried out in gut wrenching shriek before I plunged the stake into the back of the vampire that was wrestling with him.

The blood sucker crumpled to the floor before turning to ashes.

I saw blood gushing out of Paul's neck as I shifted back to my wolf. He was bitten.

Holy mother of the moon. What happens when a vampire bites a werewolf?

I didn't have an answer but Paul didn't look to good as his skin paled as he covered the wound.

"Go!" He shouted at my frozen features and I nodded before turning back and helping the others.

Kai had one pinned to the ground was tearing his limbs apart while Dylan was fighting off another.

I leapt onto the back of the one attacking Loly and pressed him to the ground.

He used his strength to push me back as he rose to his feet and knocked Loly square in the jaw.

Growling, I got to my feet and grabbed onto his head with my canines. Holding up the body, I dangled him off the floor.

But the blood sucker curled his fingers around my neck, dug into my skin with his finger nails and pulled me off. My body was tossed haphazardly across the grass as he reached for Loly whose front paw was curled against her jaw.

Then, like the sound of an angel's voice, I heard the loud rumbling of a vehicle barreling down the long and narrow road.

The tires screeched to a stop and I heard a vicious growl erupt through the still night air like thunder crackling during a storm.

Aiden.

I pushed to my feet as I saw Kai take out the vampire he was fighting with a wooden stake.

Dylan was still struggling with his but as three wolves descended upon us, the vamp looked around before taking off.

One of the wolves that just arrived chased off after the vampire but he was long gone.

Aiden's wolf easily subdued the vamp that was attacking Loly and took him out with a stake to the heart.

Taking deep breaths, I struggled to catch my wits as I felt slightly dizzy.

Aiden stalked up to me and I almost stumbled back when he nuzzled the side of his head against mine.

My wolf took comfort in his presence and touch as I felt my lungs filling up with air and my chest pain subsiding.

It didn't last longer than a few seconds before we were moving again.

Two wolves helped Paul up as we all hurried back to the large SUV, shifted and changed.

When Aiden and I were both dressed, he cupped my cheek with his right hand and I could see the worry lines on his face marking his features.

"Are you alright?" He asked as his eyes went to the nail marks on my neck.

But they were already healing up so I nodded, "Are you?"

"You nearly sent me to an early grave, but I'm fine," He said as his thumb stroked my cheek.

"Not to interrupt," Loly cut in, "but Paul was bitten and we need to get out of here."

Aiden nodded as his face contorted into a solemn expression and he led me to the passenger side.

I was happily surprised that I was getting to sit up front for once. Maybe it was a sign that he was finally not seeing me as 'immature'.

When everyone tucked inside, Aiden turned us around and sped back in the direction he'd came from.

"Is Paul going to be okay?" I asked no one in particular as I turned back to see his limp and sweaty body laying in the second row of seats with Kai and another pack member while Loly, Dylan and the other wolf sat in the first row.

"Maybe?" Kai answered as he covered the wound. "The vamp bit one of his veins but he's healing up. Hopefully it closes before he die from blood lost."

"Fuck!" Aiden growled. "I should have checked the car before. Hell, I should have come pick you up."

"You couldn't have known this would happen," I said. "They said the car was new, how would you have guessed that something could have been wrong."

"That dosen't excuse me from me from not ensuring you're brought back safely," He whispered.

As I opened my mouth to respond he shook his head and instead asked about my family.

I told him what I'd told Dylan earlier and he nodded before asking, "And did you tell Emery what I told you to?"

I narrowed my eyes at the smirk playing on his lips.

"I did."

"And what did she say?"

"I don't think you want me to say in front of your pack."

"Try me," He said and he briefly turned to me and I saw the sparkle of humour in his eyes.

I shrugged, "She said you're a dickhead and it's time to grow a pair."

His smirk was as clear as day, "Dickhead...now where have I heard that before?"

The tips of my ears heated as he referred to the time I blundered and called him that sweet endearment.

I heard Dylan chuckle behind me and I shot him a death glare which only made him laugh harder.

"What advice did she give you anyway?" I asked as I slumped into my seat.

"Not very good ones, I can tell you that," He chuckled.

I rolled my eyes, "I think that's pretty obvious."

His lips pursed in thought, "What advice do you think she gave me?"

"How to not be a dickhead?" I guessed and Dylan snorted behind me.

"How to not cry over not being able to catch a fish," Paul sputtered but the back.

"How to not growl every two seconds," Kai added.

Aiden growled and then tried to cover it up with a cough, "I know how to catch a fish."

"But you're not very good at it," Paul said.

"And I don't cry-"

"Well-"

"I don't!" Aiden cut him off. "As for growling and being a dickh ead...well that's a matter of opinion."

I turned towards the six pack members with a mischievous smile, "All those in agreement that he growls and acts like a-"

"Tate," He said while feigning hurt.

But I ignored him as everyone said a collective, 'I'.

I nudged him with my elbow, "Looks like all the opinions are in agreement."

He shook his head and rubbed his jaw but I didn't miss the small smile that was pulling at his lips.

And as I looked at him relaxing into his seat, it struck me how much I missed him.

All his brooding moods and quiet contemplation. The way he focused on a book or made sure Tourmaline was always happy.

I missed him more than I thought I would.

An hour or so later, we found ourselves safely back at the castle. Paul was a little frail but he'll be alright.

Aiden on the other hand was being exceptionally attentive. He opened my door for me, grabbed my bag and I could tell he wanted to reach out for my hand but second guessed himself and stopped before he did.

It was as if I came back to a slightly different person. He still walked as if the world was on his shoulders and growled when someone said something he didn't like, but he was also acting like a shy boy.

He looked away when I turned to him. His eyes lingered when he think I didn't notice. His fingers drummed idly when I knew he wanted to reach out and take my hand.

It was an oddity I hadn't expected.

And certainly not things a 'friend' would do, I thought to myself with a giddy smile.

"Tourmaline should be asleep..." He started but the words died on his lips as we entered the large foyer was instantly greeted by a squealing five-year-old.

"Tate!" She yelled in excitement and jumped into my arms.

I hauled her up and hugged her to me, "Hey, Princess."

She pulled back and faced me with a beaming smile, "I missed you so much."

"I missed you too kiddo. Didn't you get my message?" I asked and she titled her head in confusion.

Aiden coughed at our side as he reached out for Tourmaline but she tighten her hold on me.

"What message?" She asked.

I smiled, "For my birthday remember. You messaged and I said I missed you and we'll have cake soon."

She shook her head and looked at me like I was crazy, "I didn't message you. Dad said we couldn't bother you when you were with your family."

"Oh sweetie no. You can message me anytime. Plus I didn't have you around to celebrate with me so I was pretty bored," I booped her nose before I fully processed what she said. "If you didn't message me, then who did?"

"Dunno," She shrugged.

My eyes went Aiden and if the man was on trial, he'd be caught from his expression alone.

His eyes were darting around the room and his cheeks were rosy red.

Well, well, well... looks like Alpha Aiden really did wish me a happy birthday. Under the pretence of innocent little Tourmaline.

I couldn't help the shit eating grin on my face as Aiden took Tourmaline out of my arms and told her it was time for bed.

She pouted but after yawning a few times, she went upstairs without an argument.

When she was out of earshot, I turned to Aiden.

"Funny isn't it, how I got a text for my birthday but it said from Tourmaline," I pondered.

"Yeah, that's really funny," He said as his eyes focused on the painting on the wall behind me.

I stepped closer to him, "Did you lose your phone that day?"

His eyes met my challenge, "No."

"You could have said it was you."

"Where's the fun in that, Cupcake?" He asked as he took my hand and pulled me towards the kitchen.

"Cupcake?" I asked curiously even though it was the second time he'd call me that. "I don't remember agreeing to being called that."

"You're right," He nodded as he continued walking. "Lemon Tart suits you better. Mildly sweet but so very sour at times."

"Hey," I playfully slapped his arm as we entered the kitchen and he turned to me.

For the the first time since I've met him, I was graced with a smile. A genuine smile that took over his features and caused a tingly feeling in my chest.

I'd only gotten small smiles, smirks and a tug on his lips. But never a full smile.

Never this ray of sunshine.

"I have something for you," He said and I was still struck speechless as he pulled me closer to a counter.

He uncovered a large dish to reveal a chocolate frosted cake with candles on it.

Picking up a lighter, he lit the candles and said softly, "Happy belated birthday Tate."

I turned to him with a smile and wrapped my arms around him as I did when I'd left two weeks ago.

I heard him suck in a breath but wrapped me in his warm arms nonetheless.

"Thank you," I said.

His chuckle reverberated through me as I pulled back, "You're going to want to out those candles before we end up with a wax frosted cake."

I closed my eyes, made a wish and then blew out the candles.

"Did you make this yourself?" I asked and he nodded shyly. "Can't fish but can bake a cake. Is it edible?"

"Ha ha," He grumbled miserably. "Paul's full of shit and if you don't want the cake, I'll be happy to eat it by myself."

His hands reached out for the cake and I slapped them away.

"I never said I didn't want the cake."

I grabbed the knife and plates he set out and cut us both a slice. Aiden's was larger because I knew it was his favourite.

Hopping up onto the counter to sit, I bit into the cake and immediately died and went to foodie heaven.

"This is amazing," I moaned around a mouth full of cake.

He smiled again, "It was my mother's recipe."

"She thought you how to bake?"

"She did after she got tired me asking her to bake it almost every day," He laughed.

"Thank you Aiden," I said again. "Really, this meant a lot to me."

He simply shrugged and went on eating his cake.

"It's good to be home," I said.

"Yeah it is," He replied as his eyes found mine.

CHAPTER 15

"Hey kiddo. What are doing down here by yourself?" I asked Tourmaline who was currently sitting in the living room alone.

"Hey Tate!" She greeted excitedly. "Calypso was watching movies with me but she went to get popcorn."

"And where's Jenny?" I asked suspiciously.

Since I'd arrived last night, I hadn't seen her with Tourmaline all day. And she certainly wasn't around throwing me glares.

"Dunno," Tourm shrugged and I wanted to smile at her catch-phrase but Jenny's absence made me rather annoyed.

Which only spoke volumes about her character and level of responsibility. She had one job...

"Are you going to watch with us?" Tourm asked but her eyes were glued to the screen as I shook my head.

"Maybe later," I promised. "I'm just going to find your Uncle Aiden."

"Why?" She asked curiously.

I stared at the medical files in my hands but said, "Just wanted to borrow a book. I'll be back soon."

She nodded her head but said no more as I slipped out the door and went in search of the Alpha in the library.

Should I do did?

Would telling him about my heart condition really be such a good idea?

I was torn between the decision. On one hand, I could get Emery to pay me a visit soon and try healing me up and on the other, I didn't feel okay keeping this to myself.

But telling him meant being sidelined. I doubt he'd let me properly help with vampire related situations if he knew I had a fragile heart.

Indecisiveness still eating away at me, I held the folder behind me back as I entered the library and spotted Aiden at his desk with the lights on as dusk settled outside.

He looked up from the paper he had in his hands and waved me closer, "Great, you're here. I was about to come find you."

"You were?" I asked in confusion as I approached his desk and settled in the seat across from him. Taking care to ensure the folder was still out of his sight.

"Yes," His tone was strained as he turned the newspaper he had towards me. "Look."

As my eyes scanned the headlines in big bold letters, I felt the colour drain from my face.

Ten people missing in the last twenty-four hours.

I left my folder behind my back as I sat on the edge of my seat and flipped to the article. According to the journalist, ten individuals were reported missing after they seemingly disappeared into thin air over the night. The town where it happened was about an hour away, south of where we were.

My eyes found the steel icy blue eyes of Aiden who was staring at the newspaper as if offended him.

"What does it mean?" I questioned even though I strung together my own suspicion.

His fist were tightly clenched on his desk and I could see the veins on the back of his palms straining behind his tan skin.

"A few things," He sighed. "The vampires are up to something. They're either feeding closer or creating more damn blood suckers."

"They don't feed around here?" I asked in surprise.

"No. From what we've monitored they sporadically feed further away in the city. More humans means more crime which won't raise suspicion and put them at risk of exposure. The coastal towns around here are much less populated which is why they don't feed unless it's a stay tourist."

I rest the newspaper aside as my hand itched to touch his own.

Like the force field of a magnet that pulling me in, closer and closer, until I stuck.

Yesterday was disconcerting to me as it was. First the vampires and then Aiden's one-eighty.

I left a man closed behind shutters and a locked door and when I returned there was a welcome mat waiting for me.

The concern that had melted his blue eyes into liquid pools and the way he blushed when I discovered that he was behind the birthday message. My present was the icing on the literal cake when he pulled out the delectable chocolate dessert.

Never, in all my wildest dream, would I have even begin to think that Aiden would bake me a cake and light my candles. It only made my birthday wish easier.

A safe and long life for Tourmaline and Aiden. Nothing more, nothing less.

But despite that, I couldn't ascertain whether or not it was out of friendship or more... How I desperately wished it was more.

Which is why I kept my hands firmly places on the table as I listened to him.

"Ten humans last night was no coincidence," He shook his head.

"But they won't possibly be creating new ones..." I trailed off as I tried to convince myself. "You said yourself that they hate to create new vampire since they're erratic, wild and uncontrollable. New vamps around here would raise a lot of concern if they start killing off humans like flies."

I recalled Aiden telling me just that. Once new vampires transition, they're hard to tame since the thirst for blood drives them into a killing frenzy. Which would cause problems for any vampires, mostly the ones living in the area. And since the ones we're dealing with hadn't risked their identity getting exposed because of their quest for mermaids, I wondered what had changed.

"Unless..." Aiden trailed off uneasily as his spine straightened.

"Unless?"

"Unless after last night's attack they decided that they needed to replenish their small army. Rebuilding their empire by replacing their fallen soldiers," He mused before his eyes fell to the newspaper. "What still concerns me is why they were so reckless about it. Ten humans in one night from one town. If they fed then the bodies would have been found but since no corpses showed up..."

His abrupt stop to his sentence was completed with a troubled expression and I felt my insides twist anxiously.

"If they didn't feed then they took the humans to create more," I finished for him.

When his eyes flashed to mine, the answer was in his eyes.

His hands coiled tightly around the ends of the armrest on his chair as he nodded, "And my only guess for them taking humans this close to us is for show. The thing about vampires is their constant need to be ostentatious and flashy, at least they used to be back when there were much more of them. Showing us that they aren't afraid of human speculation and creating baby vamps is their way of saying 'game on!'"

A very dangerous game.

A power move on the carefully created chessboard that Aiden and the vampires have been been playing for years.

There was an important question that wasn't asked.

"Why now?" I queried aloud.

Aiden's lips curved up in a smile that held no humour but contained only malice. A smile that was woven to scare adults and wreak the minds of children with nightmares.

"That's the golden questions, isn't it?" He said.

"Maybe it's because your pack has killed them?" I guessed.

He shook his head, "No, we've killed a few over the years. That can't be it."

"Well, whatever their cause, I think we should start preparing for anything," I said. "You said yourself the new vampires are wild. Whether they're strengthening up or planning something more, it can't be good."

"You're right," He agreed and the trust and sincerity in his eyes would have knocked me off my feet if I were standing.

Maybe...just maybe, he was starting to see me as responsible. Not an immature teen.

It certainly hadn't went over my head that he chose to discuss this news with me rather than keeping it hidden until I found out.

Which reminded me of the secret that I had trapped in a medical file that was burning a hole through the back of blouse.

But the worry lines that was set into Aiden's forehead was enough to make me hold back.

Tomorrow, I decided.

I was not going to worry him anymore than he already was. And he was plenty right now. Throwing in a Luna with a heart condition that should not affect werewolves wasn't something that he needed added on his plate.

After all, his reasons for wanting a mate - or a Luna for that matter - had been because of his need to strengthen his pack.

It was the reason he was prepared to take Emery if he hadn't found a mate. If I wasn't his mate, things would have been much different in both packs. No doubt my family and I would have not survived the wrath of his brutally strong pack.

So, to tell my secret was to cast a dark cloud on an already stormy day. However, I didn't like keeping the secret anymore than I did exposing it.

It would be double standard of me to expect him to spill his guts while I buried my skeletons six feet under.

I had no tell him. No questions or quarrels about it.

"Aiden?" I said in a quiet voice as I sat on the edge of my seat.

"Hmm?" He asked as I pulled him out of thought.

"Can I ask you something?"

"Anything," And I knew he meant it. The clarity in his eyes were enough to tell and it warmed my heart.

"Why weren't you going to wait?"

His eyebrows pulled together in confusion, "Wait for what?"

"For your mate...for me," I clarified as I felt the blush warm my cheeks.

"Oh," He said startled by my question. I waited while he paused silently before he answered, "After Will and Amethyst died, I had Tourmaline to take care of. I didn't find my mate in the pack immediately and so I assumed that maybe I would have found her soon enough if she was younger. Leaving here to attend the annual Mate Meet-up wasn't ideal and neither was hosting it, so I never did. After a while, I just stopped searching. I'm twenty-one, I didn't expect to find my mate if I hadn't already."

I understood what he said but I didn't like it.

"And you were going to kidnap Emery? Despite her already having my brother?"

He shook his head with a guilty smile, "No. Dylan was joking around that I should take a mate to strengthen the pack and suggested going after your brother's mate. Someone who joined our pack last year told someone from another pack and the word spread like wildfire as they took the words out of context. I just played along with it to rile your brother up."

My jaw was practically laying on the table.

"So it was all a joke?" I demanded unbelievably.

He winked as the corners of his lips titled up, "Now you can say I'm a funny guy."

My eyes narrowed on him, "I think the punch line was way off its mark."

"I suppose I should have set the story straight," He said as he looked away guilty.

"But," I back tracked as I didn't mean to take away his rare and lovely smile, "you did have us running around like headless chickens for a while."

He chuckled but it came out bitterly and if there was one thing I wish I could have done in that moment was see inside his mind.

Just look into the back of head and see what he thinking. Why he was thinking it. Make sense of this quiet, contemplative man with crystal ocean eyes.

"If you didn't plan on taking Emery, then why were you there?" I asked quietly as I peeked up at him through my lashes.

Aiden's heart best firm and steadily as he leaned across his desk, closer to me. His scent of fresh waterfall and sea-washed mahogany brushed over to me as a potent combination and made me slightly dizzy from the intoxicating scent.

It was my drug in the form of natural perfume.

"I said I stopped looking, I never said I gave up," He clarified and the intensity of his eyes drew me in closer until our faces were inches apart.

My heart beat erratically in my chest at his words and my eyes unconsciously flickered to his lips.

"I wish you'd have called me during the last two weeks," I admitted something of my own. "Instead of calling Kai to check up on me, you could have just called me."

I detected the slight hitch of his breath at my confession as his eyes softened.

"I should have," A smile played on his lips then. "Technically I texted first so it was your turn to make your move."

"Texted as Tourmaline," I reminded his teasingly.

He laughed at that as he shook his head, "I still can't believe you were home for less than five minutes and already figured that out."

"All those emojis were a give away," I fibbed.

"Were they?" He asked unsure.

"Oh yeah. The kids barely use them anymore grandpa," I teased as he grumbled. "By the way, I wouldn't have mind if you said it was you."

"I'll keep that in mind," He said as he leaned away and dug through the draw of his desk. "As we're on the topic of your birthday, I forgot to give you this."

He produced a small jewel box from his desk and I was struck speechless by it.

I hadn't considered that he would have gotten me something, much less jewelry.

"Who are you and what did you do with my Aiden?" I deadpan.

He smirked with a raised brow, "Your Aiden?"

My cheeks must have been as red as a ripe tomato then as I attempted and failed to deny, "I-I..."

"It's alright Tate," He laughed as he got up from his seat and rounded his desk. "I actually like it."

I fiddled with my hands nervously as he stood before me where he leaned against his desk with the box in his hands.

With surprising gentleness, he placed his index finger under my chin and tipped my head back.

My eyes found his and I felt my breath caught at the tenderness in his eyes.

He placed the box in my hands, "It's from Tourmaline and myself."

Slowly, I opened it and was stunned to see a gold necklace with a yellow stone as the pendant.

"It's a sulfur rock," He answered my unasked question. "There's an extendable clasp at the back that will stretch enough around the neck of your wolf when you shift. That way you won't have to take it off and it will conceal the scent of your blood."

"Aiden...I - thank you," I said as I felt my skin warm with a blush. Standing to my feet, I wrapped my arms around his neck.

For the second time that I'd hugged him, he was again startled by my reaction. Yet, he didn't take long in wrapping his arms around my waist and pulling my body into his.

Every inch of me that was pressed against him felt tingly with a new sensation. Like little zaps of pleasure combined with the soothing calm of being near him.

Electrifying. Heart-stopping. Mind-melting.

It all twisted up in me and threatened to steal my breath and knock me off a cliff I wasn't sure I'll be safe falling from.

Or was it already too late for me?

As I pulled back, Aiden held a secret smile as he took the box from my hand.

"Turn around," He said softly and I complied.

Aiden's warm fingers brushed against my neck, burning a trail of fire in its wake, as he pushed my hair to the side. His hands moved elegantly and slowly as he placed the pendant against my chest and secured the clasp at the back. Knuckles dragged along my skin and warm breath sent goosebumps down my back and neck.

It was agonizing being this close to him and only being able to feel his callous fingertips faintly brushing my neck. It was like wanting to open the biggest gift under the Christmas tree but your mom saying it wasn't yours to have.

Aiden insinuated friendship but his actions were contrary to those of a platonic companion. Yet, I wasn't sure what he wanted.

Did he want me as I wanted him or was the mate bond mangling his actions?

As he brushed he neatly fixed my hair, I turned back to him only for his eyes to be on my lips.

But, as if shaking away a dream - or nightmare - he stepped back to give me an inch of space that I did not need nor wanted.

I touched the crystal as I watch Aiden hover anxiously over his desk.

Deciding to cut him some slack, I asked, "You said it would cover the scent of my blood?"

He seemed relieved by the change in direction as he nodded eagerly, "Yes. While the crystal does causes the vampires pain and wards then away, it apparently also covers the scent of blood."

"I can still smell things," I noted.

"Right, it doesn't cover all scents, only blood and only for vampires. The chemical compound affects their senses, especially

scent. It throws them off balance and makes them a but disorient-
ed so they can't pick up the scent of blood," He explained. "The
mermaids all have a crystal of their own."

"Is that why I can't pick up their scent?" I asked curiously.

He shook his head, "No, the mermaids have a muted scent
regardless. They're hard to detect by our nose but the vamps can
sniff out their blood unless they have a crystal. Which is also good
for a fight."

My fingers glided across the smooth surface until I felt the sharp
edge at the bottom. I understood exactly what he'd meant by it
also being a weapon.

"I see," I nodded along to these strange details that were
over-looked by the world.

"Any more twenty-one questions?" He asked jokingly.

I opened my mouth immediately to ask one more but closed it
as I thought better of it. Or better of how it may be perceived.

"Spill it out Tate," He chuckled reading me as my fingers twisted
together.

"Well..." I started before looking around the empty library, "I
saw that Jenny wasn't watching over Tourmaline anymore. Is she
alright?"

He shook his head as he snorted, "Only you would be concerned
for someone like her."

His comment had be taken back.

"Did she do something?" I questioned with wide eyes. "Oh man,
I knew I should have told you how bad she was at taking care of
Tourm-"

"Why didn't you?" He asked, cutting me off.

"Because she's was here before I was? Because you gave her
your trust to take care of your niece? I wasn't fully sure if she was
awful to Tourm or just awful to me."

A growl tore through Aiden's lips as his warm eyes hardened into solid ice.

"She's been awful to you?" He seethe.

Shoot, did I say that aloud?

"Forget about that," I waved him off dismissively. "Why isn't she taking care of Tourm anymore?"

His cold eyes narrowed and I knew he wasn't over the subject but he moved on.

"I could tell she wasn't a good influence for Tourmaline...and she's been trying to...get with me for years now," His last few words were no more than a whisper.

"Did she ever succeed?" I asked timidly and he shook his head. "No."

My answering smile returned a glimmer of light in his features.

"So you fired her from taking care of Tourn?"

"Yeah, Calypso said she'll keep an eye on her some days and then another mermaid will help out for the other days."

"That's great," I assured him. "I can even look after her when I'm not training."

"You would?" He asked with surprise.

I shrugged, "Of course. I grew up with my eight-year-old brothers, remember? If I can handle those two then it'll be a breeze looking over Tourmaline."

"You're amazing," He whispered under his breath.

"I know," I shrugged with a smile. "Now how about dinner because I'm starved."

He nodded with a small smile.

"Lead the way."

"Gladly," I said as I moved towards the door.

Just before I could place my hand on the door handle, I heard Aiden call me back.

"Hey Tate, you left..." His sentence was broken by a sharp inhale of breath.

I spun around and saw my medical file in Aiden's hands.

His eyes darkened as it met mine and I gulped in fear of what was to come.

Chapter 16

"Aiden, I..." I trailed of quietly as I was at a lost for words. What was I suppose to say?

Sorry didn't quite seem good enough. It would not justify why I didn't tell him. The capacity of sorry was too meager to hold the guilt that festered within me.

And maybe it was selfish of me to keep him it from him. But from the anguish in his eyes, maybe I did do the right thing but for the wrong reason.

"What is it?" His voice was strained as he stood still with the folder in his hand.

I took a tentative step closer as I realized that he hadn't read the contents of the file yet.

"It's my medical file," I said quietly and I saw a flame behind the blue of his eyes and my gaze dropped to the floor.

"I could see that, but why do you have one?"

"Because I-I...I'm..."

"Tate," He pleaded as his grip on the folder tightened.

I nodded at him as I felt the prickly pain in my chest awaken. It mockingly reminded me that it was the star of the situation as if I'd forgotten.

"Is it your chest?" He asked between clenched teeth before I could begin.

My eyes flashed up to meet his perceptive stare as I was startled with surprise. Had Dylan betrayed my trust and told him?

"You know?" I asked meekly.

He shook his head but his jaw stiffened, "No, but I'm guessing my assumption is correct? The way you always clutch your chest, it has to do with this?" He waved the file.

He'd noticed.

It was the wrong moment to feel it, but the knowledge that he'd been paying enough attention warmed me. Somehow, it made it much easier to tell him. Much more bearable to accept his reaction.

"Should we sit?" I gestured to the sofa with a nod of my head.

"No, I'd prefer to stand."

"Okay," I took a shaky breath as I looked away from him. "A few months ago there was an attack with rogues. They struck us when we least expected it and it turned pretty bloody pretty quickly. I was there along with three other wolves when nine of them jumped out of nowhere. My ego got the best of me and I went for the two big guys," I smirked at memory. I really thought I would have taken them out but they over-powered me. "I had two ribs and...and a punctured artery."

I heard his sharp intake of breath but I refused to look his way. If he dared to show me pity, I don't think I'd be able to survive it.

I squeezed my eyes shut as I prepared to reveal a pack secret to him. One that hadn't left our pack's territory since it came to be. But if I was going to tell him about this, I wasn't going to lie or withhold the truth.

"I was dying. I was as good as dead as I slipped into the arms of death. There was no turning back, no saving me. At least there shouldn't have been-"

A loud crushing sound stopped me mid sentence as I looked to where Aiden had thrown his desk lamp across the room. The yellow light was extinguished as pieces of glass was scattered along the marble floor. The shards refracted the light from the ceiling and casted a hundred sharp sparkles of light across the room in a beautifully ominous glow.

The haunted expression that shadowed Aiden's features was exactly what I worried about. If he took this as weakness. But the now broken lamp and glimmer of something else in his eyes had me perplexed.

Could it be fear that I read? Or was I not as omniscience as I thought I was?

He dragged in a long, shallow breath, "But you lived. You're alive."

The conviction in his voice had me believing that he was trying to convince himself. As if he was telling himself this wasn't a dream...or a nightmare.

"Yes, but what I'm about to tell you now is something that you can't tell anyone else. Please, Aiden, for me," I asked and he gave me a curt nod.

"Anything," He said so quietly that even my werewolf ears barely picked it up.

A small smile pulled at the corner of my lips but I pushed it aside. "Emery has a gift. All of the Lunas of the Blood Moon Pack are gifted with a power when they join the pack. Emery can heal anyone at a faster rate than any werewolf can heal. Cure any wounds that would take our life before we could heal ourselves. She saved me, brought me back to life."

Aiden was startled by this news as Emery was when she learned of her powers. A million questions took plagued his features but I held up my hand. I had to finish this before he asked anything.

"As I said, I was meant to die that very second she started pulling my heart back together. She had to be quick about it but like the miracle of our existance, she saved me. But that didn't come without its consequences."

"You're alive," He repeated sternly.

"For now," I laughed darkly without an inch of humour. "There's no science to explain how she healed my heart and because of that there's nothing to explain why I was left with side effects. Well it was only one anomoly, chest pains every now and again. It was nothing of concern as the pack doctor did all the tests he can think of, but everything was all clear."

Was. Past tense.

"Emery couldn't fix it since there was no real problem to solve. Our only theory is that, because she messed with fate and rushed to heal me, something may have went sideways. I honestly didn't mind it. A few chest pains was a generous offer in return for my life..."

"Then why do you have a medical file?" He asked between clenched teeth.

I tucked in my chin as I felt an unfamiliar wetness in my eyes that I willed away. Aiden was the first person to know what was the latest with my heart besides Dr. Adler. And somehow, speaking the words aloud made it much more real than the pain itself.

"Because the chest pains have been more constant recently. More painful. When I went back to the pack, I asked the doctor to run a few checks for me...and-"

"And?" He asked impatiently.

"And my heart rate is slowing down. It's becoming weaker. Causing more pain, making me short of breath, tired. Dr. Adler confirmed that it's bradycardia. If you read the file you'll see that my heart rate's at sixty-four beats per minute. If it goes under sixty, well there'd be a lot less oxygen in my blood cells which would lead to...bad things."

Death wasn't a word I wanted to associated it with at the moment. It was like that one friend who seeked you out when they wanted something and I'm quite tired of death wanting my life.

Aiden was completely silent and still. For a solid minute I thought that he'd either turn to stone of left the room. But his earratic heartbeat and his addicting scent was every present. As the silence stretched out, I struggled to find the courage to look at him.

Afraid that I'll see the disappoint and regret that I anticipated.

When my eyes found his, I wasn't even sure he was looking at me, but through me. Lost in thought.

"Aiden?" I coaxed anxiously.

That snapped him out of his trance as his eyes focused on me. My already shallow breath was stolen from my lungs when I registered his anguished expression.

Sorrow. Guilt. Fear. Anger. Pain.

A perfect blend.

He shook his head as if trying to clear his thoughts, "Emery's healed you now, right? Now that you've pinpoint a condition, she healed you while you were there."

The intensity of the hope in his tone sent another punch to my heart. Another infliction of pain.

"No," I said gently and when his anger became more prominent, I back tracked. "Not yet. When we left she was still weak, she wouldn't have been able to heal me even if she tried."

"But she'll heal you," He decided with such assurity, I was compelled to believe him. "We'll go to the pack tomorrow or they'll come here if you can't make the trip. Whatever it may be, tomorrow she'll heal you."

I watched as he placed the file on his desk and reached for his phone but I walked closer and placed my hand on his.

"Not yet," I shook my head. "She's weak and pregnant. I think it'll be better to give her a week before we worry her and ask her to help."

His eyebrows knitted together, "Have you not told her?"

Guilt ate at me, "I haven't told anyone."

"And how long have you known?"

"Since my birthday."

He certainly did like my answer as he shot me a sharp stare. "You've known for two weeks and you didn't think anyone should know?"

I expected his voice to be at yelling level. But the low, sharp cut of his calm words had a greater impact. Opposite of typical anger yet so much more lethal.

"I didn't want anyone to worry," I whispered. "Especially after my family went through the fight with the hunters."

"And what about me?" There was an unusual lilt to his voice. An octave higher. "Why didn't you just tell me? Or Kai? Or anyone else from this pack?"

I didn't understand him. He was more mixed up than a rubik's cube. One minute he wanted friendship and the next he seemed more concerned than was required.

"Because if I did you'd make me come back before time," Or worst, tell me not to return.

"And for good reason too," He growled as his hand under my own curled into a fist. "What if something had happened? What if you-"

His sentence broke off as he struggled to contain the Alpha that demanded to be released.

"How do think Tourmaline would have felt?" He finally asked. "Or me?"

My eyes widened at his words as my heart felt a different kind of pain. A squeeze that wasn't threatening to suck my life away. Instead it blossomed into warmth that seeped into the rest of my body.

Was it not as I'd expected it to be? Did he not care about my capability but instead feared for me?

Had I been blinded to this?

"Aiden..."

"God, Tate! It was so careless of you not to say anything. And the vampires last night-" He grimaced at the thought.

The warm blood in my veins turned to ice at his words. Did he already assume I was too weak to fight?

I kept my tone even and emotionless as I said, "You've not trusted me with your own secrets Aiden, so how am I suppose to give you the benefit of the doubt? Everything I learned about your pack was when they were already in front of my eyes."

He recoiled at my words as if I had shouted them at him. His hand slipped out from below my own as he leaned against his desk.

Head hung. Shoulders defeated. Breathing uneven.

The silence stretched out again.

What do I make of his words? Had this truly affected him to such an extent?

"Why did you feel as if you could not tell me?" He asked quietly as his shoulders slumped in and his face took on a troubled expression. "Do you...do you not trust me?"

"I do," I answered without having to think about it. My quick response surprised me. I don't think I realized when I did or just how much until he asked. I trust him but I was afraid of rejection.

I was never sure how he felt about me. An unknown mystery that tangled my decision.

He seemed disbelieving as his eyes were unfocused and staring at the floor, "Then why didn't you tell me?"

I'd hurt him. I had unknowingly hurt him by keeping this to myself. I expected that I would have been the one with wounded emotions but I ended up hurting him. It was selfish to not consider the possibility that Aiden would have been affected by this beyond having a weak Luna.

"When you met me, you implied that my age made me inferior," I muttered. "So you can imagine how I'd think you'd react when you knew something was physically wrong with me."

"I never-"

"I believe the words childish and immature were used during the first ten minutes of our first conversation."

He dipped his head lower.

"So were you not going to tell me?"

"I was," I admitted. "That's why I came looking for you and brought the folder. But, when you showed the article about the humans, I didn't think now was the best time to add to your plate...To tell you that having me as a mate defeats the purpose that you need me for."

His head snapped my way and again I saw the blaze of anger behind his irises.

"And do you think I need you for Tate?" He asked harshly.

I twisted my fingers together as I spoke my insecurity, "To strengthen your pack. A weak Luna wouldn't do that. I wouldn't be what you want. Having me around won't serve a purpose."

He scoffed, "And do you know of what I want?"

"I know that the reason you looked for a Luna was to strengthen the Oaks Pack. How am I suppose to do that if I can't even fight without losing my breath?"

"If I wanted you for strategic purposes, Tate, I would have already have you marked and bounded to the pack the first night you got here," He snarled.

My heart stuttered at that knowledge. He made a convincing a point. A point that struck my heart with hope.

"So if I'd told you that something was wrong, you wouldn't have demanded I returned? Think of me a weak pup who couldn't defend herself?" I asked. "When have you ever made me feel like I was here for some other reason beside being the Luna? Being your friend?" I spat out the distasteful word.

His expression was pained. I'd upset him even further.

When he spoke, his voice dripped with pain and regret, "Do you think of me so lowly?"

"No," I said sincerely. "But I do think that you think of me that way."

"Then you don't know me at all," He declared with a shake of his head. "When I asked you to be my friend, I had not realized how my words could have been construed. It was only when I'd said it that I'd realize how awful it sounded. I don't want to be friends, Tate. I never have."

"Oh," I squeaked, startled by this knowledge. I felt dejected and my heart felt battered. My throat had a lump that made it impossible to swallow this information. I lifted my head higher and said, "If that's what you want then I won't force you to smile and pretend to be okay with my presence here. I know when I'm not wanted."

As I turned to leave, his warm palm hand captured my arm. I sucked a harsh breath at the electrified touch of his skin on mine.

He spun me around and a smile brightened his features as he laughed quietly.

I frowned at his unexpected reaction.

"You're very obtuse, Tate," He said with a shake of his head and I scowled at him.

"I'll keep that in mind," I muttered angrily.

His grin widened as he cupped my cheek and tipped my head up, "You silly girl. When I said I didn't want as you as a friend, I meant I want more. Don't get me wrong, I do want your friendship, but not only that. Do you understand?"

I hear my heart thump loudly in my ear, feel blood rushing to my cheeks, my skin prickle to life and see every colour of the world vibrated to life in my eyes after shedding its drab and weary shades.

It was if the world woke up from a restless slumber after Aiden's revelation.

I could see he was still waiting for my answer so I nodded my head. Words were lost in the ocean outside.

"I would have liked for you to tell me without that notion in your head, but I can see why'd you think. I was an idiot for asking you to be my friend, but I was scared that I'd lose you over something stupid I would I have said," He admitted. "I don't see you as an object for making this pack stronger, I never did. It was my goal in finding a Luna, but that was before I found you."

"Aiden," I stuttered as my hand held onto his wrist that was cradling my face. "If you'd told me before... God, I really am obtuse."

He chuckled as his thumb brushed my cheek, "Nah, I'm just an idiot. Alpha Idiot should replace Alpha Dickhead, don't you think?"

I smiled, "Alpha Idiot and the Silly Girl."

"A perfect match," He winked.

I nodded shyly as I looked him in his ocean eyes, "I don't want to be just friends either."

He breathed deeply, inhaling my scent with a smile on his face, "That's good to know because I was about to go ask Tourmaline to be my wing girl."

I flicked his chest playfully, "First the text and now using her cuteness to your advantage, for shame."

He shrugged indifferently before his smile faltered, "Tate, I don't see you as weak. Not before and not now."

"Thank you," I said gratefully.

"How do you feel now? I'm sorry we argued, I should have not done that," He said guilty.

"I'm fine," I assured him. "More than fine now, actually."

He nodded as despair filled his eyes and then determination, "We'll fix this. I swear to you we'll get Emery here soon and then you'll be fine. As healthy as a werewolf should be."

I knew his words were for my comfort but I could tell he was convincing himself. He pain he felt, knowing he couldn't fix this himself must be awful. If I were in his shoes, I knew I'd walk to the ends of the earth to find a cure for him.

"I'll be okay, Aiden. Trust me on that," I squeezed his hand.

"Don't break my trust, Cupcake," He said.

Gently his other hand cupped my other cheek as I held onto his arms. He lowered my head and leaned in. I felt his breath fan my eyes lashes and I inhaled a lung full of his comforting scent. And then ever so gently, he placed a warm kiss on my forehead.

The simplest gesture stole my breath and my heart. I felt the skin on my head tingle from the brief contact. His warmth seeped into my skin and it felt like a weighted blanket.

When he pulled back, I could see the emotions swirling in hid eyes and I smiled at him encouragingly.

"Come, I'll take you to the pack doctor before we get dinner," He said as he held one of my hand and grabbed the folder.

I was falling. There was no doubt about it.

How very wrong I was.

Aiden Oaks was truly a big softie outlined by hard edges that was shaped by his tough life.

CHAPTER 17

Three days later and Dr. Nazra, pack doctor of the Oaks Pack, confirmed that my heart rate's keeping a steady pace at sixty-four.

For now.

Aiden and her had an hour long phone conversation with Dr. Adler, to which Aiden kicked me out of the room after I keep telling the three of them that I was fine. I did, however, listened through the door as they discussed causes, treatment and the effects it will have on me.

It wasn't anything new that Dr. Adler hadn't already explained to me. But Aiden did keep his promise and kept Emery's magical healing a secret.

All Dr. Nazra knew was that we had a possible solution. She didn't question it after Aiden made it clear it wasn't up for discussion. She and Dr. Adler did discuss a second option.

A back-up plan that Aiden growled at. He was fully adamant on Emery healing me...and I can't deny that I was wishing for the same.

If it doesn't work...then the next option was a pacemaker. Except I really didn't like the thought of them cutting me open to put the pacemaker in my chest.

If felt too clinical.

Too intrusive for my comfort.

Until then, I was banishing all thoughts of heart conditions, healers and devices with electric pulses.

Now, my only focus was deciding on which swimsuit to wear for my first lesson in swimming.

Little Tourm and I banded together and got Aiden to take us down to the beach today. With her cuteness and my mate magic, he was putty in our hands.

Since the last time we were down there, Aiden tracked down the issue that caused the motion detectors he has in the water to not send a signal to the alarm system. It turned out to be a short in the cables on the alarm due to it's exposure in the sun.

Now that it's sorted, Tourmaline was excited to get back into the water. I was also a little buzzed to learn how to swim...especially since Tourm promised to have a pod of dolphins swim by.

The perks of having mermaids around.

As I looked at the dozen swimsuits Calypso got for me from the human town nearby, my indecisiveness kicked in.

One piece? Bikini? Should I just throw one of the shorts and a t-shirt?

It certainly didn't help with Aiden's confession looming over my head like an animated circle of dizzying stars.

Not just friendship.

Those were his words. The exact words that's been looping around my head for past three days.

I had the urge to laugh at myself for believing that being friends was what he wanted all along.

But now that he did admit to wanting more, my insecurity rang out as I tried to find a suitable swimwear. I don't think there was a person on this planet, male or female or non-binary, that doesn't experience insecurity every now and again. It was a naturally ingrained part our mindset influenced by society's words.

So now I stood in front of my mirror wondering if anyone would question me wearing a turtleneck to the beach.

Answer leaned closer to: yes.

Ditching the eyesore sweater, that I'll probably never need in this corner of the world, I closed my eyes and grabbed a random piece of cloth off my bed.

Peeking one eye open, I cringed at the wine red two piece, but mustered what little courage I had and threw it on.

And God bless Calypso for also bringing me a few cover-ups, albeit they were either crochet or sheer.

I picked up the white crochet material and tied it up before braiding my hair. By the time I was finished, there was a knock on the door.

It flew open before I could answer it and Tourm came running in.

"Tourm, you knock and then wait for an answer," Aiden explained to his niece from his place outside the door frame.

"Sorry Dad," She called over his shoulder but she not sorry at all from the grin on her face.

"It's okay," I laughed. "You can come in Aiden."

Tourm beamed at me as she climbed onto my bed and started jumping when Aiden stepped through the door.

He stopped short when his eyes landed on me and they widened as I heard his jagged intake of breath.

"Fuck," I heard him growl under his breath. But it was low enough that Tourmaline didn't pick up on it.

She did, however, ask, "What did you say, Dad?"

He coughed as he shook his head but his eyes never left mine, "Nothing."

"But you said something," She urged.

"I said we're going to miss the surf, so you better hurry along," He waved her off the bed.

She stopped jumping as her five-year-old eyes looked at him quizzically.

"That's not what you said."

"Isn't it?" He said in confusion as fear sprung on his face and he tore his eyes away from mine.

"Dunno," She shrugged before jumping off the bed and running out the door. "I can't wait to see the dolphins!"

Aiden was staring at me with hooded eyes as I walked past him.

Right as my shoulder brushed his, I smirked and couldn't resist the urge to tease him, "You got a little drool there."

I pointed to the corner of his lips and when he lifted his hand, I laughed and quickly walked out the door, following Tourmaline.

Aiden trailed behind us without a word as we walked down to the water.

Rick, Calypso, Kai, Matt, Dylan and a couple mermaids and mermen were already down there. Including Jenny swimming around in mermaid form.

I frowned because she really was beautiful and her mermaid form just made her more majestic. But the knowledge that she had a thing for Aiden was my reason for my crabby feelings.

Had she not wanted me out of the picture, we may have been good friends.

Well...there was at least a thirty percent chance.

"Tate," Tourm pulled on my hand to get my attention.

"Yes, princess?"

"Can you braid my hair like yours?" She asked as her big blue doe shaped eyes looked up at me.

I smiled, "Of course I will."

We walked closer to the water's edge and then sat on the dry sand as I braided Tourmaline's hair into a French braid.

"All done," I told her before he turned and gave me a hug before running off again.

"Stay close to shore, Tourmaline," Aiden called and she nodded her pink hair head. Then he turned to me but the sun was to his back so I had to shade my eyes to be able to see him clearly.

He held one of his hands out for my own and grabbed it as he pulled me to my feet. The loose sand under my feet made me slip as I stumbled into Aiden.

My body was fully pressed into every dip, curve and contour of Aiden's hard and warm body. And oh boy, the physical connection was explosive.

He chuckled and I felt my frame shake with the movement as his face got dangerously close to my own.

"Ready for your first lesson in swimming?" He asked as his arms steadied me in the sand and he took a step back. Except, before I could answer, the man pulled off his shirt and bared his gloriously tan six pack of pure unadulterated abs to me.

And hubba hubba was he mouth watering.

"Tate?" He raised a brow in question and I snapped out of the trance his abdominal muscles put me in. "I think you got a little drool there?"

His thumb wiped at the corner of my lips as he smirked. I batted his hand away as I playfully narrowed my eyes at him.

"Ha ha, very funny," I shook my head as a smile played on my lips. "You know it's kind of a faux pas to repeat someone's joke back to them."

One his brow shot up as he shrugged, "I suppose, but you did smile."

"And what a beautiful smile it is," Dylan commented as he popped out of nowhere with his usual mischievous grin.

A hint of annoyance crossed Aiden's face looked at Dylan.

"Don't you own a shirt?" Aiden asked his Gamma.

Dylan looked at him warily, "Dude, we're on the beach."

"Go find a shirt."

"What? Are you insane?"

"Dylan."

"Nope."

I rolled my eyes at their back and forth, "Leave him be Aiden. His nips aren't offending me."

Dylan placed both his hands over his chest as he looked flabbergasted, "Don't look at my tits."

"I wasn't," I snorted.

"I'd hope not," Aiden grumbled jealously.

I groaned, "Can someone just teach me how to swim?"

"Could you handle it?" Dylan asked and when I gave him a confused expression he gestured to my heart. "I mean with your chest and all."

Aiden's expression soured considerably as his eyes darkened and flashed between us.

"You know about Tate's heart condition?" Aiden question with accusation laced in his tone.

"Yeah, she mentioned that rogue attack or whatever," He shrugged indifferent.

"Dylan!" Rick called out from further down the coast where there were bigger waves. "You're missing the gnarly waves man!"

My eyes caught the large waves that broke as it neared the shore when Dylan took off towards his board. The blue water foamed as it washed up to lap a few feet away from our feet before dragging back into the open blue.

A thrill of both excitement and dread creeped along my spine as if someone poured ice down my back.

I wrapped my arms around myself to ward off the chill of the terrifying thought.

When I looked at Aiden again, his expression was still dark.

"You told me you hadn't told anyone about your heart..." The hint of distrust was as plain as day in his voice.

"I hadn't told anyone about the lowering of my heart rate," I clarified and his jaw clenched. "And I hadn't told anyone in this pack about my heart either. But the first day I was here...it got really bad before I made it to breakfast and Dylan found me in the hallway."

Aiden was then in my space as his fingers lifted my face to look at him, "What do you mean he found you?"

"I mean I fell over from the pain and he found me. I didn't know what else to say so I gave him a summarized version," I shrugged. "He doesn't know everything, especially not about Emery."

"Tate..." He sighed as he closed his eyes tightly. "Jesus, Cupcake, why didn't you tell me then? What if something worse had happened?"

"But it didn't?" I suggested with a wary smile and he growled.

"That's not the point. You tell me when you're not feeling good alright? Even the smallest pain, you tell me," His eyes searched my own for a sign that I understood.

So, with a resigned sigh, I nodded, "Alright, I promise."

He still seemed worried as his eyes fluttered to the water, "Maybe this isn't such a great idea..."

"Wow, wow, wow," I grabbed his bare shoulders. "You promised and my heart's perfect."

A rose an eyebrow, unimpressed by my words.

"Well perfectly fine for its condition," I amended.

"Fine, but if your chest-"

"I'll tell you," I assured him.

He resigned the conversation as he nodded and grabbed a bottle from a bag laying with dry clothing for Tourmaline that he'd brought down.

"First rule of swimming-"

"Don't drown," I guess.

He smiled and his freckles became more pronounced, especially in the sun.

"No, but that is an important factor," He stated. "Though you should probably not try to die today."

"Duly noted."

"First rule is always wear sunscreen," He handed me over the bottle while he grabbed another. "You don't want sun burns, trust me."

Being on the sand made me feel more comfortable as I untied my cover-up and placed it on a beach chair near Tourm's bag.

I rubbed the sunscreen over my exposed skin before turning to Aiden who seemed to be struggling with reaching his back.

"Here, I got you," I said as I pushed his hands away and rubbed the product on his smooth solid back. Jesus, the man was built like a solid wall of muscle.

I felt him tense under my palms but relaxed after a few seconds when the shock wore off. Tiny tingles exploded over my hands where I touched his warm skin and I heard him inhale a shaky breath.

It was perplexing to me on how I'd managed to volunteer myself for that task without being a ball of nerves. Maybe Aiden's abs did have some sort of voodoo magic that me under a spell...or maybe I just really wanted to feel him up.

"There, all done," I said shakily as I stepped back. My nerves now sinking in.

He turned around with hooded eyes but the warm pools of his pupils spoke volume.

"Thank you," His voice was deeper when he spoke up before he looked at the water. "The next thing you need to know is how to spot for a riptide."

"Those pull you out into the water, right?" I asked as I watched Tourmaline swimming about in her mermaid form.

"Yes, it's the current that pulls the tide back from shore and into the sea. If you get caught in one they can take you out for miles in a blink of an eye and you can't swim against it," He stepped behind me and pointed towards a spot in the water. "It's more dangerous than sharks. You see the gap between the waves there."

My eyes narrowed on the water to the space where Aiden was pointing and I nodded.

"That's one way to spot the rip and if you can see just before it the water's a bit choppy," He explained. "It tends to be a narrow current but powerful even for strong swimmers. You won't get stuck in one because you won't be coming down here without me-"

"But-" I turned my head to his which was looking over my shoulder.

He shook his head sternly, "No. You can't swim and those blood suckers are out and about, so you won't be down here without me, alright."

"Fine," I grumbled.

"Great. Another reason you won't get stuck in one is because I'm showing you how to spot one. But, if for someone insane reason that do you-"

"I won't."

"If you do," He continued, "then you swim parallel to the shore until you break from it and then follow the waves at an angle. They'll help push you to shore. Got it?"

"Aye aye Captain," I gave him a salute.

His lips titled up, "Save it for when I take you out on the boat."

Excitement rushed through my veins as I squealed, "You have a boat?"

He smirked, "I'll take you out in the water some day. But today's not day."

I felt my heart flutter at his words and thanked my lucky star when it didn't sting with pain after. Maybe... just maybe my title of bad luck was wearing off slightly.

At least by a fraction.

Before we could head to the water, Kai approached us with his surfboard in hand.

"Hey, Tate," He smile as he patted my hair. I'd come to realise it was a trait of his that he did whenever he saw me. Like an older brother.

"How's the water?" I asked him.

"Warm and calm," He deduced.

But as I looked at the deep blue, it looked anything but calm. I gulped in fear at the ghastly waves. Maybe I should just stick to bathtubs and kiddy pools. Whose brilliant idea even was it that I start learning in the sea opposed to a pool anyways?

The sudden dread was a force that crumbled my earlier excitement.

"Tate," Aiden called and pulled me out of my reverie. When I looked at his concerned expression, I only then realized that he was asking me a question.

"What was that?" I asked.

He chuckled as my eyes found its way back to the ocean.

"Afraid to go in?"

"No," I answered hastily.

He had a right to give me an unconvinced tilt of his head, "So let me get this right. You're not afraid of jumping out of the car in the night to fight a vampire but you are afraid of the water."

I folded my arms and lifted my chin in defiance, "Seems like a reasonable fear to me."

His eyes twinkled with an indescribable expression as he shook his head.

Aiden held out his palm to me, "Come on, I'll keep you safe. Promise."

The sincerity in his tone and the trust I've built for him had me easily accepting his hand.

As we approached the water, I noticed Kai following closely behind with his bored.

"Do you guys honestly think I'll be so bad that I require two of you to make sure I don't drown?"

Kai looked guilty but Aiden chuckled.

"With your luck, I think we actually require about four strong swimmers to keep you alive," He teased and I playfully jabbed him with my elbow.

"How long can you hold your breath?" Kai asked as we stepped into the warm water.

"I don't know...I guess I've never been a position where I've had to time it."

But considering I grew up with three brothers and a dad, I've had to hold my breath a lot when they thought it was funny to let out their toxic gasses.

My feet were still firmly planted on the sand below my feet as we stopped where the water was a little over waist deep. Aiden's hand was still firmly gripping my own as the waves made us unstable.

Aiden had informed me that before I learned to swim, I had to learn to float so that I'll be able to keep my body buoyant.

"Do you trust me?" He asked intently as Kai got up on his board.

I nodded and he let go of my hand I almost screamed bloody murder.

"Aid-!" I stopped mid shout as his hand settled on my waist.

"Sorry," He laughed and I knew he was anything but from the sparkle in his eyes. "Is this okay?"

He meant his hands on my bare skin. And honestly, I was not okay.

I felt my skin flush, my heart flutter and my mind being muddled.

"Mhmm," I murmured and saw Kai snickering.

I dashed some water his way and when it splashed him, he just laughed harder.

"You do not want to start a water fight with me Tate," Kai smirked.

"Bring it on buddy," I said in a challenge as I moved to splash him again but Aiden kept his grip firm on my waist.

"You really don't want to do that...especially considering you don't know how to swim yet," Aiden insisted.

"Fine," I conceded.

As Aiden went about explaining how to keep my body afloat, one of his hands went to my back as the other went behind my knees. He lifted me horizontally until I was on the water's surface with my eyes shut close to block out the sunlight.

"You're not focusing," He chided without releasing me. And it was a good thing he didn't because I knew I'd sick like an anchor if he did.

His warm breath fanning over my cheek, his big palms on my tingling skin and the residual fear of the waves mixed into a powerful concoction that had my mind adrift instead of my body.

"It's sort of a hard thing to do Alpha," I grumbled.

"Concentrate, Tate. Level out your breathing and relax your muscles, the water will hold you."

"But you're holding me."

"Should I remove my arms then?"

"Don't you dare!" My eyes popped open an one of my arms wrapped around his neck and I clung to him.

His amusement didn't die from his face as he removed my arm we tried again.

This time, he did move his hands and I instantly panicked and sunk. Aiden's hands held me up before my head could go completely under and I glared daggers at him.

It took a good while out there until I finally managed to relax and allow Aiden to move his hands.

I waited to sink but I didn't. I was floating. Thank you saltwater.

When I opened my eyes, I was blinded by the sun rays and as I titled my head, I lost complete vision at the even brighter light that was Aiden's proud smile.

"You did it," His ocean eyes shimmered as the daylight refracted off it.

My excitement, however, was short lived as I felt something cool and smooth brush against my thigh.

I saw the fin breach the surface and reached for Aiden instinctively.

He eased me back onto my feet just as the creature jumped into the air and splashed us.

"Holy mother of pearl," My jaw was laying at the bottom of the sea as I watched the dolphin swim back to me.

I was in awe as he whistled and squeaked and nudged me with his nose.

Tourmaline was right behind him with an excited smile.

What it must feel like to be a five-year-old mermaid with dolphin friends.

"Flipper," She spoke to the dolphin, who seemed to understand her clearly, "meet Tate, Uncle Aiden's girlfriend."

Flipper, the dolphin, squeaked again as he bobbed his head excitedly.

Aiden, on the other hand, stifled a cough and I could feel my own cheeks heating and it wasn't because of the sun.

That conversation wasn't one that we'd broached yet and I wasn't exactly sure that it will be anytime soon.

"He's a bottlenose dolphin," Aiden informed as he changed the subject.

"You can touch his head," Tourm encouraged. "He's our friend."

I hesitated for a split second before gently brushing my hand along the front of his head.

He made a few clicking sounds before beginning to swim around us.

"He's magnificent," I said to Tourm and she beamed proudly at me.

"He wants you to come swim with his pod," She translated.

I frowned, "Maybe another day...when I can actually swim."

"He's heading to Australia now," She said sadly. "But he'll be back when he needs us."

As Tourm began swimming around with him, she sung, "Just keep swimming, swimming, swimming."

"She speaks with them?" I asked Aiden with complete fascination as Kai jumped in the water with them and passed Aiden his bored.

"Yeah, it's a mermaid thing. Kind of like our mind link," He said as he climbed onto the bored with grace and then held his hand our for mine.

I was a lot more clumsy and was both surprised and relieved when I made it on without losing half of my bikini.

My legs drifted against the water as it hung over the sides of the board.

Aiden's firm chest was pressed against my back as he began paddling us to shore.

"Are we done for today?" I asked.

"Yeah, I'll take Tourmaline to see the dolphins off since they're near the monitors. Tomorrow we can use the pool to get you to learn to hold your breath."

I nodded and when he didn't get a reply, his voice was laced with concern, "Are you alright? Is it your chest?"

"No, I'm fine," I smiled to myself as protective side came out. "I was just thinking of Tourmaline and how much she must be missing out on learning about who she is and her home. The entire ocean belongs to her and she's confined to an area that's basically a bathtub compared to the rest of earth's water."

"I know what you mean," He sighed. "And I hate those god forsaken vampires for causing that. The only thing I could do to help the situation is find something that says her blood won't help them. It's been years of research and hundreds of books, even one that claims to described how Poseidon created them, but nothing on blood."

Anger radiated off of Aiden in large bolts of electricity.

I could only begin to understand the frustration he must feel. Knowing that the best he could do for Tourmaline and her people were keep them in a castle and pray for an answer to show up in an old script.

There was no way he'd let the mermaids test the theory themselves. If they did that, they'd have to do it on a vampire and before other vampires. Therefore, if it worked the vampires gain two things:

1) A vampire to walk in the daylight,2) Proof that it works which will only make them hunt down the mermaids faster.

It was a dangerous gamble that no one would take. And who knew how much mermaid blood was even required for one vampire.

The risks were too great.

When we made to shore, I hoped off the board as Aiden went back to swim with Tourmaline.

I joined Calypso and Matt who were sitting in the beach chairs. Matt with a ukulele and Calypso with a book. Caly threw me a towel and as I patted my skin dry and relaxed into a chai, I noticed Calypso wasn't dressed for the water with a t-shirt and shorts.

"Are you going to swim?" I asked.

She shook her head and bookmarked her page, "Absolutely not."

"She hates the water," Matt grinned as he strum the instrument.

"You do?" I asked in surprised since everyone here seems to love the ocean.

"I may be from the Caribbean, but the sea is not my forte," She laughed as she eyed the water. "I much rather sit here and read."

Calypso had explained to me how her parents were from a pack from the Caribbean but they moved here when she was five and they were welcomed into the Oaks Pack. They moved back a few years back but Calypso and Rick knew they were mates by then. Since he was the Beta, they figured staying was a better choice.

"Well, I don't blame you," I nodded. "It's scary."

"You guys are insane," Matt snorted.

"So then why aren't you swimming?" I asked.

Matt's eyes flashed to the waves where Rick and Dylan were surfing and his expression fell.

"Waves aren't that good today," He shrugged as he turned back to his ukulele.

Calypso and I shared with a confused exchange but didn't push it.

"Want a popsicle?" Calypso asked as she opened a cooler.

I gladly accepted as Matt played his ukulele for us and we talked.

My focus, however, was heavily monopolized when Aiden started to surf.

His hair, that was usually tied up, was now out. Dirty blonde, shoulder length hair that made him all the more breathtaking.

Oh boy, there was at least some luck I struck when the Moon Goddess paired me with him.

He was a thing of beauty he was.

CHAPTER 18

I felt the presence of someone following me as I trekked my way through the castle to the dining hall.

The hair on my arms were raised as my werewolf senses detected movement trailing behind me.

I inhaled deeply, feeling a strong pull in my chest by the movement, and I caught the familiar scent.

"Is there a reason you're lurking in the shadows, Kai?" I asked as I abruptly stopped and turned towards him with a smirk.

He stepped out from behind a hidden alcove a few feet away from me.

"I wasn't lurking," He objected.

"Following?" I suggested an alternative word.

"Doing my job," He corrected.

"And your job's shadowing me?" I asked as my eyebrows drew together in confusion but then smoothed out in realization. "Aiden."

"Yep," He answered with a guilty smile. "Say hello to your new guard until you feel better."

I felt a spark of anger ignite under my skin, "Thank you Kai, but I don't need a babysitter."

"Then consider me your guard."

"I don't need that either," I bit out.

Kai's eyes warmed as he stepped closer to me and patted my head, "I know what you're thinking and it's not that all at."

I sighed, "So it's not him thinking I'm weak?"

He shook his head and looked exasperated, "Aiden knows you're strong. Hell even I know that after you jumped out the car and fought a vamp that first night. But, I think you should cut him some slack on this. After losing his parents and brother, he won't be able to bear another lose. Especially not yours, Tate. You're his mate."

"Do you have to make so much sense?" I frowned.

Chuckling, he threw his arms around my shoulder and guided me down the hall, "Being this wise is a blessing and a curse."

I poked him in the ribs at that before hesitantly asking, "So he told you huh?"

"About?"

"My heart."

"You have nothing to worry about with me Tate. I don't think any less of you for it. In fact, you've earned more of my respect," He squeezed my shoulders and smiled down at me proudly. "It's an honourable thing to fight for your pack and then live to tell the tale. Battle wounds make us who we are."

"Even if it makes us into weak links?"

"They don't make us weak. They make us stronger and wiser. Weakness is just a concept we say to define our insecurities and a wound is nothing you need to be ashamed of."

"Thanks Yoda," I said appreciative of his wise words. Kai was like the big brother that protected you from everyone including yourself.

I didn't need to know him long to know that about him. He was fiercely loyal and protective. He'd wage wars to see his loved ones live.

Kai was a warrior with the mind of a philosopher.

He snorted at me calling him Yoda as he went on a tangent about how the Star Wars chapters were inaccurately named according to the plot of the films.

When we arrived at the dining hall, I watched Aiden smiling in amusement as Tourmaline told him about the turtles that showed up on the beach yesterday.

I stopped a few feet away I observed their interaction. It was common to see them together laughing but each time, it did something to my heart.

Not the painful punches that has me gasping for breath, but soothing strokes that keeps me alive.

They moved around like father and daughter and in many ways they were. Seeing that only made me want to be apart of their tight-knit family of two. Not as a usurper to intrude on their time, but as someone to be there for them.

A confidant. A friend.

Someone they trust to share their inside jokes with. Someone that could easily be apart of their lives.

I must have been in my head too long because Aiden's eyes found me with concerned curiosity.

Tourmaline was speaking with Matt now and Aiden motioned me over.

Before I could take a step, he was pushing away from the table as the frown lines appeared on his forehead but I shook my head and smiled at him.

Approaching the table, I took my seat and gave his broad shoulder a gentle squeeze.

"I'm alright," I answered with a small smile, knowing the question was already on his lips.

He nodded as he pulled the various dishes over that was prepared for dinner.

"How'd training go today?" He asked and I could detect the hint of anger in his tone.

"Dylan told you," I bit out as I glared at the oblivious Gamma across the table.

"I asked him."

"Then why ask me?"

"Because I want to know why you choose you continue training when you're not physically up for it."

"I am up for it," I pressed quietly so Tourmaline wouldn't hear us speaking.

"Yeah?" He questioned with a raised brow and his grip tightened on his fork. "So then why'd you almost collapse after your chest started hurting?"

I shrugged, "That's what it does sometimes."

I pinched the bridge of his nose, "Tate, this isn't a joke. I don't want you training if you're going to overexert yourself."

"I wasn't," I insisted.

My eyes harden at my words, "All the more reason you shouldn't train."

"I need to exercise."

"You need to stay alive."

"Is that you put Kai to tail me?" I said with anger of my own.

His looked at Kai and then back to me, "Yes. He's to keep you safe. I don't think you realize just how important you are to me."

My stare softened as he melted my heart and anger into a puddle.

Just as I opened my mouth to say something, a blood curdling chorus of screams pierced the room's chatter.

My eyes immediately fell on Tourmaline who was clutching her head and covering her ears as screams of pain escaped her.

I was on my feet and standing next to Aiden who already had her wrapped in his arms.

His eyes held horror and the fear in his irises were foreign as it took residence there.

My eyes flickered across the room as I saw the other mermaids all clutching their ears and screaming like Tourmaline.

"They're here," Aiden said with a chill undertone in his voice.

Fear sunk into my spin as he moved to the foyer and we all rushed behind him.

"Who's here?" I asked in general, but no one answered as chaos ensued.

Pain was etched across Tourmaline's face as tears streaked down her cheeks and she buried her face in Aiden's neck.

"We have to get her out of her," Aiden rushed out as he looked around the foyer. Almost at a lost of what to do next.

Rick shook his head, "They're already here Aiden."

Aiden's nostrils flared and he hugged Tourmaline closer to his chest and looked about ready to yell at the universe.

My hand rubbed gentle circles on Tourmaline's back as I tried and fail to bring her some semblance of comfort. She was still screaming in pain along with the other mermaids and Aiden stood as still as a statue.

"Aiden!" I snapped at him and his horrified eyes found mine. "Do something."

My voice broke on a plea even though I was at a lost for what was happening.

"They won't stop, Alpha," Kai said beside him. "Not until she goes out there."

Aiden's growl echoed across the foyer as he passed Tourmaline to me. She curled up in my arms and clung to my neck.

"I'm not taking her out in the dark," He said harshly. "Rick get the boat, Dylan send a few guards down there with Rick and Kai," He addressed his friend but his eyes landed on me and Tourmaline, "protect them until I get back."

Tourmaline's scream came to an abrupt halt but she continued to cry on my shoulder and I hugged her small body closer.

"Aiden, where you going?" I asked, eyes wild, heart pounding.

"To bring the sirens here," He answered before dropping a kiss on Tourmaline's hair and to my surprise, my own as well. "I'm going to make it better, Princess."

Tourmaline didn't respond to him as sobs racked through her body.

His eyes assessed us one more time, "I-"

"Alpha, it's time to go," Rick said from the hallway and Aiden took off without another word.

"Sirens," I whispered.

Confusion swirled around my head like a tornado but I pushed it away, knowing that their presence and existence wasn't a good thing.

Not when the mermaids had been in visible pain.

Kai ushered me back to the dining room and I sat at the table with Tourm sitting on my lap.

I brushed back her hair and tried my best to sooth her as all the mermaids seemed to be shivering in their seats.

At least they weren't writhing in pain anymore.

"He went outside and it's night," I muttered to Kai.

He wore a grim expression but nodded.

"What do they want?" I asked as I ward off the mental images that were conjuring in my mind.

Flashes of vampire infested water and my mate at their mercy. Blood pooling in the ocean. These mysterious sirens hurting Tourmaline.

When Kai hadn't answered, I looked up at him and his eyes were on the little girl in my arms.

She's what they want.

"Are the sirens not like..." My eyes fell to Tourm and Kai shook his head.

"They're-"

"Evil," Dylan answered as he came and sat next to me. "They're a bunch of bat shit crazy old ladies."

"Old?" I was surprised by his revelation.

He nodded, "The sirens are somewhat regarded as the cousins of the mermaids. Except they're not good. They don't protect the sea life and they don't give a rat's ass about humans."

I glared his way for the cursing and he simply shrugged.

Kai thankfully took over, "What he meant is that they don't have any regards for anything except the ocean. They create hurricanes, tsunamis, typhoons, water spouts and tidal waves. They're the bad counterpart to the good mermaids."

"Then why do they want her?" I ask ad my arms became a little more secure around Tourm.

"Because she needs to control the balance. Without her in the water, the sea's dying at an accelerated speed," Dylan finished.

Tourmaline lifted her head and looked at me with fright plastered across her features.

"Tate, I don't want to go with them," She sniffle and I felt my heart constrict with a growing pain.

"Can we not leave?" I asked the boys.

They both immediately said no.

Dylan spoke first, "One it's dark outside, taking Tourm anywhere out of these walls is asking for bad fate. Secondly, the mermaids were in pain because the sirens were calling to them. That's something they can't get away from, no matter how far they go. If the sirens call, they feel the pain."

I looked at Kai and he confirmed it with a sadden nod.

"So what? We sit here while Aiden's out under the moonlight to bring them here? Aren't we suppose to prevent them from getting Tourmaline?" I all but shouted.

"No, they'll not stop their call until they see the mermaid Queen. It's best to bring them inside so that Aiden can bargain with them."

"And the vampires?"

"It's a risk he has to take."

I shook my head as anger consumed me and fright fanned the flames of my burning rage.

My heart was doing its best to weaken me while my mental state was already being shifted into different directions. It felt like someone wedged a knife right through an artery. I inhaled deeply and focused on Tourmaline.

Outside, an explosion if thunder clapped through the air and pulled a few gasps from the lips of mermaids and werewolves alike.

There were lightning in the sky, dark clouds to suggest a thunderstorm or rain to warn us. The booming explosion was materialized out of nothing. I gulped down anxiously as my heart beat in tandem with the thunderstorm.

"They're angry," Kai whispered as he stepped closer to us in a protective stance.

"You'll be alright," I murmured into Tourmaline's hair as I rocked her gently in my arms.

The room fell into an intense silence as anxiety clutched everyone's minds. An electric pulse of fear was also tangible in the air.

These sirens were trouble, I could guess as much.

Thirty minutes of werewolves on edge and the mer-folks pacing ended when everyone stopped and turned to the door.

"Let's go the ballroom," Kai said as he gestured for everyone to follow into the room across the foyer.

It was an empty large space that was created to fit royalty.

As we all gathered to one half of the room, I stood in front with Tourmaline clutched in my arms and Calypso, Kai and Dylan flanking me.

When the double door on the other side of the grand room opened, the temperature dropped significantly.

I expected to see Aiden storming in first but my heart squeezed in anguish as Rick and Matt walked at the forefront. They both had angered expressions as a group of women followed behind, surrounded by werewolves.

The sirens' eyes were glassy and sinister. Their features were cold, bleak and sharp. Almost stone like. Even though they were wrapped up in towels, their exposed skin had a glossy sheen, as if they were permanently tattooed with water.

I didn't need to search the crowd of twenty sirens to spot Aiden. No, my eyes landed on him despite having the innate need to keep my attention on the sirens. On the enemy.

His arm was wrapped around a siren with pale blonde hair and cat-like eyes.

She wrapped both her arms around my mate and leaned her towel clad body against him.

I tensed and my heart faltered at the sight.

The siren's eyes locked with mine and she smirked before whispering something in his ear that I couldn't hear.

Anger course through my veins at what was going on.

Was this a part of the plan? Did he know her from before? Did he...did he not meant what he'd said about us?

A small gasp of pain left my lips from the intensity of the pain in my chest.

Aiden's head lifted a fraction of an inch before blonde whispered in his ear again.

"He's under her call," Calypso said.

My eyes flashed to her, "What?"

"The sirens call. Her luring song," She clarified. "If she sang to him, he'd be useless against her powers."

My heart constricted even more as horror gripped me. I turned back to Aiden as he crossed the room with the girl on his arm, and I could see his usually clear blue eyes were clouded over.

As if he was under a spell.

"What should I do?" I asked hurriedly.

There must be something. There has to be something.

She gave me a grim smile, "Kiss. You have to kiss him. Only a true mate's kiss can break the spell."

More fairytale gibberish. Just great.

My first kiss with my mate was going to be to snap him out of the siren's call. To take advantage of those oh so heavenly lips without his permission.

"Why aren't the others affected?" I whispered under my breath.

"Their call doesn't work on mated wolves."

Which made sense as to why Dylan didn't go with them and explained Rick, Matt and the other wolves' being of sound mind.

As they came to an abrupt stop all twenty cold eyes zoomed in on me and the child in my arms.

Goose pimples covered the skin of my arms from the frigid temperature and the fear they invoked.

Tourmaline lifted her head and glared daggers at them but they didn't bristle.

Rick and Matt joined our side of the room, going straight to their mates, but the other werewolves kept their stance around the sirens. Aiden, still in the arms of the wrong person.

"I don't know what all the preamble is about. Your Alpha is infatuated with one of ours and so the only right thing to do is hand over the girl," The eldest siren said from the head of the group.

Tourm's arms tightened around my neck.

"You mean you had her sing to him," I spoke up and her eyes narrowed. "I'm the Luna. I'd say it's a pleasure but considering you have my mate and want Tourmaline, I don't think we're here for pleasantries."

"Luna," She said the word with distaste. "I've heard of no such thing."

But I could see the miniscule amount of panic in her eyes. She hadn't anticipated Aiden finding a mate.

"Then let me acquaint you with the word," I smirked. "It means that you can't do anything against my word while on my pack's land. It means you listen and respect my words when I say Tourmaline won't be going anywhere with you."

She laughed darkly and without humour. It was the sound of the eerie thunder that rolled across the sky during a storm. The sound that made nightmares and warned you away from dark corners.

"I'm afraid you aren't aware of who we are child."

The others laughed along with her but their features were devoid of any emotion except anger.

"I know enough," I informed as I was momentarily distracted by the blonde siren's hand running through Aiden's loose hair.

"Certainly you don't for you to be speaking without caution," She tsked.

"You can bring your storms and lightning but you forget that you're on land. Your legs won't move as fast as your tails will," I watched as she visible seemed displeased with my answer. "Oaks Pack, why don't you show the sirens the welcome they should have expected."

About fifty of them around me lifted crossbows loaded with wooden arrows made for vampire hunting. It'll work just fine for siren hunting as well.

It was a precaution I had Dylan set up while we waited for their arrival. A necessary step to put us ahead.

The leader assessed the pack and went silent for a long minute.

"Do you know how fast a tsunami moves Luna?"

"Slower than us putting an arrow through you?" I guessed.

She shook her head with a too bright smile, "Yes, but my death won't stop it from washing you dogs into the sea. And while you'll able be drowned and turned into food for the life below the surface, Tourmaline and the mermaids will return to the sea. Right where they're needed."

My heart plummeted, knowing fully well that she meant every word she said.

She took my momentary silence to continue, "So, now that you know I'm serious, it's better if you put those toys away and hand over Tourmaline."

"She not mine to hand over," I seethed with rage. Both from the sirens unexpected visit and Aiden going out there knowing he'll be easily seduced.

"She belongs to the sea."

"Which is too dangerous for her."

"We'll protect her."

"You'll all die within the first six hours out there."

Her eyes sliced me in two as she took two calculated steps forward.

Dylan and Kai stepped forward but I shook my head at them.

I tried to coax Tourmaline out of arms but she shook her head fiercely.

"I'll be right back sweetie," I whispered in her ear as I passed her to Kai.

When I was sure we was safely in his arms, I matched the siren's steps and then some.

Crossing the space, I didn't waste time in coming toe to toe with her. She didn't step away in fear but the rise of her eyebrows gave away her shock from my movement.

"What are you going to do? Fight me wolf," She sneered with an ugly smirk.

"No," I smiled as a painful fire tore through my heart. "But I may slap her."

She turned to watch where I was pointing and I took the opportunity to push her against a guard.

With her out of the way, I sprinted the few steps that separated Aiden and I.

In the split second between that action, the lyrics from The Little Mermaid played through my head but with a pronoun change.

As crabby Sebastian said, 'You gotta kiss the boy.'

My hand instinctively shot out shoved blonde away. The urge to punch her was strong, but I neither had the time nor skills to survive a tsunami.

I pulled Aiden's solid body against my own and planted my lips against his own.

They were as soft as they looked and his body heat warmed me against the icy frost of the sirens.

My hands brushed into his hair, an act I've been craving to do since I saw his shoulder length strands. My teeth coaxed his lips to respond.

And then finally, as if the magician snapped their fingers, I knew Aiden was pulled out of the trance.

His arms wrapped around my waist and pulled my body into his.

His lips responded to my own without a second though.

As if he knew I'd be here waiting to kiss him back to life.

And, I suppose I would be here for just that.

Especially when he owned lips like those.

CHAPTER 19

All too soon, we pulled away from each other, already going further than was necessary.

My eyes opened to met the piercing gaze of Aiden's that held a trust that I'd never seen there before. I jolted against him as I felt my heart lurched in my chest. The building pain was constructing itself to a massive explosion since Aiden left.

Right now, that explosive force of anguish tore through me with an intense ferocity that threatened to bring me to my knees.

Aiden's jaw clenched and the trust in his eyes was lost to the hardened worry that commandeered his features. He kept his arms firmly latched around my waist and I appreciated the support because without it, I'd be curled on the floor already.

He saved my pride by not asking if I was alright in front of our enemies. However, his rigid posture and coiled muscles suggested that he was fighting his very nature not to scoop me up and take me to the infirmary for Dr. Nazra to make me better.

Not she could either way.

Before we stepped away from the sirens, Aiden turned to the blonde siren with a thunderous expression.

"You ever do that again and the sirens will have fish guts to clean up," He admonished. "That goes to all of you."

Blonde's features shifted to something akin to a night terror to scare little children into bed. Her skin became a few shades more bleak, her cat-like eyes thinned and her lips curled over sharp, elongated teeth.

Aiden was already running on a high line and his anger was about to snap. But before he could turn the siren into shark food, the elder siren who I was speaking to before, stepped in front of the siren and sent blonde a stern narrow of her eyes.

"Pitera," The older mermaid commanded, "put your claws away. You should have known better than to lure the Alpha."

The blonde, a.k.a Pitera, sneered at the older siren with disbelief in her eyes.

And I knew exactly what that look conveyed.

"You set it up, though," I called out the older one. "You assumed Aiden hadn't found his mate yet which is why you had Pitera sang to him."

There wasn't an ounce of guilt or shame on her face. Not because she was guilt-less but because she neither felt guilty nor held shame for her actions.

"At least he got himself a smart one," She sent a chilling smirk my way as Aiden pulled me away from their presence.

As we retreated back to the werewolf side of the stand off, Aiden kept one of his arms plastered around my back while he took Tourmaline into his other arm.

I heard her sniffle of relief as she hugged him close.

"Now that you've scared my niece and threaten my mate, what exactly could I do for you?" Aiden asked rhetorically.

"We ask nothing from your kind, we simply take," The older siren said as she brushed her wild red hair behind her ear.

"Then you've forgotten our last meeting. Tourmaline won't leave this pack until the vampires are taken care off."

She snapped her sinister eyes to him, "And when exactly will that be? A month? A year? A decade? You get to sit in this fancy castle like a king while our seas are collapsing because of the humans. You don't get to decide when the Queen of the ocean returns wolf, the sea does."

"Sura," Aiden addressed her by name, "the Queen does not take orders from you either."

Tourmaline and the mermaids shrieked in pain again when Sura opened her mouth and began whispering ancient words that weren't my common tongue.

The chorus of pain echoed deep within my chest. I let out a silent curse at the weakness that my complicated heart rendered.

Aiden released his hold on my waist as he gripped Tourmaline in both his arms. I was close to losing my balance until Dylan grasped my arm and kept me upright to which I nodded to him in a silent 'thanks'.

My mind was in a daze of pain when I heard Aiden shouting, "Stop it! Stop this right now or I'll kill all of you myself!"

And immediately, like flipping a switch, the mermaids were silenced into soft sobs.

The anger rolled off Aiden in waves and my own wasn't far behind.

"I stop not because of your measly threats, wolf, but because I rather not destroy the ones that I came here for."

"You won't take her from me," Aiden growled but I could hear the slight fracture in his voice.

It was a miniscule detail that I'm sure no one picked up on. But I heard the small waver. The ounce of fear that he let creep into him.

Over his brick walls and barbed wire fences, the fear snuck in like an unsuspecting snake.

Sura shrugged, "Take her to the sea, and I don't mean this shallow coast you confine her to. Let her see the animals that die, the oil spills that are kept a secret, the plastic that travels all the way down to the Mariana Trench. I dare you to show her how our home has become a toxic wasteland for plastic."

"I know," Tourmaline's little voice responded as she untucked her face out from the crook of Aiden's neck. "I know everything that happens in the sea because the animals tell me."

Sura seemed shocked by Tourm's ability to speak, but she was absolutely perplexed when Tourmaline demanded Aiden put her down.

He put up a fight, but there was nothing he wouldn't do for her. So, he gently set her on her feet and ensured she remained standing right before him.

The symbolism of us standing behind Tourm didn't go pass them. The Oaks pack would always be at her back, warding off the evil and fighting those who dare come close enough.

The sirens' cold eyes glazed over with trepidation as they hovered behind their leader, Sura, who seemed just as confused by Tourmaline.

But the older sea-spirit was the first to bow her head to her Queen. Reluctantly, the others followed suit as one by one they showed an inch of respect for Tourmaline's position.

"I know of everything that happens," Tourmaline repeated with a diplomatic aura around her.

"Then you agree that the mermaids must return to the sea," Sura said with affirmation.

Tourm shook her head, "No. If we go back to the sea the vampires would come for us. If they get us, then there will not be any mermaids to help."

Sura bristled and anger flashed through her slit pupils, "Forget the vampires. They'll not come for you once you're in the open water. If you aren't there to restore the balance then we will not be able to stop the natural disasters."

"The natural disasters that you created," Aiden reminded her.

Sura curled her fists as an explosive thunder cracked through the air outside and left a deafening ringing in in my ear.

Aiden's hands grasped Tourmaline's shoulder, ready to pull her out of harms way if need be.

"We can manipulate the elements of the sea to do our biding, Alpha, but not all that happens are on our part," She explained with venom in her voice. "We cannot stop what nature creates on its own."

"And I cannot stop the humans from putting plastic in the water," Tourmaline informed and held her head high. "We will not come with you, Sura."

"You heard her," Aiden seethe. "The mermaids will remain here under my protection."

"Your protection," She scoffed. "Have we really fallen to such times where the mer-folk require the help of the dogs?"

The pain in my chest fueled my anger towards the siren. But, alas, my strength was no match for a war raging in my heart. Weakness seeped out of me like a toxic spill of shame.

If we needed to fight these sea creatures, I'm afraid my condition would only hamper the progress.

"Help us with the vampires and they won't need to stay here," Aiden challenged. "You'd go to the sea if it was safe, wouldn't you Tourm?"

She gave a curt nod with a spark of excitement lighting her features.

Tourmaline may not have experienced the open sea before as she's supposed to, but it was her true home. It calls to her like Aiden calls to me.

A beam that signals her home.

"And how exactly would we be able to help you?" The siren asked, intrigue clear in her voice.

"A natural disaster," Aiden deadpan with a poker face. "You said yourself that you manipulate the elements of the sea."

That won't work, I began thinking just as Sura cackled loudly.

The wolf guards surrounding her took a step forward but I lifted my hand for them to stop. Angering her would only make her opposed to helping us.

"And just what natural disaster of mine do you think would actually kill a vampire? The last I check they don't drown and I'm a siren, not a magician."

"Then send a lightning bolt to their residence. I can see that you're capable of that," Aiden gestured outside.

"Oh wolfie, how much you have yet to learn," She tsked. "I don't control the lightning, but I do control water patterns which can create a storm. If you want a lightning bolt then I'm going to have to create a lightning storm strong enough. Even so that still won't guarantee it'll hit their hideout."

"Then tell us what you know about mermaid blood," I asked as I leaned more of my weight into Dylan.

Sura flicked her wrist as if brushing off the subject, "There's nothing to say about it."

"There's always something to say," I countered.

Her lips curled as her agitation increased, "It's blood. You cut them they bleed. There's nothing magical about it...at least it's never been proven."

I hesitated before asking, "And has there been tests to prove it?"

I watched Aiden's shoulders bunch up in tension. He held his breath in anticipation.

"I don't know," She admitted as her eyes went to the wall. "Of course we'd never harm our own. The blood of the mermaids was an old folklore that was passed down from the older generations, but we never tried to test the theory since we don't heal as fast as you wolves."

I couldn't detect any waver to her tone that would suggest a lie, but then again, the sirens were clandestine creatures. The darkness to the mermaids' light.

Aiden's posture was still as stiff as a rock.

We were as knowledgeable about the mermaids' blood as we were yesterday.

"What about a siren's blood?" I suggested with a sharp tone. "Are there tales about that too?"

Thunder clapped through the sky as Sura fixed her lethal glassy eyes on me. My heart squeezed painfully in tandem.

"What are you insinuating?" She seethe.

My response time was delayed as I forced in a breath, "Right now mermaid blood is just hearsay. What if siren blood got added to the list? Don't you think the vampires would have a much easier time hunting the ones who don't have dogs protecting them?"

The wind picked up outside as it bristled a haunting whisper through castle. The air cooled further and caused the shutters to slam against the large windows into a chaotic ruckus.

The drop in the temperature, combined with the frigid air surrounding the mermaids had me sputtering with a sickly cough.

The uncontrollable, vicious movements made the pain bleed through the arteries of my heart and into my muscles. It forced my limbs to weaken until all my weight was resting against Dylan.

Sura was too wrapped up in her flare for the dramatics so she missed my visible downward spiral. But Aiden hadn't.

I watched as he flinched at my sharp intake of breath. Willing him to stay frozen as he instinctively began turning his body toward my own.

By a stroke of luck, Rick inconspicuously caught hold of the back of t-shirt and forced him to stay in place. For the last thing we needed was Sura to learn about a weakness.

"So little Luna, you want to-"

"Send the vampires your way?" I answered for her. "Why, yes. I do believe it's a good solution."

Dylan's hand on my arm tightened in a silent question. My eyes flickered to the internal battle that Sura was having and he nodded in understanding. I was getting somewhere with my threat.

"They'd never be able to get us," She tried, but her attempt was futile. Even I could detect her unconvinced tone.

"You said yourself that you're not a magician," Aiden corrected her and I smirked at the detail.

Nodding, I added, "The vampires are already dead, there really isn't anything you can do to stop them."

Sura cursed in a loud foreign tongue. A peculiar sound. But the anger that fueled the sharp note made it clear that we backed her into a corner.

"You'll regret this," She said in low monotone voice.

A whispered promise. A silent threat.

"I doubt that," Aiden said without a hint of fright in his voice.

She seared him with her eyes before turning to Tourmaline, "Don't think I'll forget this, little one-"

"Shall I escort you back to the sea, Sura?" Rick cut her off as Aiden pulled Tourmaline behind him.

She lifted her palm to silence him, "I'm not done wolf. While you may be able to throw around your threats of vampires, know that I'll be back for our Queen. A few years from now, we'll come back for her. And Luna?"

My attention was already solely focused on her and the words escaping her mouth. I didn't answer her and she smirked slightly as I clenched my jaw in anger.

"We'll take Tourmaline to the sea whether the vamps are around or not. So you better figure out how to resolve the issue."

Aiden took a menacing step towards her but Rick kept a firm grip on him.

"She won't be going anywhere," He snapped.

"Oh, she will. I'll send word when I want her in the water," Sura informed with no room for argument. "Considering this extra time a gift of mine-"

"It's not a gift," I was tempted to scoff.

"Call it what you want. But seeing as I'm leaving Tourm here for now, I do expect something in return."

A second of pure, thrilling silence sliced across the room at her unbidden request.

"What?" Aiden seethe.

"A few mermaids."

"Absolutely not."

"I think you're being a tad unreasonable, Alpha."

Aiden scoffed, "Am I?"

"Yes. We've travelled all the way here only to be greeted with hostility and threats on our lives."

"Which you started," Rick muttered snidely to which Calypso elbowed him to stay quiet.

"No-" Aiden began but was cut off by his niece.

"Yes," Tourmaline said as she pushed on Aiden's leg until she stood at the front where she could face Sura. "Four mermaids will go with you...if you protect them."

Sura's expression relayed shock at Tourmaline'a agreement. But, as the words sunk in, I could see the animosity die from her cold eyes.

A mutual understanding and compromise was met.

"Of course," Sura agreed quickly with a small nod of her head. Knowing fully it was this option or us sending the vampires her way.

"Are you sure, Tourm?" Aiden asked her and she nodded with confidence. "Any mer-folk who wish to volunteer, your Queen has spoken."

They didn't miss a beat as four of them joined the side of the sirens. I had a brief moment of disappointment when none of them was Jenny.

When their Queen spoke, they listened.

"I would say it was a pleasure, but..." Sura sneered as her words trailed off.

"The pleasure was ours," I said with a fake smile.

She ignored me as she faced Aiden, "I must say Alpha, your wife's a bit out of hand."

I was stunned by the term she used.

"It's a good thing she's not your concern then," He simply said and hadn't bothered to correct her.

Disappointed the lack of fight he put up, she brushed her wet tangled hair off her shoulder, "We'll see ourselves out then."

And without a word, the sirens shuffled through the door with the four mer-folks in tow. However, Sura couldn't leave it at that.

Before she crossed the threshold, she turned to me with a wink, "A gift for your trouble, Luna."

I didn't register the meaning of her words. What gift?

Her maniacal laughter drifted down the hallway and raised the hair on my arms as she finally left, the werewolf guards following her out.

Aiden whisked Tourm into his arms immediately as he asked, "Are you okay?"

She nodded once before her eyes found mine. Her rather untroubled eyes turned dark as fear crept into her pupils.

"Tate?" Tourm asked and the waver in her voice had me reaching for every ounce of strength I had left in me.

My hands were a bit shaky as I gripped Dylan's arm and pushed my weight out of his hold.

"I'm fine," I forced a smile for her as I managed to keep my feet firmly planted to the floor.

Aiden turned to me and I could see the relief that had been on his face, drain away.

He set Tourmaline down before stalking to me, "Tate are you-?"

"I'm alright," I assured him by reaching for his hand and giving it a gentle squeeze.

Aiden's scent of sea-washed mahogany and fresh waterfall invaded my senses and wrapped around me like a blanket. Soothing my muscles and numbing the pain in my chest.

His scent was a drug.

An addictive medicine.

A balm for my soul.

"We should get Dr. Nazra," He insisted but I placed my other hand on his chest to prevent him from moving.

From our close proximity, my head swam with the memory of our kiss. The soft feel of his lips against mine. The tingling sensation that exploded along my skin. The dreamy state that had me drowning in him.

His mind must have been in the same place as his warm blue eyes quickly glanced to my lips and back to my eyes.

Oh yeah, we were definitely sharing the same memory.

Whether his version was good or bad, however, was up for debate.

I felt tiny hand on my leg and I was forced back in reality as I saw a very concerned Tourmaline staring up at me.

Moving to pick her up, Aiden beat me to it as he lifted her back into his arms and gave me a pointed stare.

I rolled my eyes at him, but in fairness I was too weak to pick her up.

"You don't need to worry about me, okay?" I said brushing some of her hair away from her face. "I'm as healthy as a horse."

Her nose scrunched up in confusion at my analogy but she nodded anyways.

"Uncle Aiden will keep you safe," She nodded before leaning her head on his shoulder. "Isn't that right Dad?"

He nodded without question, "Yes."

The intense and sincere conviction in his eyes had my heart racing in a good way. In a way that made me feel as if I was floating instead of being lit on fire from the inside out.

A blush crept onto my face but I was saved when the guards returned to the room.

"Alpha, Luna," They called for our attention. "The sirens are out of pack territory and have returned to the water."

I heard Calypso breathe a sigh of relief, "Thank the Moon Goddess."

Nodding along in agreement, relief finally eased the pressure on my shoulders.

"For now. But, they did leave a storm," Aiden said without looking outside.

I sniffed the air and caught the subtle change. The scent of rain permeated the air as the cool earthy fragrance clung to werewolves that had followed the sirens outside.

"That was her parting gift," I realized and Aiden nodded with a frown.

"Dylan," Aiden called his Gamma to attention, "I want to oversee all our windows get covered. You know what to do."

He seemed annoyed by the request but left to it nonetheless.

"Kai and Matt, will you check with patrol for me," It wasn't a question but they nodded anyways before leaving the room.

Aiden didn't call upon Beta Rick and when I looked at him and Calypso, I knew why.

There was trepidation plastered on Caly's features as she eyes the windows. She shrunk into Rick's embrace as thunder rolled through the dark inky sky.

I'm guessing a storm here on the coast was going to be riddled with anxiety. The howling winds always said as much.

As the large ballroom emptied, Tourmaline yawned sleepily and her eyes fluttered shut.

"Time for bed sleepy head," Aiden mumbled to her and she nodded drowsy with sleep.

"I'll leave you to put her down," I said as a pinch of disappoint struck me. I'm hopped we'd be able to talk, but Aiden usually goes to his room after tucking Tourm in for the night.

"Wait," Aiden halted my steps when he grabbed my hand. "I-I..."

My eyebrows pulled together in confusion as the sudden red shade his face took on. From the collar of his t-shirt to the tips of his ears, he was flushed a deep crimson.

"What's wrong?" I asked with concern. Mistaking his flush for anger.

"Well...you see," He released my hand before rubbing his jaw, "I was wondering if you wanted to spend the night in my room?"

Eyes wide, I stared at him in bewilderment as heat started to creep onto my own face.

My mind was incoherent as I tried to formulate a response.

Or a single thought.

A sensible thought would be an excellent thing about now.

A nervous chuckle bubbled out of me at the sudden turn of event.

But Aiden must have realized where my mind was at from my blushing cheeks and wild eyes because he shook his head furiously before I could respond.

"No! No, no, that's not what I meant," He quickly backtracked as his blush deepened. "I meant that I usually have Tourm stay with me during a storm or after the sirens visit. For my own peace of my mind, I keep her within my reach just in case something happens."

Relief and hurt both waged a bloody war within me from his words.

My eyes fell to the floor as the unexpected feeling of rejection surged through me like an unwelcome guest.

"It's fine, you don't-" I started but he cut me off.

"I want you there," He interjected. "But, only if you want to."

"You don't need me close by. I can protect myself," I said with my eyes still focused on the floor, tracing the intricate details of the marble.

"I know," His two words lingered in the air. The rest of his sentence clinging to the space between us as it tried to materialize.

Tried to get me to breath air into it and see what he was trying to say.

I know...and yet I still want you there.

That's what Aiden meant. As I grabbed the words and tucked them where my heart belongs, I turned to eyes to the blue of his.

And his missing part of his sentence was etched clear as day on his face. The crinkle between his brows in a silent plea and the hope in eyes willing me to agree.

"Okay," I whispered on a breath and watched a smile transform his face.

"Okay?" He asked in disbelief.

I smirked, "You'd have to take the floor but, yes."

He chuckled nodded anyways.

"How about I go put Tourm down and you can meet us there after you get what you need from your room?"

I nodded and he left the room with a smile on lips.

Butterflies fluttered around my stomach. My hands shook in nervous energy. Heart racing at a pace that's not at all healthy for me.

The thing was, I'd never been in Aiden's room.

As I went to my own room to take a shower, I contemplated this entire evening.

The sirens, their threats, the kiss, the storm and now staying in Aiden's room.

Aiden's bed.

I pressed my hands firmly to the wall of the shower as my nerves spiked and created a dizzying spell in my head.

"Get a hold of yourself, Blackwood," I scolded myself before taking a few deep breaths.

It's not like anything's going to happen. Tourmaline would be in the room with us after all.

A wedge to stop my heart from imploding on itself by being surrounded by Aiden and his private world.

It eased the tension in my muscles a bit but the trepidation still lingered in my bones. The other questions in my head didn't make it easier.

Did his room scream toxic masculinity? Did he have a night light? Was he one of those guys that thought it was cool to have a water bed? Does he pick up after himself or was I going to find dirty laundry all over his room?

A lot could be said about a person from their personal space. And while my nerves were sparking to life, I also felt the warmth of the gesture.

Brick by brick, Aiden was taking his wall down for me. Showing me who he was and what was under his protective fortress. And that was a gift I wouldn't take for granted.

I'd keep it close to my dying heart and pray that it'll fix me up.

Dressed in my most child-like pajamas - tiny butterflies littered my long-sleeved top and striped pajama pants - I silently walked out into the hallway.

Turning to the left of the hallway, for the first time, I swallowed the anxiety that threatened to creep my throat. I padded slowly towards the large wooden door that stood at the end of the hall-way.

Beckoning me and warning me away. My eyes brushed over the detailed carving on the door. The trunk a tree was immaculately shaped out of the wood with its branches stretching across the rest of the image. A lone wolf, with its head angled towards a crescent moon completed the detailed carving. It wasn't out of place, for it befitted the enchanted castle we were in.

Just another relic to show the history of its residents.

My feet shuffled to a stop outside of the door as my hands stroked the contours of the carving. I hesitated opening the door, my confidence faltering as I overthink the situation. Wondering silently if Aiden had changed his mind.

My finger was still on the carving when the door suddenly opened and revealed a startled Aiden. He hadn't expected to see me standing there, I could tell.

"Tate, I was just about to see what was taking you so long," He answered my unasked question. "Why are you standing out here? Come in," He opened the door wider.

"Just admiring your door," I coughed out nervously.

He lifted a brow, unconvinced but he didn't directly call me out on it, "Calypso carved it."

"She did?" I asked impressed.

Aiden nodded, "She did most of the art around the castle."

My eyes found its way back to the door with a new found appreciation until Aiden cleared his throat.

"Are you coming in...or?" A frown pulled his lips down as I stood there just outside his door.

My heart raced in my chest as I nodded and took a step forwards. Ducking under his arm that held the door open, I entered Aiden's secret space with renewed eyes.

CHAPTER 20

I took in the room with a perplexed expression.

"Where's...well everything else?" I asked as I looked around at the bare contents.

To the right, a large bookshelf lined the wall from top to bottom. Ancient academia text with leather brown spines stacked each row. To the left was a giant cork board that contained articles, book pages and hand written scribbled notes pinned up like a murder investigation. A white board also hung on the wall with writing and book titles.

Beside that, there was a desk and an armchair.

And a railing across from me.

"Downstairs," Aiden answered as I approached the other side of the room.

With my hands planted on the cool metal railing, I looked down to see a king size bed with Tourmaline already tucked in and sleeping on the floor below.

I was in awe as my eyes turned to the main feature of the two story room.

The window.

Where the bookshelf ended, the staircase started to the the other floor. But behind the staircase, was a giant rectangular glass that ran along the right wall.

All the way from the top of the second floor to the bottom of the first. And beyond the thick glass was the edge of the cliff and then the sea beyond.

However, the beauty was marred by the heavy raindrops that splattered the window and the white clouds against the dark sky that signaled the storm.

I watched as a bolt of lightning flashed between the clouds in a beautifully terrifying hue of white and blue.

The chill of the siren's presence was still etched into my skin but Aiden's heat ward it away as I felt him step closer behind me.

My skin tingle from his near proximity. Tempting me to press into his comfort. To relive our brief moment of feeling alive in the ballroom.

"It won't break," His breath brushed the shell of my ear and for a moment I didn't know what he was speaking off.

When I titled my head back to look at him, his eyes were on the window.

"How are you so sure?"

A small smile played on his lips as his eyes were light were humour from a distant memory, "I tried everything to see if it'll crack."

"Everything?" I asked unconvinced.

His gaze shifted to my own with a fierce intensity, "Everything."

I smiled as I ran my hand over the railing and walked past him. My arm brushing his and lighting a wildfire of emotions in me.

"I really like your room," I said, lowering my voice, as I walked down the steps.

"You do?" He asked in surprise as he followed behind me.

"It's incredible," I breathed as I took in the ground floor.

An industrial styled chandelier hung from the high ceiling creating the effect of water droplets frozen in the air. It gave off the a soft warm glow that made the room more inviting.

Under the mezzanine of the upper floor was more bookshelves, a large sofa and a desk with more scattered paper.

Aside from those loose notes, his bedroom was pristine. Clean stone blue walls with white trimming. Bed properly made, with Tourmaline sleeping away her nightmarish visitors. Floor clear of dirty laundry. No old moldy food sitting on the bedside table.

The carpet that laid partially under the bed and stuck out at the foot was also dust free as I curled my toes in the soft tufts.

There wall to the left of the bed and opposite the glass window wall was covered in black slate stone. The texture uneven by the natural dips of the stone and a single black door laid against the giant wall. It was pushed slightly open and I could see the tell tale signs of the bathroom.

The only other door was the one between two book cases under the mezzanine. On the wall opposite of the bed. That was either the closet or Aiden's secret lair he used to hide his emotions.

The latter seemed more probable.

Picture frames lined the wall above the desk, but there weren't any other personal touches.

Except for Aiden's many novels. From this point, I was betting he could give a local bookshop a run for their money.

"So you really like it?" I detected the nervousness in his tone as my eyes fluttered around curiously.

I nodded without turning to him and let out a little laugh, "That's what I said. I honestly can't believe you've never let me in here before."

"You were always welcomed in."

Now I did turn to him as I narrowed my eyes, "Hmm, I guess you failed to pass along my invite."

"Can I be honest?" He asked as he worried his lip between his lips and I stop shuffling my feet in the carpet.

"I'd prefer if you were," I nodded for him to go on.

He rubbed his jaw as his blue eyes shifted to the wall behind me, "I didn't want you to feel pressured. You were still seventeen when I basically forced you here-"

"Almost eighteen," I corrected, but he ignored me.

"It still wasn't right. I should have given you time. Waited for to be ready to come here on your own. I wasn't going to shove you in a room alone with me after that," He shook his head as guilt ate away at him.

I imagined after what he'd been through, finding a mate must have added to his anxiety about loss. Of course he'd want me to immediately be in his pack territory, that was where he felt the safest.

The best place to keep me safe along with his niece.

"Aiden-"

"I'm sorry I pushed you away," He concluded.

My heart fluttered in a pain-less way for once and I couldn't help the grin on my face.

I didn't hesitate as I cupped his cheeks and forced his blue eyes to mine.

"Two things," I smirked, "one, I wanted to be here and two, thank you."

He shook his head, "You don't need to-"

"Just accept it, Aiden," I rolled my eyes as he blushed. "It meant a lot to me, regardless."

"While we're on the topic of gratitude, I need to express my thanks to you as well," His eyes sparkled to life as it lightened in shade.

"I know, I basically saved your butt from Sura and her slimy sirens," I shuddered at the thought of them as I dropped my hand from Aiden's face.

But he unexpectedly caught it before entwining our fingers.

"That too," He agreed and I looked at him in confusion. "I meant thank you for pulling me away from the siren's call...pulling me back to you."

Now it was my time for my cheeks to be rosy red as I flushed.

But there were questions that rattled at the back of my head. Before I could ask, Tourmaline stirred among the blankets and Aiden tugged on my arm gently towards the sofa.

I followed with ease since I needed answers for my questions.

Curling into one side of the sofa, Aiden sat on the other, keeping a wide berth between us.

My fingers twisted together as I watched him from the corner of my eyes and asked, "Why'd you go with the others if you knew the sirens could put you in a trance?"

He pulled the elastic out of his hair before brushing his fingers through the shoulder length strands.

Without turning to me, he said, "It's my responsibility. I had to take charge."

"Even if it meant putting everyone in danger by making yourself vulnerable?" I looked at him fully then.

"I knew you'd pull me back," He confessed.

"You what?" I gaped at him.

The corner of his lips tipped up in a secret smile as he looked at me from beneath his lashes.

"Was the kiss that bad?"

Rolling my eyes I stretched my leg out and poked his arm with my toe, "That's not what I meant and you know it."

"So it was good?" He smirked as he lifted an eyebrow.

I groaned in mock frustration as I tossed my head back and stared at the ceiling. In actuality, I was saving myself from Aiden's heated gaze on my warming cheeks.

His Atlantic blue eyes always seem to make my resolve weaken.

"I'm kidding," He chuckled. "Ask me what you want to."

Slowly, I brought my gaze back to his watchful eyes, "Why'd you go to the sirens knowing the danger?"

"Because they needed to think they had the upper hand," He shrugged. "When they got me under the trance, they assumed that they had the advantage since the wolf leader is in their control. If I didn't do that, then they would have never stepped inside the castle and continue to torment Tourmaline and the mermaids until they all went into the water. That's not something I was going to let happen."

I nodded in understanding, "Why didn't you tell me?"

"I was going to, but I was worried you'd have not agreed to...kiss me."

Snorting I looked at him like he grew two heads, "That's absurd."

"Is it?" He challenged as a shadow of doubt passed over his features.

"It is," I snapped as I scooted closer to his side of the sofa. My knees pressed to side of his leg as I commanded his undivided attention, "Contrary to popular belief, old man, I don't find you totally unappealing."

"Oh, not totally, but just a little," He rhetorically asked with a shake of his head.

With a pinch of my fingers I smiled, "Just a tiniest, miniscule amount."

"And the rest of me?" He questioned with intense interest while humour played in his eyes. "The parts you don't find unattractive."

I waved my hand dramatically, "Considering you're like, what, fifty years my senior? I'd say you're like an old lovable grandpa."

Pressing my lips together, I tried to contain my laughter as Aiden's face contorted into absolute disdain of my words. His expression turned sour at the unexpected statement.

He seemed at a lost for words and I was forced to press my palm to lips to quiet my laughter.

Aiden's posture softened at my giggles and then he was chuckling along with me.

"Jokes on me for treating you like an immature teen all those weeks ago."

I shrugged with a smile, "I had to teach you your lesson for that."

He didn't respond as his eyes traveled to the window.

"I wasted that first week. Then you were gone and now that you're back, I can't stop worrying about you for so many reasons..." His voice echoed his pain.

The sudden shift in conversion gave me whiplash.

Taking his hand in mine, I said, "I told you that Emery-"

"I know," He cut me off and I could see the determination in him. "I'll call your brother first thing in the morning. They'll have to leave immediately to reach here before nightfall."

"We don't need to rush them," I disagreed with a shake of my head.

"Dylan told me, through mind link, what happened to you while the sirens were here," He gulped as his grip on my hand tightened. "I didn't have to turn around to know you were in pain, I could almost feel it. I'll be damned if I let you go through that again."

Silent and without preamble, I leaned forward and pressed a whisper of a kiss on his cheek.

When I pulled away, I saw the welcomed surprise on his face.

"Tomorrow, you'll tell me about the sirens," I said before yawning as the day's events caught up to me.

He took a minute to get his words together, and when he did, his voice was raspy, "I'm taking you somewhere with me tomorrow."

"Oh?" I muttered in shock.

Smirking he got off the couch and pulled me up as well, "It involves the boat and food."

"I can get behind that," I nodded in delight.

"Good," His eyes sparkled to life. "The bed's yours and Tourmaline's. I'll take the couch."

"You don't have to, I'm more than fine here," I gestured to the couch.

He gently pushed me towards the bed.

"Don't be absurd Tate, just take the bed."

"But-"

"Tourm is comfortable with you already, you don't need to worry it," He insisted before turning the lights off.

I stood at the end of the bed as I watched him go back to the sofa and lie down.

"Night, Cupcake," He called as I crawled into Aiden's bed.

The following morning, the sky cleared, the rain stopped and Aiden called my brother.

Thane wasn't too delighted to hear about the development in my heart situation. I didn't see it necessary to worry them over it when I was miles away and they were recovering from a war with the hunters.

Not to mention Emery was pregnant and I couldn't afford to have her use her energy on healing me when she needed it for herself and her little bean.

But after hearing Aiden's overexaggerated description of my pains, they left immediately and was set to arrive this evening. Before sunset.

The question of it Emery's power will heal my heart again was to be determined. The anxiety that clawed at me until I knew which direction my destiny was going to take me would have probably caused my heart to go into another spiral of pain.

However, Aiden's instructions to get dressed and be down on the beach in a half-hour, had my mind otherwise preoccupied. I wasn't sure if it was an intentional distraction or not, but I welcomed it with open arms.

Now if only I knew if this was a date type of boat ride or a 'I have something to do and I'm taking you along with me' type of boat ride.

My decision on an outfit would at least be easier as I threw threw my jeans haphazardly behind me and onto my bed.

And then, like an angel that she is, Tourmaline skipped into the room.

"Help me?" I asked and her genius five-year-old mind had my outfit chosen in five minutes.

A cream coloured linen pants that was ankle-length, a thin white short-sleeved cotton linen blouse and brown sandals to match.

I looked the epitome of a modern sailor woman.

"You look really pretty, Tate," Tourmaline smiled up at me when I was all dressed.

"Thanks kiddo," I picked her up as we headed downstairs.

I walked to the courtyard as I saw Calypso swiping her paint-brush on a canvas. Her t-shirt and jeans were covered in paint stains as she turned to us with a smile.

Taking in her painting, I realized just how talented she truly was.

"What's this one called?" Tourm asked her as I set her down.

It was an abstract visual of a woman perfectly painted in hues of brown. Her style of painting was represented her African heritage which each brushstroke.

"I'm thinking Ansellia," Calypso mused as she pointed to the background of the image. "This is a Leopard Orchid and Ansellia Africana is the scientific name. It's my mother's favourite flower."

Tourmaline grabbed Calypso's hand and grinned, "I love it!"

"It's beautiful," I commented in awe because I lacked any artistic ability.

I blame my parents for that.

"Anytime it rains, I could never sleep. So I paint," She revealed with a shy smile.

"And make me stay up with her all night," Rick chuckled as he stepped out of the back door with two mugs of coffee.

He handed one to Calypso and she swiped some paint unto his cheek.

"You're my muse," She said.

"I'm the person you boss around to wash your brushes and get you new paint when you run out," He challenged and she shrugged without denying it.

"That does sound like me," She mumbled before turning to me. "Don't you have somewhere to be?"

I nodded as butterflies took up rent in my tummy.

But my eyes went to Tourmaline who was still admiring Calypso's art piece.

"Don't worry, we got her," Rick promised as Kai and Matt joined us outside with toys in hand.

Between the four of them, I have no doubt that Tourmaline will be safe until we're back.

Kai patted my on the head, as he does, "Be safe, kid."

"And have fun, but not too much fun," Matt said as he waggled his brows at me.

Tourmaline titled her head in question and I took that as my cue to leave as the four struggled to explain why Matt would not want us to have fun.

As I made my way down the long staircase that was rested against the side of the cliff, I took account of how calm the water was.

The storm blew over in the early morning light. The only remnants of its existence was the rain drops that coated the windows of the castle of the leaves that were blown off trees in the courtyard.

Aside from that, the sky was clear and the water was inviting.

But today wasn't for swimming. Not when I saw Aiden standing in a fancy boat in the water.

When he saw me approaching, he jumped into the water, getting his legs wet, and met me on the sand.

Aiden was dressed in a navy cotton cargo shorts and a white t-shirt and looked absolutely delectable.

"Ready?" He asked with excitement.

"When you said boat, I expected something a little more like a sail boat," I pressed my lips together to contain my laugh.

He pressed his hand to chest in mock hurt, "You don't like my boat?"

"I never said that," I scrunched my nose as I kept my eyes on the boat. "But it seems a bit too fancy for your taste."

"It is," He agreed as he shook his head with a smile. "It's also not a boat, it's a thirty-three feet Riva Aquariva super yacht."

My jaw unhinged at the word 'yacht', but did I expect from the man who lived in a castle?

"Did you just say-"

"I did, but it's also our fastest boat. It's just the two of us today and I'm not taking any more risks."

My heart warmed at his concern.

"Now would you prefer to get your pants wet or do you want me to carry you?" He asked as he stretched his arms out towards me.

The butterflies intensified at the thought of being that close to him. Shaking my head, I begrudgingly refused his offer.

I didn't want to seem as if I couldn't do something as simple as get to boat without help.

Disappointment dulled his excitement a fraction, but he did held his hand out for me.

I removed my sandals before grabbing his hand and letting him lead me into the water where the boat waited for us.

The sandbar dipped into deep water by the time we were knee-deep in, which meant that the boat was closer to the shore and we didn't need to get anymore soaked.

As I tried to boast myself unto the main deck of the boat, my arms shook and I slipped. Aiden's firm grip was on my waist as he kept me upright.

My strength and energy was depleted after the intense chest ache my heart decided to put me through last night.

"Are you okay?" The concern in his voice was palpable.

"All good," I chuckled nervously as I gripped the boat with shaky hands again.

"Do you...do you want me to-"

"You can boast me up, Aiden," I chuckled as his hands hesislated on my waist. But as his hands lowered to my thighs, I immediately chocked on air as my chuckles turned to coughs.

The place where his hand rested burned with a delicious intensity from the contact.

My face reddened and it wasn't from the sun.

With ease, he lifted me out of the water and onto the boat without strain before hauling himself in.

"You really need one of those wooden decks that leads into the water," I said as I got to my shaky feet and inspected his boat.

"I'll look into to getting one," He noted.

"Tell me about your fancy yact," I grinned to him when he shot me an annoyed expression.

"The back of the boat," He pointed to a large white surface of the main deck, "is called the stern. The engine's under there in this boat. The front of the boat is called the bow and there's a latch on there that opens to the hull where the lower deck is. There's nothing more than storage and a seating area down there."

I looked passed the boat's windshield that was behind the steering wheel and eyed the long bow of the boat that seemed rather inviting.

We stood on the middle of the main deck with a u-shape seating framing the back and then two seats the fancy dashboard. One at the wheel and a passenger seat next to it.

"Layman's terms would have been preferable."

"You'll get the hang of it," He said as he moved to the chair at the wheel of the boat. "But, right now, safety first."

Aiden grabbed an orange life jacket off the seat and held it up for me to put my arms through.

I raised a brow at him and shook my head, "No way am I wearing that."

"Tate," He pressed.

When I didn't budge, he tried again.

"Please, for me," His clear blue eyes did some sparkly thing that had me hook, line and sinker.

"You're not playing fair," I grumbled and he smirked as if he knew exactly what he was doing.

Holding my arms out, he slipped the jacket over my arms before strapping me in.

"Just for my piece of mind and your safety."

"I can swim," I said in a high pitch tone.

"Sure you can," He amused me. "Now take a seat, I'm about to start her up."

"Wait, where's yours?" I asked with a pointed stare.

He snorted, "I don't need one."

"If I'm wearing one, you're wearing one."

"I can swim, you can't."

"Precisly, if you fall overboard and get swept into a current, I can't help you."

"That won't happen."

"It might."

He pursed his lips in mild annoyance before relenting, "Fine."

I grinned as he lifted one of the seats at the back and produced another life jacket from the hidden storage.

When he finally got it on and started the engine, I took my seat.

"What's her name," I asked as the boat started moving out into the open sea.

"Irene, my mother's name," He stated with a shy smile.

"I love it," I said as I sat back as the boat sped up. "Now, where exactly are we headed?"

"To the human town up the coast. A few days ago Matt was able to track down a human fisherman who apparently had an affair with a mermaid."

My eyes boggled out of my head, "Who did what now?"

"His name's Earl and back in the sixties he miraculously recovered from chronic kidney disease. The medical records were shut tight, but there were a few locals that talked about his recovery," As the boat dashed across the flat surface of the water, Aiden's voice grew louder over the wind. "Some of them claimed it due to the lady on his arm who made him change his life around, but I don't think love can be a cure."

"Can't it?" I questioned with wonder.

"Not medically, no," He shook his head.

"You're very pragmatic for a connoisseur of novels and poems."

"Would you rather I be optimistic and foolish?"

"Optimism doesn't equal stupidity," I said sternly.

He shook his head at himself, "You're right, but when the world is stacked against you...well you start to loose faith."

A shift in his demeanour had me reeling back. I could almost see the walls around him stacking up on the jagged edges I'd manage to break down.

My heart squeezed in protest and quickly changed the topic to keep his mind away from the dark place he was going, "Tell me more about this Earl guy."

His eyes were focused on the water with a fierce intensity, "After Matt did some digging around the newspaper archives in the human town, Dylan hacked the computer system at the hospital. Earl's test went from the fifth stage of chronic kidney disease and needing a transplant to being cured in a week."

"How?" I asked the question he was shying away from.

"Blood transfusion after he got into a fishing accident," His tone was grave.

The haunting look in his eyes shredded my own faith into bits.

"But, there wasn't anything to say whose blood it was, only that it was donated to the hospital that day. No record of a donor's name or a list of visitors that day. As if it just appeared," His fists tightened on the wheel.

"And the woman?" I asked as anxiety ate away at me. "Is she still alive?"

He shook his head, "She died when she was forty-two. A car accident during a storm night."

"And how old is this man?"

"Seventy-nine."

"And he didn't relapse?" As awful as my thoughts were headed, I couldn't stop. I willed Aiden to say 'yes' despite how cruel that sounded.

Because if he said yes, then there was still the possibility of the mermaid blood being a gigantic hoax. But is he said no, then this was the truth we didn't set out to discover.

As the silence stretched between us, I had my answer and I didn't like it anymore than my cruel thoughts.

"We don't know for sure," I shook my head as my fists curled into itself.

"That's wishful thinking," He corrected.

"Aiden?" I snapped and his eyes flickered to me for a second. "Be optimistic with me. Just this once."

He didn't respond with words but after a minute, I could see the crack in his resolve. The harsh lines that sharpened his features softened as we sped against the salt-water wind.

I sat back in my seat as I watches the ripples in the water move at a fast succession from the moving boat. The sun glimmer its reflection on the ocean blue surface.

The colour of Aiden's eyes when he was in the sun.

Water splashed on the windshield of the boat, my pants leg dried from the wind and my skin warmed under the morning sun.

Yet, there was a question that bothered me as my eyes tried to see beyond the blue water and into the deep abyss below.

"How are you sure there aren't any vampires under the surface?" I asked Aiden wearily.

"From our monitoring of their behaviour, we've concluded that they feed heavily during a storm," He said with a factual tone.

I turned to him in surprise.

He smirked, ready to answer my question before I asked, "It's easier for them not to get caught when there's a lot of rain. Storms always seem to hit the worst at night, which means the vampires come out when everyone goes inside to bundle up. Those left wandering around alone are easy targets for the vamps. Getting rid of the body even easier with the beach is so close."

"So they just dump the body off a cliff?" A chill set into my bones at the new information. Unease crawling along my spine.

A wordless nod followed by, "They make it seem as if they drown. After we heard about it we thought that it was too big of a coincidence that that much persons will drown in one night. We kept an eye out the next time there was a storm and we saw it ourselves...they're wild savages when they drink blood."

Bloody images of a pile of pale corpses plagued my mind. A day nightmare that left my skin crawling.

"Look, we're almost there," Aiden's voice pulled me out of my revere.

I looked up as we broached the side of a cliff and the extensive scenery of village came into view.

It didn't sit up on the cliffs as I'd expected. Instead, the landscape sloped downward at sea level.

Blue and red roofs covered most of the houses. White restaurants sat on the edge of the water. Boats lined the dock and local fishermen hauled coolers of ice on and off their boats.

Seagulls swooped down into the water, kids ran about on the pebble shore.

It was a scene stolen straight out of a movie.

"It's..." I was at a lost for words as Aiden maneuvered his boat into the docks.

"Beautiful?" He suggested.

"Magnificent," I concluded with a grin.

"I thought you'd like it," He eyes twinkled happily.

"Love it," I corrected.

I took a whiff of the air and smelt nothing but Aiden, the beach and humans.

"We're safe," He whispered for my ears only as fishermen walked along the dock.

"I know, but I've never been around much humans before either," I laughed nervously as I took off my life jacket and slipped on my sandals.

Pocketing the key to his boat, Aiden slipped on his shoes and I couldn't contain my laugh.

He looked up at me with a curious expression.

"Are those loafers?" I asked between a laugh.

He rolled his eyes at me, "Boat shoes."

"Uh huh, whatever you say old man," I teased.

"I'm starting to believe that you have a thing for calling me old," He said as he held his hand out for my own and I happily accepted.

I shrugged, "Just getting your age right."

But before we stepped off the boat, he pulled me closer to him, chest to chest.

"Tate?" He said with eyebrows drawn. "You don't have to worry about anything, okay? Not when you're with me."

I wiggled my brows at him, "Trying to impress me, Alpha?"

"Is it working?" His eyes twinkled.

"Maybeeee," I lengthened the syllable.

He held onto me firmly as I began turning away. "And about earlier, it's just hard to think that something will go right when everything seems to be slipping through my fingers."

In response, I tightened our intertwined fingers, "But I'm here now and you're not getting rid me any time soon. So, share your burden with me, because I could handle it."

His lips quirked up, "I'll keep that in mind, Cupcake. But now, I do believe I mentioned breakfast?"

"Food, yes. I'm starved," I exaggerated as I pulled him to the dock.

He helped me out from the boat and then steered me in the direction of a little cafe.

The humans we walked by paid us no heed as I'm sure they were accustomed to tourists popping by all the time.

"This place sells the best breakfast sandwiches," Aiden informed as we entered the shop.

The delicious aroma of fresh baked bread and grilled sausages wafted through the air. I was near salivating as we joined the line.

"Would it be weird if we bought five?" I whispered to Aiden.

He chuckled, "I highly doubt they'll question it."

"I meant five for me, alone," I corrected.

"I hope not because I can eat about eight," He worried his lip between his teeth.

Unconsciously, he released my hand and wrapped it around my shoulder as we moved up.

A simple gesture that almost made me stop breathing.

Aiden must have caught on to his movement because he tensed up next to me.

I kept my eyes on the back of the person's head in front of me and Aiden also didn't look my way.

We remained frozen, me not breathing and him not moving.

He waited, with most of the weight of is arm off my shoulder, for me to say something.

I didn't.

And when he realised I was okay with it, his posture relaxed and his arm rested comfortably around me.

We got our thirteen sandwiches, no questions asked, and made our way to the beach where there were a few benches.

"You haven't told me about the sirens yet," I reminded him.

Nodding, he handed me a cup of coffee before explaining.

According to Aiden, the sirens showed up the morning after Tourmaline was born. News of the Mermaid Queen's death had circulated.

They demanded Tourmaline be handed over, but after losing every last part of himself, Aiden wasn't about to give up his niece.

The sirens were angry but the werewolves were livid. The mer-folk, even more so and they were the ones to get the sirens to back away at Aiden's request.

You see, the Oaks Pack has protected the mer-folk since Will and Amethyst took over the pack. Now that they were gone and the sirens had done nothing to help them with their ongoing battle with the vampires, they knew whose side they on.

So, they forced the mermaids to retreat with the promise of getting Tourmaline in the water soon.

Aiden wasn't sure how but he knew Amethyst's death was the driving force behind their rage and determination to keep Tourm safe.

Sura and the other sirens hadn't shown their faces since. Not until last night.

He knew they'd come back for her but he had not known when.

Now, we can only hope my threats keep them back until we rid ourselves of the vampires. Or at least until Tourmaline can fend for herself.

"Ready to find Earl?" He asked as I dabbed the corners of my lips to wipe away any sauce stains.

"Did you get an address?"

"It's off the main road and about ten minutes from here," He said as he stood up and held out for my hand again.

Before Aiden, I didn't see the need as to why couples always held each other's hands. It seemed a basic gesture. Simple. Unwarranted. Nothing that could provide substance for any real comfort.

After I met Aiden, I realised just how much that gesture meant. And just how much I craved it the minute he let go.

The gesture of touch, in any form, was neither simple nor meaningless. It was complex and unintelligible. Because it didn't need to make sense.

It just needed to provide an abundance of the emotion that we were unwilling or too scared to convey through words.

A touch was a silent man's language. It was Aiden Oaks' personal form of communication.

The first day I met him, I'd stripped him off that by telling him not to touch me. And he'd listened as his accidental contacts were all well... accidental. They were tense and hesitant.

Which may have been why we were unsure about each other.

Taking his hand, I said through my touch, what I was unwilling to say through words.

And he got the message as he squeezed my hand and tugged me closer to his side.

For the next ten minutes, we walked silently towards the house where the old fisherman resided.

We took a left on the main road that was stretched from the shops at the beach to inland. From there, the road grew quieter as the houses became more sparse.

At the edge of the street, Aiden finally nodded towards a relatively medium size one-story home with a wrap around porch.

Old boats were stacked up in the driveway and the paint was chipping from the walls outside the house. But the grass was freshly cut and the front porch was dust free.

There a bucket of fresh fish laying by an old wicker chair with a knife awaiting to be used.

I nudged Aiden and gestured to it. His eyebrows were drown together but then he shrugged.

"He must have been cleaning his morning catch," He said before rapping his knuckles against the door as we waited for Earl to come out.

We waited and waited.

Five minutes and not a creak inside the house.

"He must be out in water," I guessed.

"He's old."

"Not dead," I pointed out before pressing my ear to the door. "There's no one inside."

Aiden rubbed his temples as he turned back to the front lawn.

I, slipped a bobby pin from my hair. Bending my knees, I fiddled with the hair piece in the lock.

"Tate!" Aiden hissed behind me when he realised what I has doing. His voice dropping considerably low as if someone would catch us. "We can't go in, that's breaking and entering."

I snorted, "Not if we don't get caught."

"I'm certain that's not how the law works," He grumbled.

Turning to him I smiled as the lock clicked open, "Stay outside then."

I contained my laughter as he cursed behind me when I pushed open the door.

The foyer was dark but my werewolf picked up the typical human touches around the room.

Unopened mail, rain boots at the door, keys hanging off a nail.

"It stinks in here," I fanned in front of my nose as the scent of fish clung to the air.

"Well he is a fisherman," Aiden said, right at the heel of my foot as I turned towards a hallway. The place I knew would have what I was looking for.

The walls were lined with images of boats and waves and trips.

I halted my movement as my eyes caught the distinct red in a picture.

A woman, around thirty or so, dressed in the latest sixties apparel and standing on the beach where Aiden and I had just been.

But it wasn't her bell-bottom jeans or tie-dye shirt that caught my eye.

"Her hair," Aiden said in a chocked whisper.

It was the blazing, unnatural red ends of her hair. Her roots were the same but most of it was, I guessed, dyed black.

The red wasn't that of a natural ginger. It was vibrant and fluorescent.

Mermaid hair.

I turned to him slowly, devastation grabbing me in its clutches at what this most likely meant.

His eyes remained unmoving and focused on the image. As if he can will it to be fake.

"Aiden..." I tried to find my words but I was at a lost.

"We should look around. See if he kept any documents on her," He said, voice strained.

I touched his arm as we turned to move up the staircase in the foyer.

But before we could get far, a crashing metal sound disrupted the still silence in the house.

My ears rang with sound of tools rattling from the backyard.

Aiden was in front of me at once, pushing his way to the back-door.

"Stay here," He said but I was hot on his trail.

"Heck no," I whispered as I followed him through the kitchen and then out the back door.

Aiden was already moving towards a tool shed tucked away between some overgrown bush.

The doors were wide open but not yet within our range of site.

The wind bristled and kicked up the scent of fish that was around the house.

Giving away to a much more foul odour.

We immediately froze, but it was too late.

My eyes locked onto the figure in the shed as the scent of fresh blood and rotting flesh invaded my senses.

CHAPTER 21

I stared, wide eyed, into the glimmer silver eyes that will haunt my dreams from that moment forth.

A vampire held an old man's neck to his blood-stained mouth. The man's eyes wild with fright, his lips open on a silent plea. The life draining from his eyes.

I felt sick to stomach, urging myself to look away, but my muscles locking me into place.

Earl turned as white as a sheet. His skin ashen and his pulse no longer beating.

The vampire dropped his dead body to the floor of the shed. It made a sickening cracking noise. The sound of bones breaking. A skull cracking.

Beside me, I vaguely became aware of Aiden shifting. Tearing his clothes to shreds and leaving his awful boat shoes busting at the seams.

His canines gripped my blouse and yanked me back, fully saturated in the dazzling sun.

But my eyes were frozen on the vampire. His black hair perfectly smoothed back and three-piece suit pressed to crisp lines.

The only sign of his true monster nature was the glistening sheen of blood on the corner of his lips which he brushed off with his thumb before licking it clean.

Aiden's wolf nudged a wooden stake into my hand as the vampire edged his way around a work bench and closer to the door of the tool shed.

His movements were slow and deliberate. As if trying not to spoke us.

As if we were the prey and he was the hunter.

He can't step outside. He can't walk in the sunlight.

Those were words I chanted in a silent prayer. Manifesting my thoughts into being reality.

And it must have worked as he grabbed an extra-large black umbrella and opened it up.

Just like that, he covered himself and took a step outside. Careful not to let the sunlight touch him.

Aiden's wolf growled low and dangerous at him, a warning. My grip on the dagger tightened as I ran through the training I've done for the past week.

The blood sucker stopped right outside the door with a smile.

His skin was bloodless and pallid. Cheeks lacked that ruddy tinge and skin admonished of the glow from a warm tan. Lifeless and sickly. Unnatural and eerie.

"Wolf," He greeted with a thick French accent and a nod of his head.

Aiden responded with a snarl, saliva flying out between his canines. He positioned himself slightly in front of me.

Always protecting.

"You're alone," I called out as I picked up on only his scent. "Brave of you to be out during the day.

His silver eyes flickered to me with a spine-chilling gleam. His nose turned up to the air as he sniffed.

"Ahh, so you're the magnificent creature Aiden's found," He grinned.

I faltered at what he said, surprised by his knowledge of us.

But I supposed he's known of Aiden seeing as he was the were-wolf between the vampire and their mermaid blood.

He spoke again as if reading my mind, "My vampires have told me all about you...well your blood in particular. Old Earl there was tasty, but a bit bland with his A positive blood. You ma chéri," He sniffed again, "are incredibly sweet."

Blood type O negative was in fact like a rare aged fine wine for vampires. It's apparently one of the rarest blood types.

Just my luck...

Before I could give a retort, he said, "But you have a bleeding heart."

That had my heart speeding up.

Bleeding heart?

Aiden didn't like his words at all, which made him low his body and ready to pounce.

"Uh, uh, uh," Vampire man enunciated as he unwrapped a silver chain from around his wrist. A silver cross dangled at the end as he lengthened the chain.

The sinister gleam of the silver metal had me grabbing a fist of Aiden's black fur, holding him in place.

While I had no doubts about our ability to take him on our own, adding silver to the fight was asking for a miracle.

My muscles were still weak, my heart could start its untimely pain feast at any moment and vampires are still strong.

Experience-wise, my first fight ended with a dislocated shoulder and my second was a stroke of luck by having the others with me.

If this creature got the chain around Aiden, we'd be done for.

"What do you mean?" I asked with a still face, but I felt my nose flare at the thought of him knowing more about my health than myself.

Swinging the chain in a circular motion, he shrugged, "You're sick. Dying, really."

Aiden growled a few decibels too high. I flattened my hand on his wolf, mild panic washing through me because of two things.

1. His growl could garner unnecessary attention from neighbours and well, there's a dead body a few feet away from us.

2. A vampire, who has the strangest ability to read my heart and blood with a sniff, just told me that I was dying.

"You're lying," I snapped, the waver of my voice betraying my lack of conviction.

He snickered, a nasally quality layering the sound.

"Of course, you don't have to trust me, I barely trust myself at times," He sighed heavily. "By the time you do realise I'm telling the truth, you'll be dead."

Dagger clutched in my hand, blood boiling, rage coursing through me - I sprang off my heels to bury the wood in his chest.

But Aiden's canines clutched the end of my blouse and pulled be back just as the vampire's chain whipped it in front of my face.

The stinging heat and pain that the silver promised, kissed my cheek in a faint whisper before it was yanked back into the bloodsucker's hand.

"A weak heart isn't your only weakness, wolf," He goaded me on.

My muscles protested as my anger fuelled my wolf to come forth, but with great control, I pushed the beast back.

Knowing I needed to be in human form to bury the dagger in the vampire's chest. Opposable thumbs were, unfortunately, something we didn't have in wolf form but was important in getting the dagger where we wanted it.

"A flimsy umbrella isn't going to protect you from the sun," I retorted through clenched teeth.

"Oui, but it does provide some reprieve."

I stared at him in complete contempt and disdain.

"Why are you here?"

"I live here," He rolled his eyes.

"I'm not sure 'live' is the correct term to be used in conjunction with you."

Aiden whimpered at my side, tugging on my blouse to move away, but I stayed put as the vamp snorted in response.

"I've been around for over four hundred years and you honestly believe I haven't heard sad excuse of a joke?"

I narrowed my eyes on him, anger burning through me, egging me on to attack.

"Your lack of life is not of interest to me, but the lives of humans are. Including him," I pointed to the cold corpse laying in the tool shed.

The vampire shrugged, "Wrong place at the wrong time."

"This is his house," I bit out between a growl.

He sighed, almost as if his hundreds of years of life is finally catching up to him, "Your wolf boy there is une tête carrée...an idiot. You're not the only ones searching for answers. I heard about this useless human and well, he proved useless of course."

"How?" I barked at him.

"Tsk tsk," He scolded and licked his lips. "Answers don't come for free mademoiselle. Let me have a taste and I'll tell you anything."

Aiden's paws dug into the dirt, his eyes shifting on the blood-sucker, calculating his movements for an attack.

The vamp caught on as Aiden lunged at him.

Aiden knocked the vampire onto his back but the lecherous creature kept one hand on his umbrella and flicked his other to wrap the chain around Aiden's right front leg.

He snarled lowly as the silver cut into his flesh.

Pushing my muscles forward, I sprinted towards then. The wooden stake in my hand, poised and ready to kill.

When the vampire's deadly silver eyes caught my sluggish movement behind Aiden, he pushed the big wolf off him and scrambled back into the shed. Careful to keep his umbrella covering his skin and tightening his grip on the silver.

His smirk was sinister and his messed-up hair and rumpled clothing gave way to the demon that he was. The chain pulled as he tried to tug Aiden into the shed with him.

My mate struggled to stay in place as the silver sent blood trickling down his leg.

I didn't stop and think as I grabbed the chain with my bare hands. A swear tore from my lips as the biting fire blistered my palms.

Aiden whimpered but I continued holding the chain as I tried to tug it loose. Only to realise that the cross attached to the chain was weaselled between a few beaded links, making it impossible to unhook.

The vampire laughed cheerily at our struggle, fuelling my anger which sent shot of familiar pain through me.

Not now, I yelled at my heart.

But as usual, it never listened to a word I said.

So, this time, instead of ignoring it, I welcomed it. Used it to boost my dangerous level of anger.

The chain was thin, but the pain was immense.

Sweat broke out on my forehead as I tugged to the chain, trying to rip the links apart.

Excruciating pain sliced through my chest.

My breath grew heavier, more laboured than the one before.

The feeling of suffocation from my lack of oxygen enriched blood entwined with the inferno my palms felt from the silver and the heart wrenching torture, all shocked my body into hysteria.

The shot of adrenaline that tore through me gave me the last ounce of strength I needed to break the chain. The vamp went stumbling back as the tension in the chain broke.

My hands were sore and burnt, red gashes slashed across both palms.

I felt my knees buckling beneath me, but Aiden stuck head under my arm and supported my weight before pulling us back from the shed.

Further into the sunlight and away from the vampire.

His laughter died slowly on his lips but he kept an arrogant smirk plastered on his pale lips.

"You broke my rosary," His voice lacked any emotion that would suggest he actually cared for it. But it wasn't as if he'd need it, for no God would allow him into their kingdom.

"You'll survive," I bit out between the pain, wishing Aiden was in human form to help me verbally battle this creature.

"But you will not," He grimaced. "Unless you want me to do something about that..." He licked his fangs. "I can change you or maybe just end your life now to prevent you from going through the pain you'll have to endure later."

The thought didn't even have a nano second of living in my mind as I shut the thought out.

I shook my head, "I'd never become something like you. I won't give up my humanity to prey on the innocent."

"Humans are not innocent," He scoffed.

"Earl was," I gritted out as Aiden licked the palm of my hand.

Providing a cooling relief on the slow healing wound.

My body fell further into his, but he kept me upright, his own wound healing just fine.

Vampire man shrugged, "I consider uselessness a sin."

It was ironic, how saintly he carried about himself yet he was the walking, talking spawn of the devil.

A creature created to kill for blood. Innocent or otherwise.

"And Earl here was rather useless," He continued. "I showed up to find out about his mermaid and before the man could even scream, he was trying to take my eye out with a fishing hook. Didn't give up anything about her but when I said 'mermaid', oh boy the look in his eyes were thrilling."

He closed his eyes and vibrated as if recalling Earl's face and taking immense pleasure.

"But then he was having a heart attack. Tragic really, I had to rush my meal of him before his blood ran cold. Then you two showed up," He rolled his eyes at us. "So, that brings us to why you're here."

Dread sank into my stomach as he paced the tool shed, his umbrella in hand and acting like a cane.

"You're here because you want to know what I know of course, but the thing is you were late. So, I'll just spell it out for you, free of charge," He stopped right in the middle before facing us. Face upturned with regal angles to his skeleton. "Earl was healed with mermaid blood. The golden question is, how..."

Aiden's wolf went rigid. His muscles coiled and his body turning into a slab of stone.

"You see, I do want the answer to that question. Desperately. But as summer draws closer, the sun is making my skin itch. So at this point, I really don't give a shit. I'll have the Mermaid Queen's blood one way or another," His smile sent a chill down my spine and his words tore a hole in my heart.

"You'll never have her," I snapped just as the scent of rotting flesh grew in the air. The scent drifting from the thick tress behind the tool shed.

"And it looks like we have company," the vampire laughed.

Aiden starting moving then. His focus snapping back into place.

I stood on my own two feet as he grabbed his wallet and boat keys from the pile of his shredded clothing.

Then he lowered his body for me to climb on and I didn't hesitate as the stench of more vampires grew.

But before we bounded out of the backyard, the vampire called to us.

"Wait!" He yelled and Aiden reluctantly stopped at the end of the side path that went to the front yard. "Anvi sends her regards."

Aiden bared his canines at him, his body shifting to back and fight. But I firmly gripped his fur and steered him back to the path.

My palms burning in protest of my grip. Still unhealed.

Reluctantly, he growled lowly before bounding away as the sound of the quick footsteps of the other vampires grew louder.

The name 'Anvi' rattled around my head with vague familiarity.

As we crossed the front lawn, I panicked as the street stretched out before us without a hidden alley in sight.

I don't see how a big wolf running around with a girl on its back won't raise eyebrows.

"Did you have to tear your clothing?" I whisper-yelled at him.

He grunted in reply before taking off down the middle of the street.

My heart raced in my chest as I listened for the sound of on-coming vehicles or footsteps on a front lawn. The fierce pounding only heightening my struggle to breathe.

Our luck, that had seemed to vanish, finally bloomed again as we made our way through the street and then finally finding an alleyway that led to the shops at the beach.

Aiden stopped and lowered his body for me to get off before placing his wallet in my hands.

His red eyes were distressed and wild with panic. But they conveyed one thing: hurry!

I nodded before sprinting out of the alleyway and then slowing my steps as I made my way to a clothing shop.

The opinions were limited and very tropical beach chic. And despite my fear and agony, I couldn't help my chuckle as I grabbed a Hawaiian shirt and a swimming trunk.

Making my way to the counter, the human girl paid me no heed until I pulled out some cash and winced as the edge of the bills grazed my sore palms.

Her eyes turned worried as the cash fell out of my hands and exposed my wound.

"Fell off my bike," I blurted out before she could ask.

She nodded, unconvinced, but lacking the drive to press me further.

I tapped my feet impatiently as she bagged the clothes with what felt like slow motion movements.

With a quick thanks, I all but sprinted out of the store, scared of being apart from Aiden too long.

If anyone had walked into that alleyway...

But as I approached there were no signs of human distress, and I slipped in between the narrow passage.

Aiden's wolf slumped in relief when he saw me.

Turning around, I gave him his privacy to pull on his clothes before his hand was grabbing my own and pulling me towards the dock.

His shirt left unbuttoned in his haste to get off this vampire infested part of the coast.

"I forgot shoes," I mumbled as his bare feet trudged across the gravel road.

"It's alright."

"And your hand," I winced at the laceration on his wrist. Dried blood crusted on his skin.

His eyes shifted to his own wrist but when he caught the sight of my palms, he sucked in a raged breath.

Aiden face washed anew with guilt, but we didn't have time to say a word more as we quickened our pace when we reached the docks.

"Get your life jacket on," He said as we jumped into the boat and he began undoing the rope that anchored us to the dock.

I planted myself in my seat as my trembling fingers tried to buckle the life jacket in place.

In under a minute, Aiden had the boat untied and started, manoeuvring us away from the human town.

We moved faster this time, in a rush to make it back to safety despite knowing we were safe once under the sun.

But what could be under the sea...under the boat, was terrifying.

The motion of the boat bobbing along the water made my stomach queasy and my heart lurched every time water splashed onto the windshield.

Maybe coming face to face with the vampire had something to do with my fear or maybe it was the fact that he'd told me I was dying.

Both would make sense, but I knew in my gut that those reasons were as truthful as if I said the sky was green. A lie and an excuse to shadow the thing that I didn't want to accept because of how real it almost came to be.

Losing Aiden.

If there were more of them or if I couldn't break the link...we'd not have made it out alive.

My life was as good as gone with my sentence from the vampire, because if Emery couldn't fix me then my time was wearing to its end.

But Aiden couldn't die. He had Tourmaline and a pack to take care of and while I'm still alive, he had to remain alive too.

Because I don't think my heart would be able to take it if he died and I had to live.

As if sensing my thoughts on him, his pained eyes found mine. Stretching his hand out, he gestured for me to come to him.

And I did.

He kept one hand on the steering and steady me with his other hand on my waist before pulling me to sit between his thighs. The seat was big enough but Aiden hold on me was firm.

The warmth of his exposed chest seemed through my thin blouse and into my skin. A soothing touch that drastically eased my inner turmoil.

"Are you alright?" He asked, his voice husky with emotion. Taking the back of my palm, he turned it over before he squeezed his eyes shut for a second. "Fuck!"

My breath caught at his outburst. Cursing for Aiden was rarer than an occurrence of a blue moon.

"It'll heal," I whispered as his ragged breath fanned across the left side of my cheek.

"You shouldn't have been hurt in the first place. I put us both in danger by attacking," I could hear him grinding his teeth.

Aiden's explosive anger was simmer just below the surface. Waiting for something to trigger the eruption of his rage.

I turned my head to him, and pleaded with my eyes, "Just hold me."

The burning dark blue his eyes were, lightened in shade as a fraction of his anger dissipated.

Nodding, he released my wrist and flattened his palm on my stomach, pulling me further into his warmth.

Lowering my head, I placed it in the nook of his neck. Inhaling his scent and simultaneously easing my pain.

His stiff posture from being wind up eased as he rested his chin on head. Taking in my scent as I was doing to him.

"What's my scent?" I asked out of the blue.

"Pink summer berries, bergamot and tropical hibiscus," He answered without missing a beat.

I smiled against his neck, brushing my lips against his skin as his grip on me tightened.

"That's very specific," I teased. Hoping it would help him release his stress.

But I knew there was nothing I could do to help his anxiety with the biggest information we learned.

The human, Earl, was in fact healed by a mermaid.

"You're addicting," I felt his breath on my hair, taking a deep inhale of my scent.

Trailing my nose along his neck, I placed a kiss below his hair, "Thank you for wanting to protect me."

"You don't need to thank me."

"And you don't need to protect me," I countered as I rested my head back on his shoulder.

He huffed, "As if that would stop me. Whatever that thing said back there...I don't believe him. Emery would heal you and you'll be fine."

Bleeding heart.

The word rang out in my head, startling me back to the realization that we'd have our answer to that by tonight.

Emery and Thane would be here by sunset and I wasn't sure if I dreaded or welcomed their arrival.

Shaking the thoughts away, I said, "That's not important right now. We have bigger issues to deal with."

"Your life will always be important to me," He growled.

"And my life will be worth nothing if we don't figure out how to stop the vampires. There's still so much that we don't know about the mermaid blood," I sat up and shifted so that my arms wrapped around his neck. "Aiden, what are we going to do?"

He must have detected the despair in my voice or the trepidation in my eyes because he softened under me.

I knew how hard he was trying to keep it together when he responded with, "We could move to Sweden or Iceland during the summer. Watch the midnight sun chase away the vampires."

A humour-less smile touched my lips, "And in the winter?"

Pupils contracting, the darkness filled his eyes again. His expression clouding over like the sirens themselves conjured up another storm. This one more deadly than the last.

His lack of a response was answer enough. That's as far as this conversation will go right now.

For I knew, the only thing that would truly calm him was having Tourmaline in front of his eyes, alive and safe.

The name 'Anvi' still haunted me, but I would just have to wait until we get back on land.

"He'll never have her," I enunciated as we continued pushing against the waves to get back home.

CHAPTER 22

I stared down at the gauze on my hands that Dr. Nazra just wrapped up. My super healing had not worked.

My palms were blistered and aching. Soothed only by the burn cream that she applied.

I didn't just have a bleeding heart, I also had a broken body.

When I looked into the mirror of the vanity, exhaustion marred my features and my skin was pallid like that of a bloodsucker.

But the fear was washed away along with my pain. I made sure to scrub at it in the bathroom, a feat made difficult by only having the use of my fingertips. After we got back, everyone was all over the castle, so we didn't call a meeting just yet. The shock of the morning still in our systems.

I sent Aiden to find Tourmaline, knowing that was what he needed to get his head on straight. Myself, on the other hand, needed to rid the stench of the vampires permanently out of my system.

And when I walked out of my bath, Dr. Nazra was there with a bandage and a stethoscope. Sent up by the Alpha's behest.

"Are you sure the pain has subsided?" Nazra asked once more as she stood at the door.

I plastered on a small smile and nodded, "I'm fine Nazra, thank you."

"Let me now if your chest starts to hurt again," She said pointedly before taking her leave.

She didn't make it far down the hallway before I heard her footsteps stop and whispers start.

I sniffed him out before I could even hear his husky voice.

"She's okay?" Aiden asked, tone agitated.

There was a hesitant pause before she answered, "Mostly, yes. But her healing has slowed down drastically. To the rate of an average human's healing ability."

A rough intake of breath had me on my feet. The need to walk out there and convince Nazra to tell Aiden that I'm hundred percent okay.

But the truth was what he needed. Truth and trust were what Aiden valued above all else.

"And her heart?" He started to get snippy.

"No improvement," She informed.

"At least it's no worst," He mumbled, but lacked conviction. "Thank you Nazra. I'll see you down there for the pack meeting."

"Alpha."

In less than a blink of an eye, Aiden rasped his knuckles against my door.

"Come in," I said on a sharp intake of breath as I accidentally pressed my palm to my stomach.

The unease of where we stood on the matter of the vampires made me fidget in my spot as he entered. But as I took him in, a few butterflies managed to chase away the unease.

There he stood with a tray of food in his hands and a distraught expression on his face.

"I thought you'd be hungry," He said quietly as he took in my bandaged hands but said nothing.

He didn't have to because his expression said everything. The fine lines that creased his forehead in worry and the stubborn pucker between his eyebrows that told me his mind was waging a war and the set of jaw as he grind his teeth in agitation.

"I am, thank you," I stretched my hands out for the tray in reflex. A movement that made Aiden wince as his grip tightened on the tray.

Quickly, I hid the bandaged palms behind my back. Guilt ate at me for my physical incapacity because I knew the visual was just another reminded of both my underlying conditions and the massive vampire problem.

"Never hid from me, Tate," Aiden surprised me by saying as he lifted a hand and brushed a strand of my hair behind my ear. "Don't you dare hid your pain from me, ever."

"I just-"

"I know," He cut me off with a nod, "and I appreciate it. Now let me take care of you."

I shook my head, "Tourmaline-"

"Is fine," He pressed as he nudged me to sit on the bed. "She's with Kai and Matt...I haven't told her about the news yet."

"She's brave," I laughed without humour. "I can already see her putting on her brave face and leading her mermaids into action."

"Too brave, just like her parents," Aiden said with a small smile as we sat. "I thought soup would be easy on your stomach."

I nodded but held up my hands, "Well, it's too bad I can't hold a spoon."

Aiden rolled his eyes at me, "Then it's a good thing you have a mate."

Without preamble, he lifted a spoon of soup to my lips with intent focus. The gesture was intimate and sent my heart into a warm frenzy.

A good frenzy.

"Aiden," I shook my head, "you don't have to."

"I want to," He said earnestly. "Please, let me take care of you."

"You take care of everyone enough."

"Ahh, but you're not everyone. I haven't been taking care of you enough..." He trailed off in thought.

Knowing that he wasn't going to move the spoon away and being useless without the function of my hands, I opened my mouth and accepted his offering.

Maybe it was his close proximity or maybe it was the warmth of the soup, but the chill that was in my bones before, drifted away.

Although, I suspected it was the heat of his burning blue eyes that sparked the fire in my blood. An odd sensation that sparked the air between us. The mate bond shaking off its deep slumber and letting us know that it's there.

Waiting ever so patiently for us to connect the dots the between us.

"I don't know how to tell them," Aiden whispered with a strained breath.

"Aiden..." I struggled with my words as I was caught off guard by his petrified expression.

It was very unlike Aiden. A sudden flaw in what I was considering a still piece of art come to life.

His eyes were unfocused as he stared at the ground. A crease between his eyebrows that weighed heavily with worry.

An otherwise poker faced or assured Aiden was now plagued in a distress that I didn't know how to solve.

"I've failed them," He shook his head. "For the past five years I gave them empty promises of finding the solution that this whole mess was false. That somehow, I'd find the words that would state it was all a myth."

"You couldn't have known. None of us did," I reminded him.

"I...I..." His words drifted into a silent breath.

A brief pause followed, which was only disturbed by my erratic heartbeat.

Dazzling blue eyes, plagued with the stress of keeping a pack alive, snapped towards me with a silent plea.

"What do I do?" He asked as my answer would be biblical.

A holy prayer that would save us.

"First," I cleared my throat, "we tell them. Emphasis on we."

He nodded but he still didn't seem anymore appeased, "And then what? There's little we can do now besides fight."

"Wrong," I shook my head.

"I was kidding about chasing the midnight sun. I can't uproot the entire pack again."

I rolled my eyes at him, "Well, it's a good thing my plans revolve around staying here."

He seemed unsure as he asked, "What do you mean?"

"Anvi," I muttered and watched a spark lit his eyes. "She was Amethyst's best friend right?"

I recalled where I heard her name from before. It was my first day here when Tourmaline mentioned Anvi's disappearance.

Aiden nodded as he turned his body fully towards me, visible distress lines creased at the sides of his eyes, aging him more that his rushed maturity has. I internally cursed my bruised hands for robbing me of the ability to comfort Aiden with touch.

"Yes," He nodded. "It slipped my mind that he mentioned her...I couldn't think past getting you to safety."

I felt the corner of my lips twitch at his unconscious revelation.

But the sentiments were cut short as the brief story of the mysterious disappearance of Anvi plagued my mind.

"Tourmaline mentioned that she disappeared right after she was born, which was why Jenny took over," I said in more of a question.

"She did," He declared. "One minute she was putting Tourmaline to sleep for the night and by morning she was gone. There wasn't any vampire scent in the castle and mermaid scent is too god damn hard to track. She disappeared.

"At first we thought she went into the water and the other mermaids looked but she was nowhere to be found..." He rubbed his jaw in agitation. "After a while, we suspected it might have been the vampires, but we weren't sure until today."

"That's it then," I pointed out as he gave me a dubious look.

"I don't follow."

"If the vamps had Anvi all this time, then they would have tried her blood. But the vampire we met today, along with all the others you came across for the last five years, didn't step into the sunlight. And I suspect it wasn't for a lack of trying."

He didn't take long to process my train of thought as his eyes widened in realization.

"But the human..." He mused. "How would it be possible?"

"I don't know, but I think I know who might," I watched as his expression darkened.

Knowing what had to de done. A petrifying thought.

"What if the bloodsucker was bluffing?" He questioned.

I shook my head, "He insinuated that she was alive. We need to rescue her, if not for more answers then for her life. Who knows what she's been through for the last five years?"

He went silent but I could see the wheels in his head spinning. Thinking up a solution that could explain the spider-web that we've been tangled in.

No words were spoken again as he brought the spoon of soup back to my lips.

A few minutes later, he finally concluded, "They don't know why Anvi's blood didn't work. For five years they've been holding her hostage because they don't know. I doubt she'll have any answers of her own."

"But she might have an idea."

"I don't know, Tate. Finding their hideout is one thing, going in and leaving Tourmaline here unprotected is another."

I was perplexed by his sudden pessimistic attitude.

"Aiden," I whispered to draw his eyes back to me. "Tell me what's bothering you?"

His eyebrows drew together in a pained expression as he shook his head, but I pressed on.

"The vampires won't get to her-"

"It's not that," He cut me off before drawing in a deep breath. "Today...today I could have lost you. If anything ever happens to you, Tate-"

"Nothing would."

"But if something did, I don't know what I'd do with myself. I don't know how I'll be strong enough for Tourmaline," He admitted.

His usually clear blue eyes were clouded over with fear and doubt and it broke me inside. To know that losing me was something to take this Alpha of a man to his knees.

"You're not going to lose me, I promise you that," I swore. "So let's forget about that and focus on getting some answers, okay?"

He nodded but I could still see a trace of doubt in his eyes and the weight on his shoulders. As he lifted the last spoon of soup to my lips, I stopped his hand with my bandaged palm.

"Aiden, I don't need a perfect heart to know that I..." I trailed off as the I killed the words on my tongue, not ready to vocalize those thoughts.

"Know what?" He prompted with intensity.

My eyes flickered briefly to his chest, where his heart lay, before returning to his eyes and switching my words, "I don't need a perfect heart to help you find a way to keep Tourmaline safe. And we will keep her safe."

He surprised me with a small smile, "You don't need to tell me because I know you'll do anything to keep her safe. It's who you are."

Not giving myself much time to overthink it, I threw my arms around his neck and pulled him towards me. I received a chuckle in return and that sound alone would be enough to repair my heart.

"Thank you," He whispered into my hair, but I didn't know what for.

Gently squeezing me to him, I knew once we had each other, we'd get through this.

Damn the vampires and the sirens and my heart.

No problem was ever solved without difficulty.

Once we had gathered everyone into the large ballroom, they took the news as expected.

Everything fell into disrepair.

The wolves were agitated and the mermaids were shocked with fear.

Question after question were thrown at us about the vampire we encountered.

"And you said he had a French accent?" Dylan asked.

Kai rolled his eyes at him, "I highly doubt his accent is of any importance after her attacked our Alpha and Luna."

Dylan's jaw ticked as he said, "Now you see that's what makes me a good Gamma, I pay attention to the details."

"I-"

"Leave it be," Matt cut his mate off as he steered him to the side.

Kai shot daggers at Dylan who only smirked in response.

I looked to Aiden who didn't catch the little riff as Tourmaline was interrogating him with her own questions. For a five year old, she was cool and collected about it.

But I saw the fear in her eyes as she grabbed for Aiden. It didn't last long, though, as she felt the duty to protect her people and her uncle.

With maturity that she should not have to endure at such a young age, she went into action by gaining as much information as possible.

"And you're sure it was a mermaid who saved the human?" She asked for about the tenth time since we explained.

"I'm pretty sure she was kiddo, her hair alone gave it away," Aiden answered patiently.

"So the mermaid blood heals them, what do we do now?" Calypso asked as Rick hugged her from behind.

Aiden and I exchanged a glance before I announced, "We didn't reveal everything we know."

The room fell into silence as all werewolf and mer-folk eyes fell on me with intense curiosity.

"There was a mermaid that went missing five years ago," I watched as they processed my words slowly. Jenny pushing her way to the front of the crowd with wild eyes. "Anvi's her name... she's alive."

A chorus of gasps and mumbles resounded across the room, but there was one person who grabbed most of my attention.

Jenny was motionless and unblinking as her shoulders dropped in what I can only guess was relief. Much like the other mer-folk...but something about her expression was different.

More intense.

She took a stumbling step closer as she asked, "I-is she alright?"

"I don't know," I answered honestly.

"But you're going after her right? I mean she's an important member to our group," Jenny tried to school her emotions as she straightened her spine and plastered on a poker face.

"We plan to," I said but she gave me a doubtful look.

Weary of my words and in need of assurance, she hesitantly asked, "You swear?"

I studied her behaviour for a brief second before nodding, "You have my word."

She appraised me with a tinge of respect, "Then what do we have to do to get her back."

"Before we discuss that, we should look at what her being alive means," Aiden interjected. "If they had Anvi all this time but no vampire, that we know off, has stepped into the sunlight, then something isn't adding up."

"The mermaid blood doesn't work?" Rick asked, perplexed.

"It does, but it doesn't," I answered. "There's something missing that we don't know."

"But we think Anvi might," Continued Aiden.

"Shit," Rick responded. "How do we even find her?"

"That's our next move."

"We'll never find them," Dylan sighed. "It's been ages that we've been tracking their hide out and we haven't succeeded yet."

I smiled, "The operative word being 'yet'. We'll find them because all of our future depends on keeping the mermaids out of their hands."

"Tate is right," Tourmaline nodded as she grabbed my arm. "We have to find them."

"Rick, get the tracking team together and Dylan we'll need the maps," Aiden started delegating. "If anyone have any other questions, your Luna will be here to answer them all along with the mermaid Queen."

Aiden shot Tourmaline and I a wink as he left with his ensemble, but not before giving Kai his instructions.

"Keep them safe," He patted his friend's shoulder.

Kai nodded dutifully as he walked to our side. Ready to defend and protect.

However, no one stepped a foot out of the ballroom when we heard the front doors open.

"Wow, Tate didn't say she lived in a freaking castle," A very familiar female voice echoed through the hallway.

"Show off," My brother grumbled.

Aiden rolled his eyes at Thane's comment but gestured his head to the hallway with a smile.

A grin broke out on my face as I took his cue and ran towards to their voices.

CHAPTER 23

"Emery," I released a breath of relief at the sight of her and my brother standing in the foyer.

Finally, I thought, finally I can have my heart and body back.

They both grinned as I approached, having not seen each other in weeks.

"Hey dork," My brother greeted with a smirk, but as I lifted my hand to flip him off, all traces of humour disappeared.

"Tate, your hands?" Emery questioned with worry.

Hurriedly, I wrapped my arms around her as my brother's eyes searched behind me with building rage.

"Where is he?" Thane growled as he side stepped us and moved towards the ballroom.

"Wait, you doofus," I moved away from Emery and blocked his path. "There's a lot that we need to explain."

Thane's brown eyes, the exact as my own, boiled with fury, darkening as it shifted from my hands to an approaching Aiden.

"Did he do this?" Thane asked lowly.

"What?" I looked at him as if he grew another head. "Of course he didn't!"

"Tate," He growled as he took another step. "Has he hurt you?"

I placed my forearms on his chest and halted his movements, "Aiden wouldn't dare. You need to calm down."

No sign of calm was evident on Thane's features, so I looked at Emery for help.

Her own eyes were watery as she couldn't take her gaze off my gauze hands.

"Thane, glad you could make it," Aiden said behind me but I could detect the sizzle of hostility in his tone. His hands appeared from behind me as he lifted my arms off my brother and gently shifted me to his side, keeping an arm around my shoulder.

"If you dare-"

"Thane," Emery stopped her mate as she assessed me. "It's because of your heart, isn't it?"

Aiden beat me to the explanation as he said, "Our pack doctor has determined that Tate's heart is slowing down her healing rate. Her blood is not as oxygen enriched as it should be which is making her lose her werewolf regenerative healing."

"My sister can speak on her own," Thane bit out.

"Sweetheart, relax," Emery entwined their arms as Thane sought comfort in her. "I'm sure Aiden is only trying to ease the pressure on Tate."

"I always knew I liked you more than your mate," Aiden joked as Thane's anger flared.

"If you-"

"Thane!" I snapped at him. "Aiden's telling the truth... I-I can't heal as fast anymore."

Aiden held me tighter against him as my voice dropped.

"Jesus, Tate," Thane swore as he ran his hands through his hair wildly. "Why didn't tell us when you were back home?"

"Because the pack had been through so much and Emery was still unconscious. I didn't want to add to your plate."

Aiden released me as Thane reached out to wrap me up in his arms, "We're family, we don't keep things like this, no matter what. Okay?"

He cupped my cheeks and waited for me to agree.

"Okay," I promised.

His eyes were pained but he took my answer as he straightened to his full height, "If you're wondering, we haven't told mom yet, didn't want to worry her, but dad knows."

I nodded in understanding as a little voice erupted behind us.

"Uncle Aiden?" Tourmaline's voice questioned as she looked curiously at Thane and Emery.

"You have a niece?" Emery asked.

"He has a niece?" Thane growled in surprise.

"So not the time brother," I elbowed him in the rib since my fists my indisposed.

"I thought you didn't have any siblings?" Thane questioned my mate.

I had considered what Aiden would say to my family when they family arrived. My delay in having them both come here didn't just stem from Emery's recovery, but also because I didn't want Aiden to feel pressured into having to disclose his deepest secrets.

Not only are they my family, but they're the Alpha and Luna of another pack. While they would never hurt me or my new pack, I experienced Aiden's doubt in strangers. Especially when it came to the little pink-haired angel standing by his side.

Loss is something than runs deeper than any wound and Aiden's hurt was bone deep. Opening up easily is something I would never force him into or expect him to give easily.

Yet, as we all stood there in the midst of uncertainty, Aiden continued to stupefy me.

His blue eyes were set deep but shining clearly. The force of breaking his own fortress walls downs caused him to hesitate a bit, making him unsure of his decision. But when sultry eyes found mine, I could see the last remnants of doubt fade away as he gave me a subtle nod.

"We have a lot to discuss," He said, holding his hand out towards the living room.

Thane was also taken back by Aiden's shift in direction and willingness to cooperate. But, in good sense, he nodded.

"Wait, I have to heal Tate," Emery held onto my arm.

"How about I get you something to eat while we talk and then we can get to it?" I suggested as I watched her small baby bump. "I've got to ensure my nephew is fed."

Emery sighed comically as she rubbed her stomach, "That actually sounds amazing. Eating for a werewolf baby has also become my main task these days."

I nudged her to Thane, "I'll be back then. Help me Tourm?"

She nodded happily before Emery called me back.

"And Tate?" She smiled sheepishly. "If you have chocolate ice-cream, I'd kill for some."

"Love, that really isn't good for you," Thane chastised.

Emery pinched his arm, a bit aggressively, as she snapped, "It's your kid . I didn't crave ice-cream before you got me pregnant."

Thane held the fear of God in him as he gently wrapped his arm around his mate's shoulders, "Have I told you how much you scare me?"

"Thane," She growled.

"I mean - how much I love you," He corrected.

Aiden rolled his eyes at them as he looked at me, "I'll take care of them."

I sent him a wink before going to the kitchen and having one of the pack member, Smith, help me gather up a tray filled with food. And chocolate ice-cream.

"Tate?" Tourmaline asked as we stood in the kitchen.

"Yes, Princess?"

"Is that your brother and sister?"

I wrapped my arms around her and managed to scoop her up before setting her on the counter, "The ugly guy is my older brother, Thane, and the girl is his mate, Emery."

She frowned, "I wish I had a brother."

"Oh sweeties," I expressed as my heart tore in two for her. "What if I told you I could find a pair of rascals that will be just as good?"

Her eyes widened with excitement, "Are you having a baby?"

I couldn't help the outburst of cough as I also choked on air. My eyes watered and I could feel a blush coating my cheek as I shook my head, as gently as I could control it.

"No," My voice went unusually high before I cleared it. "No, I'm not."

"Not yet?" She pressed.

"You're way too good at getting what you want kid," I narrowed my eyes playfully at her.

She grinned, knowing exactly what she was up to.

"However, I do have two other brothers. They're eight, only three years older than you."

"Really?"

"Really."

"Can I meet them Tate! Please?" She pouted.

"As soon as they can visit, we'll invite them over."

"Yay!" She squealed as we made our to the living room, following behind the pack member who helped. "What's their names?"

"Teddy and Thomas."

"You all have names with T's," She pointed out cleverly. "Just like me!"

"I know," I agreed. "You're already apart of our family and I think my crazy mom will agree."

Tate giggled in her palms as we entered the room, capturing the attention of the others.

Emery looked at Tourm and I with a knowing smile. Thane still seemed confused.

But Aiden...his gaze never seemed to not have my head spinning.

"Is that all I can do for you Luna?" The pack member asked.

"Yes, thank you, Smith," I shook Aiden's spell off of me as the boy left the room.

"Oh! My ice-cream," Emery clapped happily as she started with dessert.

"Love-"

"Don't you dare say a word, Thane."

He held his hands up in defence and mumbled, "It's a good thing you're self healing."

"That's right."

"So?" I looked between the opposite sides of the coffee table. Aiden sat in an arm chair near the bookshelf while Thane and Emery across from him in a large sofa. The setting sun outside cast the room in a golden tint as its light filtered through the large windows running along the wall opposite of me. "What have you found out so far?"

"He's said nothing," Thane rolled his eyes.

"I was waiting for you," Aiden replied gently as I took my seat in another armchair, right next to him.

Tourmaline, on the other hand, took a seat next to Emery and lifted her tiny hand, "May I?"

Emery grinned with delight as she took Tourm's hand in her own and placed it on her stomach.

Her little face broke out in a wide grin and her eyes were filled with so much joy. There weren't anyone pregnant in the pack, nor is there any other kid her age or younger around. The youngest, aside from Tourmaline, were five kids around seven.

She got along with them just fine, but I don't think she's ever experienced meeting something with an unborn child.

I briefly wondered is the lack of children in the pack was related to the uncertain future of the pack's fight against the vampires. It would be a dangerous world to raise a child in.

Tourmaline innocent question of me being pregnant turned in my head as I looked at Aiden, who immediately had his eyes on me.

He too had a small smile on his face. One of the rare ones.

My expression must have gave away my the fact that something was on my mind as he lifted an eyebrow at me in a silent question.

Smiling, I shook my head at him.

"What are you going to name her?" Tourmaline asked.

"It's a boy," Emery corrected. "And I was thinking Eros."

Tourmaline's eyebrows pressed together before she smiled, "I like it."

"I still think Thor's a better name," Thane pipped in.

"And I think your car will look nice in pink," Em replied.

"It actually might...the jeep looks great," He mused.

"Thane-"

"I know," He kissed her forehead. "No superhero names."

"It's actually a God," Aiden pointed out. "And how do you already know the gender?"

"It's a Blood Moon Pack thing," Emery rolled her eyes. "Stupid patriarchy."

He nodded before letting out a deep breath, "Well, how about we get started?"

"Wait," Emery stopped him as she got up and walked over to me. "I hate to see you like this, Tate."

"Emery, what are you-?"

She shushed me as she unbandaged my palms, causing the stinging to breath a new wave of pain into my system as the gauze was stuck to my wound.

"Flapjacks," I cursed as my eyes watered and unable to say the real word when Tourm stood right there.

"You're hurting her," Aiden growled as his palm gripped the handle of his chair.

"She'll be okay," Em promised as she grabbed both my wrists and sweet relief rushed through me. Eliminating all the pain.

I watched as the skin healed up perfectly on my hands, as if this morning didn't exists.

She released my hands when she was finished, looking a tad faint. Thane had her in her arms already as she reached for the glass of juice.

"Just needed a good warm up before I get to the heart," She said. "No one back home has allowed me to heal anyone since the coma."

"And for good reason, now sit," Thane helped her.

Aiden's larger hand gently took my own as he brought it up to his eyes, inspecting every inch of my oddly pale skin as if he couldn't believe his eyes.

"It doesn't hurt anymore?" He looked up at me.

"No, it's perfect," I said as the tingle of his touch had me giddy. "You're-"

"Sure?" I took the words out of his mouth as he nodded once, "Yes, I'm fine."

"Good, that's good," He breathed a sigh of relief but the weight of getting my heart fixed still stuck around.

Tourmaline also took my other hand and, in an oddly similar fashion as her uncle, inspected my hand.

"How about you tell us what you wanted to while I rebuild my energy?" Emery suggested.

Everyone sobered up as Aiden nodded. I kept my hand in his hold as he began telling them about his past. Each nightmare being relieved through his mind as he recounted the death of his family members.

The dark blue-grey walls of the room darkened as twilight faded into the night sky. Casting the room in a gloomy atmosphere that reinforced the cold past that Aiden lived. The bookshelves of old text and the shaggy carpet not providing its familiar warmth that was desperately needed in the room.

Emery and Thane reacted just as I did, but a little more dramatic. Well, Thane was the drama queen as he demanded to know why the Oaks Pack kept the vampires a secret.

As Aiden supressed his pain and concealed his every emotion, I rubbed gently circles on the outside of his hand with my thumb, while also hugging Tourmaline close to me when she planted herself on my chair.

Finally explaining all that he had, he sighed, "Now you know of all the skeletons that live in my closet."

Thane shook his head with a matured expression, "Doesn't matter, I'm not going to divulge."

Aiden snorted, unbelieving.

"Look," Thane sighed as he grabbed Emery's hand. "You know my wife's most precious secret, so I don't think I'm in any position to be telling yours. Not to mention my sister lives here now. I won't put her or your niece in danger."

"You're really not going to tell anyone?" Aiden was unconvinced.

"You have my word, Aiden."

My mate pondered my brother's serious tone for a moment before he nodded. His features were to askew for me to determine if he actually believed my brother or not. But Thane's face was as clear as day.

His eyes held a new found respect for my mate.

"And we'll help any way that we can of course," Thane continued. "I'll search our archives for any books that might help."

"I've checked your library already," Aiden stated.

"We have more hidden away."

"Then I'll be eternally grateful."

An understanding passed between them. Silent but strong wiled.

"Now, what we truly came here for," Emery smiled as she pat the seat next to her.

Aiden lifted a sleeping Tourmaline off my arms as he placed her on the empty settee.

I sent a quick prayer up to the Moon Goddess, hoping that it worked.

"You ready?" She asked as Thane and Aiden looked on nervously.

Aiden looked sickly green, as if he was going to throw up.

"I'll be fine," I promised him with a smile.

He gave no reply as he stood on the opposite side of the coffee table, one arm folded and the other pressing his knuckle against his lips.

Emery's soft hands laid above my heart as she closed her eyes and focused.

Calm immediately beheld me, allowing me to a good deep breath.

It must be working.

Emery's lips titled up.

For a split second.

Before it dropped and I felt the excruciating pain that signalled when my heart was about to act up.

I gasped for air as tears leaked out of my eyes, unable to stay trapped behind my shut lids.

She pressed her palms with more force as she cursed.

"Heal, damn it!" She yelled.

I felt like my windpipe were crushing as she kept her hands on me. Urging my heart to heal.

But it wasn't. I could fell it not healing.

It wasn't like the last time.

The time she healed me and saved my life.

"Shit," I heard curse. "Stop. Stop it! You're hurting her."

"Sweetheart stop," Thane said, his voice catching at the end.

Her palms were immediately removed from my chest and I was engulfed in strong, warm arms.

I clutched my chest as the pain threatened me. Willing my nose to soak in the scent of fresh waterfall and driftwood mahogany.

"Shhh, Cupcake," He whispered in my hair as he hugged me from behind me. Arms wrapped around me as he held me tightly to his chest. "Doctor Nazra will be here soon. You'll be alright."

"Emery?" I heard my brother ask in panic. Searching for answers as I was desperately was.

Why didn't it work?

Her voice were filled with tears and I didn't dare open my eyes as she said, "I-it felt like it was starting to work...b-but it stopped. It won't heal. I- Thane, I don't know what to do."

"She'll be alright, Love," He said to her but I could hear the pain in his voice and the quiet sobs that Emery tried to stifle.

"Yes. Yes, she'll be fine," Aiden's voice wavered, but the conviction was crystal clear. I clutched his arms tight as I felt the pain slowing ebbing away. "She has to be alright."

I opened my mouth and my voice came out all croaky and broken, "I think it was j-just one of those chest pains."

Opening my eyes, Emery and Thane's expression broke me further than I felt.

I couldn't be healed.

That sunk in slowly as Emery's words echoed in my head.

Bouncing around like a ton of bricks, wanting to crack my skull open as the pain in my chest threatened to do with my heart.

I was broken.

Emery, with her God like powers, couldn't save me.

Aiden's hands were clammy and trembled slightly as he held onto me. His palm gently turned my head to face him.

My eyes took in his jagged expression but the determination was set like stone on his face. However, that didn't prevent his eyes from being watery and his hands from shaking as he contined to assess me.

When I caught my reflection in his pupils, I felt another piece of myself slipping away.

What I saw in its reflection was nothing but a shell of who I once was.

While the wound wasn't visible, I could still see it etched permanently onto my soul.

The pain was like strokes of the worst colour imaginable streaked across my face. Consuming me in its horrid world. Turning me into something less like me and more like it.

It was the slow death of my wolf.

And of Tate Blackwood.

CHAPTER 24

"Where's Emery?" I asked my brother as he entered the infirmary.

"Asleep," He sighed heavily. "She wore herself trying to find a way to heal you."

"She shouldn't be. If she could have healed me, it would have happened."

"That won't stop her."

"I know," I muttered guilty.

It was unbecoming to throw oneself a pity party, but I couldn't prevent the unyielding guilt that chipped away at my insides.

It festered like a plague as I watched those I cared most for run themselves mad trying to find a way to fix me.

But what if I couldn't be fixed? More specifically, what if I couldn't be fixed for the long run?

My focus shifted back to the pitch black sea outside. Only catching glimpses of the dark water as the light from the lighthouse spun and reflected its light off the waves.

Once my heart stopped aching, Aiden scooped me up and raced to the infirmary. He had Dr. Adler, from Thane's pack, on the phone in no time while Dr. Nazra checked up on me.

Now Aiden was interrogating them both on what could be done and how quick we could do it.

Plan B wasn't discussed before, as we were all betting on Emery to heal me. A simple solution to a complex situation.

I should have known it wouldn't have worked.

Yet, I had hope.

And now I felt empty.

Like a hollow tree trunk.

Withering and drained of life.

Or like autumn leaves falling from from the branches as their dead shells drifted to the ground.

"We can put her on some medication, see if that will slow down her accelerated decline in health," Dr. Adler suggested over the phone.

"But that wouldn't be a solution, just a short term treatment," Dr. Nazra added.

"Then what do we do?" Aiden asked, agitated as he paced near the phone.

"She'll need a pacemaker," Dr. Nazra said. "It's a small device that sends electrical signals to your heart to help control your heart rate."

"That sounds like a good solution," I piped in.

It actually sounds like a much better solution than being drugged up on meds for who knows how long.

Dr. Nazra gave me a sad smile before she explained further, "It won't be that simple, the pacemaker has to be surgically implanted under your skin."

Aiden's feet stopped abruptly which almost made him fall before he caught himself.

I could see the colour draining from his face as he shook his head, "Not unless there's a high success rate."

"Pacemakers are a common procedure and it has a high success rate. It's usually the main solution to bradycardia as it regulates the heart rate to a normal pace," Dr. Nazra answered before a troubled expression crossed her face. "I've never had the need to perform an operation of that nature...given our species."

"Dr. Adler?" Aiden questioned.

The old man sighed over the telephone line, "I'm afraid I haven't either. Cardiology wasn't my strongest area, but I know who the top cardiologist is in the country."

His blue eyes found mine, clouded with desperation, "Would it be safe for him to operate on her? Given her DNA?"

"Doctor-patient confidentiality would prevent him from speaking of Tate's case, but I don't know if it will be enough to stop him from divulging the information, or taking test samples."

Aiden slammed his fist into one of the steel medical tables, creating a crater the size of his fist.

"Aiden," I whispered, pained to see this torturing him.

He turned to me instantly and I stretched my hand out to him, beckoning him to where I sat on the exam table.

Like a moth to a flame, he drew closer to me, resting his forehead against my own as he entwined our fingers together.

Breathing in his scent, I allowed myself to be comforted by him and he took comfort in me. The warmth of his skin soothed my skin, the sound of his deep breathing was in tandem with mine - sharing one breath.

Thane didn't growl or hit his chest in an act of brotherly protection, and for that, I was grateful.

Gleaming blue eyes, like those of a thunderous sky, met mine with determination.

"Mermaid blood," He whispered to me as he found a sacred treasure. "We'll ask the mermaids to help."

I straightened my spin as I pulled my head away from his.

"No," I admonished with finality.

"Tate," Aiden warned. "It's the only thing that may be able to cure you."

"At their expense," I countered. "I won't ask them to give me their blood when they need all their energy to protect themselves from the vampires."

"Technically," Dr. Nazra inserted, "they'd only have to give a pint, which won't make a big difference in how they feel or operate. People donate blood everyday."

"Not mermaids," I pointed out.

"I think we should hear them out Tay," Thane said. "They have a point."

Aiden nodded appreciatively to my brother while I shook my head vehemently. Not was so not the time for them to finally be in cahoots.

"If we use the blood, we'll also be able to test whether or not the mermaid blood works," Aiden went on.

"Seems like a solid option to me," Thane agreed.

"Great, then we'll get a mermaid in here now."

I grabbed Aiden's forearm and yanked him back to me with fire in my eyes and heat in my voice, "No."

He opened his mouth to offer a rebuttal but I cut him off.

"You said the merfolk are fragile creatures. My life is nothing compared to ensuring their species survive," I stated. "I'm not going to be the one to risk even one life of a mermaid."

His eyes softened and the crease between his eyebrows smoothened out as he looked me as if with new eyes. There was a clarity about his expression that made my breath catch in my throat as this curiosity in his eyes assessed me. As if looking for something or maybe now seeing something that hadn't seen there before.

The beat of silence between us seemed to break the high tension that had settled in the room when we entered.

And ever so slowly, the corner of his lips tilted as his long eyelashes fluttered over his blue eyes that seemed to shift between shades every time I looked at them.

"You're real stubborn, you know that," His voice held amusement as the corner of his crinkled and he slowly shook his head.

"You say that as if it's a bad thing."

"It's not."

"Then I guess I win this argument."

He shook his head as all traces of amusement vanquished from his eyes.

"Stubborn doesn't equate to being right in this situation, Tate," His neck strained with a simmering anger as I once again tried to refute him.

"You can't-"

But he cut me off with a searing statement that left my skin feeling blistered and tore at my heart.

"I refuse to dig another grave for someone that's important to me," His voice was grave, like a bleak gray sky over a casket of flowers. "I won't go through that again...no matter the expense. Do you understand me?"

The way he held my eyes made it seem as if he was asking something much deeper. Something more profound that he hadn't put into words. But, he was also pleading with me to listen so that he won't have to experience the immeasurable pain of losing someone he cared for.

And for that I couldn't fault him. Not now and never again.

I squeezed my eyes shut as Aiden's pain from the past that still lingered today like a fresh wound, passed through me. With a gentle nod of my head, I heard him release a breath that he's been holding.

It was shaky and very unlike Aiden.

How could I have ever called him Alpha Dickhead was beyond me.

"We can try," I enunciated as I peeled my eyes open.

Aiden didn't hesitate as his eyes moved to the good doctor.

"We can have a merfolk give her blood now?" He asked.

Dr. Nazra nodded with certainty as she and Aiden immediately went in search of blood donor.

"Don't move a muscle," He said sternly before he rushed after her.

I rolled my eyes at his back as Dr. Adler's voice carried through the phone line, "Hello? What do you mean by merfolk?"

I turned to Thane, who immediately grabbed the phone.

"I'll call you back, Adler. In the mean time, I would like your complete discretion and not a word to my family."

"Of course, Alpha," Dr. Adler responded at once before Thane hung up the phone.

Dr. Adler was a honest man and a loyal pack member to the Blackwood pack and his Alpha. Which is why I trust that he'd keep on his word and not share our secret.

However, while Dr. Adler posed no threat to divulging the mer-folk secret, I had two questions weighing heavily on my shoulders.

One: What if it doesn't work?

Two: What if it does work?

Both questions had terrible outcomes. Neither I was ready to face.

"Tate? What's wrong?" Thane asked with concern as he sat beside me on the exam table.

"Nothing," I shook my head and he gave me an unbelieving look.

"You don't think it will work?" He questioned.

I offered a shrug, "I don't know."

His eyes, the ones that were just like my own, squinted as he assessed me. His expression was troubled as if he couldn't come to a conclusion.

"Stop staring at me doofus," I pinched his arm.

He winced at my action, "Ouch!"

"You know what?" I said with a grin. "That mad me feel much better, can I do it again."

"Hell no," He said in a high pitched voice as I did it again. "Jesus, Tate!"

I snorted, "How did you not see that coming?"

"I... you know what, good point," He frowned. "It hasn't been that long since you've been home and I'm already losing my touch."

"What touch? You've always been the loser in our sibling rivalry."

He flipped me the bird before he shook his head, "I missed you kid. We all do."

Nodding, I swallowed the lump in throat, "I miss you all too, mom especially."

After a pause he finally turned to me, "Why didn't you want the mermaid blood?"

"Because it's not right," I clarified.

"It's just a bit of blood, they'll be fine within the next day," He said before pressing me. "Tell me the real reason."

I glared at his untimely observational skills as I formed my thoughts into coherent sentences.

In the end, I could only mutter one thing,

"I'm scared."

Thane seemed perplexed by my statement, "Of what?"

"The results!" I exclaimed. "Don't you see? If it doesn't work then I'm as good as dead...but if it does work, then the merfolk are as good as dead."

For once in his life, my brother was speechless.

Not a word left him as he sat there in the aftermath of my words.

"The vampires will come after them anyways," He whispered after his prolonged silence.

"And we'll have nothing to stop them with. No proof or evidence. My being alive would give them all the proof they need that it does work."

"How? They don't know you're sick," He said, but when I didn't offer a reply, he grabbed my shoulder and shook me. "They don't know that you are sick, right?"

I shook my head slowly, "We meet one of them in the human town up the coast. He could sniff out my dying heart like a dog with a bone."

"Shit!" He swore as his went eyes turned to steel. "Then if it works you can come back home with us, just for the time being. They won't know you're alive."

"No," I jumped off the bench and felt a bit woozy as my legs wobbled.

"Tate," Thane held onto my elbow to keep me upright, but I ripped my arm away and padded closer to the window.

I made sure to enunciate my words with as much finality as I could muster, "I'm not leaving here. If it works or if it doesn't, you can't make me leave and I won't leave."

"Fine," He gave in easily. "But answer me this, if it doesn't work, how are you so sure you'll find your evidence? Aiden said himself that he's been searching for years."

I didn't answer him.

How am I sure we'll find any proof?

"You think he'll blame you if it doesn't work," He whispered behind me.

I spun around to refute his statement but something inside of me acknowledged that what he said was true.

My eyes fell to floor and my eyebrows pulled together. It may be an irrational fear, but was it not an acceptable assumption?

"I don't have a relationship like Emery and you. I can't just woo him with promises of a future and my charm. This isn't some romance novel where everything will end perfectly."

"Sister," He shook his head protest, "I'm not for romance novels, but I can tell when a man is in love."

My eyes shot up to his as I threaded cautiously, "W-what do you mean?"

"He loves you," Thane grinned.

I shook my head vehemently, which only made my head spin, "You don't know him."

"You're right, I don't. But I have seen the way he looks at you, the way he was gripped with fear when Emery couldn't heal you. I think you've stolen the poor man's heart."

I glared at his shit-eating grin, while my insides knotted together in excitement and horror.

Excited at the prospect of being loved and horrified that my bad health would end the situation in a tragedy.

"You're not angry?" I asked instead, recalling my brother's over-the-top protectiveness earlier.

He seem to think on it before he answered, "No. Quite frankly, he's earned my respect after I heard what his pack has been through. What he's been through. He has to be a strong Alpha to keep his pack surviving to this day."

"I'm shocked you admitted that," I said in surprise but he lifted his hand.

"I'm not done," He stated as he rose to his feet. "Mostly, Aiden has earned my respect for taking care of you. Not as an Alpha, but as your mate. As he should. Defying his own rules to keep you safe."

"His rules?"

"I imagine his vow to protect the merfolk includes him not asking them for their blood. So, yes, he's breaking his rules for you."

As a lost for words, I shook my head at my elder brother, baffled.

"Since when did you become wise?"

He gave me a sad smile, "Almost losing a mate and child can do that to a person."

I grabbed him in a hug, not realizing until now how much I needed my family at this time. Especially my older brother.

"Thank you," I said to him, but it felt to weird so I ended with, "idiot."

He chuckled just as the door to the infirmary opened and my mate stepped in with a merman trailing behind him.

Aiden's eyes held concern as he spotted us.

"What happened? Are you alright?" He rounded the tables in a flash to get to me.

"I'm fine, much better now," I assured him.

His troubles were not eased as he guided me back to the table, "You shouldn't be standing. If you need something, tell me."

"What if I need to stand?"

I saw the smile pulling at the corner of his lips as I sat down.

"Then stand when I'm around to catch you."

His eyes sizzled with an under current that seemed as strong as a riptide. Catching me unknowingly and dragging me out to sea.

I felt the blood rush to my cheeks, especially with Thane's words ringing in my head.

He loves you.

Swiftly, I turned my attention to Dr. Nazra to save myself from Aiden's curious eyes.

She was instructing the merman to sit while handing him a juice box. The steel-colour hair man grumbled as he snatched the drink from her and plopped down into the chair she pointed at.

"Aiden?" I asked. "He his doing this of his free ill, right?"

Nothing in his expression changed as he nodded in affirmation. But I wasn't sure if he was telling the truth given that the merman seemed annoyed to be here.

"I don't think-"

"He'll be fine," My mate assured me as he wrapped my cold hand in his larger, warmer ones. "We're not sure if your blood type has to be matched with the merfolk, and he's one of the only two with O negative."

"Who's the other?" I asked.

His expression shifted to annoyance as he said, "Jenny."

"The merman will do," I chirped, happy that it won't be Jenny's blood flowing through my veins.

"Aiden, why don't you get Tate something to much on to keep up her energy," Dr. Nazra said.

Aiden seemed unwilling to leave the room again, but he dutifully moved to get me something before Thane stopped him.

"Don't worry, I'll get it."

Aiden nodded in appreciation before pulling Dr. Nazra's office chair closer to me and taking a seat.

"Your hands are cold," He noted as he rubbed them between his hands. "Scared?"

"Of the blood? No, I've never been frightened of needles."

"Not the needles. Of what happens after," He clarified.

"Are you?"

"No."

My eyebrows lifted in bewilderment.

"How can you not be?"

"Because if you're healed then I know that I can face anything with you at my side."

"I wish I had as much faith," I admitted.

"Do you not think it will work?" He asked, confounded.

I shook my head, "I don't want it to work."

I listened as he inhaled a shaky breath, "You'd rather leave me than having the blood work?"

With all my might, I forced a glare at him, "I'd rather die than give the vampires a reason to come after the merfolk."

His hands dropped mine and cupped my face, "And I rather die than have you fade in front of me."

My heart beat erratically in my chest at his confession. At his wild blue eyes on me and the earnest truth painted on his face

With a shaky breath I said, "If I promise you something, will you give me a promise of your own?"

Surprise marred his featured from the unexpected shift in our conversation. I could see his hesitation weighing down on him heavily.

But I needed his word.

With a curt nod from him, I said, "I'll promise you that I'll try. I'll try my hardest to stay alive and do as I must to heal my heart...but only if you promise that you'll not worry about me."

His eyes went colder than a glacier as he bit out a sharp, "No."

"Please," I begged, "just promise me that you'll focus on keeping the pack safe and let me worry about me."

"I can't and won't give you a false promise. That's not who I am," He said as he pulled away from me.

"Then be as honest as you can be," I said grabbing his hand again, refusing to lose his touch. "You have enough on your plate and I refuse to burden you."

"Burden me?" He scoffed loud enough to draw the merman's attention to us, but Aiden ignored him and Dr. Nazra's presence. "God, Tate, don't you get it?"

Baffled by his pained words, I went quiet.

"I care for you, more than I want to admit at this time," His confession stole the breathe from my very lungs and the heart from my very chest. "So, I can't promise you that I won't worry, but I'll promise that I won't smother you."

I wanted to his pull him by the material of his t-shirt and kiss him, but he leaned closer to me and kissed my forehead.

Heat blossomed over my forehead at his actions and I couldn't help but fall a little further for him.

He loves you.

Thane came with a glass in his hand and an annoyed expression on his face as Dylan strolled in behind him with a tray of food.

He must have found Dylan in the kitchen and knowing how assertive, or pushy, the Gamma can be, I'm sure he grabbed the tray and piled it with food.

Leaving my brother, an Alpha, brewing in anger.

"Tate," Dylan said with a disapproving shake of his head, "why exactly didn't you tell me that you were undergoing a blood transfusion? You know I'd be here to support you."

Aiden grabbed the tray from him set it down beside me as he began assembling a sandwich with the cutlets on the tray.

"It was...a spur of the moment decision," I clarified with a smile as I accepted the sandwich from my mate and the glass of soda from Thane.

"Nevertheless, you know if you've told the entire pack, we'd all be here to support you," He said with a stern expression.

"You shouldn't be here," Thane cut in. "The last thing my sister needs is to be crowded right now."

"It's fine, really, I don't mind the company."

"Eat," Aiden instructed, giving Thane and Dylan a warning glare.

So I did while watching the blood of the merman be extracted by a needle in his arm. From where I sat I could see the merman grinding his molars, squeezing his eyes shut and inhaling ragged breaths.

The merfolk weren't built like werewolves, so I expected he was neither accustomed to pain nor had a tolerance for it. And with a large needle in your arm, I imagine it would hurt a bit.

About ten minutes later, Dr. Nazra was carefully extracting the needle from the merman's arm and covering the spot with a pressure bandage.

She immediately placed the pint of blood in a cooler of ice before getting another juice box for the merman and some fruits from my tray.

"You might feel slightly dizzy, so you should eat something and remain sitting in that chair until I say you can move," She instructed before turning to me. "Luna, are you ready?"

"As I'll ever be," I answered as she pointed to a medical chair for me to sit in.

She reclined my chair back before she started prepping for the blood transfusion.

Aiden pulled his chair next to me and kept my right palm between both of his. Worry lines were set into features with a pucker between his brows. I could practically hear how fast his heart was beating.

"I'll be okay," I assured him.

His lips were in a flat, troubled line as he gave me no response but a comforting squeeze to my hand.

My brother's expression was also troubled as Dr. Nazra removed the blood from the ice and hooked it up to an intravenous line. She inserted the needle into the crook of my arm, directly into my blood vessel.

"Does it pain at all?" She asked.

I shook my head in response as she began running through protocol by monitoring my blood pressure, temperature and heart rate. She also ensured that I told her if I was experiencing any of the symptoms that she listed.

I didn't know if it was hyperactive imagination or not, but I could feel the blood of the merman flow into my bloodstream. Thick, warm blood rushing into the red lake of my body.

It was agonising process. The waiting. The building of my anxiety. Watching Aiden struggle to keep his patience in check.

The constant questions from him and Thane.

Are you feeling okay? Just fine.

How are you feeling now? Still fine.

'Fine' being my synonym for 'exactly the same'.

But I remembered my promise to Aiden. To try. To give it my all.

So with every ounce of faith in me, I prayed and hoped. This had to work, I was betting everything on it. For Aiden.

This blood had to be the key to putting me together again.

Two agonizing hours later, the last drops of blood entered my system.

And Dr. Nazra's heart monitor remained unchanged. Slow beeps echoed through the room, signalling my slow heart rate.

No one said a word as she removed the intravenous needle from my arm, a bruise surrounded the area where the needle was but Dr. Nazra assured me before that it was common and would disappear quickly.

But as the bruise remained, I knew for certain that the blood didn't work. For if it did, my werewolf ability would have healed it faster.

While she bandaged my arm, Dylan was the first to ask the doomed question.

"So doc, did it work?" His voice was filled with curiosity.

Her sad eyes turned to me, "No, it didn't."

A lump formed in my throat as I nodded my head curtly. My eyes were wet but I refused to shed a tear for myself. This wasn't the end, it was just the last magical solution.

There were other means to which I would be able to live for years to come. Maybe never as a werewolf, but I'll still be alive.

But would be alive mean I'll still be me? Still be living?

For what's a werewolf without her wolf? It's like a human without her soul or a mermaid without her tail.

A dark, festering crack was spreading inside of me. Dragging me into forbidden thoughts of a dreary life.

Aiden's tight grip on my hand reeled me back into the infirmary as he spoke between clenched teeth, "Did you do everything correctly."

"Of course, Alpha," She replied seriously. "I would never takes risks with our pack's Luna."

"Then why didn't it work?" He snapped angrily.

I squeezed his hand, "The same reason it doesn't work for the vampires. It's all a myth."

"But the human," Dylan pipped in with confusion. "How was he healed then?"

I shrugged, "What does it matter, he's dead now."

And I might be soon enough.

"Should we discuss a potential cardiac pacemaker?" Dr. Nazra asked after she patched me up.

I was drained of all of energy. After putting all my faith in one thing, I had little life in me left to clutch onto a false future.

"No," Aiden said firmly as he got to his feet. "Tomorrow we can talk, but right now Tate needs to rest."

Thane was quick to help my exhausted body up, but Aiden kept his grip on me firmly.

I knew his mind was probably in a restless state with my results and so I didn't push him away with my words, even though I wanted to. I wanted to tell him to I was fine on my own so he'd save himself from worrying over me...even though I desperately craved his nearness.

Some very contradicting feelings.

However, I knew he hadn't promised to stop worrying over me, I held onto his arm a little too tightly as I shook my brother off.

"We'll be fine, you should go be with Emery," I assured him.

At my mention of his mate, he didn't fight me, knowing that I needed my mate right now.

"I'll see you tomorrow," He said instead before leaving us.

"Come on, I'll help you to bed," Aiden said gently as he wrapped an arm around my waist and supported most of my weight.

Despite having fresh blood in my veins, I felt drained.

As we hobbled out of the infirmary, I turned to thank the merman, but only just noticed that he was already gone.

I couldn't find any words in me to say to Aiden. None to comfort him or myself. So our journey up the stairs and to my room was deadly silent.

As we reached my door, I realised how desperately I wanted to stay in his room again. The comfort of his soft sheets against my skin, the sea-washed mahogany and fresh waterfall scent lingering in the air and gentle sound of crashing waves outside lulling me to sleep.

But as he opened the door and led me to my bed, I torched the idea.

I barely registered him asking if I was feeling okay and if I needed anything... only nodding and shaking my head until he stepped towards the door.

"Goodnight, Tate," He whispered painfully as he walked out the door.

A sob tore me at that point. Traitorous tears spilling over my eyelids like an overflowing dam. Like a ceaseless torrent of rain during a storm.

The weight of all the hope I had put into the mer blood working came crashing down in full force. It was a hard pill to swallow after counting on it to work.

Now I was left with was a dying body and empty promises.

The thought of the pain I was going to put everyone I cared about through caused another cry to pass from my lips.

Emptiness blossomed inside of me like a well, dark and seemingly endless.

My door slammed open and I watched as the light from the hallway spilled in through my teary eyed vision.

I quickly wiped my tears away as I watched a determined Aiden stalk back inside.

He didn't ask another question as he scooped me off the bed bridal style.

"Aiden?" I questioned alarmed.

"Fuck the promise," He growled. "I can't stop my feelings for you and if ensuring you're safe and happy and is me smothering you, then so be it."

I couldn't stop the small bubble of laughter that arose to my lips as he marched us towards room. Pressing my nose to the crook of his neck, I inhaled his comforting scent, feeling at ease.

He was gently with me as he laid me on his bed and turned off the lights before sitting next to me.

"Tell me what to do, Tate. Tell me how to make this better," He pleaded in anguish as he brushed a fresh tear away from my cheek.

I shook my head, unable to come up with a solution to ease both of our pains.

"Just lay with me," I whispered as I shuffled around to make space for him.

"Are you sure?" He asked.

"It's all I need right now."

Nodding, he pulled off both of our shoes before laying down beside me, ensuring he didn't cross any invisible boundary.

But there weren't any on my part, so I lifted my hand to touch him, and when he didn't pull away, I shifted closer to him. He wrapped his arm around my waist and pulled me even closer.

I had not realised just how cold my skin was until I was pressed against his werewolf heat. My lack of blood of an efficient blood circulation stealing my natural warmth from my skin.

I could tell he wanted to ask more...say more, but he held off.

How do I tell him that I don't feel like myself? That I haven't been feeling like myself for awhile now. How do I say that I feel like a shell of my former self?

Instead, I ask something that's been rattling at the back of my head.

"Why haven't you suggested that I go home with my brother?"

His arm tightened around my waist as he let out a small growl, "One, this is your home now and secondly, why the hell would I do that?"

"So I won't get it the way. The vampires are enough of a problem."

"Precisely, they're problem and you're my mate. I don't know how I can make that any clearer to you. I don't care if you're in perfect health or not, you're still my mate and I'm not going to just shrug of that fact."

"Good, because I already told my brother that I'm never leaving," I admitted and I felt a chuckle of relief reverberate through him.

"Rest, Cupcake. Tomorrow is a new day," He whispered as he rubbed my back and lulled me to sleep.

CHAPTER 25

I awoke with a start as the remnants of a terrible nightmare faded from my memory. The bright light of the sun washed through the tall window in Aiden's room.

It ran the length of two stories and provided a most dazzling view. The clear blue water and the sandy beach calling my name. If only the deep blue beyond didn't hide any possible blood craved creature that would pull me below the surface to my death.

"Good morning, sleepyhead," Aiden chuckled as he walked from his mini office area across from the bed. His expression shifted as he looked at my frazzled state, "What's wrong?"

"Nightmare," I said on an exhaled breath as I took him in.

He was freshly clothed in a pair of jeans and a dark blue t-shirt. But what really had my heart going was his hair. Untied and still damp from his shower.

No matter how long I've known Aiden, I don't think he'll ever not make me nervous. It wasn't his blonde hair or surfer boy beauty that caused my brain to turn to mush, even though it did contribute to it. It was him; his smile, his eyes, the way he smelled.

It was the way he held himself as Alpha and yet allowed Tourmaline to place a tiara on his head for a tea party. The way he sat for two hours holding my hand and taking my mind off the blood transfusion. His perseverance and dedication to reading every old text to find a solution that may not even exist.

And I know it didn't make much sense, it didn't to me, but he made me nervous in the best way.

It was as if he saw me. Not my skin and bones or my spoken words.

No, Aiden saw deeper. He saw past the tangible aspects of myself and somehow, he seems to like what he sees.

"What was it about?" He asked as he sat next to me on the bed.

"I can't remember," I said yawning. "What time is it?"

"About eleven."

My eyes boggled out of my head, "I slept in."

"It's fine, you needed the rest."

"But Emery and Thane-"

"Are fine. They're with the others in the backyard."

I dragged my hands up my face and into my hair as I shake my head, "Last night felt like a bad dream. As if it didn't really happen."

Taking one of my hands in his, he said, "You don't have to worry about it. I'll see that every medical thing is taken care of."

"If you're trying to bribe me into making me like you any more, then I don't know if that's possible," I admitted as I turned my gaze away from his ever perceptive eyes.

The faint hitch in his breathing was the only sign that my words affected him.

Until he turned my hand and lifted it to his mouth. Gently brushing his warm lips against the inside of my wrist.

"Good to know," His breathed into my skin, causing goose-bumps to rise along my arms.

"S-should we go meet Dr. Nazra now, for a check up?" I stammered, willing my brain to form coherent sentences.

He nodded before immediately shaking his head, "Wait, before we go, I wanted to ask you something."

I gestured with a tilt of my head for him to go on.

"I don't want you to be alone at anytime from now."

Rolling my eyes, I asked, "Where would I possibly go? Plus you already have Kai shadowing me when you're not around."

He scratched the back of his head as his eyes focused on my hands, avoiding my gaze.

Maybe I made him just as nervous as he made me.

"Kai's the best person to protect you and I trust him. But there's still a large gap of time when you're on your own."

"I'm not letting you put a guard in the bathroom," I warned.

He snorted, "Trust me when I say I don't want that for you either."

"So then what are you talking about?"

"You should sleep here."

My eyes widened as his unexpected words shocked the my train of thought out of me.

"Your room?"

"Yes."

"Would I sleep on the couch?"

"No, you'll sleep right here," He said patting the bed we sat on.

"So you'll sleep on the couch?" My voice went up an octave above its usual frequency, no doubt betraying my nervous excitement.

He smirked with a shrug, "I don't mind the couch, but it's up to you."

"It's your room, I can't put you out!"

"You're not, I rather be in the same room with you in case anything were to happen."

Warmth blossom through me at his concern. Unwarranted, but welcomed nonetheless.

"I'm not going to make you sleep on the couch," I decided as my eyes lowered to his lips.

His smirk deepened to a full grin, "Good, because it would be a shame to not put this large bed to use."

Something about the tone he used when he said those words made it sound as if he was implying something else.

"So I guess I'm moving in," My fingers fiddled with the bed-sheets, a nervous tick.

"And you're welcome to everything in here...except my stash of chocolate cake in the mini fridge."

My eyes flashed up to his dead serious expression and I threw my head back into in a fit of laughter. Aiden's deep laughter soaked into my like a caress.

As my laughter died down, warmth blossomed in my stomach like hot liquid.

His mouth was on mine and his hand was in my hair before I either of us could have said another word. His lips were soft and gentle. Setting a languid pace as he coaxed my mouth open.

I tasted the bitterness of his morning coffee on his lips. The caffeine wasn't send any jolts to my body the way his touch was.

Desperate to crawl into him, I buried my hands in his hair, feeling the cold damp strands between my fingers.

A deep, almost moaning, growl passed from Aiden's lips to my body. His left hand moved from my hair to my neck while his other curved around my waist and pulled me to his lap.

Natural instinct had me wrapping my legs around his waist as his fingers lowered to my hip before slipping under my t-shirt.

Tingles shot up my spin as my skin flushed from his touch and his warmth.

Aiden was always so warm. Like the sunshine while you were in the water down on the beach.

With gentle precission, he rubbed slow circles onto my back, causing my fingers to tighten their hold in his hair.

He touched me with a kind of reverence. His lips moving from mine to make its way to my jaw and down my neck. A prayer on his lips that whispered the name of a false god.

"Tate," He moaned with a lingering kiss on my collarbone before pulling back.

I knew this is where our session was going to end, so I quickly silenced him with a last kiss to his lips before jumping to my feet and heading for the stairs.

"Be careful!" He called after me seriously but I could hear the amusement in his voice.

After a shower, I startes gathering a few of my belongings into a bag. Even though I didn't arrive with much nor have I been here long, I've accumulated quite a bit.

A task better left until later, I decided.

When I headed to Dr. Nazra's office, Aiden was already there discussing pacemakers.

My mate turned to me with a secretive smirk and a glass of orange juice. Mental images of being on his lap caused a red blush to heat my cheeks.

"Luna," She greeted me with a comforting smile. "How are you feeling today? You look a bit flushed."

"Not any different, just a bit tired." I narrowed my eyes at Aiden as he held on his laughter behind Nazra's back.

As she ushered me into a chair, she brought out her equipment to run a few tests.

"It must be from all the metal exertion you had yesterday," She answered before turning my arm to see the dark bruise of where the needle was yesterday.

A physical sign that the mermaid blood had not worked, or else it would have healed.

While she ran through a few test to ensure my body was reacting to the blood transfusion well, Aiden was drilling her with questions.

I didn't have it in me to listen to the discussion. The conversation of treatments to prevent me dying only my heart sink and my throat close up.

With all my might, I'll keep my promise and try to live. But I trusted Aiden enough to ask all the right questions while I wrap the fact that I'll probably never shift again, around my head.

It wasn't something that was easily digest. Not being able to be yourself. To roam around freely in my true nature.

To have the feeling of the soft earth beneath my paw or the wind between my fur. The echo of other creatures running alongside my wolf. My heart racing with life instead of reminding me that I had to slow down because of the jolts of pain.

For a split second the idea of being immortalized into a vampire crossed my mind. And for that split second I felt completely and utterly disgusted with myself.

While their strengths emulated those of a werewolf, their trickster minds and cunning lifestyle was one I would never resign myself to.

I'd never feast on innocent humans to satisfy a sinister crave. And I most definitely would not give up the glorious sunshine to find comfort in the moon.

The Moon Goddess herself would turn off her light before watching her child turn into something other.

"Your vitals are looking good, no sign of any allergic reaction to the blood, but your blood count has increased because of it which is good. Hopefully you'll feel a bit warmer now," Dr. Nazra explained as she pulled me out of my reverie.

I nodded, noting that there wasn't any exceptionally good news.

"Is there anything else I'll need to do today?" I asked.

She shook her head before asking, "Not unless you'd like to discuss the pacemaker process. I was planing on calling Dr. Adler from your brother's pack so we can find a specialist."

"We're thinking on having a human operate and then wiping their memory with a plant that your old pack has," Aiden clarified.

The plant in question was only used during the ritual where my brother found Emery. While it does erase the memory of humans, it only clears their last twenty-four hours.

So the doctor consultation and operation had to be done all within a day. I wondered how we were going to do that.

"Let's just all take a break today," I sighed. "Yesterday was intense and I think we can pick this up back tomorrow."

"Cupcake-"

"Please," I pleaded, "I want to be apart of this conversation, but I just want us all to take a day."

His eyes softened and he nodded, "Okay, but tomorrow we start sorting through the next steps."

Dr. Nazra didn't seem as if she was going to take a break today though. After all there weren't patients in her infirmary to attend to, so I suppose she'd prefer to get buried in what she likes best - the medical practise.

"Don't forget to take a break Nazra," I reminded her with a smile as I dragged Aiden out the door behind me.

Once we were in the hallway, he dropped a kiss on my head, "I have a few things to take care of today, but Emery and Calypso are in the backyard. Tourm is doing her lessons for the day and I think your brother went out to the beach with Rick and Dylan."

"Oh, is there anything you need help with?" I asked with concern.

He shook his head, "Just needed to follow up on a few books I've been searching for on the internet."

I took his hands in mine and ran my palms up to his shoulders, "Tell me if you need help, okay? I don't want to be a bur-"

"You aren't and you'll never be," He said sternly. "Now get your beautiful self out of here before we rehash what happened this morning."

Smirking, I brushed a strand of his hair away from his eyes, "Are you trying to make me stay or leave?"

"Both," He placed his finger under my chin and tipped my head up to brush his lips against mine.

With reluctance, he pulled away and turned my shoulders so that I was facing the way to the staircase that led downstairs.

Emery and Calypso were both lounging outside in chaise lounge when I found them.

"Tate!" Emery gasped before rushing to her feet and pulling me into her arms.

Calypso was right behind her as they peppered me with questions.

"Are you okay?"

"How are you feeling?"

"Thane said it didn't work."

"Do you know why it didn't work?"

"Guys," I chuckled with my hands ups, "slow down."

Gesturing them back to their seats, I took the other chaise next to Calypso.

Before I could explain everything that I knew, a pack member showed up with a loaded tray of food and Kai trailing behind her.

"Luna," the pack member greeted as he set the tray before me. "Alpha Aiden requested that I bring you breakfast."

"Thank you," I said earnestly, feeling horrible that Aiden disrupted the wolf's day to bring me food.

I was a Luna, but I was far from being high handed.

The tray had an assortment of dishes. A bowl of steel-cut oatmeal topped with fruit and walnuts was the largest with a bowl of Cheerios and another with sunflower seeds. A mug of steeping tea accompanied the food with a sticky note attached.

'Eat. -A.'

If only I could mindlink him, I'd let him know that I preferred chocolate waffles with coffee that was as strong as the one I tasted on his lips this morning.

But unfortunately we haven't quite reached that stage yet.

I'm also assuming the healthy looking food was all good for the heart.

Kai patted my head in the affectionate way that he does, "Morning Luna, I'm glad to see that you're looking good today."

I grinned up at Kai, who's become a good friend of mine, "Thanks Kai. Where'a that mate of yours?"

"He's helping Aiden in the library, but I'm just here to protect and serve," He said with a little bow as he backed away from us and pulled out headphones from his pocket. "So you guys can have your girl time without me listening," He explained.

I nodded to him appreciation before turning to Calypso and Emery.

They both gave me knowing smiles as they gestured towards the plate.

"Anyways," I started before explaining the blood transfusion and my bad luck striking again.

Emery went into full doctor mode, but she apparently already met with Dr. Nazra this morning and discussed everything. She tried to find a reason for why it didn't work, but she wasn't getting very far.

It didn't work.

As for the whys and hows, I don't know if we'll ever have answers. Not unless Aiden can weasel out an answer from his research.

If the blood theory wasn't spoken and passed down orally through generations, then there had to be some record of it in text right? At least I hoped so.

There's only been brief mentions of it in a couple of Aiden's books, but no answer. Just questions that we were already asking.

"How's the baby?" I refocused the discussion on Emery and it didn't go unnoticed as she shook her head at me. But nonetheless, appeased me.

"He's doing great, the morning sickness is finally over. Honestly, thank goodness for five month pregnancies with wolf babies. I have no idea how humans get through nine," She rubbed her little bump affectionately.

Calypso suddenly seemed withdrawn. A dark cloud of emotion causing her expression to become sorrowful. Mournful even. She wrapped her arms around her waist and squeezed her eyes shut.

Emery noticed as well as we both sat up.

"Caly?" I asked gently placed my hand on her arm.

She blinked her eyes open in surprise as if not realising that she had withdrawn.

"Yes?" She shook her head as she straightened her spine. "I was just..." Words seemed to fail her as her eyes grew wet.

"Hey, hey. You don't have to explain," I assured her as I sat next to her on her chair and Emery followed suit, wrapping her arms around her.

Calypso gave me a grateful smile but turned to Emery, "A child is a blessing, cherish it and congratulations."

"Thank you, that means a lot to me," Emery squeezed her hand.

"I haven't spoken about this in a while," Calypso started as her eyes drifted to the open sea, "but I lost my baby over a year ago. Miscarriage."

"Oh Cal," I pulled her into a fierce hug, not able to form enough words for comfort, for I know they'll never be enough.

"It's okay, I'm fine now," She assured me with a little laugh as she brushed a stray tear away. "Sometimes I just get a bit overcome with emotions when I think about what could have been.

"It happened early on in the pregnancy, but Rick and I had been trying for a long while. When it happened, we were both so happy, so grateful...and then just like that our baby was gone. It got between us for awhile, but Rick wouldn't let me grieve alone. He'd give me the moon and stars if I asked for it."

My heart broke for Calypso and Rick, to want something so much and then have it stolen away from you. Not something materialistic, but rather a part of them. Building a family. Creating a tiny human to call their own. That was a great pain that I knew I could never understand.

"For a long time it hurt to even think of trying again," She touched her stomach. "I told myself that it happened for a reason. There's no place for a baby in the castle now. Not when there are vampires lurking around. So we decided to hold off on a family for now."

The weight of the situation with the vampires increased in size by Caly's pain. It wasn't just the merfolk who were affected by the bloodsuckers, it was everyone in the pack.

By looking around the castle, anyone can see that there's a lack of children running around. No one younger than Tourmaline.

Everyone had to put their lives on pause, for who knew how long, until this was sorted out.

A wave of fierce and powerful determination took seed inside of me. The kindling from a spark.

For Calypso and everyone else who had to suffer at the hands of the vampires were going to get their lives back.

Even if I had to do it with a pacemaker in my chest, I was going to fight for them.

Gathering her hands in my own, I made an oath to her.

Not a promise or empty words.

"I will find a way to either get rid of them or have them leave us alone. That is my oath to you as Luna," I swore.

The tiniest bit of light sparked in her eye and I could see her belief in me.

And that was all that I needed to know that I'll try my damn hardest for her and our entire pack.

CHAPTER 26

I t's been a few weeks since Thane and Emery reluctantly left to go back to their home. The promise of my heart problems being kept between us were our parting words.

Since then, we've been planning my surgery and I've been spiralling.

Dr. Nazra had me on a special diet to mitigate any further damage to my heart. She and Aiden have also had me on a lockdown.

I wasn't to exert myself and I had to get frequent check-ups.

But it was neither the bland food nor their acts of caring that left me feeling like there was a bottom-less pit in my stomach.

Feeling sick almost all the time and experiencing shortness of breath dragged me to a dark place. I imagined that it would be hard for a sufficiently capable wolf to go from running miles and training to being confined to a human body and bed rest.

Some days I could feel my fur itching beneath my skin and heat of wolf's body pushing me to just shift.

I was the daughter of an Alpha and the Luna of the Oaks Pack, I couldn't be sitting around all day while my pack strategize and trained around the clock.

Letting them protect me wasn't the sign of a leader, but of a dictator. If they had to trudge through this thick mud that was finding a way to defeat the vamps, then I was going to get dirty as well.

Finding ways to be as strong in human form was a challenge, however, necessary. Once I had the pacemaker in my chest, I won't be able to shift again.

And maybe that thought scared me more than I'd like it too.

For now, though, I had some time. However little it may be.

I didn't know if it was just my bad luck or a rare stroke of good luck, but there's to be a wait until I could have the surgery done.

One, we still needed to get a doctor that was good enough for Aiden and two, we had to acquire quiet a lot of O negative blood for the surgery.

Not a single wolf in the pack had O negative, so we were required to seek it through the human blood bank. Of course, there was a waitlist for the rare blood type.

So, it was just a matter of time.

Until then, I had a chance to shift into my wolf. Aiden wasn't having it, but after a few sneaky kisses I managed to get him to relent.

However, a deal is only as good as a compromise and his ask was for us to go down to the lighthouse.

There was a field where the lighthouse stood and no human eyes to catch the sight of our wolves.

Plus, it was close enough to the castle.

Tourmaline insisted she joined us and then the ball kept rolling until Rick, Calypso, Matt and Kai all decided to have a picnic.

Rick and Calypso recently converted a campervan which they dying to try out, so now was a good a time as any. Matt and Kai took a jeep loaded bikes, at the behest of Tourmaline while Aiden drove one of his cars down.

"So, are you two going to get married now?" Tourmaline asked from the backseat.

Aiden's hand squeezed my own from where our hands were entertained on my lap.

I turned and caught her excited grin while my heart beat with anticipation at Aiden's response.

A traditional human marriage was customary among were-wolves, but I had no idea how the Oaks Pack did it.

"Tourm," Aiden said with a slight warning in his tone.

"But you love Tate, don't you Dad? And she has to stay with us forever."

Her eyebrows creased as if the thought that Aiden would refute her words troubled her greatly. I could also tell from Aiden's pressed thin lips that this interrogation from his niece wasn't one he wanted to participate in.

So, I took the plunge and saved them both, "You know I'm never going anywhere. Who will invite me to tea parties if I leave?"

With that Tourmaline was placated as she grinned brightly before diverting into discussions about her next soirée.

In the few minutes it took to get to the lighthouse, there were already a few wolves there who ran the perimeter to check for any bloodsuckers. With a bow to their Alpha, they spread out along the edges of the open field that lead to the beach.

Since there weren't any motion detection device down here, going in the water would be a miscalculated risk.

Not unlike going to the water at the castle.

When I stepped out of the car, I basked in the gloriously bright sunshine that was uninhabited by clouds or buildings. Just the open sky, the salty sea breeze and warmth on my skin.

My eyes were closed and my face lifted towards the golden light when I felt the piercing and heated gaze on my face.

Dipping my head away from the blinding sun and opening my eyes, I saw Aiden staring at me in awe.

"Go," He gestured towards the lighthouse, "I'll get Tourmaline settled."

I shook my head with a smile, "A few minutes to help wouldn't kill me."

Aiden sent me a disapproving look as I picked up Tourmaline in my arms along with a basket.

She giggled her melodious tune, made even sweeter by the magical notes of her being a mermaid. A fact never forgotten by her enchanted pink hair.

"Tate, are you going to shift into your wolf?" She asked excitedly while curling her fingers around my brown hair.

I nodded with a smile, "Though I'd much rather be a mermaid."

She lit up at my words, a compliment of sorts.

"Then you'd never have to hold your breath or need Dad to help you swim," She covered her mouth as she giggled at my lack of swimming abilities.

I couldn't help but laugh along with her because she couldn't be closer to the truth.

As I set her on her feet and spread a picnic blanket for her, she began animatedly explaining how other-worldly the undersea was.

Her words lacked no detail as I pictured myself in the deep blue. Corals, shells and seaweed littering the sand floors. Fishes, turtles and crustaceans breathing life into the world as they swam around like a busy main street. The merfolk houses built of volcanic rocks and obsidian

Tourmaline also spoke of an abandoned castle, left to the cold sea when her mother and their people had to flee. A palace carved from a large formation of quartz crystal. A gem of the sea that is buried away from human eye. Lost as the city of Atlantis.

It was embellished with pearls, corals and gemstones. Surrounded by underwater sea stacks that were carved into homes for the lower courts. A palace that once had many inhabitants, but now echoed with the memories of the ghosts that resided there.

From what I could tell, the merfolk had an affinity for gemstones, seeing as both Tourmaline and her mother Amethyst were named after beautiful stones.

What troubled me most was Tourmaline never having been to her ancestral home. Not once stepping foot into the castle as the Princess, now Queen, of the sea. All her words being passed down from the description and fond memories of the older merfolk. None her own.

Aiden's heavy gaze had me shifting my eyes away from Tourmaline to over her shoulder. Her uncle was trying very hard to hide his rare smile from his face. Happiness coated his face, but his tense muscles and weighted shoulders told another story.

The pain of our lives still hung over our heads like a sharpened sword, waiting to be lowered and put to use.

I wanted him to be happy. I wanted everyone here to take their minds off reality and just be content, even if just for today.

He finished getting the bikes out of Calypso and Rick's van before joining us on the picnic blanket. Tourmaline was already once seaweed sandwich in.

When he sat down, I was already passing him a bowl of fruits and Tourm handing him a bottle of iced tea, as if we've done this a million times before.

"What were my two girls talking about?" Aiden asked innocently while causing my heart jump with life.

"Nothing," Tourm said as she looked at me with a mischievous smile.

Aiden reached over and ruffled her hair in response, causing her to screech in delight and bat his hand away in a mock fight.

When he turned to me his eyes were assessing me, "How are you feeling?"

"Fine," I rolled my eyes but appreciated his concern. "I'm feeling good today."

My words or my facial expression must have convinced him because he nodded towards the lighthouse where the others were headed to shift.

"Go, I'll stay with Tourm," He said encouragingly.

I didn't need to be told again as I got to my feet as the others came from the other side of the lighthouse in their wolf form.

Majestic creatures born from our Moon Goddess.

Adrenaline pumped through my veins, quickening my steps as I rounded the building and stripped out of my clothing.

The familiar crack of bones made my muscles sag in relaxation as my wild, uninhabited nature awoke after what felt like a long slumber.

Dark grey fur sprouted from my skin and the teeth in my mouth sharpened to canines while my nose lengthened to a snout.

It was a welcomed diversion from reality.

The thick fur warmed my cold skin as I trooped happily back to the field and joined my fellow wolves. Calypso's fur was an amber tone, almost gold, while her mate's was red with a streak of light grey on his left side. Kai sported beige fur with his back and the tuft of his ear shaded in an earthy brown while Matt was a tricolour of different browns in an almost ombré pattern.

Each uniquely identifiable, but I still lacked the ability to communicate with them. A challenge that could only be overcome when Aiden and I mate.

A task yet to be done, but which I was surprised hadn't happened yet. When mates find it each other, it's an instantaneous connection. The deed was done in a week's time at most.

Yes, we had our differences at the beginning and then there was the age thing Aiden wasn't comfortable with, we were on better terms now. In fact, the way he wraps me in his arms every night and wakes me up with a kiss and a cup of juice was enough for me to think that were in a good place.

A really good place.

Given that my heart always sped up whenever I was with him or how my blood heated when he brushed his fingers against my skin and not to mention my mind losing all function when he turned those blue eyes on me.

I could drown a thousand deaths in those ocean eyes of his and he can resurrect me each time with his lips.

Those same eyes tracked me as I crossed the field and joined the other wolves.

My chest gave me a slight discomfort and my breathing was already becoming laboured, but I tried to ignore my heart and control my breaths.

A simple task like shifting wasn't going to best me. I refused to let it.

So, with a controlled expression and light steps, I ran around the wolves. The pent-up energy my wolf was used to exerting everyday was too charged. My footsteps hurried and the need to run ahead burning within me.

I was training with the pack, but after the blood transfusion didn't work, Aiden had me under castle arrest.

No training in human form and definitely not in wolf form.

If a vampire were to attack, I'd be as helpless as a human. Well, a human might be able to outrun me given that they wouldn't be out of breath in mere seconds.

Tourm got on her bike and I slowed my speed as she rode alongside my wolf. Both of us doing laps around the field.

Every now and again she'd reach her little hand out and brush it along my fur, marvelling and the giant creature before her.

She was always brave, never fearing anything, especially the wolves. Tourmaline was, after all, part werewolf herself.

About five laps in, the pain in my chest amounted into an unbearable burning like that of a block of ice attached to my skin. I slowed my pace, letting Tourmaline get ahead of me as she began chasing Kai and Matt around.

My head spun and I pushed my lungs to take in as much air as possible in hastened gulps. But it felt like I couldn't get it into my body fast enough. I felt my body sway and ensured I was nowhere near Tourmaline. My legs buckled under me faster than I could think and my body crashed into the earth.

A whimper escaped my mouth in a wolfish tone as I curled up on myself. The pain unendurable and excruciating.

I felt like retching as my head spun. Dizzying circles made the sky shift in odd angles from my peripheral.

Squeezing my eyes shut, I heard Aiden's yell from across the field. His scent getting closer and closer as his hammering foot-steps ate up the dirt.

I didn't dare open my eyes, afraid the spinning would get worst. Afraid I'll see the pity and unbridled anger on Aiden's face.

Afraid he'll tell me about how much I should be careful and not prance around a field in my condition.

One day. One day was all I asked for.

"Tate? Tate open your eyes for me, Cupcake," The pleading in his voice had me doing as he asked.

Concern was mostly visible on his face, but the scorching anger was in his eyes.

Before he could spew a lecture at me, Tourm was there with a bottle of water. Aiden helped me get it into my mouth as I tried to catch my breath. A task that proved to be more difficult than I would have ever thought.

Aiden placed his fingers on my pulse, counting in his head the number of times my heart beat.

"Should I call Dr. Nazra?" Calypso's concern voice travelled over to me and I turned to see that they were all rushing towards us, now in human form.

I shook my head gruffly and Aiden's eyes narrowed on me, but he didn't contradict me.

"You need to shift," He said instead as he got to his feet.

His hands went to my sides, helping me rise, but my wolf was much bigger than his human form. Although, his strength was unbound.

My legs were sluggish as he guided me back towards the light-house where my clothes were discarded.

When he stayed put on the other side of the lighthouse with me, I gestured my head for him to go but he shook his own.

"I'm not leaving you in your condition."

Condition. I detested the word.

It held no good connotations. Only solidifying the fact that I wasn't okay. My condition.

The words stuck to my skin like an icky slime, making me uncomfortable and disgusted with my own person.

Certainly, it doesn't help with my self-confidence either. Which further makes me annoyed with his stubbornness as he stood there.

I screamed in my mind at him to turn around, but of course he couldn't hear me. So, I screamed again, 'I wish you'd like me in spite of my condition and not because of.'

It wasn't as if he wanted me sick, not at all, but how was sure that what he felt wasn't entirely out of pity? Seemingly, it was odd to consider that given that we'd admitted as much as liking each other. And maybe I was pessimistic because I always thought the worst.

Sometimes the worst was always better than a disguised lie.

Pushing my snout against his shoulder, he finally relented and turned away from me, but he remained rooted to the spot.

"You shouldn't have been running around like that, Tate," He started as I shifted back into my human form.

Vulnerability gripped me with its frightening claws as I scrambled to throw my clothes on. The act of being naked around your mate, even if he's not looking at you, was an intimacy that we haven't explored yet. And because of that, my breathing became even more laboured with the fear of my own body.

An oddity considering werewolves were shameless with their state of nudity when needing to shift at a moment's notice.

When I was dressed, Aiden turned around with his mouth open, no doubt about to pick an argument with me.

But his mouth snapped closed as he crossed the distance that separated us. His capricious behaviour had me off-kilter as the anger washed away from his face.

"Please," I detected the fear in voice. A strange gravely sound that almost brought me to my knees. "Please, don't scare me like that again."

I was nodding without thought as he cupped my cheeks, unable to form a coherent thought.

"How are you feeling? Is your chest still paining?" His eyes searched my own for the answer.

"I'm fin-"

"Don't say fine," He shook his head. "Not to me."

That caused me to smile, "My chest is sore and my head is still spinning, but I could breathe."

He nodded, "We should get you back home."

"Aiden, no. I'll just rest, let Tourmaline have some time to play. She's been to confined in the castle."

He was uncertain, his muscles tense as he seemed unsure of what to do.

"I'll be good once I sit down and eat something," I reassured him.

"Are you certain?" He brushed my hair away from my face.

"Positive."

Aiden still kept his eyes on me as he took my hand and led us back to the picnic blanket, worried that I might fall over.

Once I was sat, he piled me with all the nutritional snacks he packed. Meaning, everything that was good for my heart.

If only it could prevent what has already happened.

By the time my head stopped spinning in circles, everyone was riding around on their bikes. The guards still stationed on the perimeter on high alert.

There weren't any vampire activity since our run in with the French bloodsucker in the human town, and that gave me a sense of foreboding that something bad was about to happen.

Either they were waiting to attack us for information or they building an army to steal the merfolk. Whichever it was, it wouldn't end without blood being spilt.

I watched as Aiden raced Tourmaline around, her little legs trying to peddle faster than her uncle. And he let her win each time.

If something were to happen to me, at least he'll have Tourmaline. They'll have each other. My only reprieve in the situation.

Rick was peddling around with Calypso, both seemingly happy while covering the pain of their lost child. I don't know what their plans looked like in the future, but I only wanted them to be happy.

Matt and Kai were also on their bikes, but they off to the side in a silent debate. I could tell from their expression that they were arguing through their mind link.

I shifted my eyes away from them, not wanting to be a spectacle at their private conversation.

The only person missing was Dylan.

Apparently, the cars in the garage needed their monthly check-up, a job that Matt usually deals with, but since our car had died on us when I returned from visiting my family's pack, Dylan was adamant on running this month's check. He alluded to the issue being Matt's fault for not ensuring the cars were all properly charged.

Kai didn't take too much liking to the accusation of his mate.

The tension between them was usually intense, but seemed to rub Kai the wrong way. I wondered if Kai and Matt's argument was about that.

Aiden hadn't mentioned anything, but there's a silent conflict between Kai and Dylan. I noticed it the moment I stepped into a room with the two of them.

I just couldn't figure out why.

Sneakily, I walked over to the tall lighthouse, glad to see that the steps were intact. I gently walked up the winding steps, Aiden's voice in my head telling me not to walk too quickly.

When I made it to the top, I found a giant lightbulb at the centre and windowpanes lining the walls, creating a panoramic view. It was breath taking.

From up here, I was at the height of the seagulls as they stalked their prey in the water. The ocean stretched out as the deep blue met the bright sky. Aiden and the others were tiny dots in the field.

But one person was missing from our entourage.

I smelt him before I saw him.

Turning around, Kai gave me an embarrassed smile as he reached the top.

"Busted," I tsked.

He held up his hands in surrender, "I'm at the mercy of my Alpha. He just wants you to be safe."

"I know," I answered as I turned back to look out at the ocean, leaning against the railing. "I don't mean to worry him; I just hate sitting around for long."

He patted my head as he stood beside me, "Trust me, he'd still worry if you were sitting in the castle doing the most mundane task."

"He shouldn't."

"That won't stop him."

"And what about him? I don't suppose I could ask you to instead keep him safe?"

"I'm afraid I won't be able to split myself in half," He gave me a smile. "Plus, I rather shadow you. Aiden can get snappy when he's annoyed."

My brows furrowed, "Is he often annoyed?"

"He used to be more often, before he met you," He informed me with a knowing expression.

My cheeks turned scarlet at the admission. Without knowing Aiden before I met him, I can't compare his behaviour.

From the stories I heard, the ones that gave him his nickname of Alpha Dickhead, I was perplexed on how he was that person. Aiden was far from the ruthless leader that everyone whispered about.

Needing the conversation off of myself, I decided to push my luck.

"Kai, can I ask you something?" I turned to him.

He must have assumed I meant something about Aiden, because he nodded immediately, "Of course."

I twisted my fingers together as I asked, "What's up between you and Dylan?"

Kai's expression immediately darkened like storm clouds rolling in as he hunched against the railing and kept his eyes on the ocean. His jaw was clenched and I could the muscles on his neck straining as he kept himself in check.

"I shouldn't have asked," I decided but he shook his head.

"No... it's fine," He answered before inhaling deeply. "I just forgot that you haven't been in the pack that long."

I placed my hand on his shoulder in support, "You don't have to tell me if you don't want to."

He didn't say anything as he scrubbed his hands down his face and said, "I was the Gamma before Dylan."

My eyes sprang open widely as I stood there frozen in shock. Of all the things I expected him to say, that wasn't one of them.

Before I could ask more, he turned to me with a sombre expression, "That's all I'm willing to discuss."

I nodded respectfully, but my mind was wheeling around with so many questions.

The main one being: What happened for Dylan to get the title?

CHAPTER 27

C hapter 26 Summary Recap: While Tate awaits receiving blood to undergo a heart operation, Aiden takes her and the rest of the crew to the lighthouse. There, Tate gets to finally shift into her wolf. This doesn't last for long as the energy spent on transforming and running around leave her spent and quickly out of breath. While she's shifted back to her human form and goes into the lighthouse, Aiden orders Kai to keep an eye on her. During there conversation it is revealed that Kai was the Gamma of the Oaks Pack before Dylan claimed the title. Kai refuses to speak further on the subject, leaving Tate with questions of what happened in the past.

Sitting across the table from Kai made the questions in my head bounce back to life.

Kai was the Gamma of the Oaks Pack before Dylan. That sentence in itself made no reasonable sense.

For starters, I don't believe Aiden would have permitted a challenge against his Gamma. However, if Kai accepted the challenge in the name of pride and honour, then the possibility of him losing the fight would be next to none existent.

Not unless his opponent was a Gamma from another pack or someone of higher ranking. There are a rare few that might be able to best the greatest warrior of a pack, but Dylan didn't strike me as one of them.

He was great on the field, sure, but I've also seen Kai fight. Kai's technique was almost innate. He moved with the grace of a swan, the agility of a hummingbird but the ferocity of an eagle. Kai's footwork was unmatched in the pack while Dylan's tactics can be predictable at times.

So, that begs the questions: What happened and why has been kept a secret?

Kai refused to answer my questions, going as far as keeping a wide berth between us whenever he's shadowing me, in the days since he revealed that secret.

And I get it. It's his secret to tell, which is why I haven't asked again or questioned anyone else about it.

But since two and two weren't adding up to four, I had to figure it out. If only to put my mind at ease.

Turning to Aiden, I noticed that he's left his plate untouched. A dark, troubling shadow shrouded his features in a menacing edge.

My blood may be low, but he was the cold one today.

"Aiden?" I placed my hand on his arm, startling him back to reality.

"Hmm?" He murmured expectantly, as if he didn't hear what I said.

"Are you okay?"

If smiles were a product, then the one he gave me was a cheap knock-off brand sold for an inadequate amount. Too tight and not reaching his eyes.

"Distracted is all," He answered before getting to his feet. "I'm heading out to train the others, but I'll see you later."

A forehead kiss later and he was nearly bolting from the room.

Tourmaline shared my same troubled expression as her uncle left the room, but she simply stole the cinnamon roll from his plate.

I moved to follow him, my concern growing, but Calypso stopped me as she grabbed my elbow.

"He didn't tell you, did he?" She asked with concern.

My heart stammered in my chest, causing a pinch of pain to ignite. Biting down the torturous inferno, I said, "What do you mean?"

Caly seemed unsure of herself, wondering if she should tell me what Aiden hadn't. Quiet frankly I was surprised there was something he refused to share yet again. Especially after assuring me that he'd tell me things from now.

Everyone around our table seemed uncomfortable, a bit afraid and weary about what Calypso was about to say. Their eyes darting back and forth at each other. The pain in my chest became more pronounced as I waited with baited breath.

When no one at the table advised her against it, she spilled the beans.

"Today's the anniversary of his parents' death."

My eyebrows shot up in surprise and the unabashed guilt surged forward at not knowing. How could I have been so obtuse to miss the signs that Aiden's mood became darker since yesterday? How could I have not known to be there for him when he needed me most.

Just as he's always there for me.

"Thank you, for telling me," I said, my voice monotonous as I got to my feet. Fully intending to find Aiden and give him whatever comfort I could.

"Wait," Calypso stopped me again, "you should know that he's never in a good mood on this day of the year. Alpha Aiden's mood only declines as the day move forward and I'm afraid that he can be harsh without meaning too."

My lack of knowledge on his temperance made a chill set into my veins. I could never be afraid of Aiden, but I was worried I would do the wrong thing which could set him off. And if he said something to me that was uncalled for, I'd fear that he'd only make himself feel worst.

"You don't think I should go after him," I whispered, a clash of emotions at war inside of me.

She shook her head with a sad smile, "I'd never tell you that. If it were Rick, I'd never leave his side unless he asked. But I don't want you to go in blindsided either."

I grabbed her hand in my own and gave it a thankful squeeze, knowing that I owe this woman a lot more than she would expect.

"Leave, Tourmaline with us," Matt said. "We'll watch over her while you ensure Aiden doesn't bite someone's head off."

Tourm's eyes sparkle to life, "Matt, can you teach me the guitar? Pleaseee."

She gave him her best puppy dog face and I knew that she was perfectly content for the day.

I slowed my steps as I walked towards the training field, second guessing myself on what to say to Aiden if we're in the field surrounded by the pack.

He wasn't in bed this morning when I awoke, but I had dismissed it to him being an early riser. I should have known something was up because since I moved into his room he's never left until I was awake and he was sure I was okay.

Yet, this morning when he'd said barely any words to me, I didn't think far enough to see him suffering in silence.

At the field, he was nowhere around.

Spotting Dylan, I waved him over.

"Where's Aiden?" I questioned.

The Gamma shrugged, "He was supposed to be here after breakfast, but he hasn't arrived yet. Although, I'm sort of glad or else he would be busting my chops about now." He grimaced at the thought of it, only solidifying Calypso's description of his dark mood today.

"He lost his parents Dyl," I said more to myself than him.

"Yeah, I know," He sighed as he grabbed my shoulder and I tensed under his touch. "But you shouldn't look for him, he's never in a good mood."

He must have felt my anxiety as he dropped his hand and gave me an assessing expression as I said, "Aiden's my mate."

"More reason he wouldn't want you with him."

"He's never hurt me and I'd never leave him to hurt on his own."

Dylan's eyes softened as he nodded, "You're right, I just don't want to see either of you accidentally hurt each other."

"We won't. I won't let us," I replied, feeling at ease when he offered me an encouraging smile.

"You're right," He relinquished. "Go find him, maybe you're the antidote he's needed to help calm him."

I nodded as I took a step away from him before stopping and letting out a sigh, "I'm sorry. I didn't mean to go off on you."

Shrugging he said, "It's okay. He's stressed out, so I can only assume that it's affecting you through the mate bond."

With a grateful smile, I waved before heading back.

I couldn't help but be troubled by the sinking feeling in my stomach when I was with Dylan. Knowing that Kai's vague explanation had me choosing sides when there wasn't one to pick.

I still didn't know the full story, so putting walls up against either of them was silly. Especially since Aiden trusted both of them.

The need for power from Dylan could have just been that, needing power. Not particularly in a negative light either. Wolves aren't always satisfied being under the control of a few and wanting to better oneself in the pack was nothing new. Nor was it a reason for me to distrust either of them.

A fight was conducted and the winner was given the title. Something that occurred way before I even met the pack.

Kai's disdain for Dylan was also justifiable. No one liked being bested. Especially not a Gamma wolf.

I used to trust my gut. But that was before. Before, when I trusted that I'd be healed by Emery and everything would be fine.

After, my faith diminished into the ashes of a dead flame.

Shaking my head, I forced the thoughts aside, knowing it wasn't a necessary concern. Not when my mate was hurting and hiding and we had vampires threatening our pack's survival.

Aiden was where I thought he'd be, buried in the ancient novels of the 'mythical' creatures of the world in the castle's library. Head bent low, brows troubled, lips pursed, hair tousled...but his eyes were unfocused.

The bright blues were ashy, dull of colour. Dark circles rimmed the underside of his eyes, making it appear sunken into his skull.

"Aiden?" I whispered ever so softly.

His head snapped up in surprise, not realising that I'd been standing by the door all this time.

Shaking away his hazy expression, he looked at me expectantly, his voice rough, "What is it? Are you alright?" I could see his concern growing as his eyes swept over me, looking to see if I was hurt or in pain.

Quickly, I shook my head and moved deeper into the room.

"No, I'm fine."

"Ohh..." He trailed off absentmindedly as his fingers fiddled with the corner of the pages.

"You didn't eat breakfast," I edged my way around his desk, but he kept his head bent low.

A reply didn't come until I brushed my hand through his golden hair. Startled, his head swivel to me as if he'd forgotten that I was standing there.

"Have I ever told you how jealous I am of your hair?" I questioned with a smile, slowly getting his attention on me.

He shook his head as his eyebrows drew together, "That's absurd, you're the most beautiful person I've met."

Turning back to the pages of the book in his hands, I was left speechless and blushing while he went about his task. His tone was factual, as if it wasn't something to be questioned or queried and he certainly didn't seem hesitant to state those words.

Covering his hand with my own, it occurred to me how much Aiden has become a part of my life. How much I've come to be dependent on his presence in my life and how much I'm willing to fight to keep him safe.

He may act like a wise old man, but he still had the heart of a boy.

Tugging on his hand, he seemed unrelenting to move, but after a brief hesitation, he complied and followed me over to the sofa with his book still clutched in his hand.

Folding my feet under me, I sat as close to him as I could get, basking in his heat while hoping my meager presence could provide him a sense of comfort.

"Are you sure you're alright?" He asked as worry filled his beautiful eyes.

Nodding I said, "Read me something?"

Surprise flittered across his features, but he nodded once, "What should I read?"

"This," I pointed to the book he held.

"Poetry?"

"I want to hear your favourites," I smiled.

His eyes softened before he silently kissed my forehead and wrapped one arm around me, pulling me to his chest, "This is a new favourite of mine. To my wife by Oscar Wilde

I can write no stately poemAs a prelude to my lay;From a poet to a poemI would dare to say.

For if of these fallen petalsOne to you seem fair,Love will waft it till it settlesOn your hair.

And when wind and winter hardenAll the loveless land,It will whisper of the garden,You will understand."

Aiden's soft voice comforted me as his warm breath fanned the top of my head. His words filled with uncovered meaning, which I was desperate to determine.

Wilde's poem may hold one meaning, but Aiden's perception and deliverance meant another. And to unravel that truth meant digging deeper into our relationship. One that could very well end when my heart decided it was quitting time. The end of which meant Aiden getting hurt as he lost someone else.

Am I selfish enough to do that him? Should I sow seeds into a relationship that is surrounded by storms? Could I hurt him to such an extent?

"Why is it your new favourite?" I whispered as I shut my eyes and listened to his steady breathing.

His lips brushed against the shell of my ear as he leaned in and said, "Because I read it on a beautiful day, sitting next to a beautiful person where I've never felt more at peace."

As he inhaled deeply, I realized he was holding onto that breath as he waited for my response.

Admitting that I understood the underlying meaning to his words meant hurting him. But leaving the hurt for later meant stabbing him in the heart.

In that moment, I could have turned in his arms and confessed how much he's made me fallen in love with him. Despite how little time we've been together, in the grand scheme of things, I was unquestionably, deeply and madly in love with Aiden.

A love that was irreversible in every way.

So instead of burdening him with those feelings, I chose the lesser of two evils. After all, my time was limited and the sand in the hour glass was almost at its end.

"Read me another?" I asked, surprised at voice's steady tone.

I felt his body stiffen just the slightest and I wanted nothing more than to take back the last few seconds, but I stood my ground as he moved on to poems that didn't say I love you in as many words.

A few poems in and he finally sighed, "Who told you?"

"The others," I answered.

"Yet you've still managed to come up here after hearing about how snappy I get today?"

"I'd rather your curt words than none at all," I admitted. "Would you tell me about them?"

There was a long pause and I worried that I may have overstepped. With my back still pressed against his chest, I had no indications of his thoughts as I couldn't read his face.

Finally he said, "My mother was a warrior. She was either running around or teaching my brother and I how to fight. Anytime we made trouble she'd grumble about always wanting a daughter." He gave a little laugh at the memory and I couldn't help but smile at the sound. "I have no doubt that she'd have loved you. She'd have appreciated your persistence to live.

"Dad was...well he could be harsh. Where mom would cuddle us after teaching us how to rip apart a rogue, dad would tell us to get to bed so we can do better tomorrow. Despite his coldness, he loved Will and I. He'd always smile whenever my mom walked into the room, no matter if she was about to yell at him. He did everything for her. Believe it or not, he was also the reason my mom started baking chocolate cake daily. It seems as if I have inherited the addiction.

"The day they - the day I lost them... I fought with my dad. Becoming Alpha was never in the plans for me, it wasn't something I wanted, but with every day Will didn't return, the more likely it was that I was to be the next Alpha. My mom was already heartbroken over Will not being home, and seeing Dad and I like that only made things worst. I wish, for just one moment, I could see them again... even if it's to apologize. That was never something I got to do and I've regretted it since. For a long time I also resented Will for leaving his job to me, now I wish he was alive to make the choice himself. At least the knowledge of knowing he was happy and breathing would be enough. Now-

"Now, they're all gone. God, I really miss them," His voice cracked.

I escaped his arms, needing to be the one to hold him. He covered his face with his palms to supress the pain he lived with every day as his breathing became laboured. Wrapping my arms around his giant frame, I held onto him tightly. No words seeming to be good enough to comfort him, no expression wise enough to ease his pain. So, I pressed my forehead to his hair and let him grieve as he knew how. Hoping my presence was enough to provide an ounce of relief.

Time faded away as the clouds blew through the blue sky and the waves broke as it approached the shore before being swept back to the ocean.

Finally, Aiden lifted his head and turned to me. The pain which has been reflecting in his eyes since he lost his family was even more pronounced today as his eyes were hollowed out and his skin pallid from his grief. The scalding brand in his heart ached even more on days like these and I had a frightening thought of what my death would do to him.

"I promise you this, Tate," His voice was rough as he spoke the words, "I won't lose you, not to your own heart warring against my every effort or the vampires that threaten our livelihood. I won't lose you like I lost my family and I'd do whatever it takes to keep you safe, even if it means giving you my heart in return...because you already own it."

"Aiden-"

He shook his head with a smile tugging at lips, "You don't need to say anything. Not today."

I cupped his cheeks, appreciative of the fact that of all the werewolves in the world, it was him the Moon Goddess paired me with.

"Thank you," I said sincerely. "For everything, especially this."

I placed my hand over the left of his chest, feeling the steady rhythm of his heart. Its strong beats a lullaby for me.

"Thank you," He corrected, "for making today not suck as much as it has for the past several years."

CHAPTER 28

"Do you actually know how to bake?" Kai asked from over my shoulder as I tried to pick out egg shells from my bowl.

"Less talking, more helping," I jabbed him in the rib.

Groaning, he backed away from me, "One, ouch that hurt. Two, I've been commanded to keep you safe not helping you in lighting the castle on fire."

"Fire? What fire?" I laughed uneasily, cross-eyeing the bowl of chocolate I tried melting earlier.

One minute it was melting perfectly, then the chocolate seized and then there was smoke which was caused by a small fire.

"You almost burnt my t-shirt," He pointed to the singed end of his shirt which was a result of him getting close to extinguish the blaze.

"Then you shouldn't have gotten that close," I flipped my hair over my shoulder before painstakingly pulling out the shells.

I can cook just fine, but when it came to baking, my lack of luck followed me. Forget homemade cake, I couldn't even bake a cake mix without it becoming too dense.

Kai sighed as he grabbed an apron and pulled out some chocolate from the refrigerator. I grinned as he gave me a glare from across the kitchen.

"You do realise he could bake a better chocolate cake than anyone in this castle, right?"

I nodded, "How long has it been since anyone baked him one?"

Kai gave it a thought before answering with, "I guess the last time was his mother."

"I know it won't be as good, as it may be inedible-"

"Any crunchy from all those egg shells," He added with a wide grin.

"Hey!" I detested. "Crunchy or not, I want to do this for him. It's...it's my way of saying many things with no words at all."

His eyebrows drew together in confusion, "As in?"

"Thank you?"

"Why would you need to thank him?"

"For giving me the best time at the end of my life," I replied.

"Tate-"

"If you say I'm not going to die then I'll burn your hair next," I countered and he frowned at me. "We haven't received the blood yet and who knows how long it'll take. Every day I get weaker, less me."

"You and I both know he'll turn the world upside down before he let something happen to you."

"That's why I need your help," I said seriously.

"I need to retire," He sighed, placed his hands on the counter before straightening his spine and nodding. "Lay it on me."

"If...no, when, something happens to me, I need you to remind him to stay in control. Help him in remaining focus and protecting Tourmaline. Would you do that for me?"

With a sad smile, he nodded, "You have my word, Luna."

"Great," I let out a breath of relief, "your next task is helping me ensure this cake at least appears delicious."

He snorted as he lifted the bowl of chocolate off the double boiler.

Just as he was about to set it down, it drops to the floor and shatters to pieces. Kai clutched the right side of his abdomen as he fell to his knees.

"Kai!" I screamed as I run to his side.

His face was contorted in pain as he gasped for a breath.

"Matt," He struggled to mutter between his clenched teeth. "Matt's hurt."

Kai placed his hand on the ground to push himself to his feet, cutting his palm on a broken piece of glass as he went. He stumbled as he kept a grip on his side and hurried out the door.

Rushing behind him, I followed as he pushed his way through the castle to the door that led to the backyard.

As he broke into the sunlight, Aiden and Rick were carrying a bloodied Matt up the steps from the beach.

"What the fuck happened?!" Kai yelled as he rushed to the side of Matt.

His mate was unconscious, a wooden dagger protruding from his abdomen.

"Let's get him inside first," Aiden said lowly.

Kai looked about to kill someone, but he relented as they hurriedly got Matt to the infirmary.

Standing outside the door, I was joined by Calypso and other wolves as we listened to Dr. Nazra dolling out instructions to save Matt.

Aiden and Rick exited the room, both covered in the deep red of their pack member's blood.

"How's Matt?" I asked anxiously, the image of both him and Kai flashing in my mind.

"Dr. Nazra's working on him, the stake just missed his lung," Aiden said.

"And you? Are you okay?" I grabbed is shoulders and turned him around to ensure he wasn't wounded.

"I'm fine," He assured me before anger flamed in his eyes. "It was a vampire."

Everyone drew in a shaky breath as I asked, "In daylight?"

"No. This one was hiding in the boat we have in shed down on the beach. We don't know how it got past border patrol, but it climbed out and attacked Matt in the dark room. I don't know how long he was in there but he was still strong, used Matt's wooden dagger and stabbed him. The only reason he was in there was to do the weekly cheek to ensure no one stole our boats."

"Is it dead?" I felt my anger surging forward.

"Not yet, we have the shed surrounded from the outside. I have to go back and take care of it," He said lifting his hands to brush back my hair but stopping short as they were smeared with blood.

"Go, I'll take care of things here," I assured him.

"Tourmaline?" He asked with worry.

"She's in the pool with the mermaids, safe."

With a nod, he and Rick rushed back to the beach.

"I'll go keep an eye on Tourmaline," Calypso said and I thanked her.

Calling the remaining wolves forward, I began delegating tasks.

"I need someone to go the control room and review all the footage from the past week to see how and when the vampire got here. I need another to go Kai and Matt's room and prepare for Matt to be transferred once Dr. Nazra approves it. I'm sure he'd want to be comfortable as he recovers."

As they left, I spotted two faces I knew I could trust.

"Loly and Paul, stay behind. The rest of you are free to go," I smiled gently at the two wolves who accompanied me on my trip from my old pack to the coast.

"Luna," Loly greeted with a bow. Paul was still hesitant of trusting me, which I appreciated since it meant he truly cared for Aiden and the Pack's wellbeing.

"Here's what I need you two to do," I lowered my voice as I stepped closer to them and outlined exactly what I needed them to do.

They were both surprised by my request, but they agreed nonetheless. I could sense a million questions from them, but I promised it will all make sense in good time.

"And not a word of this to anyone else," I enunciated.

They bowed and left to their tasks.

Kai stepped out of the room, his eyes bloodshot and his shirt scarlet red with dried blood. He seemed lost and confused, unsteady on his feet.

I wrapped an arm around him and guided him to the bench that was outside the door before going into the infirmary.

The rusty scent of blood knocked into my senses as I entered the blinding white room. I could hear Dr. Nazra and two other wolves behind a curtain working on Matt.

With a silent prayer to the Moon Goddess, I grabbed a tweezer, a bowl of clean water and some gauze.

"He's- he's going to be alright," Kai stammered, on the brink of tears, as I stepped out of the room.

Relief filled me as I took the seat next to him and grabbed his wounded hand. The skin was already trying to grow back and if I didn't remove the shards of glass now, he'd have to reopen the wound later.

"I should go down to the beach," He tried to pull his hand away but I kept a firm grip and I began pulling out the pieces.

He winced as I shook my head, "No. Aiden's got it covered and you should stay here with your mate."

I could tell he was struggling with his need for revenge and need to stay with his mate. In the end, he nodded and stayed put, allowing me to clean his wound.

"There was so much blood... he- he could have died, Tate," He expressed, his voice filled with fear.

"But he didn't," I reminded him. "He's safe and that's what's important right now."

"I should have been there, I should have been protecting him."

"How would you have known?"

He held no answer, frustration, desperation and anger lining his face.

Silence unfolded over us and he kept his head bowed as I offered any amount of comfort that I could. The thoughts of when next something of this magnitude would happen and whose blood will line the floors of the castle.

This had to end. It wasn't simply the matter of protecting the mermaids anymore, it was freeing everyone from living a caged life.

Kai will live with this memory haunting him every moment he's away from Matt, Calypso and Rick would always fear the thought of conceiving a child with the possibility of a war on the horizon and Aiden would overwork himself every day to ensure nothing touches Tourmaline or his pack.

And everyone will die trying, not knowing if it meant anything at all in the end.

Rushed footsteps padded its way to us from around the hallway, startling both Kai and I. Bracing myself for the worst, I gripped Kai's arm as the person rounded the corner.

Dylan's cherry face had me breathing a sigh of relief as he rushed over to us. His joyful expression took me off guard as he waved an embellished piece of paper at me.

I felt Kai's muscles tense under my grip and the onslaught of anger that rolled off of him was almost tangible. My eyes cut to him for a split second, only to see dark pupils filled with unadulterated rage that's been boiling for too long.

Squeezing his arm, I got to my feet and blocked his sight from Dylan as I greeted the Gamma.

"Tate, I've been looking everywhere for you!" He said with excitement as he passed me the paper.

The piece of cardstock was embossed with gold lettering that read 'birthday invitation'. Turning it over, I realised that Dylan's birthday was two weeks away and we're apparently hosting a formal ball. Dress code: evening wear and theme: vie et mort.

"I didn't know it was your birthday so soon," I said with a small smile. "What does vie et mort mean?"

"Life or death, seems fitting for a birthday party, doesn't it?" He seemed proud of himself and I rolled my eyes at the irony of the theme.

Kai snorted behind as he rose to his feet, "Every day the pack lives with the fear of death and you have the audacity to not only throw a party while our Luna is sick, but also give it such a gruesome theme?"

Chuckling, Dylan shrugged in return, "If you're afraid of a few blood suckers and the possibility of having some actual fun then I guess it's much better that I'm the Gamma now."

"You little-"

"Not to mention the fact that you couldn't even keep your own mate safe," Dylan tsked as he looked at the doors of the infirmary.

Kai was on Dylan before I could intervene, slamming him into the wall, causing all the invitations to go flying around me. He strangled Dylan as his fists turned white before the Gamma landed a punch on his left cheek.

Stumbling back, Kai wiped the blood off lip before looking at Dylan with a murderous gaze. The Gamma shot his arm out to punch Kai, but he dodged before grabbing Dylan's arm under his left armpit and slamming his elbow into his nose.

Blood gushed out as Kai shoved Dylan into the wall again. Cursing, Dylan charged at Kai once again, only for Kai to grab his right arm and bend it over one of his elbow. Kai used his other hand to pull on Dylan's bent arm until I heard a sickening snap.

"Kai!" I yelled, but he didn't listen as Dylan dropped to the floor, expletives leaving his lips.

Using this to his advantage, Kai dropped over Dylan, pressing his knees to each of Dylan's arms, before sending punch after punch at his face.

Droplets of blood began splattering the floor as I marched to the men and grabbed Kai's wrist.

"Enough," I commanded.

I lacked the real command of Luna as I haven't been initiated into the pack yet, but Kai immediately stopped at my words, heeding the authority of my voice. His shoulders were trembling with bottled up rage that hadn't been spent yet.

Getting to his feet, he stalked over to the bench and sat down, wiping his bloodied fist on his t-shirt.

"I want him out of here!" Dylan raged as he struggled to get to his feet. Lending him a hand, I assessed the damage that Kai wreaked on his face. A split lip, a broken nose, a deep gash across his left cheek, a cut on his brow and a broken arm. "He and that mate of his!"

Kai's eyes snapped back to Dylan but I shook my head at him.

"That's not going to happen," I informed him and Dylan seemed confused so I enlightened him. "Matt was just attacked and given your history with Kai, he decided to take out his frustration on you."

Dylan's eyes went to Kai behind me and a questioning gaze flickered over his eyes. Whatever answer Kai gave him, caused him to relax a fraction before his outrage flamed again.

"That's not an excuse for attacking his Gamma," Dylan finally said.

"No, but neither is it an excuse to kick him out of the pack," I made clear. "Go find someone to help you clean your wounds and straighten your arm so it can heal properly, Aiden and I will discuss Kai's punishment."

"I should be the done to dole that out, he broke my arm after all."

"And he'll be dealt with accordingly," I repeated and I could see the need to fight against me on his face.

"Fine," He relented. "But I'm waiting on the verdict."

Finally, he limped away, walking all over his fancy invitations.

Turning to Kai, he winced when he saw my anger.

"We need to talk," I growled as I led the way to the library. He swore quietly, but nevertheless followed behind me.

A sharp pain shot through my chest as I pushed the door to the library open. Biting the pain back, I pinched the bridge of my nose as I held back the tear that threatened to escape my eyes.

"I shouldn't have done that," Kai said solemnly.

I kept my back to him as I bit out, "You think? Attacking the Gamma has serious consequences."

"Maybe if he wasn't so full of himself all the time, I wouldn't have felt the need to punch him."

Chuckling without humour, I leaned my weight against Aiden's desk before facing him, "Punching him was one thing, but you broke his arm."

He nodded, eyeing me carefully, "I'll accept whatever punishment you lay out."

Sighing, I shook my head, "First, you're going to tell Aiden that I've increased your patrol duties, starting from tonight and you're to train the early morning rounds."

He seemed pained by that, but lowered his head and nodded anyways, "Yes, Luna."

"Kai?" I called his attention and he looked up. "I'm kidding."

Bewildered he looked around the room as if searching for someone else who must have spoken the words.

"You're what?"

"Kidding," I repeated. "I don't expect you to leave Matt's side so soon."

"Thank you," He said sincerely, his demeanour relaxing.

"But if anyone asks, that's the tasks you were given."

"Understood."

"However, your real punishment is finally telling me why you and Dylan are always butting head."

Fear sparked in his eyes, "We don't-"

I raised my hand to cut him off, "I just watched you broke his arm without much difficulty, if you expect me to believe you lost your title to him in a fight, then you better have an excellent excuse."

"It's been five years and no one questioned it," He chuckled darkly.

"Everyone must be used to the contempt between you two, but I could see it's much more. Tell me what happened."

The doors to the library were slammed open as Aiden entered with wild eyes.

"The three of us need to talk," He announced before closing and locking the doors.

"Is everything okay?" I asked with concern.

He nodded and then shook his head as he approached Kai and I. Noting his pack member's busted lip he pointed and asked, "What happened to your face?"

"Dylan and Kai decided to have a little fight, I already gave him his punishment," I said, telling Kai with my eyes that this discussion wasn't over.

He gulped but discreetly nodded.

"You'll explain later," Aiden waved us off before going to his desk and turning on his laptop. "There's something you both need to know, and it is to never leave this room."

Kai and I looked at him intently, the anxiety in his eyes making me even more worried.

"The vampire that paid us a visit today had a lot to say," He clicked through his computer as he explained. "It appears he's been hiding out here sometime between our last check into the shed and now, waiting to attack and deliver a message."

"What message?" Kai said between clenched teeth, the anger of not getting to kill the vampire himself showing.

"First, he said they'll be paying us a little visit soon."

"Aiden-"

"That won't happen," My mate stopped me as he grabbed my hand. "I already informed the pack and we have a meeting tonight to increase the security of the castle. They'll never get in here."

I squeezed his hand, knowing that if anyone were to keep us safe, it would be Aiden Oaks.

"Then what's so secret?" I asked.

He eyed the door and listened to ensure no one was nearby as he waved us closer to him.

"The damn bloodsucker let something slip. He said the boss will here for Esprit d'eau douce," He slammed his fist into the desk as he said the words.

"What does it mean?" I pressed.

"Freshwater spirit," He translated. "At first, I thought he meant Tourmaline and the other mermaids, but the name sounded familiar."

"The book..." Kai said as Aiden turned his computer screen to us.

The screen showed an illustrated image of an old text, the title being 'Esprit d'eau douce', the cover was a deep rich blue with a depiction of a woman with a crown on her head. Except where her legs should be, two mermaid tails extended and curved around her elbows.

"What is that?" I asked.

"In French, they call them Mélusine. A woman who turns into a serpent from the waist down, they call it a spirit of freshwater in Europe. Others may refer to it as a mermaid or siren with twin tails," Aiden explained. "We haven't been able to find much on them, the mermaids here all but call them a myth. But, from what we have figured out, they're said to be the oldest sea creatures, giving birth to both mermaids and sirens. That was until they all went extinct, along with this text."

"We thought it didn't exist," Kai said exasperated. "Does it exist?"

Aiden sat down, "We've searched everywhere for it, and this is the only image we could find. An old drawing that was found centuries ago stuffed in a bottle that was recovered from a sea wreak. I thought the book was fake, that the Mélusine were just another useless piece of information, but if the vampires are looking for it..."

"Then it must be real," I deduced before turning my eyes away from the screen and towards my mate. "The vampire we met in the human town, he was French."

Nodding Aiden rubbed his jaw, contemplative, "He must be the head of the coven. It explains how he knows about the book. What worries me is his age."

"If he's as old as time, he could have existed alongside the Mélusine," Kai sighed.

"Exactly, which is why we need to find this book before he figures out we don't have it."

"We've looked everywhere."

Aiden shook his head, "We haven't looked in France."

"I have. I emailed every book store, library and vintage shops around France. I also paid hefty sums to black market dealers to get me information," Kai said.

"Ahh, but it won't just be sitting around with a price tag," Aiden said decidedly. "If this book has information on the blood of mermaids, then there's a lot more it must hold. Which means it's been hidden."

"And how do expect we find a book that's essentially not real in a foreign country?" I side eyed him.

Aiden smirked at me, "Tell me Kai, what punishment did my girl give you for fighting with Dylan?"

"Extra training and patrol hours," He answered.

"That's harsh, Cupcake," Aiden frowned at me.

I shrugged, "He broke Dylan's arm."

Aiden was surprised by this news as he sat up, "You what? Are you out of your mind?"

Kai bent his head, "I'm sorry, Alpha. I'll accept any punishment you give me."

My mate sighed heavily as he got to his feet, "How about I send you to France?"

CHAPTER 29

It's been four days since Kai and Matt left for France.

Matt recovered within a day, his wounds healing fast due to our capability of accelerated restoration of health. Aiden also put on a grand show of banishing them both from the pack's territory temporarily.

Seeing as it hadn't been done before, given no one ever attacked a high ranking pack member, it caused quite a stir. However, Dylan was placated as he found Kai's punishment fit for the crimes he'd done and the pack was working overtime on reinforcing our defences.

No one had the time to question the decision or the whereabouts of Kai and his mate. Which was a blessing as the trip to France was only something Aiden and I knew about. Calypso and Rick had questions, I could tell, but they dare not ask Aiden as he made sure his decision was unwarranted of interrogation.

When I'd ask him why he kept it between us, he said, "You're the Luna and I trust your judgment. As for Kai, he's been by my side since the day I was born and the only day he failed me was when he lost his title. But maybe that mistake could used to our advantage now as he has no reason to stay on the pack grounds and he even gave me a reason to send him away."

"You trust him with your life?" I asked.

He nodded without hesitation, "I trust him more than anyone else. It's the reason I assigned him as your guard."

And I trusted him too. In the short span of time, Kai managed to become a brother to me. A fourth brother to add to my mischievous siblings.

While Kai and Matt searched for the book, I was doing my own digging with the help of Loly and Paul. The situation I had them monitoring seemed rather normal. Yet, there was a nagging feeling inside of me that told me to keep looking. That if I kept my eye on it, I'd have solid proof of what I suspected.

Until then, I had to bid my time.

So, my task today was scouring old books Aiden had stacked in his rooms for anything on the Mélusine or a possible indication of where they resided. Currently, Kai was exploring the rural coastal towns in search of any sea creatures that grew a tail when go into water. If they still exist, it seemed likely they'd be living somewhere quiet and less populated. Especially if they had the book and are also hiding from the vampires.

Aiden asked me to stay with Tourmaline for the day as we went about his daily tasks, but the little mermaid insisted she didn't need me as she swam around with the other mermaids in the pool.

If I dare to say it, Tourmaline was becoming like a daughter to me. I didn't know how it felt to be a mother and neither would I dare to compare myself to her mother, but I did know that I'd protect her with my life.

As much as I liked waking up in Aiden's warm arms in the morning, I also liked when Tourmaline wiggled her way between us and wake us up as the sun rise on the horizon. There's nothing better than the sound of Tourmaline and Aiden's laughs as they tickled each other and started a pillow fight.

It just didn't feel like the day started until I hear that sound or see their bright smiles.

Pouring myself a cup of water at Aiden's desk in his room, I heard a knock from the door above. Unfolding myself from my seat, I took the stairs two at a time before answering the door.

"Jenny," I greeted without an ounce of enthusiasm.

She didn't seem to interested in me either as she passed me Tourmaline's flip flops, "She left this by the pool."

Taking the tiny shoes, my eyebrows drew together, "Isn't she in the pool?"

Jenny looked at me weirdly and shook her head, "Tourmaline left the pool about ten minutes ago, she said she was coming to you."

Fear gripped my insides as I looked at the green haired mermaid in the eyes.

"Are you sure?"

"Yes. Why where is–"

I dropped the shoes and pushed Jenny aside as I bolted down the hallway. Flinging Tourmaline's bedroom door open, I quickly assessed that she was not in there either.

Flying down the staircase, I went to the empty living room and kitchen, my breathing already laboured and my heartbeat pushing itself to its limits as pain pierced its way through me.

"Tourmaline!" I shouted in the hallways as I padded towards the backyard.

I expected to see guards on patrol at the cobblestone staircase that led to the ocean, but it was void of anyone.

"No," I mumbled in fear as I ran down the ever long stairway. "Please don't be in the water."

Step after step, I felt my heart squeeze just a bit tighter, threatening to cut the life from my body.

As my bare feet hit the sandy shore, I caught the tinge of pink a few meters away from shore.

"Tourmaline!" I shouted and by some miracle, she looked up at me with a smile. A turtle was by her side, netting wrapped around its body. I was already knee deep in the water as I called, "Come here!"

She nodded her head at me, about to swim back.

But as my miserable luck would have it, a hand shot out of the water next to her elbow and pulled her small body under.

I cursed as I pushed my body into the water, all of Aiden's words on swimming coming back into my head.

With a gulp of air, I dived into the ocean and pushed my way to Tourmaline. The saltwater stung my eyes as I tried to see where they went.

She was fighting against the bloodsucker as he pulled her further down, but she was so close.

Maybe it was the adrenaline or my need to protect that little girl, whatever it was, I pushed my body to hers. I grabbed the sulphur stone pendant Aiden got me for my birthday and pressed it into the arm of the vampire.

A surprise yell left his lips, muffled by the water, but he released her long enough for her to swim away.

I grabbed her arm and pushed her towards the coast as I swam up for air. When I broke to the surface of the water, Tourmaline turned back to watch me, "Get back on land!"

Fear was written all over her face, but she was a fast swimmer and would be safe. As I paddled my way after her, I caught sight of Aiden's horrified face as he ran across the beach. I was still further away from shore, feeling the current pulling me back towards the ocean, but I watched as Aiden pulled Tourmaline out before coming in after me.

"No, Aiden!" I shouted at him, just as I felt a cold hand grab my ankle.

I was barely able to hold my breath before I was sinking to the bottom of the ocean. Trying to fight against the vampire was quickly expending my energy and making my body exhausted. Its grip was like an iron shackle and its dead weight was like an anchor.

Aiden appeared below the surface as he swam past me and delivered a blow against the vampire. The hand became slack around my ankle long enough for me to push myself back to the surface.

As I gasped to inhale a breath, I realized Aiden wasn't coming up behind me. First Tourmaline, and now my mate.

I was going to kill the damn blood sucker.

Diving back under, I peeled my eyes open to see the vampire gripping Aiden by the neck. My mate's blue eyes were wide, his hair floating wildly around him as if he were an angel.

And ever so slowly, his eyes shut as his body stopped fighting. Neither the pain in my chest or the burning of my lungs could have stopped me then as I broke the necklace from around my neck and stabbed the piece of stone into the back of the vampire.

It easily pierced the stone like skin he had as his body began to convulse in a series of spasms before sinking like the Titanic.

Wrapping my arms under Aiden's, I pushed our bodies to the surface, his weight pushing me down and fighting against my efforts.

Please be alive. Please be alive. Please be alive.

The fear I experienced was unlike any. When I was attacked by rogues in my old pack, I felt a sense of justice in fighting them. When I realised something was wrong with my heart, I experienced hope that it could be fixed. When I got the news that my body was failing me, I was happy to have my last few moments with Aiden.

But as I struggled to keep both of us afloat, the big waves slamming into us at a merciless pace. Watching my mate's eyes shut from unconsciousness, I thought my heart was being ripped to shreds. I felt the sick tremble of fright crawl through my veins and poison my body. I could feel the bile rising in my throat at the thought of not hearing his laugh again or seeing his blue eyes watch me from across the room.

I thought that if I had to know what death felt like, this moment would be the best comparison. A synonym for heartbreak and loss.

As if, by some stroke of a miracle, just as my arms became weaker, I heard the whistling sounds of dolphins.

The sea creatures surrounded us, pushing our bodies to the shore at a speed only they could reach.

As we hit the coast, I pulled Aiden onto the sand bank and began performing CPR. Tourmaline was wrapped in a towel, tears streaming down her face.

"Tourm, I need you to count for me," I instructed gently, needing to bring her focus elsewhere.

She quickly nodded, tears still in her eyes, as she began counting the seconds as I pressed on Aiden's chest.

"1, 2, 3..." She mumbled between sobs as Aiden's eyes flew open and he began coughing up water.

Turning him on his side, I patted his back as he heaved the saltwater from his system.

Tears pricked my eyes at the sight of him alive. Both of them were alive, and that was all that mattered in that moment.

I heard footsteps running down the steps and towards the beach, orders being shouted to ensure we were safe.

"Come here, sweetie," I called Tourmaline over through a sob as I wrapped my arms her, keeping an eye on Aiden.

I kept rubbing his back as he inhaled a deeply, breathing life into the both us.

"Aiden," I moved to wrap my arm around him, but he shifted his body out of my reach and grabbed Tourmaline.

Retracting my hands, I understood that they both needed each other, especially Aiden as the situation was his worst nightmare come to life.

"Are you alright?" Aiden voice cracked as he checked Tourmaline over.

She nodded, tears still flowing down her cheeks.

"Alpha!" Dylan yelled as he skidded to a stop before us, eyes wild.

"Are you all alright?" Calypso asked, wrapping a towel around my shoulders.

"We're okay," I answered.

"What happened?" Rick asked, eyes on the condition of all of us.

Aiden's eyes cut to me, a fire ablaze in them, ones I'd never been on the receiving end of before. Waves of blistering heat radiated off of him and scorched my skin, setting my insides on fire. He couldn't possibly think-

"Jenny, take Tourmaline to her room. Calypso, get two more wolves to guard her room and I want Dr. Nazra to give her a check up," Aiden instructed.

Calypso seemed unsure of leaving my side as she said, "Both of you should come along as well, given Tate's condition and you could have secondary drowning."

"We're fine, take her," He passed off his niece into Jenny's arms as the rest of wolves, excluding Rick and Dylan marched back to the castle. I nodded for Calypso to go, knowing that she saw Aiden's anger and was only concerned.

"Dad?" Tourmaline asked, scared.

"I'll be with you in a moment," He promised her as we both got to our feet.

"Tourmaline?" She looked at me, stretching her arms out, but Aiden stepped between us. "Take her."

Jenny was quick to follow orders as she left with a confused and frightened Tourmaline. If my heart wasn't already aching, the sight alone would have left me broken.

Finally giving me his full attention, I knew that this was a losing game. That no matter what I was about to say, he'd already formed his opinion.

"Tate," His voice was frosty as he addressed me, "what did happen?"

"I- I don't know," I answered vehemently as I shook my head clear of the fright that I just experienced.

He scoffed, his lips blue and his voice horse, "You don't know?"

I reeled back from his anger, unsure of what was happening, "There was a vampire in the water and-"

"I know," He bit out harshly, "I know there was a vampire in the water, it nearly killed my niece. What confuses me the most, is why she was in there in the first place. Why, when I'm sure I asked you to watch her today."

"I was going to-"

"Going to?" He snarled. "Then I guess that makes it okay."

I grabbed his elbow and stepped closer to him, "Let me explain, damn it!"

His jaw clenched as he pulled his arm away from me and gave me his back as he walked a few steps away.

Taking his silence as my opportunity, I said, "I went to her and she said she didn't need me, so I left her in the pool. I knew she was safe there, so I didn't bother to stay, but I should have because you asked me to and because I care for her."

"Letting her out of your sight is a lousy way to show that."

"Aiden, I'm sor-"

"Don't you dare say that," He snapped as he turned back to me, the anger in his eyes fading into hurt. "Don't say sorry, because those words means nothing to me after watching my niece almost die, or worst yet, get abducted by those filthy blood suckers."

"I don't... I don't know what else you want me to say," I said earnestly, pressing my palm against my chest as the pain ebbed on.

When he didn't reply, Dylan walked to my side and asked, "Is it dead?"

I nodded, "I stabbed him with the sulphur stone from my necklace."

My mate's eyes shifted to my bare neck, possibly thinking that after I tried to get his niece killed, I purposefully lost the birthday present he got me.

"Alpha, what should we do?" Rick asked hesitantly, afraid Aiden would snap at him next.

"Get the wolves that were supposed to be patrolling the beach and send them to my office. Dylan, take her back to her room," He gestured to me.

"Aiden, wait. Tell me what's happening, please?" I begged as I tried to reach for him again but he side stepped me. Confusion and hurt burned as twin flames inside of me. Unsure of what just happened between us.

But an answer didn't come my way. He didn't even so much as look at me as he walked away.

The breeze that blew from the ocean chilled my body as I was standing in soaking wet clothing. Yet, it still wasn't as cold him. I didn't freeze nearly as much as I did when he stared at me with anger.

Beautiful ocean eyes once stared at me, now all I received was the icy frost blown in from a winter storm.

As Dylan wrapped an arm around me and escorted me back to the palace, I didn't react, I didn't speak and I dare not make a sound. For if I did, I fear the entire palace would be filled with my screams of pain.

The hallways that led to Aiden's bedroom and my own seemed like a trick question waiting to eat me alive. In the weeks that's that I've spent sleeping in his room, most of my belonging moved with me. Now, as I stared at his door, I questioned if I belonged there at all.

It wasn't as if I was meant to last here. No, my fate had other plans for me. So, why did it hurt so much to stop in front of old bedroom door instead of going to Aiden's? Why was his anger towards me hurting me so much that I felt as if my heart was on fire and my lungs were filled with water? Why was I feeling this way when it was all for the best?

And it was, wasn't it?

I vowed not confess any feelings for him, knowing the day I die would only torment him worst. Us fighting, his anger... it was all a blessing in a disguise. At least if he hated me, my absence would hurt less. And then he'd be alright.

He'd never have to weep for me. If anything, it would be one less burden.

It was on that day, at that moment that I decided.

I won't try to make amends. I won't bridge the gap that tore us apart.

Looking at Tourmaline's room door across from my own, there were two guards stations at the front, and I knew that I'd never be able to be callous towards Tourmaline. If she needed me, I'd go running.

Taking a step towards her door, the guards took a step forward to stop me. Regret in their eyes, but under oath towards their Alpha.

"Take care of her," Is all I said as I turned my back and went to my room.

Before I could close my door, Dylan's hand shot out and stopped me, "Are you okay?"

Nod.

"Are you sure?"

Nod.

"But Aiden, I've never seen him get that angry with you before," He commented, confusion plaguing him. "Isn't it odd?"

"No," I whispered as I lowered my head. "Tourmaline was in danger, I could have prevented it."

"You couldn't have," He shook his head and patted my shoulder. "But what does it mean for the both of you?"

I shrugged, "It means he won't be hurt when I die."

"Tate-"

"I'll see you later," I closed the door on him before he could say anymore.

I crossed my cold, bare room and went into the bathroom. Turning on the shower, I slid to the floor and pressed a fist against my lips to stifle the sobs that racked through my body.

Could have really been that careless to turn my eyes away from Tourmaline? If I'd just stayed in the pool she'd not have went into the ocean. She was a smart kid, and she knew it was forbidden, but she was only five and if a sea creature called to her, she'd never leave it suffering.

As a tear rolled down my cheek, I forbade the others from spilling over. Yet, as the pain in my chest ebbed away at way, my body reacted in the only way that made sense. It cried even when I didn't want to.

Struggling to get to my feet, I gripped the sink and slipped as my other wet hand couldn't find purchase on the tile floor. I was a crumpled, soaking wet and teary eyed mess.

The door to my bathroom opened, startling me as I hadn't heard nor smelt anyone entering my bedroom.

"Luna!" Dr. Nazra's eyes widened at my position on the floor as she hurried to my side. "Are you hurt?"

Wiping the tears from my cheeks, I shook my head and tried to give her a smile, "No, I'm okay."

"Let me check your heart," She grabbed the stethoscope from around her neck.

I stopped her hands, "How is Tourmaline?"

"She's shaken up, but other than that she's alright."

"Aiden," I said, "he lost consciousness under water, you should give him a check up before you start on me."

She smiled, "I would not like to lose my head today."

"You won't," I assured her.

"I heard," She informed me before listening to my heartbeats. A minute later she said, "I think he was only worried about you."

"I'd like to believe you."

"Believe in him," She said cryptically before pulling out a needle and a small bottle. "Is your chest still paining?"

Silently, I nodded to her, perplexed by her words. Dr. Nazra injected me with a pain killer before helping me up and into the bathroom.

"You really don't need to do this," I said as she helped me get my t-shirt over my head.

"I know, but you're my Luna and my friend," She simply said.

"Thank you," I said earnestly.

If anything, I was glad I had others around me if I couldn't have Aiden.

CHAPTER 30

I had a dream.

I was swimming the big ocean. There were creatures of all shapes and sizes. Mermaids and sirens all swam around me.

There was everything I'd wished for.

But nothing at all.

Because Aiden wasn't there.

Neither was Tourmaline.

If I didn't have them, then it wasn't a dream at all. It was a wicked nightmare.

In the days that passed following the incident at the beach, Aiden and I kept clear of each other. We were socially distancing as if the other had the plague.

Yet, no matter how hard I tried staying away from him, he was there at every turn.

In the kitchen? Aiden.

Library? Aiden.

Backyard? Aiden.

Living room, which no one uses? God damn Alpha Dickhead.

And you know what, he was a Dickhead. A gigantic piece of chocolate cake that fell to the ground before I could taste it.

Why, yes. I was both at my 'anger stage' and I just witnessed Rick tripping and sending a plate of chocolate cake crashing to the ground. And as he set the other plates on the table, everyone grabbed one before I could snag myself a piece.

There was none left.

When Aiden baked cake for everyone, not a single serving was left for seconds.

I placed my fisted hands on the tables as I glared daggers at Rick, and he had the audacity to smile sheepishly at me before hurriedly eating his undeserved share.

Had my mate not been peculiarly angry with me, I would have gotten the first plate. Quite actually, he would have baked one especially for me. But, yet again he was a conceited knuckle head.

Tourmaline grinned at me from across the table as I'd taken up residence in Kai's seat. I gave her my best smile despite the pain I felt of not having spoken to her in days and my lack of chocolate goodness. She scooted her plate towards me, not being that big of a fan of cake, but Aiden made a show of stopping her plate and turning to her.

He hadn't looked at me all night. Actually, he hadn't looked at me since that day on the beach and I'd be lying if I said it didn't hurt. He'd all but forbidden me from having contact with Tourmaline. She was either with Jenny and the other mermaids or with Calypso. Either way, she always had wolves guarding her. Ones who refused to let me speak with her let alone give her a hug.

How I've missed her little hugs. Or the way she'd giggle at the slightest thing or wake me up every morning to braid her hair.

"I put a seaweed filling in your piece," He told her and her eyes lit up at that. I guess eating seaweed was a mermaid thing because she could never resist.

While she dug in, I witnessed the most abnormal behaviour. Aiden kept his slice of cake untouched.

He didn't lift his fork. The dude wasn't even looking at it as he kept his eyes on Tourmaline, and his arms folded across his chest.

Calypso nudged me with her elbow and gestured to Aiden. I shook my head, not knowing what was up with him.

Aiden refusing chocolate cake was the equivalent to him refusing a first edition copy of his favourite piece of literature. Absurd in all sense of the word.

I may be equally at odds with him as he is with me, but it doesn't mean I've erased my feelings for him or my concern. And I was worried about him.

Fighting a battle with myself, I contemplated needing to talk to him and giving him a wide berth. Both options stemming from me trying to protect him.

As if he could feel my eyes on him, his gaze shifted to me. I was momentarily dazed by the sea of emotions that were displayed in his eyes. They were all jumbled in a stormy sea of blue, promising to wreak havoc upon me.

Just as quickly as his eyes were on me, they were gone. His walls going up as he got to his feet and excused himself.

The sting of his absence lingered in my heart as I felt hollowed out.

Calypso grabbed my hand and gave it a squeeze as I watched him walk away. The sight of his back was becoming all too familiar.

I didn't see a reason in sitting at the table anymore, so I got to my feet and walked to the kitchen, everyone's eyes on me as I went. News of Aiden and I's fight had spread like wildfire in the pack and now everyone knew we weren't on speaking terms.

How was I supposed to prove myself as an efficient Luna when I couldn't help in combat and the Alpha hated me?

Sighing, I opened the door of the refrigerator and peered inside, hoping to see a piece of cake, but coming up empty as Calypso came into the kitchen. She was brandishing a plate of cake, the one Aiden left.

Lowering her voice and standing close to me, she whispered, "Aiden left this for you."

I chuckled, "Thanks for trying to make me feel better, but I don't believe you."

"The both of you are giving me whiplash," She tsked as she handed me the plate. "Believe it or not, it's the last piece and those were the Alpha's orders."

I glared at the piece as if it were Aiden, "Then why didn't he give it to me himself?"

Patting my shoulder, she said, "Maybe you should ask him."

"What does that even mean?" I called to her as she walked away with a smile.

Staring at the cake, I wished it gave me the answers to the questions I had. Does this mean he wanted to talk? Should I go to him? Was this his way of apologizing? If I go to him, will it be okay? Or was my decision to not hurt him better?

Maybe, just maybe, this cake was meant to be symbolic. The first time we met, I was angry at him for bossing me about. The memory overwhelmed me as I thought about how he brought me a piece of cake and we made a truce. It was the first moment I got a glimpse of the real Aiden. The one I've been falling for all this time.

The gentle soul that held my hand when I got a blood transfusion and read me poetry. I want that Aiden back.

I grabbed two forks, believing that the cake was our way of reconciling, and headed the way Aiden left.

My feet were hurried as a smile pulled at my lips. The first thing I was going to do was chew him out for treating me with so much contempt. The second was to run into his arms. His warmth was something I missed, even if it was only a few days ago that I've last had it.

I spotted two figures in the courtyard, the outside area at the centre of the castle. As I got closer, I immediately recognized Jenny's green hair and my mate's blonde locks. Skidding to a halt, I stopped just next to the door, giving me a view of both of them.

"Aiden, I need to know," Jenny grabbed his arm.

Aiden's back was to me so I couldn't see his reaction, but he didn't pull away from her either, "It's not something I have an answer for right now."

"Then when will you?"

"When I get more information."

"And when will that be?" She said in frustration. "When will you stop wasting time and find Anvi?"

"I don't even know if she's really alive."

"But the vampire said-"

Aiden held up his other hand as he turned towards me. My focus was on Jenny's hold on him and as he followed my line of sight, he yanked his arm away from her.

Were they discussing the vampire situation? Was Aiden colluding with Jenny about what's going on as he's left me in the dark? I neither know about Kai's progress nor Aiden's plans.

Jenny huffed when she saw me, "Can't you see we're having a discussion?"

"Jenny," Aiden said to her menacingly. "Leave us, we'll discuss this later."

She rolled her eyes at him, but otherwise left without another word.

"What are you doing out here?" He finally asked when she was gone, his tone not unkind.

"I guess I was partaking in wishful thinking," I said quietly, walking closer to him as his eyes caught the slice of cake.

He must have caught onto my direction of thinking as he inhaled an unsteady breath, "Tate-"

"It's fine," I shrugged. "I shouldn't have expected you to be anything but indifferent."

He opened his mouth to say something, stopping and then finally scolding me, "You shouldn't be outside at this hour anyway, it's dark and cold."

"Perfect place for me then."

"Don't ever say that," He growled as he stepped closer to me and began taking off his jacket. Just as he was about to throw it over my bare shoulders, the door opened behind me.

Aiden quickly pulled his jacket away, draping it over his arm and stepping far away from me. His cold front back with blistering force and I contemplated if nearly drowning caused him to become bipolar.

"Did I interrupt something?" Dylan's voice asked as he entered the courtyard.

"No," Aiden answered sternly. "I was just heading inside."

Dylan stood between Aiden and I as his eyes shifted from one to the other, "I'd rather if you two didn't fight."

"Stay out of it," Aiden snarled.

Dylan lifted his hands in surrender, backing away, "I'm just concerned."

"You shouldn't be," I clarified. "Because nothing's going on between us. In fact, I just came out here to tell Aiden that I'll be leaving."

That quickly grabbed Aiden's attention as his eyes snapped to me.

"You're leaving?" Dylan sputtered in surprise.

Nodding, I kept my eyes on Aiden, "If we don't get the blood soon to do the operation, I won't have long. Dr. Nazra already said that the rate of my heart beat has dropped significantly. I'd like to spend my last days with my family. The people who love me."

I watched as he balled his hands up, knuckles turning white and veins bulging against his skin.

"You're going to let her leave?" Dylan turned to Aiden hysterically.

While my mate's body was strung tight, his expression was stoic, "So you're going to just up and leave? Don't forget you've made a commitment to this pack. You're their Luna, and you wish to simply drop your responsibility and leave them?"

Leave 'them'. Not 'I'.

"That's not fair, Aiden," I growled at him.

He went silent, knowing I was right.

Walking to him, I shoved the plate against his chest until he held onto it, "I've never made a commitment as you've never made me Luna. You don't want me here, so why would I stay? Why would I continue to roam the castle as if I were a ghost when you don't want me?"

"I've never..." He stopped short, eyes ablaze as he looked at Dylan before focusing on me. "Do whatever you feel like, Tate. Who am I to stop you?"

With that, he walked away. Once again leaving me angered, confused and heart broken.

I didn't cry. I didn't even blink as I watched him go.

"Let's go inside, hmm?" Dylan said softly as he guided me back into the confines of the castle. "Are you really going to leave?"

I shrugged, "It seems my stay here was bound to come to an end anyways. Why not leave while I'm still breathing?"

He nodded but mused, "Stay until my birthday at least?"

"I don't think-"

"Please?" He pouted.

"Fine," I agreed. "But I'll leave after that."

"I'm sure you will," He smiled as he began telling me about his birthday preparations.

CHAPTER 31

Calypso stood before me, a big smile on her face as wolf after wolf set boxes wrapped in ribbons on my bed.

"What in the world is going on?" I asked, confused by the organized chaos that has erupted as Dr. Nazra also stepped into the room with make-up bags and hair styling tools.

"Just the essentials for getting ready for tonight," Calypso said as she opened a large white box and pulled out a stunning gown. It was a deep gold with a black paisley pattern that looked as if it were etched into the material. A high collar framed the neckline, the cap sleeves structured at an angle and the train at just the perfect length.

Approaching her side, I stared at the intricately designed piece with awe, "We're supposed to dress in formal wear..."

The thought had completely slipped my mind given the last week. I'd forgotten to ask Calypso about getting a dress for the ball and now the casual sundress sitting in my closet seemed blasphemous to even be considered.

"Did Dylan not drill it into your head that he expects us to look like royalty tonight?" She asked, a secret smile playing on her lips.

Scrubbing a hand over my face, I groaned, "I completely forgot. You wouldn't happen to have an extra dress, would you?"

Calypso's shape differed from my own, but once I could zip it up, I didn't mind.

"If you think I'm giving you an old dress to wear, then you don't know me at all," She wiggled her eye brows as she grabbed another box and inched it closer to me.

"You bought me a dress?" My throat closed up as tears pricked my eyes. Calypso had become one of my best friends, and it hurt me to know that I'd be leaving in the morning when I promised her, I'd find a way to resolve the issue with the vampires.

How was she supposed to have confidence in bringing a child into this world when I couldn't even keep my promise or stick around long enough to even try.

"I placed the order, yes, but I didn't buy nor pick it out."

"Then who?" I asked confused as she wiped a tear away from my eye.

"Alpha Aiden," She revealed.

The confession sobered me up, sparking the rage that I've began harbouring for him. Yet, somewhere deep inside me, I also felt elated. How could he act so callous towards me and then go and do something like this?

"Was this before or after the beach?" I queried.

"After."

"Tell me his behaviour is confusing you as well," I pleaded with her and she nodded without hesitation.

"I don't know what he's up to, but he's hurt you. Which is why you need to put on this dress as armour, kill him with your attitude without letting on to how much you're hurting and he'll know exactly how wrong he was."

I nodded, knowing she was right and feeling emboldened by her words.

My palms became sweaty as I tugged on the ribbon on the box before ever so slowly peeling the cover back.

In my periphery I could see Dr. Nazra taking a photo of me as I gently picked up the tulle garment. The long gown was a soft shade of light brown with a pink undertone. The entirety of the dress was covered in embroidered flower applique that ranged from pastel pink, blue and lavender. Vines and sparkles filled the dress and created a whimsical yet earthy feel to the dress. Where the skirt was layered with tulle, the bodice and flared sleeves were translucent except for the boob area. To top it off, a silky piece of ribbon wrapped around the waist.

It was the most beautiful dress I'd ever have the honour of wearing.

"I don't think I can pull this off," I shook my head as I ran my fingers along the details.

Dr. Nazra laughed as if it was the most absurd thing she'd heard today.

"There's more," Calypso said as she handed over three more boxes.

I opened the bigger one first and pulled out a pair of beige stilettos with a golden heel and metal vines and flowers detailing the side of the shoe and wrapping around the heel.

"Aiden picked out all of this?" I asked in disbelief.

"He did," She nodded. "If only Rick was so colour coordinated, it would save me a lot of time."

The next box I opened contained a rose gold necklace with matching earrings. When I opened the last box, there was a note and another piece of jewellery.

'And when wind and winter hardenAll the loveless land,It will whisper of the garden,You will understand.' - Oscar Wilde.

It was a piece of the poem he read to me that day in the library. The one that quietly spoke of love like a forbidden whisper. Why would he send this now? And why only the last stanza? What is it that he wants me to understand? Does he want me to believe his coldness has an explanation, that I should somehow know what it means?

Shaking my head, I tucked the note into the box, not wanting to think of the cryptic words. Instead, I picked up the bracelet that didn't match my dress, but rather, several yellow sulphur crystal charms dangled around the band. Unbiddenly, a small smile tugged at my lips.

I had lost the necklace Aiden gave me for my birthday when I used it to kill the vampire and save my mate. I guess this way, I wouldn't have to lose all at once. However, I won't be needing it anymore. The Blood Moon Pack didn't have vampires hunting them, so there was no use for it.

Shutting it back into the box, I left it on my bed, fully intending on returning it along with the note to its owner.

"You won't wear it?" Dr. Nazra asked.

"No," I shook my head. "I won't need it where I'm heading."

"Well, if you won't accept his gift, then you're going to have to accept the gift Calypso and I got for you," She smirked as she headed to the door.

Two wolves walked in and then stepped aside as a grinning Tourmaline came into view. She launched herself at me at a speed I didn't think was possible for a five-year-old.

"Tate!" She yelled as I scooped her up in my arms and gave her a tight hug.

"Tourm," I said, choked up as I kept her cradled. "How are you here?"

"Seeing as you're leaving tomorrow, we thought it would be best if you two got to spend the day together," Calypso answered as she nodded to the wolves who were guarding Tourmaline.

They bowed and left the room, but I could sense them standing right outside.

"Thank you," I said to Caly and Nazra.

Tourmaline lifted her head from my shoulder, her eyes glistening, "You said you won't leave."

"I know, Princess, but it's time for me to go home."

"What about, Uncle Aiden? What about me?"

"I'm sorry, Tourmaline. I'm really sorry," A tear slipped from my eyes, causing her lips to tremble.

Those were the only words left that I could say. The only words that meant something.

"Would I never see you again?" She asked.

"Someday," I promised. "Until then, I'll write you letters and whenever you miss me, just look at the stars. I'll be among the brightest."

She nodded her head, unable to say anything else. I didn't know if she understood the meaning behind my absence, or if she knew I was dying, but she put on a brave face as she wiped my tears with her little fingers.

"Don't cry, Tate. I'll write you letters and when we finally fight the vampires, Uncle Aiden and I can come visit you," She smiled.

I didn't say anything, simply smiling and brushing her hair behind her ear.

"Enough tears," Calypso said, brushing away her own as they rolled down her cheeks. "We have to get ready."

"Tate, can you do my hair?" Tourmaline's eyes were bright as I set her on her feet and went to my vanity table.

Calypso, Dr. Nazra, Tourmaline and I spent the rest of the afternoon getting ready as I did everyone's hair and Calypso did the make-up. Tourmaline talked my ear off, telling me about everything I've missed the past few days. She also explained that when she left the pool that day, she heard a turtle calling to her for help.

No one was there to stop her, so she went into the ocean. With that, she also thanked me for saving her that day and apologized for leaving the castle. Five years old, yet the epitome of being well mannered.

Very unlike her Uncle, who haven't thanked me for saving his life, but instead growled and threw the blame on me.

By the time late evening rolled around, we were all dressed in our finest. Tourmaline in a pink ballgown fit for a queen with pieces of tulle draping from her shoulders as a cape. To top it all off, she also wore a tiara, adorned with pink tourmaline gemstones. Dr. Nazra wore a lehenga that glimmered under the light. The outfit itself being a pale blue with intricate silver beading and crystals while her shawl was an array of yellow, red and purple which somehow matched perfectly.

Calypso left first, going to her mate who waited for her to help him with his tie. Tourmaline followed after her, knowing that Aiden will be looking to escort her to the ballroom.

"Shall we?" Dr. Nazra asked as she held her arm out for mine.

Grinning, I looped my arm with hers as we made our way to the first floor.

As we stood at the top of the grand staircase that led to the foyer, I spotted my mate. My breath was caught in my chest as my gaze landed on him. Automatically, his ocean eyes found me, an expression between awe and regret claiming his features.

"Chin up," Dr. Nazra whispered to me as we made our way down the steps.

My palms felt sweaty as we got closer, Aiden's eyes never leaving me. With much difficulty, I tried to remain stoic as I assessed him. He wore a stone grey, three-piece suit with a tie that matched my dress tucked into his waistcoat. However, instead of a typical suit jacket, he donned a long matching wool coat with gold embroidery lining the lapels and edges of the coat.

"Isn't she pretty?" Tourmaline tugged on his arm as I stood before them.

Aiden seemed momentarily lost in his own thoughts, but quickly coughed before nodding.

"Maybe you should tell her," Tourmaline pretended to whisper to him, but her voice remained loud. She was one genius kid.

He hesitated before fixing his eyes on me and saying, "You look absolutely beautiful, Tate. Truly, incredibly and irrevocably beautiful."

I bit the inside of my cheek, trying to cause physical pain instead of the pain he was inflicting on me from his words.

Pretty words that didn't make much sense to me.

"Thank you," I gave him a curt nod.

He bowed his head, his eyes dropping to the floor as Tourmaline grabbed Dr. Nazra's hand and pulled her towards the ballroom.

I began to follow them, but was quickly pulled back as Aiden's hand held onto my wrist and led me towards the hallway behind the staircase.

My heartbeat was erratic as we stowed away into a dark enclave. Aiden placed both of his hands at the sides of my head, caging me in. His intoxicating scent of sea-washed mahogany and fresh waterfall wrapped around me like a fog of my favourite perfume. It was heady and I was drowning in it as his deep blue eyes anchored me down.

"Aiden," I whispered as his warm breath fanned my eye lashes.

"Can I kiss you?" His strained voice asked, his breathing shallow. Pain lacing his tone.

Maybe it was the confines of the dark hallway, how gorgeous he looked tonight or the absence of his familiar touch over the last few days. Whatever it was, it had me nodding. It had me cupping his cheeks as he pressed our lips together. A hunger building between us as I grabbed his shoulders and his hands went to my waist.

Both our hands searching, our bodies flushed, our breathing shared as we used the other for oxygen.

It had my heart hammering.

My pulse racing.

My breath staggering.

Kissing him was like kissing death. It was my cold lips trying to latch onto his warmth which promised life. My trembling, feeble frame clinging to everything that won't be there in the afterlife. It was not wanting to leave my body, yet being enticed by the angel of death himself. Wishing for that moment of reprieve that will end my pain and heartbreak.

Simple words on my dying lips wanting to ask, would you love me in the afterlife? When my body went cold, my skin pallid and my soul was set free. Would he love me then?

"Tate," His voice was rugged as his kisses moved down my neck. Each peck a blistering scorch to my skin.

He continued his ministrations as he moved back to my lips, a hair breath away, and pleaded, "Don't leave. Don't leave me. Please."

My heart lurched in my chest, causing my body to seize up as an iron clad grip tightened around my heart. Eyes pricked with tears, I coughed as I shoved Aiden back, but I kept my hands fisted against the lapels of his jacket.

"Tate-" He moved to cup my face, but I pushed his hands away, completely breaking our physical connection. "Are you alright? Cupcake, please, tell me if you're okay. Should I call Dr. Nazra?"

"Stop," I begged as I blinked away any emotion that gave away my pain. "Just stop it, Aiden."

His face contorted into confusion, eyebrows drawn and eyes worried, "Stop what? Did I hurt you? Fuck, I didn't mean to-"

"Stop pretending," I clarified with a whisper, leaning against the wall as I tried to get the pain to subside. "We've kissed, it doesn't mean you have to act as if you're concerned. So quit it, please."

Aiden's jaw clenched, "I've never pretended when it came to my concern for you. You should know that."

"Should I? Why would I ever think that when you've done nothing but hurt me for the last week," I tore into him.

"You've been hurting?" His voice croaked.

"Don't act surprise."

"I though you understood. The poem, didn't you get it?"

"The poem?" I scoffed in disbelief. "You expected me to understand the arbitrary reason you've been treating me like this because you sent me a piece of a poem?"

His eyes burned, "If not the poem, then you should know how I feel. How I've felt about you since the day we met. I told you myself that I'd do anything to protect you."

"That's not fair," I shook my head, straightening my back. "How do you expect me to know how you're feeling if you haven't told me yourself? How, when you've not even made me your Luna? How is that you protecting me?"

"Tate," He whispered, voice broken. "I'll explain. I'll explain everything, but I can't right now. Just stay, baby. Stay, for me."

I hesitated, the need to comfort and protect my mate fighting against my own self-preservation.

Finally, I said, "If you tell me what's going on right now, I will."

He shook his head, "Not yet, I can't tell you yet."

"Then we've lost, Aiden," I said calmly. "Tomorrow I'll leave and you'll never have to worry about me again. You won't have to protect me and I won't be around to endanger Tourmaline."

"You saved her."

I smiled, despite the situation, "Didn't feel like I did when you blamed me."

"Cupcake-"

"I'll see you inside," I excused myself, escaping the darkness and hurrying to the ballroom.

My throat felt as there was a lump in it and my eyes burned with unshed tears. I wished for loved, but I hadn't taken into consideration the heartbreak that came with it.

Inhaling deeply, I got my bearing and entered the ballroom. The chandeliers were turned on, casting a warm glow to the room. Silk curtains draped the windows that lined the wall on the left and framed the picturesque sea outside. Tables with candles and elaborate floral arrangements littered the room, leaving a large space at the centre for dancing.

The gold and red accents of the decoration complimented the white marble floors and walls perfectly. A live band playing classical yet whimsical songs at the front of the room.

If it was my last night at the castle, at least I could pretend to be royalty.

"Tate," Dylan greeted with a smile as he approached me. His suit was velvet blue with a black pattern. His jacket long and his brocade waistcoat styled with a cord like rope which wrapped around his waist.

"Happy Birthday," I hugged him. "You look the epitome of fashion."

As he thanked me and as we parted our hug, I saw a faint frown on his lips and his nose wiggled. Quickly, he shook whatever thought he had in his head away and smiled.

"What do you think of my handiwork?"

"It's..." I looked at the room again in amazement, "it's something else. As if you pulled it straight out of an actual royal ballroom."

"I did have some help picking out decorations," He admitted with a laugh before being whisked away by someone else in the pack.

Walking around the room, I greeted the other wolves and mermaids. All dressed to the nines. I spotted Jenny standing by the window, her eyes darting around the room as if looking for someone. Her dress was a deep emerald green with layered fringe. It hugged her body, showing off her shape.

When her eyes landed on me, she quickly averted her attention. Her behaviour had me on alert. She wasn't one to look away from me, no, she always looked at me with a bored expression.

Instead of approaching her, I found Loly and Paul in the room and without words I gestured to Jenny.

Loly nodded, knowing that I want her to keep an eye on Jenny. Paul kept his focus on my other suspect.

I had my suspicions about what was happening around us for a while. First the vampire attack when I first came to the castle, the car dying on us when I returned from visiting my family, the sensors in the ocean being tampered with, the vampire finding out about the human man who was cured, Matt being attacked and then the latest incident with Tourmaline.

It was too much to be a coincidence. Too many variables being set up just perfectly for these accidents to happen.

After Matt was attacked, I was almost sure someone in the pack was setting us up. Which is why I had Loly and Paul investigating every incident I just listed and also keeping an eye on the person I suspected.

It was a long shot, which is why I've kept it a secret. Blaming someone for being disloyal to the pack had severe consequences. I had to be sure before I made my claim to Aiden.

As the night rolled out, I watched from my seat as everyone danced. Rick swept Calypso across the dance floor with smooth moves, Dr. Nazra found herself a dance partner and Tourmaline danced with the mermaids.

Aiden twirled her around the floor a few times, his dancing flawless as always.

When he wasn't dancing with Tourmaline, he sat across the room and kept his blue eyes focused on me. It was unnerving and caused goosebumps to rise on my skin.

Dylan appeared in front of me, hand outstretched for mine, "A dance, my lady?"

I didn't want to dance with anyone but Aiden, but it would also be incredibly rude of me to not accept his offer. After all, he was the only one to ask.

Smiling kindly, I accepted his outstretched hand. However, instead of leading me to the floor, he led me to my mate.

Aiden looked up the both of us in confusion as he growled, "What?"

Dylan smiled mischievously, "As my birthday gift, I'd like my Alpha and Luna to finally kiss and make up."

Too late for that, I thought. We already did the kissing, but we have yet to make up.

Aiden's eyes blazed, the same thoughts rushing through his head, I'm sure.

"I don't want-" I began, but Aiden got to his feet.

"The pack is already anxious at the prospect of their Luna leaving, seeing us together will put their minds at ease," Aiden rattled off as he held out his hand for my own.

"That's the spirit," Dylan bellowed as he places my hand in Aiden's.

My mate gripped my hand tightly as he escorted me to the floor. The tempo slowed and I felt everyone's eyes on us as he slid one of his hands around me and kept the other firmly griping my hand.

With one hand on his shoulder, he pulled our bodies closer as he started to lead.

"Did you ask him to get me to dance with you?" I asked.

"No."

I don't know why the truth of him not asking for my hand hurt more, but it was tearing into me.

"When I leave," I began, feeling his body stiffen under my hand, "do me a favour and remind Tourmaline how much I wish I was here with her. That I loved her."

He nodded, "I will."

"Thank you."

"You're not wearing the bracelet I got you."

"I won't need it when I leave here."

"So, you're really leaving?"

"Will you tell me what's going on?"

"No."

"Then there's no reason to prolong the inevitable."

His hand tightened around me, his body rigid as we swayed.

"If you think I'll let you die, you're wrong."

I didn't ask what he meant by that, or how he could possibly revive my heart.

Silently, I laid my forehead against his chest, breathing in his scent.

I could hear his breathing shallow out, but he didn't move me away as the song continued on.

All too soon, it came to end and we both pulled away from each other. Turning without a word more.

Tourmaline caught up to me, tugging on my dress, "I need to go to the washroom."

"Let's go," I gave her my hand as we made our way out of the ballroom.

The toilet was far down the hallway, on the opposite side of the ballroom, making Tourmaline pull me along at a jogging pace.

When she was all finished and we started making our way back, I caught the faintest scent of a rotting corpse.

As we moved further along the hallway, the scent became strong and my heart hammered in my chest, my footsteps faltering.

"Tate? What's wrong?" Tourmaline asked as she looked up at me.

I couldn't get the words out. Couldn't put that fright in her.

"Stay quiet and follow me, okay?" I whispered to her as I slipped off my heels.

There was another hallway to my left which led to a longer way towards the pool area, but there was no foul scent. If I got her to the pool, she'd be safe given the passcode encrypted iron door and the sulphur that covered the exterior.

Picking her up, I hurried us down the hallway, wishing that I was connected to the pack through mind link.

As we made our way through the castle, I heard footsteps behind me as the vampire scent got stronger.

They were following us.

"Tate?" Tourmaline asked, real terror lacing her voice as she looked behind me.

I could almost sense the dead eyes of the vampire staring at my back just as a loud crashing sound reverberated through the castle. Sounding as if it came from the ballroom.

I sprinted, taking off at a speed I thought nearly impossible, my heart burning up and my lungs struggling for air.

The vampire laughed behind me, almost mockingly.

As I winded my way down another hallways, I pushed open a door, revealing a storage room packed with boxes and books.

Shoving Tourmaline inside, I said, "Hide."

The pure horror on her face was one I'd never be able to forget. Tears leaking down her cheeks and hands reaching to grab me as I moved out the door.

I closed the door silently behind me and ran back the way I came from, putting distance between us and moving closer to the vampire.

Tourmaline's scent was invisible, but mine wasn't. I couldn't be totally sure if the vampires could sniff her out through my scent on her when I carried her, but I wasn't willing to risk it.

And there was only one way to cover up my scent.

I pulled an earring off my ear, cursing myself for not wearing the sulphur bracelet Aiden got me. Using the small, but sharp tip of the earring, I placed it at the inside of my arm, slicing my hand open from below my elbow to my wrist.

Just as blood starting seeping out of my hand, dripping to the floor below me, the vampire caught up.

He smiled at me and licked his fangs, "Now, now, now that's not playing fair, is it?"

"Says the damn blood sucker who broke in," I spat as fresh pain blossom from my wound and stabbed straight through to my heart.

"Where's the girl?" He snapped, coming closer to me as two more figures appeared behind him.

The French vampire, the one Aiden and I met in the human town smiled at me as if we were old friends.

"Tate," He greeted me by name. "Whatever have you done?"

The person who came with him stepped closer, laughing a familiar tune.

Dylan stood next to him, hands in his pockets, looking relaxed.

"You!" I growled, hatred boiling in my blood at the sight of him. "It was you all along!"

Dylan was my suspect. The one I had Loly and Paul tailing for the last two weeks. I should have trusted my gut and told Aiden.

"Luna," He greeted mockingly. "Where's the kid?"

"Now, Dylan, let's not be rude to the wolf," the French vampire tsked. "Tell me child, why in the world did you cut yourself?"

He took a step closer to me and I immediately back tracked, my feet stepping into my warm, sticky blood on the floor.

"My mate's going to kill you," I threatened, placing my palm over my wound.

Blood spilled out anyways, making me dizzy, causing the ebbing in my heart to pound at a rhythm it hadn't before. This was going to be my end.

"Aiden couldn't even see through my lies, do you really believe he could kill us?" Dylan scoffed. "He's also an atrocious actor, couldn't even keep up his anger facade with you."

"W-what are you talking about?" I heaved, feeling the pain run through my entire body.

"I was the one to set up Tourmaline's kidnapping and he knew it. I'm guessing he put on a show of hating you so I won't go after you next, but I knew he was lying. Of course, it was confirmed today when I caught his scent all over you."

I shook my head, this information making my mind spin and had me feeling sick.

"How could you?" I snarled. "After everything the pack has done for you."

His smile dropped and he bared his teeth at me, "They've done nothing. Even after I kicked Kai's ass, Aiden refused to exile him. He even trusted him more than me."

"For obvious reasons," I growled and he moved to me with a fist raised but the French vamp held him back by the collar of his jacket.

"Take me," I spited out, begging to feel the blood lose. "Leave everyone else, and you can take me. I'll tell you everything I know."

"Do wolves have a natural inability to lie?" The vampire asked with a smile. "You're useless ma chérie, and you're practically already dead."

"I'm more alive that you," I said as I struggled to suck in a breath. My arm was on fire, the scent of rusty blood and its sickly warmth making my stomach turn. My knees trembling as my body got weaker.

"She had the girl with her, must be somewhere around here," The vampire who was following me said.

"Kill her, we'll find the mermaid," French blood sucker commanded.

Dylan folded his hands with a wide grin, "You first, then your mate will die and I'll get the thing I wanted from the start. The pack."

"You're weak, you'd never be able to kill Aiden," I grinned as the first vampire stepped into my line of sight and sniffed the air.

Licking his fangs, he said, "O negative, my speciality."

He pounced on me in a heartbeat, knocking me to the ground. The back of my head felt warm, blood trickling out of it, I'm sure.

"I won't have to kill him, he'd do it himself once you and that little pink hair fish is dead," Dylan said as he kicked me in the rib.

I howled in pain, coughing and fighting for a breath. As the French vampire moved beyond my line of sight and closer to where I hid Tourmaline, I screamed.

I screamed like my life depended on it, hoping someone heard me.

The vampire back handed me across the face, but I didn't let that or my lack of oxygen stop me.

He grabbed my wrist, his cold, dead hands like iron claps, pinning it the ground as his lips went to neck. His deadly stanching causing me to gag.

My heart felt it was truly being ripped from my chest. A fine bladed carving knife slicing away every muscle and tissue around it, prying it from my chest. My veins went from being lava to feeling ice cold.

This time my lungs wreaked havoc as I screamed for Aiden. Begging for him to save Tourmaline. Begging for death to take me already.

And maybe I was already dead. Maybe I was dreaming of possibilities. Hoping he'd be here.

Pounding footsteps grew closer and closer. From a faint pad of a feet to booming thunder. I heard the loudest and greatest stampede coming towards me. Faster and faster.

My eye lids were heavy as I watched Aiden come flying around the corner, his pack behind him.

Wild, inhabited murder in his eyes.

My angel of death had arrived.

Aiden was on the vampire in a flash. My screams fading to silent pants for air. He snapped the blood sucker's neck with ease, driving a wooden dagger in its chest as the others rushed towards where Dylan and the other vampire went off to.

"Find them both and kill them," He bellowed as he dropped to his knees before me. "Tate..."

I tried to smile at him, wincing in pain at my chest and trying desperately to catch my breath.

"Y-you're here," I grabbed his shirt.

"You're going to be alright," His voice broke, a tear slipping out of his eye as he shrugged out of his jacket and wrapped it around my wounded arm, getting it stained with my blood. He scooped me into his arms them and wrapped me in his warmth. "Stay with me, Cupcake."

"Tourmaline," I coughed. "S-she's in the storage closet."

He nodded to someone as the world began fading around me. Sounds quieting to a buzz.

"Nazra?!" He growled in torment the good doctor appeared before me, pulling out equipment from a bag. "Help her. Save her. Please."

Aiden kept me close to him, words tumbling out of his lips as he caressed my cheeks.

Visible fear in his eyes. Sweat on his brow. Tears in his eyes.

"Don't leave me," He kept whispering. A reverent sound on his lips.

"N-n-never," I coughed. "I-I love..."

The words died on my lips as I left his arms and welcomed the cold and inevitable death.

CHAPTER 32

Aiden's POV

"Don't leave me," I whispered to her, my voice cracking up.

"N-n-never," She coughed up. "I-I love..."

I watched in horror as her warm umber eyes fell close and she slipped away.

"No!" I growled, tightening my hold on her feeble, unconscious body. "Tate!"

"We need to get her to the infirmary, she's lost too much blood," Dr. Nazra said, eyes worried yet keeping herself focused. "Alpha, I have to tell you, we still don't have O negative blood for a transfusion."

Her words sliced through as she began shouting for someone to track down a human from the closest town.

"Give her my blood," A voice said above me. I watch as Jenny walked around to us, determination in every step. "I have O negative blood."

I stared at her in confusion, knowing she held a deep hate for both my mate and I. Why was she suddenly offering to help?

"What's your condition?" I interrogated, knowing that she was up to something.

She straightened her back, knowing exactly her condition that needed to be met, "Swear to me that you'll find Anvi, and I'll give my blood to Tate."

I glared at her, seething with rage at the odd request, but also helpless, "Fine."

"No, I want you to Alpha swear," She emphasized.

I hoisted my mate up, getting to my feet and cradling her in my arms, being sure to mind her head, "I, Alpha Aiden Oaks, swear to you that I will find Anvi."

She nodded, appeased, "Let's go."

I didn't know whether she simply wanted Anvi back because she was a mermaid or if there was something more. And that was information I didn't have time to find out before making an oath.

Not when it came to my mate.

With each step I took to the infirmary, it felt like someone was breaking the bones in my body.

Each time the sound of her heartbeat slowed or she took too long to breath, I felt my throat constricting as if someone held me up by the neck.

This was all my mess.

If I had only kept her by my side. If I had told her what I thinking. If I begged her just a little more to stay. Maybe then we wouldn't be here.

Now I held her unconscious and cold body in my arms as I raced through the castle. My head filled with 'ifs' and 'maybes'.

And if she died... well then, I didn't know what I would possibly do with myself.

Entering the infirmary, Dr. Nazra was already grabbing everything she needed. Other wolves having already set up the needles for the transfusion.

"Set her down here," Dr. Nazra instructed.

Laying her down, I prayed to a God. I didn't know if any existed. Be it the infamous Moon Goddess who birthed us or a Saint who humans prayed too. I didn't know if they had many faces or if there were multiple Gods. In that moment, I would have bowed before all of them and give my life for hers.

And if they refused, I'd be the Orpheus of this life and follow my Eurydice to the afterlife. I'd show death what she meant to me, and they could either have both of us, or neither.

"We're going to have to perform a direct transfusion because of the blood loss," Dr. Nazra said, gesturing Jenny to have a seat next to Tate.

She explained as her hands moved meticulously. Inserting the needle into Tate's wrist, stopping her blood from flowing out and then connecting the other end of the tube to Jenny.

I was moved away from Tate as Dr. Nazra and two other pack members who studied in the medical field moved around Tate.

"Alpha, you should step outside," The good doctor said.

"No," I shook my head vehemently, the thought alone bringing on more dread. "I'm not leaving her."

Dr. Nazra's eyes filled with sadness, but she shook her head, "I have to examine her and you pacing around wouldn't make it easier for us."

I felt my throat constrict, my legs turning to heavy steel bars that anchored me in place. I wanted to stay, but I needed her alive.

Dragging my feet and my heart, I pulled myself out the door, rage slowly building within me.

As the door swung shut behind me, I was instantly in the eyes of at least fifty pack members. All of them huddled in the corridor, anxious eyes and worried faces.

I couldn't pull myself together in front of them. The air in my chest felt caught as my lungs struggled to take a breath.

"Everyone, go to your rooms or report to duty," I heard Calypso saying. Her always quiet tone was now stern as she sent the crowd away.

When the last person left, I drove my fist into the wall opposite me. The marble cracked under my fist, sharp edged cutting into my skin.

"Alpha..." She said gently, staying back.

"Tourmaline?" I croaked, trying to pull my shredded thoughts together. "Have they found her?"

"Yes, and she was calling for you," She responded.

Staring down at my injured fist and the deep crimson red of Tate's blood that coated my skin and soaked my clothes, I shook my head.

"Later," I said, unable to move much further away from Tate or have Tourmaline come see me in such condition. "Calypso, would you please stay with her tonight? Take her the pool area with guards. Ensure the door is sealed."

"Yes, Alpha," she said before I heard the clicking of her heels disappearing down the hall.

Turning my back to the cracked wall, I kept my focus on the door of the infirmary. Desperation making me want to march back inside and offer my own heart in retribution.

Sacrificing my life for hers. An unfitting punishment for my cold front towards her. No, I deserved a slow and painful punishment, but at least if she had my heart she could live.

And every day after I'd spent my life atoning my sins in the darkest depths of Hell.

My thoughts went darker and darker as the seconds passed by.

The hallway growing cold and silent. A foreboding echo lingering in the walls at my every breath.

It felt like my own personal Hell. Every faint heartbeat of my mate's I heard from where I stood, her scent covered by the metallic stench of blood, her breathing ragged and too slow to be of much use. A torment created personally to pierce my soul over and over and over.

Yet, not long had passed and when the two wolves helping Dr. Nazra stepped outside and left the room.

They were silent, heads bent as they scurried down the hallway.

Dr. Nazra stood at the door, gesturing me inside with a grave expression.

"We should talk," she said quietly as I entered. My eyes went straight to Tate.

An oxygen tank was secured to her face, a neck brace around her neck and her arm stitched up.

My knees threatened to buckle and I would have too if Dr. Nazra didn't grab my elbow.

"Tell me," I said, my voice sounding like an old boat engine.

"Jenny's blood wouldn't be enough. Given Tate's already pre-existing condition, the amount of blood she lost and a fractured skull, there isn't a high chance of survival. We can't take care of her head while she's undergoing the transfusion and as of right now, we're simply bidding time," she said, and I could see how much the situation is also affecting her. "The only way is if the mermaid blood works. And we've tried this before."

My hands curled into fist, my stomach dropping to my feet as she confirmed the thoughts that had already been swimming in my head.

"No," I growled menacingly, scaring Dr. Nazra into taking a leap back. "You have to save her."

"There's nothing-"

"Please," My voice dropped into pleading whisper. "Please, tell me there is something we can do."

"I'm sorry," she said, her expression firm but her voice trembling.

A gut-wrenching pain tore into me. I can't lose her.

Not her.

Going to my Tate, I grabbed the hand which wasn't being used to get the transfusion and sank to my knees.

I didn't care if Jenny's cold eyes were on me if Dr. Nazra heard her Alpha apologizing.

"I'm sorry," I said to Tate. Kissing the middle of her palm. Her skin was pallid, lacking the tinge of blood that should be circulating in her body. She was cold, no warmth to her stillness. "I'm sorry I couldn't protect you. I should have saved you."

Defeat slowly began sinking its claws into me as I felt warm tears trail down my cheeks. I couldn't protect anyone I loved.

They call it Alpha Aiden's Protection Program, yet I couldn't protect anyone that mattered.

Not my parents. Not my brother and his wife. And neither could I protect Tate.

I didn't get to tell her that I love her or that I'm sorry. That I'll eternally be sorry for putting her through all the things I've said and didn't say.

That I was only trying to protect her, but instead I royally fucked up. That instead of keeping her safe, I all but left her in the hands of danger.

Wrapping her hand in my own, I leaned my forehead against the bed, thinking of how I'd dreamt of offering her a ring one day.

Now her hand felt too small. Too skeletal. And she wasn't here to plan our future.

Jenny gasping caused me to turn my eyes to eyes to her. Her own eyes were focused on Tate's arm where she cut herself open.

The thread that Dr. Nazra used loosened and un-stitched itself. And as if someone was taking an invisible needle and thread to her arm, her skin began pulling together and healing.

"Dr. Nazra," I bellowed, unsure if I was seeing this right.

"I'm seeing it too," She answered, eyes wide as she walked towards the bed.

"She healing," Jenny said in astonishment. "My blood?"

"There's no other way," Dr. Nazra confirmed, both her and I looking at Jenny.

"What are you?" I questioned.

"A mermaid," She answered immediately, confused by my question.

"Then why the hell did the mermaid blood from last time didn't work?"

She seemed at a lost as I was as we watched my mate begin healing.

I got to my feet, wondering if this was real, a figment of my imagination or if I'd finally gone mad.

The latter options seeming more likely.

"Impossible," Dr. Nazra said as the colour in Tate's skin swirled to life. She moved to remove the needle from both Tate and Jenny, stopping the blood flow.

My heart felt suspended between crashing to death and soaring with elation. Flexing my hand, I welcomed the pain in my knuckles which told me I was conscious. That what I was witnessing was as real the oxygen in the lungs. I caught the change in her heart beat, speeding up to that of a person alive, and ever so subtly her breathing matched. No more struggling to catch her breath.

Dr. Nazra removed the oxygen mask from her, followed by the neck brace.

I felt my heart beating in tandem with my mate's. Felt the rush of life in me that only she could provide.

I wasn't going to lose her. Not to Dylan and those God forsaken bloodsuckers.

"Why isn't she waking up?" I asked, my voice pleading as I watched her become whole again.

Dr. Nazra shook her head, "I've never dealt with mermaid blood before, but if it was wolf healing then her body would need time to process the changes. In a matter of seconds, she was revived back to life, I'm sure she'll awake soon enough."

I didn't like that answer, needing to see Tate awake and speaking.

"Do you know what this means?" Jenny asked, her voice drowned in fear. "If word gets out..."

"It won't," I clarified, a plan formulating in my head.

She snapped at me, "How can you be so sure? Dylan's been your Gamma for years and yet he got away with so much."

Jenny stabbed a match stick into the coals that held my guilt. Fanning the flames so that it burned me up from the inside.

"You promised you'll save Anvi, you can't go back on your word," She pressed.

"I won't," I snarled, turning to her. "And no one is going to find out that the mermaid blood works because today my mate died."

Both Jenny and Dr. Nazra stared at me in utter confusion.

"We don't know why your blood worked as opposed to the other we tried, and as if the pack wasn't already in danger, this knowledge is just going to stir the pot for trouble. Until we can make sense of what happened and how to use this against the vampires, Tate being alive stays between us," I shifted my focus on the both of them, ensuring they understood my words.

"How do you propose we keep her away from a castle filled with wolves?" Dr. Nazra asked.

"We'll move her to the Queen's quarters," I said.

Over the past five years, the wing of the castle where my brother and his wife, Queen Amethyst, lived has been sealed off. No one wanders into that side of the castle under my command.

When they died, the hallway became cold and I could hear their laughter echoing off the walls. See their faces in the trinkets they kept. It haunted me to go there, so I closed it off.

Everything they left was still as it was. Clothes stills hung in the wardrobe and bed still made. I couldn't make myself move a thing. When Tourmaline was ready, she could stay there, since everything in those rooms belonged to her.

But being a coward, I couldn't face it.

As we waited to ensure Tate was fully healed, I kept her hand in my own and waited for her to open her eyes. I willed her to look up at me with those brown eyes of her.

Holding on to hope that she'll still be her. And when she awakes, I'd never let her go again. I'd never let her hand go. I'd never turn my back to her.

I sent Jenny to check the corridors while Dr. Nazra gathered anything she'd need when we transferred Tate before grabbing clothes for her.

When it was time, I picked her up, now being in the frame of mind to take in how light she felt. Had she been eating? Had she been sleeping alright?

I didn't know and the only one to blame was myself.

As I carried through the castle, careful to not make a sound, Tate's new warmth felt like an oddity. She was always cold, her hands always searching for mine to keep warm.

"I'm going to keep you safe," I whispered a promise to her.

When I made it into the bedroom, I see the dust that had settled over the belongings of my family. Pictures of Will and Amethyst scattered through the room.

Jenny had placed clean sheets on the bed and Dr. Nazra stood with a fresh change of clothes for Tate.

Setting her down, I left the girls to get Tate out of her dress, the beautiful material now stained red. The image of her walking down the steps towards me was now tainted with the one I saw when I found her. The heated memory of us in the enclave under the staircase was now brandished with vivid feel of her warm blood on my hands.

Looking down at my palms, I couldn't stop the sob that tore through my lips at the sight of the dried blood. Her scent clinging to me as a reminder how close I was to losing her.

Ferocious guilt ate at me, tearing away at my skin bit by bit, consuming my insides whole until I felt hollow inside. Yet, despite that I couldn't help but also cry in relief.

Relief that she was cured.

Relief that I'll be able to hold again if she had me.

If she decided to stay.

Tate was still unconscious.

Dr. Nazra said she was in perfect health. Her heart miraculously healed. Her veins filled with all the blood she need. Her breathing even and steady.

I spent the night at her bedside, hoping she woke up.

When the sun crested over the ocean, I knew I had to deal with the repercussions of choices.

Entrusting Jenny, of all people, I left her to watch over Tate. I needed Dr. Nazra at my side to explain to the pack that Tate didn't make it.

As we gathered everyone who were unoccupied into the ballroom, my steps faltered when I saw Tourmaline holding onto Calypso.

I couldn't put her through the torture of believing Tate was death, only to confuse her later when she would find out my mate was in deed alive.

Mind linking Calypso over, she followed me out the door with Tourmaline. As soon as my niece was in arm reach, she threw herself at me, tears leaking down her cheeks in quick succession.

I hugged her tightly, another wave of guilt attacking me for not going to her sooner. When Calypso left us and everyone was securely inside the ballroom, I put enough distance between me and the other wolves to ensure they couldn't overhear us.

"Tourm," I whispered, my voice cracking as I watched her cry. Her nose snotty as she wiped it on my clean t-shirt.

"Is Tate alright, Dad?"

I gave her my best smile, "She's alive, but asleep."

Her eyes lit up, but tears still flowed, "Is she really?"

"Yes, but I need you to promise me something?"

She quickly nodded and as I explained to her that we had to keep Tate's healing a secret, I could see she was confused, but knew it was important. Tourmaline was smart for a five-year-old, so I knew she'd keep it a secret.

By the time we made it to the ballroom, my eyes took in the forgotten decorations and party paraphernalia from Dylan's doomed birthday party. Of course, he threw a celebration in honour of attacking my Tate. Disguising his foul plans under the pretext of setting up a ball.

And as I looked back on the theme of the party he boasted about, I couldn't contain the spark of rage it set off. Vie et mort. Life and death, as if he was simply gambling on the lives of the innocent.

Keeping Tourmaline's face pressed against me, to conceal her emotions from the pack, I made my announcement.

"If you didn't witness what took place last night, then you've probably already heard," I began. "Last night, during the attack, Tate was left alone with my niece. In that span of time, the vampires were able to infiltrate the castle. In protecting Tourmaline, Tate put her own life in the hands of danger."

I stopped, the memories roaring to life in my mind like a film reel. I didn't need to put on an act for my pack, not when every emotion I felt were true.

"She died last night after the attack," I revealed, pain lacing my voice as I struggled to enunciate the words. It hurt me to even speak the vile sentence. I had the urgency to knock on wood to ensure my words stayed just that and didn't come into fruition.

Silence fell around the room, no one spoke or even breathed. While they weren't connected to Tate through the pack, she had become a part of their lives. She was always around; helping when needed, listening whenever someone had something to say, encouraging the pack when she was hurting.

This was yet another blow to their lives after losing so many. And I prayed when the time was right, and I could tell them Tate was alive without risking her, the mermaids and the pack, they could forgive for me.

One by one, I heard cries began and questions started to be asked.

Dr. Nazra stepped up and began using medical terms to explain. In layman terms however, she said that Tate lost too much blood which couldn't be replenished by Jenny's donation, coupled with a head injury.

Someone asked if the Blood Moon Pack would retaliate for not protecting their own, a very reasonable question, yet one I hadn't thought to get an answer to.

"My mate was already suffering with her heart before she got here, so I assure you we will not be fighting any wars with them," I said as I made a mental note to call Thane and explain what had happened. Of course, it would be prefaced with, 'your sister is alive'.

After the pack meeting, everyone approached me with their offer of sympathy and condolences. I felt disgusted with myself for playing them as I had, but it was a necessary evil.

When Loly and Paul stood before me, their expressions held guilt. I knew nothing good was about to come out of their mouths, so I passed Tourmaline to Calypso, telling her to grab Rick and meet me in the library.

"What?" I bit out, staring between the pair.

Paul was first, explaining how my mate asked them for a favour. To keep tabs on Dylan and find dig up anything they could on a handful of incidents that took place while she was here.

"She had already suspected him, but he must have known we were following him, because he kept trace clean," Loly said.

"She knew," I said in astonishment. She knew and yet she hadn't told me. "Was this before or after the beach incident with Tourmaline?"

"Before. The day Matt was attacked down at the beach," Paul clarified. "He didn't leave the castle, but I saw him on the phone a few times. He spoke in French, but I didn't know what he was saying, so I brushed it off as him planning his party."

I felt my eye twitch, but couldn't exactly blame Paul when I hadn't paid enough attention myself.

"Did you find anything else?"

Loly nodded, "All the accidents were wiped clean. No trace of a scent, no fingerprints, all camera footage wiped. But, after last night's attack, I realized that I missed something. Dylan was a correlation in everything that occurred. The day we brought Tate to the pack and got attacked, he knew we were arriving, the day she came back from visiting her family, he insisted on going to pick them up and the car broke down. Kai frequently checked the cars, so there is no way he wouldn't have spotted something if it was wrong.

"Then when you found out about the human who got healed, Dylan knew the name of the man. He knew the day when Matt always checked the shed on the beach. He had access to the water motion sensors we have. He appeared out of nowhere one day and decided to gun for Kai's position. Why? And how did he win Kai? It just doesn't seem possible that he could when he was a rogue."

Truth was, I had asked Kai how Dylan won him that day. My friend simply shrugged and said Dylan was clearly stronger than him. And that day I knew he lied to me, but I never bothered to figure out why. Maybe I assumed he never wanted the position, or maybe he'd wanted to leave the pack after we were suddenly in the middle of a mermaid and vampire war.

Whatever his reasons, I should have asked the harder questions. I should have found out.

The day Tourmaline was attacked in the beach, I had a hunch that it was Dylan. His behaviour had already begun to be off the day Tate arrived. His moves became too erratic. Yet, I still didn't puzzle together that it was him until that day.

When a guard I posted in the backyard mind linked me to inform me that he'd been moved to patrol duty because Dylan thought we needed more bulk in our protection, I didn't question it. Dylan was after all the Gamma, and I had trusted his judgement. But when Jenny came running to me in the training field, telling me Tourmaline was missing and Tate went after her, my mind was already set on the culprit.

But I knew if it was Dylan, he had more up his sleeves and he'd be in contact with the vampires. Which was something I could use to my advantage if he thought he was playing me, but I had secretly switched the game on him. I also knew he would try to attack Tate next, going after the people closest to me.

Which was exactly why I thought treating her cold before him would throw him off. I thought he believed I blamed her for putting Tourmaline in danger, he'd leave her alone and focus his target elsewhere, make it easier for me to protect both my girls.

Then of course, she decided she should leave and tore my heart out of my chest. Clueing Dylan in on how I actually felt, which left my mate on the brink of death.

"There's one more," she said. "Last night, before the vampires attacked, Tate asked us to also keep an eye on Jenny."

I felt a fist on heart tighten and my vision momentarily blurred as I tried to keep a stoic expression. I'd suspected the sea witch of being cunning, after all she made me form an unbreakable promise to her in exchange for her blood. But if Tate asked these two to monitor her, then she would've had a reason why.

"Is that all?" I asked between clenched teeth.

Both of them nodded and before dismissing them, I thanked them both on behalf of Tate. As soon as I stepped away, I was already mind linking Dr. Nazra to go to Tate and stay with Jenny. The mermaid couldn't be trusted, but I also couldn't go to that part of the castle at the moment since everyone's eyes were on me. However, mermaids' strength was relatively none existent on land, so I was sure there was little she could do with a werewolf in the room next to her.

That, and she saved Tate and counted on me to save Anvi. If she harmed Tate now, she knew the deal would have means of being called off.

Pushing the queasiness in my stomach down, I raced to the library to find Rick. When I finally opened the door, I was greeted with a sight that had me seeing red.

Books were scattered all around the room, pages torn to shreds, my desk in ruins and stationery littering the floor.

"What. In. God's. Name. Happened?" I growled each word.

Rick scratched his head in confusion, "This was the first place they came when they entered the castle, maybe they were searching for a book?"

"Is there a book they should be searching for?" Calypso asked. I could see the tear stains on her cheeks and her redden eyes, both from mourning the fake death of her friend.

Sighing, I began tidying up and said, "There is much I haven't told both you."

"What exactly?" Rick asked.

Pausing with my efforts, I turned to them, knowing both my Beta and his wife had to know what was going on.

"For starters, Tate is alive," I said to them both.

Tourmaline smiled from her place next to Calypso as both her and Rick gasped.

Chapter 33

I awoke with a foreign sensation pulsing beneath my skin. Warmth blossomed through my body, blood flowing through my veins which once felt as if held ice. My breaths came easily, in a steady pattern instead of the laboured pants. The rhythm of my heartbeats consistent and without faults.

My eyes flew open with those thoughts, landing on the very unfamiliar ceiling. Deep violet covered the ceiling, reminding me of the sky while an angry storm blew through, leaving chaos in its path. An elegant chandelier sat at the middle, its warm lights glimmering off the iridescent surface of the ceiling.

Had I possibly crossed into the afterlife?

Lifting my left arm into view, I was baffled at the sight of arm whole and intact. No scars, bruises or wounds marring my skin.

Automatically, I flew up into a sitting position, a surge of strength and energy fueling me. Power that I hadn't felt since before I was attacked by rogues in my old pack. Before all the bad luck had starting pouring down on me.

When my gaze fell to the right of me, Aiden's bent head was laying on the bed next to my hand. He was slouched over, sitting on a chair that didn't appear comfortable. His hair was disheveled, messily tied into a bun. He now sported a short beard, there were dark circles under his eyes and his eyebrows were furrowed, as if he his worries followed him into his dreams.

Assessing the room around us, I wasn't sure where we were in the castle. It was neither Aiden's nor my room. Yet, it appeared lived-in from the trinkets that were scattered on a large vanity table, shoes neatly stacked by the door and a few articles of clothing hung on a room divider. From my vantage point, I could see there was a layer of dust that coated everything. As if they were untouched for years. Sitting and waiting for its owner to come dust them off.

There were picture frames lining the walls, and when I looked closer, I knew exactly where I was, but not why. I instantly recognized the couple in the photos. A man with shoulder length, dirty blonde hair and a pair of blue eyes the exact shade of my mates and a woman who was ethereal, godly and definitely the Queen of the Sea, Amethyst, with her purple hair.

Looking back towards my mate, I wondered what in all of the seven seas had actually happened. If he was here, and I was alive... what exactly transpired between the time I cut my arm open to now.

A million questions infiltrated my mind, sending me in a tailspin as I sorted them in my head. Dylan, my wounds, Tourmaline, vampires, the book search. There were so many things to be discussed.

Moving my fingers to Aiden's cheek, my eyes landed on the charm bracelet around my wrist. It was the one that contained pieces of sulfur crystal, which Aiden had gotten for me in replacement of my necklace.

Coldness seized my movement as the memories of Aiden begging me to stay plagued my mind. And with that came the recollection of his behaviour and Dylan's claim.

Had he truly been trying to protect me?

I feathered my fingers through his hair, gentle as to not wake him up. Tracing a loose strand, I used my finger to follow the shape of his brow, down his nose bridge and across his cheek bone. Mapping out every detail of him with my touch, burning the image into my mind.

When his eyes fluttered, I quickly snatched my hand away, folding both of them on my lap as I waited for him to wake up.

Aiden blinked the sleep from his eyes, scrubbing a hand down his face before he sat up and noticed I was watching him.

I caught the subtle sound of his breath caught, his motions freezing and his eyes unblinking. It was as if he was afraid to move in case the image of me disappeared.

"Tate," His voice was caught between a breath, barely audible.

No words left my lips as he engulfed me into his embrace. His scent wrapped around me, his grip tight and a his breath ragged as he inhaled. After a few minutes, he pulled away, hands cupping my face.

He looked me over - eyes moving over me, head to toe, as he checked for any wounds.

"Are you okay?" He asked, checking my arm where my cut was, feeling my pulse. When I nodded and he was sure there was no visible signs of injury, he slumped in relief."You're okay. You're alive," He chanted, as if needing to verbally confirm that the sight before him was real.

I placed my hands on his wrists, gently lowering his hold on me, "Aiden...w-what happened?"

"The vampires attacked you," He choked out, tears in his eyes. "There was so much blood...I almost lost you. Why did you harm yourself?"

His eyes were wild as he looked me over, lowering back into his chair so were eye to eye. I felt his emotions overcoming me, the terror that filled his eyes chilling my bones.

"I couldn't let them find Tourmaline, and using my blood was the only way to cover my scent on her," I said. "Is she safe? And the vampire? Did you catch them? Dylan, he's working with them too."

Nodding he wiped tears from his eyes, looking up at me, "Tourmaline is safe, thanks to you, again. The vampires got away, we found an access tunnel in the basement they must have used. Dylan took off with them."

Relief filled me with the news of Tourmaline, but confusion and unease still whirled inside of me at the thought of the vampires gaining access to castle so easily.

"A tunnel?" I questioned for further clarification.

"We didn't know it was there, but it leads down the beach, Calypso found some old blue prints, but they weren't mapped. However, the wood used as support beams are old, so I suspect it's been there since the castle was built. A wall was built over it, maybe from when Amethyst took residence here, I'm not sure. Dylan must have found it and started quietly chiseling away at the concreate since he's been in the pack. He wouldn't have risked using a power tool to create noise and it explains why the vampires only snuck in that night," He explained.

I used my fingers to massage my forehead, this new information creating knots in my stomach.

"I suspected he was working with them," I said, not looking at Aiden. "I had Loly and Paul tracking his movements, but they couldn't find any traces he left behind. Last night I also had them follow Jenny-"

"Not last night," Aiden stopped me as he shook his head. "You've been unconscious for five days."

I gaped at him, "Five days? Why? How... how am I alive?"

The thought swirled through my head like a stampede. The blood lose, my heart problems, my perfectly healed hand. I looked at Aiden for answers, not entirely sure I was actually alive or if this was a hellish nightmare I'm having from six feet under.

Before he could answer me, another thought struck me like a blazing iron rode piercing through me until it cut right through. Pressing my hand to my cheek, I checked my temperature before lowering my find to the pulse point on my neck.

Warm skin and a beating heart. Definitely did not turn into a vampire, thank the Moon Goddess.

"The impossible," He muttered under a breath. "You were badly injured, with the wound you inflicted on yourself and a cracked skull, Dr. Nazra said you wouldn't make it. As you know we didn't have any O negative blood...not until Jenny offered hers."

"Jenny?" I blinked in surprise.

"She offered to give you blood for a transfusion, we didn't have any other options left. What we didn't expect was for her blood to heal you."

"I don't-...am I cured?" I questioned as disbelief filled me.

He nodded, a smile lighting his face, "You're cured. Safe. We don't have any answer on how her blood worked compared to when we tried the first time, but you're healed and that's all that matters right now."

A thousand thoughts swirled in my head. I was whole again. I was Tate once more. No more chest pains or short breaths, no more excuses for holding back. It was a gift of another life, a reason to fight even harder.

Jenny was many things, but she'd saved me. And for that I owed her much more than a thank you.

"If her blood didn't work... I don't know what I would have done if I'd lost you," He expressed, eyes dropping to the floor. "I couldn't go through with another funeral."

"Aiden," I whispered, reaching my hand out to him.

Before my hand landed on him, he was out of his chair and on his knees. His grief-stricken eyes found mine, the blue irises were a raging storm, an angry ocean that was stirring up a monstrous storm. His expression was reverent and repentant, pleading.

"I'm sorry," He said, honesty lacing his words like the antidote to a poison.

It stung, to finally hear him say the words. Words I'd almost given up on hearing after he refused to explain what was going through his head. What plans he had and wouldn't share.

"I could never ask for your forgiveness, because I don't deserve it. Yet, I'll be selfish and beg you with every single thing in me, to not leave. For me."

Holding his eyes, I took my time to choose my words carefully, piecing together my emotions and feelings that's been dormant while I was unconscious. It's been five days for him, but it was only yesterday for me when we were kissing under the staircase and he was pleading with me to stay. I'd had little time to think.

"Dylan said something." His nostrils flared at the name, but he waited for me to explain. "He said that your behaviour was the result of him. Of you trying to protect me from whatever plans he had for me. Is that true?"

"After what happened with Tourmaline, I suspected he would go after you next," He confided, eyes regretful. "I should have told you, and for that I couldn't be more sorry. Even after all that, I still couldn't protect you. As your mate I should have kept you more safe, not hurt you."

"You should have told me."

"I wanted to, but Dylan has been in the pack for years. I wasn't sure if anyone was aiding him in plotting against the pack, or if he was simply spying through other means. I couldn't take the risk of him figuring out that I was on to him, not when it would compromise your safety," He explained. "I figured if I kept you away, he wouldn't go after you and if I eased off him, he'd slip up with his plans. I thought you would have understood, after I told you I'd do anything to protect you. The poem..."

And when wind and winter hardenAll the loveless land,It will whisper of the garden,You will understand. - Oscar Wilde

Only knowing what I know now, do I finally understand the words he meant for me. When there was coldness between us, a lack of love, it was because he had a reason and he'd want me to understand. He expected me to understand.

"The poem," I continued his sentence while shaking my head, "didn't make any sense to me. You never explained what it meant to you, and I lack the ability to read your mind."

"Then you should have at least trusted my feelings for you," His voice pleading.

"What feelings?" I questioned with a spark of anger. "You haven't told me anything about how you've felt."

His winced, something akin to fear and pain lining his features as his voice softened, "How do I simply put that you're everything to me? That you're the oxygen that fill my lungs, the heartbeat in my chest, the thoughts in my head and the single most important thing in my life? How do I tell you that I would have torn my heart out clean and given it to you just so that you could live? Tell me, how could I have said all that and burden you with my feelings when I didn't have a way of saving you? How could I have made you feel like you had to stay for me when I had nothing to offer you? Not a safe home or a way for you to live painlessly."

Something wet and warm hit my bunched up hands that laid on my lap. When I looked, I realised tear drops were dripping down my cheeks. Quickly, I dashed them away, expecting my chest to constrict and bring on an onslaught of pain that had become synonymous with my tears. But all that was gone now, because I was saved.

"I didn't mean to make you cry," He said remorsefully. "I just got you back and of course the first thing I do is upset you."

I shook my head, my throat constricted by my emotions and tears.

"I meant every word I said."

"I know," I croaked.

"I'm sorry."

"I know," I whispered. "But you hurt me, Aiden. You found my weakest spot and you cut me deep, inflicting new wounds every time you turned away from me. Wounds that always bled each time I remembered that you blamed me for Tourmaline."

With shallow breaths he finally said, "If I could take it all back, I would. There are many things in my life I wish I could re-do if I had the chance, but hurting you is my biggest regret. The truth is, you saved Tourmaline and I that day. I knew that the moment it happened, yet I twisted it to blame you while you were already suffering. I hurt you in indescribable and insurmountable ways, and for that I'll forever be sorry."

He didn't have to ask for forgiveness, but it was his. If the last attack was meant to be a teachable lesson, it was that life was unpredictable is many ways. And it was too short to live with regrets and holding back. So if he's not holding back anymore, I wasn't going to either.

I was going to live with every breath I was given and I was going to love with every beat of my heart.

"Aiden..." I whispered, words coming short of what I wanted to say.

"There's one more thing I have to say," He placed a hand on mine. "This is neither the situation nor the place in which I'd imagined telling you this, but I refuse to wait any longer. Not when I've hurt you so much and almost had you slip through my fingers."

"What?" I asked.

"I love you," He proclaimed, his words clear, exact, final and lacked any room for questioning or misinterpretation. "I have loved you from the moment you jumped out of the car and started fighting with a vampire despite not knowing what it was and lacking the training to deal with one. And everyday since, you've only made me fall harder, deeper."

My eyes widened by his declaration, my heart fluttering to life in my chest. It was the first time he said it, yet it felt like familiar words he'd been whispering to me all this time.

Looking at him now, the brick wall which I fought hard to break through was finally gone. Not a rubble in sight. No more hiding himself from me. It was simply Aiden Oaks before me.

I pulled my hands from under his and grabbed his arm, pulling him up and onto the bed with my renewed strength. He seemed surprised by my ability to haul him up next to me, but before he could say a word, I was on him. Once his back hit the headboard, I climbed onto his lap and tucked my face into the crook of his neck. Aiden wasted no time in returning the embrace, his clasp strong and unyielding to let go. I basked in his familiar warmth, soaking up the feeling of his muscular body pressed against my soft one.

"I missed your stupid face," I said.

I heard a contented sigh from him as he said, "I missed you too, Cupcake."

"I know," I grinned.

There was a brief pause before he pulled his head back and looked at me with a bemused expression, "Did you just call me-"

"Stupid face? Yes, I did."

He chuckled at my curt response and I revealed in the sound.

"I love you too," I finally said, hearing his breathing stagger.

He took my face in his hands and brought his lips to my forehead, "Thank you."

I smiled, a small sense of peace settling into me, "So this is what it's like to be in love."

"I suppose it is," He smiled, a genuine one that lighted up his face, softening his hardened features.

I could bask in the peace all I wanted, but there were many more information I had to catch up on starting with, "Have Kai and Matt returned? Did they find any mélusine or the book?"

"They haven't contacted me since the day after the vampire attack," I could see the concern written all of his face, hear the worry lining his words.

I narrowed my eyes, "What was the last thing they said?"

"Kai found a lead in an old sea side book store. The owner said he'd about the mélusine during his time as a coast guard back in the day. According to him, there had been sightings on the coast of the city Brest in France. When Kai speculated it as a folktale, the man denied that it was anything but as he was sure he'd seen one himself during a night shift."

"They're real?"

"It was decades ago, so Kai wasn't sure about finding them. I'm beginning to worry that something happened to them both, but I have no way to reach them and sending a wolf after would be dangerous," His muscles were rigid, bunched up in tension under me. "I asked Jenny if she knew anything about them and she said they were the oldest sea witches, long gone from earth."

The mention of her name reminded me of why I'd been suspicious of her. She may have saved me, and for that I was grateful, but there was no denying she knew something the night of Dylan's birthday. Her panicked expression, her eyes flickering around the room as if waiting for something cataclysmic to happen.

"She shouldn't be trusted," I stated to my mate.

Knowledge and respect filled his gaze as he nodded, "Yes, about Loly and Paul, they told me about your secret suspicions."

"I wanted to tell you, but-"

"I understand," He assured me. "Accusing Dylan without proof would have only caused tension within in the pack - I hadn't exactly been honest about my thoughts either and it's time to change that. We need to work together, as a team, or else we'll only hurt each other and the pack."

I held out a pinky finger to him and he smiled as he wrapped his own around mine, "Deal."

"Deal."

"Have you questioned her then?" I asked.

"Not yet. Loly wasn't sure why you'd suddenly suspected her, but I have a feeling she's been up to no good. I thought it would be best to wait for you to interrogate her."

I frowned not liking the idea of being the one to throw accusations when she'd cured me with her blood, but it had to be done.

"Fine, but only after you get me some food. And lots of it."

"Your wish is my command, but you're going to need to move of me."

I shook my head, "Take me with you."

He stilled his movements as features hardened, "There's something else I forgot to mention."

I squeezed his arm, a sense of unease rushing through me, "What?"

"The night you got attacked, everyone assumed you wouldn't make it. When your body did respond to the mermaid blood, I decided it would be best to keep it from the pack until we have an explanation and a plan. It's not that I don't trust them, but after Dylan..."

"Aiden," I said, my voice as sharp as a razor blade, "what exactly do you mean you kept it from the pack?"

I could feel my eye twitching as I assumed exactly what had happened.

"I told them you didn't make it," His voice was meek and guilt ridden.

"You Dickhead," I almost shouted, realising that was the reason I was in here instead of his or my room. He winced at my reaction, but I went on, "How could you tell them I died? How do they even think I'm dead when they could smell me? Wait, you didn't spray me with skunk spray, did you?"

I lifted the collar of my dress and gave it a sniff, relief filling me when I confirmed he hadn't sprayed the odious scent on me to cover my wolf scent.

"Dr. Nazra and Jenny helped me moved you that night, when everyone went to their bedrooms. We were sure to cover your scent and this wing of the castle has been closed of for five years, it's far away enough where no one would scent you. It's a mess

I made, so don't worry about the pack later on. We just need to figure everything out before we share the news."

"Good grief," I tugged on my hair, "I don't know if that was a good move. A lack of trust in the pack could have serious consequences."

He stopped my hand and held it between his, "It may not have been the best strategic Alpha move, but I wasn't thinking as an Alpha. I was thinking as your mate. If word even reaches the ears of the damn blood suckers, do you think they would attack again, strong this time, to get their dead hands on you?"

I blew out a harsh breath, seeing his logic, but not loving it.

"Okay, but we have to let them in on it soon."

"Once we figure out a plan. If Kai doesn't call soon, I'm thinking-"

"I'll go look for them."

"No," He said flatly. "It's too dangerous, and I'm not letting you out of my sight again. If they don't return soon, I'll call a local French pack to help find them."

"That will require explaining," I reminded him.

"I'll fib as much as I can, but we have to get them back. I owe them both an apology, and Kai needs to reinstated as Gamma."

The guilt in his eye was as clear as the water in the ocean outside. I gave him a sad smile, "They'll call soon, I could feel it."

He kissed the crown of my head again before getting to his feet and going to fetch both my food and Jenny. With a warning to stay in the room, I sighed at the fact that this was now my doom. Faking a death was more troublesome than dying. At least then my ghost could roam, but now I'm stuck in a dusty room that didn't belong to me.

I found a new tooth brush in the en-suit along with a fresh change of my clothes. When I was scrubbed clean and my breath my minty fresh, I stared at myself in the mirror of the bathroom.

My skin was no longer the garish pale tone, but instead bronzed to it's natural hue. The worry lines I hadn't taken notice of before were gone. My cheeks didn't look sunken in, and my eyes weren't hollowed. The image that stared back at me was, Tate Blackwood. The real Tate, not the sick Tate who waited for death and was shit out of luck.

Reality crashed into me, like a sudden burst of fireworks sparkling beneath my skin. It set me alive and fueled the energy in me. The fire let my wolf howl with delight, making me want to shed my skin for my fur coat.

I was ready to run. To catch the wind between my fur and the grass beneath my paws. Paradise was right outside and wanted to bask in its glory.

Yet, now that I was no longer counting down the days I had left, I couldn't move from this regal room.

The thought struck something deep within me, but I knew I had to be patient. All this time I'd wanted to defeat the vampires. To bring peace to pack, let the mermaid go back to the water and create a safe place for Calypso to raise a child. Now was my chance to help them.

The sound of footsteps heading my way excited me along with the scent of food.

Giddy with excitement, I entered back into the bedroom and five and a half bodies piled in.

Tourmaline was on me in an instant, her arms looped around my neck. Calypso and Dr. Nazra were right behind her, wrapping me in their arms as we group hug. Another body joined the hug and I realised Rick, with teary eyes, had also joined.

Jenny was standing by the door, a nervous expression on her face as she twisted her hands together. Aiden was grinning from ear to ear as he held a large tray of food.

"Okay, let my girl breath," Aiden chuckled. "I have to feed her."

They let me go, except for little Tourmaline, who now had tears in her eyes.

I calmed her down, gently stroking her hair and telling her that I'm alright. Aiden did a good thing in letting her know that I was alive. If he'd led her to believe I was gone... well I wouldn't like to imagine the emotional scar it would leave on her.

We spent the next hour catching up - and by that I mean everyone was making a fuss over my wellbeing.

Dr. Nazra informed me that she'd been administering intravenous injections to keep my body sustained. IV needles that were connected to long tubes never worked for us wolves as our skin demanded regrowth. Hence, a daily injection was needed.

Calypso filled me in on the pack's way of coping with my 'death'. When she mentioned a private ceremony with only the heads of the pack in attendance, I shot daggers at Aiden. He dropped his head at my glare, remorseful.

While they talked, Aiden made sure that I was eating. Each time I stopped, enraptured in the conversation, he took the utensil out of my hand and shoveled more food in my mouth.

I hadn't a clue which emotion was stronger; my annoyance with him or the fluttering feel of my heart at having his full attention and care.

When the tray was empty - which wasn't a difficult task to accomplish given I gained my werewolf appetite back - Jenny finally cleared her throat and walked further into the room.

"I have somethings to say," She dipped her head. I was momentarily silenced at her willingness to begin the hard conversation.

"Go on," I prompted.

"Dylan wasn't the only one who was working with the vampires. I was as well," She confessed, not able to meet my gaze.

Aiden growled, moving towards her, but I grabbed his arm. This little mermaid had some serious explaining to do.

"When Anvi went missing, Dylan approached me and told me that the vampires had her. That they're keeping her alive, once I played by their rules," I could practically feel the growing tension in the room as Jenny spoke. "So, I joined hands with him, doing whatever it was they wanted. The day all went to beach, Dylan told me to mess with the motion sensors since he couldn't leave his scent around. He was also the one to tell the vampires when you'd found Tate, and orchestrated the ambush. That also includes the time he messed with the car before volunteering to pick Tate up at the airport. For whatever reason, the vampires never attacked him, so he never worried

"He also had Matt attacked a few weeks ago. His vendetta against Kai and Matt... I don't know why he was against them like that. But his goal was to become Alpha."

"What?" Rick barked, anger lacing his tone.

I could imagine the betrayal he and Aiden felt, knowing their best friend had been screwing them over to become the leader.

Jenny shook her head, as if confused herself, "He never explained why, and I knew better than to ask. But that was his goal, to get rid of Aiden and send Tourmaline to the vampires."

Aiden's muscles bunched under my hold, fighting to restrain himself.

"When Tate was found, he went a bit ballistic. He wanted to kill her the night she came to the castle, but getting away with murder would be harder as her room was next to Alpha Aiden's. His moves became sloppy, he was always planning some scheme to attack everyone."

"His birthday?" I questioned.

She nodded, "We knew you were dying, but he didn't want you to die on your own. He wanted to weaken and hurt Aiden so that he could easily win the Alpha position. So, he finally got the tunnel open in the basement and planned every detail to the 'T'. Your blood was meant to be drained that night."

"Is that why you were anxious that night?" I asked, recalling her behaviour.

Her cheeks flamed, "I was getting a bit antsy with them. They hadn't shown me a picture of Anvi to prove she was still alive, let alone allow me to meet her. I wanted so bad to tell you, to prevent this from happening, but I couldn't risk her life."

"Why would you do all that for her?" Aiden asked between clenched teeth. "You even made me promise to find her."

That was news to me, but now I was equally as curious.

Jenny gulped, fidgeting before revealing, "Because she's my mate. Something only the mer-folk are aware of."

"You and Anvi are mates?" Calypso clarified.

"Yes," She answered before she lifted her head pleading to Aiden. "Which is why I made you promise. You have a mate of your own, and I imagine the connection is not so different from that of a mer-folk mate. So you must understand why I need to get her back. To save her."

Aiden still seemed confused as he asked, "If Anvi is your mate, why have you been..." his eyes flickered to Tourmaline and me before he cleared his throat, "trying to like me."

Green envy grew on my vines, ready to lash at the mermaid for pursuing my mate.

She snorted, "Trust me, it was as painful for me as it was for you. Dylan instructed me to..." her eyes also went to Tourmaline as I imagined her next words were going to be, get you in bed, "make you like me before I..." she gestured to Aiden before placing her finger at her neck and made a motion of slitting her throat. Her game plan was seduce and murder. "That way he'd become Alpha and I'd trade Tourmaline for Anvi."

My blood boiled thick with rage at her confession. Kai had a point in not trusting Dylan, as his intent all this time was betrayal for power. Yet no one suspected the green haired mermaid.

"Why did you give me your blood?" I snapped at her, not liking the fact that my body was now contaminated with her sinister blood. "Why, after all that, are you telling us this now?"

She titled her head up, finally meeting my eyes, with determination, "You could call me whatever you'd like, but I'm not a killer. I gave you my blood because if you died, I'd have that on my conscious. And I also had a bargain I needed to strike with your mate, and my blood was the perfect leverage I needed."

"You knew it would heal me?"

"No," I could tell she wasn't lying. "I only offered because Dr. Nazra didn't have any of your blood type. I didn't know it would have worked since the last time you tried it hadn't. But now that you're alive and awake, you have to help me get Anvi back."

I shook my head, "Why should I?"

"Because I saved your life," She stated.

Everyone went still, Aiden being the only one who rose to his feet and let out a menacing growl.

"We will help you," He clarified. "But you have betrayed my pack as well as your Queen in the worst way possible, and for that you will be banished from this castle we get your mate back."

There was no fear on her face as she nodded. Desperation was a wicked thing. Blinding and deceitful.

CHaPTer 34

S itting in the sliver of sunlight that peeked through the thick curtains was how the last two days of my life went.

I hadn't expected sitting still in an old room would make me become an impatient person, yet here we are. I was itching for some fresh air and to finally shift into my wolf.

However, that couldn't be done as my mate faked my death to his pack. Now, I was left sitting here all day with the company of Tourmaline, Calypso, Dr. Nazra or Jenny. Never all at once though. Tourm visited with either Calypso or Aiden, and the others visited in between. It would be too risky if they all came at once instead of on a rotation.

The time I loathed the most was when Jenny showed up. I found it impossibly difficult to thank her or even speak to her. She was just here out of obligation to keep me company while the others went about their daily tasks. And even if she was here out of concern, I'd never be able to forgive her for plotting to kill my Aiden or trade Tourmaline's life for her mate.

"Wouldn't you have done the same for Aiden?" She had asked that morning.

I was just polishing off the hearty breakfast Aiden sent up for me when she'd directed her question at me. The food turned to concrete in my stomach as she voiced the words.

What would I have done?

Responsibility to protect my mate and guilt of harming others both clashed inside of me.

"If I had to hurt others to save my mate, then I don't believe I'd be any better than the ones who wanted to harm him in the first place. And I don't believe he'd forgive me for hurting others for him either," I answered her.

She lifted her brows, not at all surprised by my answer yet she neither believe it, "So you'd leave the person you love to die at the hands of your enemies?"

"No, I'd cut my enemies' hearts out with the help of the ones they wanted dead." I stated pushing my plate aside. "I'd be wise enough to know that I stood no chance against a cave of bats, so I'd seek help from those they wanted me to hurt. Isn't that what you're doing now?"

"I'm not a wolf," She snapped. "We don't plan wars or strategize about killing others."

"Then it's time you learned. Vampires are the prime enemy of your people, Jenny, you have to adapt to your situation. If you don't, you'll lose your mate and the rest of your people while you continue to be their puppet," I said. "I won't forgive you for attempting to kill my mate or Tourmaline, but I'll help you because I want my revenge just the same."

"You act as if you've never messed up in your life."

"I have," I answered, "but never in a magnitude that required me to harm a child."

Jenny went silent as she turned her head away from me. Her green hair curtaining her face from me as she peered down at the floor.

That was how the rest of the morning went by, Jenny sitting across the room from me, a book in her hand but not turning any pages. I, for the life of me, couldn't decide if jabbing myself in the eye or jumping off the balcony would provide more excitement than pacing the ever stuffy room. I didn't think my mind was that morbid, but anything to mix it up would be heavenly.

When Jenny finally left, Dr. Nazra stayed at my side for the rest of the evening, but she fell asleep an hour in our conversation. I don't blame her, ever since the castle was attacked everyone had been on edge. Patrol was tightened and training was pushing on a constant rotation. Training in the Oaks Pack wasn't easy two-step defences and throwing punches. Nope, the trained warriors fought as if they were in a war. Quick healing and stamina allowed for this, but when the injuries became too deep, they required Dr. Nazra.

She's been in the infirmary all day after pulling night duty on patrol.

When I looked to her sleeping form, I couldn't stop the burst of guilt in me. I should be running patrol. I should be protecting my pack the way a Luna does. Yet, I was stuck in this ivory tower, nothing to do but sit and rot.

Finally, night rolled around and I sent her back to her room. A Luna's order to take the night off, even though my words hold no official capacity of authority.

Not five minutes after she'd left, Aiden finally clocked in. He forwent his comfy and dustless room to keep me wrapped in his arms at night. Those moments were the highlights of my day.

When he stepped through the door, looking tired and rugged, I couldn't help but throw my arms around his neck and twine my legs around his waist. He let out a tiny 'oof', but returned the embrace as he wrapped me in his arms.

"Hey," I whispered his ear before pulling back and catching his small smile.

A smile that lifted his shoulders as if I took the weight off them.

Silently, he went over the bed, laying us both down on the soft mattress yet keeping me wrapped in his arms.

"Hi," His warm breath fanned across my face, making me blush at both his nearness and the way his eyes sparkled while looked at me.

"How was your day?" I asked as my fingers brushed his long hair at his neck.

Groaning, he pulled me closer, held me tighter. "I want to tell you that everything if fine, that I have everything under my cont rol...but I'd never lie you, Tate. Not ever again."

I cupped his cheek, smoothing my fingers over his stubble, "Then don't."

Nodding, he opened his heart to me. The brick wall no longer standing between us.

"It's tiring. The pack seems to be more suspicious of each other. Dylan's betrayal left a nasty scar in our pack's minds, making us wary and distrustful. Even if it wasn't his intention, he chipped away at our pack mentality."

The fire in his eyes screamed for blood, a vengeance for his people and his pack's pride. And I was going to do everything in my power to help him get it.

"Let me help you," I said and he immediately started shaking his head. "Aiden, let me come back, please. I can't sit here all day knowing those damn leeches are preparing to slaughter us, to take Tourmaline."

His expression was pained as he held my hand that was resting on his cheek and slide it to his lips where he pressed a tickling kiss.

"I want you by my side, Tate. I need you there. But I can't risk your safety or Tourmaline's or the pack's. You were an ounce of blood away from death, if you came back now they would know," His teeth grinned together, eyes holding mine as he readied for a fight. "I won't put you in a position to get hurt ever again."

The anger in my blood that wanted to protect my mate and pack simmered at his statement. I knew he was right, was explained the situation before, but how could I sit here. Worst yet, how could my very existence put everyone in harm's way. We each had to pick our battles in life, and this time I chose to back down. Because this was a fight I'd neither win nor wanted to face the consequences of if I did.

So instead I pressed my lips his, taking him by surprise. The shock didn't last long as he wrapped his arm around my waist and opened his mouth to my demanding tongue.

Aiden didn't kiss with hesitation anymore, now he kissed me like a starved man whenever we were alone, and I can't deny that I've haven't been equally as ravenous for his soft lips on mine. Our breaths mingled, our hands explored, our feeling deepened.

It was never like this before. I think my ill heart played a significant role in that. It made Aiden cautious of touching me, of going to far in case my heart speed up and caused the rippling pain to tear into my chest.

Now that I was fully healed, and maybe it was my close brush to death, or the fact that we were finally on the same page about our feelings...whatever it was, it awoke a deep burning of want in the both of us.

A searing desperation of need that had me moaning into his lips and had his large palms pressing into my back sensually as our bodies aligned.

I returned the kiss with as much passion as I received, curling my fingers in his dirty blonde hair and gasping as his hands curved against my waist and traveled lower.

He pushed my leg back as he rolled me under him, his movements smooth and cautious to not break our kiss. Aiden's weight pressed comfortably against me. Pulling away from my lips, he grinned down at me before pressing kisses all over my face causing me to giggle.

My laughter soon turned into gasps of air as his fingers explored my body, his little ministrations sending pleasure coursing through me.

My hands left his hair, trailing down his back and then edging it's way back up under his t-shirt. I felt his muscles flex and his abdomen shudder when I raked my nails over his skin. Aiden let out a growl, his kisses moving to my neck.

As his hand toyed with the hem of my t-shirt, I nodded at his silent question. He took my answer in stride as his palms stroked up my stomach before hovering over my chest.

"This okay?" He paused to ask.

"Yes," I said breathlessly.

His calloused fingers traced the edges of my bra and I felt the sharp teeth of his canines scrape against the juncture of my neck and collarbone. The area where my mark would sit.

Aiden stilled above me as my eyes flew open in realization. He lifted his head into my view and I saw that the sharp teeth were in fact the ones he'd used to mark me. My mate was all to quick to sit back, pulling his hand free from my shirt as his teeth shrunk back to its human shape.

"Shit," He swore, dragging a hand down his face. "I need to be more careful."

My heart thundered in my chest, racing from our fiery exchange of kisses, as I nodded my head in agreement.

You see, my fake death not only stopped me from helping my pack, it also stood in the way of Aiden and I going all the way. If we did end up sleeping together Aiden would surely mark me, and if that happened, then the pack would be aware that they now had a Luna. We had to come clean about our pack about me being alive before we go barreling in with them suddenly getting a zombie Luna. Couple that with the fact that we also can't tell them I'm alive until we know how the mermaid blood works has left Aiden and I in a constant state of having to hold back on our desires.

His expression was pained, "Don't get me wrong, Cupcake. I want to - god do I want to - but-."

I sat up and kissed his jaw, "I know, babe. I don't blame you. I just really want to leave this room and start killing some blood suckers."

He chuckled, "And here I thought you wanted to leave so you could finally jump me."

"That too." I grinned as the heat between us simmered down.

Even though I was bold enough to admit it, I could feel the tips of my ears heat from a blush.

Aiden simply kissed the shell of my ear without dragging out my response to him.

"Tomorrow you'll get into contact with a pack in France?" I asked quietly.

"If Kai doesn't contact me, yes."

The underlying fright in his voice was almost undetectable. His best friend was missing and he didn't have to the means of going after him.

I wanted to say that Kai and Matt were going to be alright. That they'd call before the sun rises tomorrow. But I couldn't do that. I couldn't whisper false promises and fill my mate's head with an empty sense of hope.

"I should go take a shower," He finally said, lifting away from me. Aiden pulled his phone from his pocket, placing it on the bed next to me as I sat up. "In case they call."

I nodded silently as he grabbed a fresh change of clothes and headed to the en-suite.

Glaring at the blank screen of his mobile, I willed it to ring. To ping with a text, light up with the indication that Kai emailed him a location or a photo. Anything would be better than the silence he'd given us.

By some odd stroke of luck, I watched in utter confusion as the phone's screen awoke with life. A soft jingle echoed from the speaker and it vibrated against the mattress.

No name. Local number.

My finger was sliding the screen to answer as I pressed the phone to my ear.

"Alpha?" A familiar voice called through the receiver.

"Kai?" I asked carefully. My mind unbelieving that I had actually heard his voice.

"Tate!" He answered. "Where's Aiden? I need to speak to both of you. Privately if you could."

I was on my feet already, moving to the bathroom.

"Kai," I said through a heavy breath. "Holy shit, you're okay?"

He chuckled, "Trust me, it hasn't been a pleasant time." I wanted to asked more, but he went on in a rushed tone. "Could we make this quick? I don't want to stay on the line for long."

"Yes, of course," Startled, I pushed the bathroom door open despite hearing the water going.

Aiden jumped in surprise at my sudden intrusion, his hands flying to cover his groin. As a question formed on his lips, I held out the phone, "It's Kai."

His eyes were wild as modesty left him and his hands fumbled to turn off the shower. Grabbing a towel, I threw it at him as he exited the glass enclosure and wrapped it around his waist.

The phone was on speaker before he held his hand out for it, "Kai?"

"Alpha," He sighed in relief. "Look, I know we have much to discuss, but we can't speak over the phone for long in case anyone's tapping in."

"Kai," Aiden snapped his friend into attention. "Are you and Matt okay?"

"We are," He answered and Aiden's shoulder relaxed with relief. "There's a lot to explain, but I need you to come to me."

"Your number says you're local."

"We're in a small town a few hours up the coast." Aiden and I exchanged a curious glance before Kai went on. "I'll drop you the location, but we don't have much time. You'll have to leave by sunrise, and ensure you're not followed."

"I'll be there."

"And Alpha... look, I know you trust Dylan, but I don't. So, don't let him see you leave and for God's sake check the car you use before you do. He could have installed a tracker or messed with the battery again," I could hear the frustration in Kai's voice along with the hope that Aiden believed him.

"Trust me Kai, there's a lot we need to tell you too," I answered. He'd left before Dylan's doomsday of a birthday party, so he was yet to catch up on to the Gamma being officially kicked out of the pack.

The silence that followed clued me into his shock at the turn of the conversation, but he quickly composed himself and said, "I'll see you tomorrow and we'll talk then."

Aiden ended the call and before he could say a word, I said, "I'm going with you."

He pressed his lips together, looking aggravated, "Fine, but if something happens-"

"It won't."

"But if it does," He pressed as he held my shoulders, "you run okay. You run as fast and as far as you can, preferably into the sunlight."

My fingers reached out and grabbed the towel that was wrapped around his waist, dragging his wet skin flushed to me, "If you think for one second I'd ever leave you, then you haven't been paying attention, Alpha."

His lips brushed my hairline as he said, "Ohh, I've been paying attention, but I won't stop the hope that someday you'd actually listen to me."

"Where's the fun in that?" I grinned at him before asking the question we're avoiding. "Do you think they found the Mélusine?"

With a pinched eyebrows he considered, "If they haven't then it's something close enough. Hopefully they have the answer as to why Jenny's blood healed you."

"Would they...do you think it's a trap?" I worried my lip between my teeth. I trusted Kai with my life, and I knew Aiden did as well. Maybe it was the sting of Dylan's betrayal or the odd circumstances of Kai leading us way from the castle, but I felt on edge.

"Kai wouldn't do that," Aiden decided. "If by some chance they were captured, he'd find a way of telling me through that brief phone call."

I nodded, knowing he was right. Yet I couldn't shake the feeling that after tomorrow, we were in for a fight that would end with spilt blood. Whether it stopped at wolf blood being lost in battle or merfolk blood being stolen by vampires, I had yet to see.

At some point this battle had to end. I'd prefer it in be sooner rather than later, because it was time for the Oaks Pack, my pack, to live.

"We should take Dr. Nazra with us," I said.

Sighing, he nodded, "I'll mind link them to meet us."

Over the next hour, Aiden and Rick argued over this strange meeting, which was to be held at a small, rural town according to the coordinates Kai had sent. I could sense the distrust that Aiden had mentioned earlier, it was written all over Rick's expression.

I could tell Rick was still dealing with Dylan's lies, seeing as they'd become brothers as Beta and Gamma, but Aiden reassured him that Kai wasn't Dylan. Calypso also butted heads with her mate as she wanted to tag along, worried over our safety. I'd never stop her from wanting to help, but I agreed with Rick on this matter, she has to stay in the castle.

The danger of the situation was already unknown, if anything were to happen to Aiden or I, Tourmaline would need Rick and Calypso. The pack would need them.

Tourmaline, we'd also kept out of the conversation but Jenny, however, followed Calypso up here and now she also demanded to tag along.

"The last thing we need is to watch out for you if we have to fight," Aiden said, refusing to let her go with us.

She glared at him, an argument on her lips, but I started before she could say anything.

"We should let her go," I told Aiden, who turned to me with shock as did everyone else. Despite what I'd said to Jenny earlier, about her bad decisions made to protect her mate, I knew I'd do anything to keep Aiden safe. "If the mélusine are here, I think it would be best to have a mermaid with us. Maybe they'd be more amiable to our situation and help. Plus, her determination to save Anvi - while not the right approach - is admirable. She'd do anything for her, which means she won't be a liability."

"Thank you," She said to me.

I nodded once, the bite of her plot against us still fresh in my mind.

Aiden raised his brows at me curiously, but I simply shrugged.

With that set, we were officially a party of four, Aiden, Dr. Nazra, Jenny and myself.

Calypso left shortly to check the car for any possible tracking devices or faulty systems, while Aiden and Rick gathered weapons to kill blood suckers. Jenny looked up the small town, noting it was mainly a port for transporting vessels and a harbour for local fishermen, while Dr. Nazra went back downstairs to feign a headache and put one of her trainees to oversee the infirmary. This way, she'd be in the clear to easily disappear tomorrow.

I, on the other hand, planned my escape. If I had to leave the castle undetected with the others tomorrow, going out the front door was not an option. As I looked out the window of the castle, I determined it was also not an option. Unless, I'd wanted to break my neck on the way down.

"I'll cover you," Jenny's voice called from behind me.

Turning away from the window as I lifted a brow in question, "I think that green hair of yours will track more attention than not."

Scoffing, she shifted her attention back to the laptop where she was booking the hotel rooms, "I meant with my blood, unless you'd rather jump through the window."

"I'd rather jump through the window," I said, making a face at her idea.

"You'd only need a little blood, since us merfolk have subtle a scent. Not that I have much to spare anyways, seeing as I gave you some not that long ago."

"Your blood has more than been replenished by now," I rolled my eyes at her.

"So, I'll take that as a no?"

"It's a yes," I sighed, having no other option. "Why are you so keen on helping, anyways? Aiden already agreed to help get Anvi back."

"And for theat I should be thankful," She said seriously. "My life hasn't been all rainbows and dolphins. I left my home behind when Queen Amethyst moved us here, I lost my family when I was young and my mate was stolen from me while I was blackmailed. And yeah, maybe I deserved some of it for doing shitty things, but if I intend to get Anvi back then I need to help those who'll help me. Most importantly, I need to become the kind of person who she'll love, because Anvi will never forgive me once she learns what I've done over the pass few years. I know she'd hate me if she knew I put Tourmaline in danger."

"I can't say she won't," I said honestly, "but what would she say if she knew what you'd been through for her? What you've done at the hands of the vampires to ensure she stayed alive?"

There was a clarity in her eyes then, the scrunching of her brows as tears brimmed her eyes. She'd never thought about it that way.

CHAPTER 35

"S it still, would you?" Jenny chided.

"You're literally rubbing blood on my arms, what do you expect me to do?" I grumbled as I made a face at the cup of blood she held. As if she was some Picasso, she used a brush to apply the warm, sticky blood on my arms.

I wasn't squeamish at the sight of blood, hard to be when you're a werewolf, but the idea of being painted in someone else's blood had my tummy protesting to return my breakfast if I didn't stop the artwork from happening.

"That's enough," Aiden commanded to Jenny as he walked into the room. "I couldn't smell her coming up here, so she should be safe."

"You couldn't?" I asked amazed that the mermaid blood could cover the powerful scent of a mate.

Aiden nodded grimly, not seeming pleased by his lack of sensing me by scent.

"Are we ready?" I asked, watching as dawn soon approached beyond my bedroom window.

"Dr. Nazra is already in the car and Rick is clearing the gate the north entrance so we could exit quietly," He explained before turning to Jenny. "Leave us."

She didn't question him before walking out, her footsteps fading down the corridor.

Aiden approached me slowly, reaching out and pulling me to him, "I need you to stay at my side when we get there, okay? Don't leave with anyone else."

"I promise," I pecked his lips.

"And don't trust Jenny," His eyes bore into mine as he said it. "I did promise to help her get her mate back, but after all that she has done, I don't trust and will never trust her. Not even with a single strand of your hair."

"I don't trust her either," I agreed. "But she won't betray us again, not if she truly wants to see Anvi."

He nodded but I could still sense his wariness, "If there comes a situation where we must split up..." his voice trailed off as if he couldn't conceive that notion. Simply not wanting to speak it into existence.

"I know," I gulped over the lump that formed in my throat before answering, "run."

"That's my girl," He praised before dropping a kiss on my forehead and then led us to the garage. Only being five in the morning, most of the pack was asleep. Guards were stationed everywhere but the maze of corridors we took to the garage. Carefully situated to allow our silent exit from the palace grounds.

In the next half hour we loaded whatever weapons were needed together with extra clothing, because for a werewolf you can never be too certain you won't have to tear your clothes apart while shifting. By the time we were clearing the castle's gate, the rays of the morning sunrise was already streaming through the car windows.

"Keep the blood on you," Aiden advised when he saw me trying to rub at the already drying blood on my arms. Reaching out, he took one of my hand in his, easily steering the car with the other, "Just in case."

"Hate to break up the cute moment," Dr. Nazra teased as she stuck her head between the front seats, "but how are we sure this isn't a set up? And what could Kai have found that would help?"

Aiden and I exchanged a glance. We hadn't exactly explained where Kai and Matt was to anyone except Rick, Calypso and Jenny. The fear of losing our last hope had kept our lips sealed.

"They're called the Spirit Of Fresh Water," Jenny said from the backseat. "The Mélusine."

My eyes shifted to her in the backseat as Nazra sat back to listen to her. Jenny's eyes were distant and her lips were tilted up. As if she was reminiscing about an old memory.

"Growing up in the sea, as a mermaid, we were always told about the Mélusine. They were honored, worshipped, feared and our ancestors," Jenny explained, hero-worship lingering in her voice. "The Mélusine were said to have two tails, some even claimed they flew but that was a myth. They were the creatures of the sea, they had no reason to venture into the air. But they were also said to be the first life of the ocean, powerful beyond belief, so much so they could have wreaked havoc on the world's coastlines with only a hum.

"However, as humans began exploring the sea, it was only time until the Mélusine became infatuated with legs. Some no longer wanted to swim, they wanted to walk through field of flowers, feel the earth between their toes and bask in the sunlight. Before long they began mating with humans, using their sea shanties to lure them under. Those children then became what we know today as mermaids and sirens." She smiled as she said her next sentence, "Queen Amethyst used to say that the mermaids were birthed from one of the Mélusine's tail, while the sirens were birthed from the other. That's why we all have one tail and a pair of legs that could walk on land."

"If they truly were so powerful how haven't I heard of them until now?" Dr. Nazra asked, furrowing her brows.

"Ah, the question everyone asks, but it isn't the right one," Jenny smiled sadly. "If the Mélusine wanted legs, their children wasn't the way to go. Although mating with humans did cause an eventual decline in the birth of pure blooded Mélusine, there was a dark secret. The ones who desperately wanted legs used an ancient folklore to get their wish. It is said that Poseidon himself had granted them a book of their origin, holding everything from how their existence came to be and how to protect their species. One method of protection was to drag anyone who seeks them harm into the bottom of the ocean. Once death took that creature, the Mélusine would then be free to adapt to their likeness. Think of it as shedding a layer of skin to become like that creature so they could then use their skills against others who wanted to harm them."

"So if I wished you harm, you'd simply have to drag me into the ocean and kill me and then you'd be able to transform into a wolf?" I asked curiously.

Her eyes met mine in the mirror, a mischievous smile on her lips, "If the legend if true, then yes."

A chill settled into my blood at the thought of such powerful creatures existing.

"But I'm not too keen on smelling like a wet dog for the rest of my life so I'd rather not drown you," Her back handed comment was expected, but I could tell it was her way of simply saying she was not going to kill me. At least by drowning. "If you haven't figured it out already, some of the Mélusines saw the human who were procreating with the other Mélusines as a threat to their extinction. So they began killing both human men and women who were mating with other Mélusines, thereby gaining legs. Of course this didn't sit right with their sea folk partners, thus beginning an inter-species war. The children, mermaids and sirens, were hidden away from the war, but the Mélusine were said to have eventually died either in the war or from age.

"There were rumours that a group of them survived, but I've never seen nor met one. If they are alive then I resent them for not helping my people when we faced extinction ourselves."

Jenny raised an interesting point. If her ancestors were alive, and held the power her stories claim, why haven't they helped? Why didn't they stop the vampires before the slaughtered the mermaid queen?

Dr. Nazra was the first to break the silence that had settled in the car, "Are you saying they found the Mélusine? Or the book they had?"

"Kai didn't say," Aiden answered. I could see the gears turning in his head by how much information Jenny had revealed. Of course any new information wasn't pertinent to us now, as Aiden had knew of the books existence long before. "I never kicked Kai or Matt out of the pack, I sent them to find the book or the Mélusine."

"Where?" Dr. Nazra asked.

"France," Aiden and I said the same time.

"What could they have found?" Dr. Nazra asked the question that was on all our minds.

Our journey took four hours. The further we drove along the coast, going from one town to the next, the less populated the area became. Grand houses which exuded old money slowly shifted to small homes before large warehouses surrounded us. In the ocean, clear waves also gave way to big ships as we approached our destination.

Soon enough, the town's sign came into view. Black Rock Bay.

"Where are we meeting them?" I asked Aiden.

"There should be a local bed and breakfast around here. The only one in town." He pulled up his GPS and we were about five minutes away.

Not long after, we parked at a quaint little house that looked as if it didn't hold more than four rooms.

It sat at the ocean's edge, its backyard being the beach.

"It's... cute," Jenny gave us a weary sigh as she looked at the building before us. "They're not going to kills us are they?"

"No," I rolled my eyes, then I looked at Aiden, unsure. "They aren't, right?"

He chuckled at my furrowed brows, "No, Cupcake, you'll be fine by my side."

"I think the Alpha is right," Nazra mused as she opened her door. "It hardly seems the place for a horror film."

As we each piled out of the car, I catch the shadow of someone peeking between two curtain panels at the front window. Not a minute later and Kai had pushed the front door open.

His expression was grim as we approached and I could sense the tension in Aiden's shoulders as he took the lead and closed the gap to his best friend.

That furrowed expression on Kai's face melted away into a large grin as Aiden embraced him in a hug only a brother could offer.

"I missed you too, big guy," Kai chuckled as he pulled away and yanked me in next. But the hug was short lived as he held me at arms length and sputtered, "Your heart..?"

"All healed up," I confirmed.

"And she has me to thank," Jenny added which made Kai tilt his head in wonder.

"You figured out how mermaid blood works?" He sputtered as he shook his head. "So you're telling me I've been to through hell trying to find a solution and you found the answer?"

"Not quite," Aiden frowned.

I explained, "We did a blood transfusion after I was attacked by a vampire, we don't quite know the logistics of it. Unless, of course, you have the answer."

Matt showed up then with a bewildered expression, "Attacked? Vampires?"

"What happened?" Kai asked.

With a heavy sigh, Aiden looked around before saying, "Let's take this conversation inside. I'm sure you didn't call us out here for no reason?"

His eyes shifted to Jenny, untrustingly, "We got something... or should I say someone."

Aiden's eyes met mine as we reached for each others hands. This was it, our last shred of hope.

Quietly we filtered into the house that was plastered in floral wallpaper and grandma décor. It was chic, in a mildly cottage core by ocean side style.

"No one at the front desk?" Asked Aiden.

"The owner went out for her lunch time walk with her guide dog." Kai responded. Aiden quirked a brow at him but Kai simply shrugged, "You said to be discreet, and Mrs. Lu can hardly see and definitely can't hear. She's a tough one but definitely not a blood sucker."

I relaxed at that, feeling assured there were no spying eyes, listening ears or lecherous vampires lurking in the corners.

That was until I heard the quiet whispers of two women in the upper level floor. Oddly enough, they smelt like Jenny... not a scent to be traced. My eyes turned to Aiden as his flicked up to the ceiling. This was it, the moment Aiden and his family had been searching for for ages, the answers lied with whatever they had for us.

"We can trust them?" I asked.

Matt smirked, "Oh, I think you're going to like what they have to say."

Without further preamble, we ascended the staircase before being led to an upper-level sitting room.

Was it...? Could it truly be?

As we stepped into the room, one by one, the atmospheric integrity of our reunion was compromised by our astonishment at what we saw before us.

Two women who appeared to be in their fifties, which I assumed based on their slightly graying hair, fell silent as they rose to their feet. However, it wasn't the gray streaks that had my eyes widen, rather it was the fading jewel colour tones at the ends. From my sneaking suspicion their hair didn't appeared to be bleached and dyed.

"Mélusine," Jenny whispered before instantly dropping to a knee and lowering her head. They were her heroes and ancestors after all.

They both smiled, seeming relieved at Jenny's presence.

"Rise, my child," One said as she lifted Jenny to her feet. "I'm so very glad to meet you, daughter of the sea."

"You can call me Jenny," She stuttered.

The old woman smiled at her, "my name is Neriss and this is my sister Ossine."

"How?...Why?" Jenny's eyebrows drew together as her words stumbled together in a rushed mess.

"What she's trying to say is, we have many questions," I helped.

"And we have all the answers," Ossine replied, putting a hand on Jenny's shoulder. "I'm sorry Jenny, that we didn't help any sooner."

Neriss approached us as then, tentatively, "You must be the Alpha and Luna which Kai and Matt speak so fondly off."

Aiden nodded and stretched his hand out, "Aiden, Alpha of the Oaks Pack, and this is my Luna, Tate."

"You're the one that raised Queen Amethyst's child?" She questioned and when Aiden confirmed it, she happily accepted his handshake. "Then for the little Queen's sake, we will tell you all that we know, come sit."

Even as we sat, Aiden kept his hand firm grasped in my own and I knew from that hold that he was nervous.

Kai cleared his throat as silence settled over us, "Why don't Neriss and Ossine first explain where they've been and why they haven't helped yet."

Looking at them expectantly, Ossine began. "I'm sure the mermaids have at least heard the stories about the Mélusine over time. While I'm not sure what new rumours have been in circulation, the one about our ancestors mating with humans is true.

"Centuries of this happening has led to our people becoming weak and being hunted for our blood and power. Most of the offspring today is either born into the Mer-Folk or the Sirens, while there are a handful of pure blooded Mélusine remaining. Our parents settled in a small corner of France many decades ago, covering any trace of our origin to protect ourselves. We no longer had the power that thrummed in our bodies, just two-tails and many vampire and humans alike trying to capture us.

"That is why we stayed hidden because our numbers are small. We wished to help the mer-folk many times, but putting our own lineage at risk was too steep of a price, especially after what happened to the mermaid Queen."

Jenny shook her head, "But why didn't you send us a message? Reach out in some small way?"

Neriss looked down guiltily, "We should've but we did not know you were seeking shelter with the wolves. Our only connection to the ocean is through a school of cardinal fish and they hadn't spot the mer-folk in years after informing us of the vampires that hunted them. We have two-dozen of ourselves, no power or connections, there was no way we knew how to help without endangering our families. If we'd known you had a pack behind you, I would have contacted you sooner and maybe formulize a plan."

"Luckily we're here now, thank to your friends Kai and Matt," Ossine smiled. "These boys went through hell finding us."

"They almost killed us," Matt laughed at a memory.

"Our lives were spared after we told them about Tourmaline and the vampires. I also told Neriss and Ossine about the attempts made to save Tate's life in the past, why don't you begin by telling us what changed?" Kai said.

Aiden, troubled by having to recall this painful memory recounted what happened only a few days ago, squeezed by hand before saying, "One our wolves was secretly working with the vampires. Unbeknownst to us, they carved out a passage in the castle and while trying to get to Tourmaline, they attacked Tate." He stopped and inhaled a deep breath before continuing, "Jenny offered her blood in an attempt to save Tate in exchange to helping her get her mate back."

"The medical procedure was conducted in the same way," Dr. Nazra added.

"Ahh, it all makes sense now," Kai grinned.

"How?" I asked curiously, desperately.

"Jenny gave you her blood willingly," Ossine stated. "The very core of the earth lies within the nature of free will."

"Will?" Aiden mused, sitting upright.

Neriss nodded, "Will - free will - is a God damn powerful thing. Something us sea folk has held paramount for centuries. It's why humans experience such devastation from the sea when they pollute, kidnap and kill the marine life. When they cast their filthy nets, and take away the freedom of those creatures, the sea pays in retribution. The earth's balance isn't simply the right and wrong, it's also the will of it's creatures. It's why climate change is on the brink of its unreturnable point. When greed takes away the will of mother nature, no one can stop her from wreaking chaos."

"So you're saying the key to using Mermaid blood is having the mer-folk be willing to give it up?" I asked.

"Indeed. I suspect without that knowledge and plagued with danger at every turn, those mer-folk who gave you their blood before did so out of duty for protection but not from their free will."

"So that was the answer?" Dr. Nazra asked skeptically. "But how can possibly make sense?"

Neriss smiled at that, "How do werewolves transform? It's not a simple answer, my dear. It is just the way of the world."

"And what of its healing properties? The vampires believe it can be used to cure their affliction towards the sunlight," Aiden asked.

Ossine laughed, "Those bloodsuckers are not stupid, but they're not smart either. Mermaid flood can cure them but not in the manner in which they believe."

"What my sister said is true, the blood of the mer-folk heals them in the most extreme sense. So, if they are willingly given mer-blood, they won't just be able to walk in the sunlight, they'll lose their immortality and power. Rapid aging would immediately set in until they achieve the age they are biologically meant to be. In the end the blood will leave them frail and dead in a matter of seconds." Neriss shrugged.

"This is a lot to unpack," I whispered under my breath.

"You should have said something before," Jenny's voice was strained with hidden anger. "My ma- my mate has been held captive by those monsters for the past five years. Can you imagine what this information could have done?"

Ossine shook her head, "Even if you knew of this and gave the vampires your blood willingly, what then? One would inject the blood and then die, and what of the rest? They will see their dead comrade and then lay havoc on the mer-folk knowing they can't be saved. The Mélusine bloodline is almost at its end, we cannot have the mer-folk meet a same fate in a faster manner.

It would take them seconds to kill you because whether you accept it or not, Child, the folk of the sea are not fighters. We are not innate killers like these wolves or the vampire. Our voice is the only thing we can use to cause destruction, but for the undead, neither a tsunami wave nor a siren's voice can drown them. Our nature is too harmonious to attempt fighting them head on."

Aiden's shoulder sank in invisible relief as his eyes sparkled with mischief, "While I'm not your biggest fan to withholding that information from us which lead to the deaths of my brother, sister-in-law, and many of my pack... I think there's a solution to this situation."

Kai chuckled as if reading his mind, "Do tell."

CHAPTER 36

Not long after the Mélusine disclosed their ancestors' secrets to us, they were off. And while they could simply swim across the Atlantic with a shiver of sharks for protection, they chose the human way of transportation, airplane. It was undoubtedly the less scenic and more mundane way of doing things, but it was by far the safest. No one knew they were sea creatures and traveling during the day and out of the water ensured their secrets were kept.

Having a dwindling population made them a paranoid bunch.

When we were sure they were safely checked into the airport and were waiting to be boarded, we decided it was best to set off ourselves before darkness caught up to us.

Kai and Matt had their own car so Jenny and Dr. Nazra decided to hitch a ride with them.

"Are we sure this plan is going to work?" I asked Aiden, concerns over all the ways this could go wrong plagued my mind.

It wasn't that long ago my brother, Thane's pack were in arms against a fledgling of humans. A battle that left blood spilt and my brother on the brink of death despite thorough planning.

Aiden took my hand in his, keeping our entwined hands on his thigh, "There's never a guarantee, but this our only shot. If this works, maybe... just maybe, we can put an end to this damn fight."

I squeezed his hand three times, "Then we'll fight. Once you lead us, we'll win. I know it."

"I can't do it alone, Cupcake. I need my Luna at my side," Aiden turned towards me with a shy smile before gazing back at the road.

"I'm not your Luna yet," I clarified.

"Oh? You don't say," He said in mock surprise. "You trying to tell me something, Babe?"

I rolled my eyes at him, "What I'm saying is, yes."

"Yes too?"

I poked his cheek with my free hand, "Keep messing around and I'll make you find a new mate."

He let out a deep chuckle, daring me to do just that. But when his eyes briefly flicked to mine, I saw a sparkle of need there.

"When we get back, we're telling the pack you're alive. If I have to go another day without being able to reach you through a mind link, I'll go crazy," He swore.

My cheeks reddened, knowing what was to come, "Aiden, I've never... I mean I haven't done any of that before."

He shrugged, "Neither have I."

"You haven't?" My eyes widened.

He laughed at the intonation of my voice, "Why do you sound so surprised? Between raising a kid, being pushed into the role of Alpha and keeping vampires from killing my pack, it's not like I've had much time on my hands. I didn't exactly have my mate at my side either."

I really loved this guy.

Aiden, the wind in my sails and the sunshine on my beach. Falling in love with him was like the crashing of waves on a shore and the warmth of the summer at sunset. Hectic at times, but a sweet sea breeze that kept you wanting more.

That's my man, who was not so much of a dickhead anymore.

I quickly stretched up and kissed him on the cheek to show just how much I appreciated him.

Aiden's ears turned pink in a blush and I couldn't help but laugh.

"So, now that you have your Luna, what about a Gamma?" I asked.

"You think he'll accept if I ask?" Aiden's voice held hesitation, unsure of his decision.

"He's your best friend, and your Gamma before Dylan came along. I think he'll be happy you thought of him for the position."

"That's just the thing, though. I allowed Dylan to steal that from him, something which never should have happened."

I held onto his arm reassuringly, "There was little you could have done. Dylan challenged him and Kai accepted. According to pack law, you couldn't have intervened."

"Maybe," He sighed. "But, I don't want him to think I don't value his position or embarrass him by bringing up the past."

"Ask him." I said. "You'll never know unless you ask."

He turned to me with a smile, "When did my girl get so wise."

I gasped, "You thought I wasn't before?"

He shook his head vehemently, "No, that's definitely not what I'm saying."

This is going to be a long trip, I thought fondly with a smile.

We arrived back at the castle just as the sun began to lower over the horizon. I was seeing the pack in a much different light than I did from that first day I was brought to the castle.

Beside the time of day being different, the ease of knowing how many people here I loved and the possibility of finally giving peace to the pack filled me with a new found energy.

I was buzzing with the new life given to me.

No more rotting smell of bloodsuckers or nightmares of their deadly silver eyes. Aiden and I were going to give Tourmaline the life she deserved. One where she could swim across the ocean to her mother's home and play along the seashore at any time of the day.

"You ready?" Aiden's eyes glittered in the setting sun as we exited the car together.

The several pack members who were on patrol outside, stopped in their tracks to look at us with boggling eyes. Their expressions were further mystified when Kai and Matt, former exiled members, pulled up beside us.

Aiden chuckled beside me, sure enough they were sending their questions of a mourned Luna through the mind link.

"I'll explain in the pack meeting," He informed aloud for my benefit. "Those on patrol, I'll have someone filling you in while the meeting is going on. But don't lose focus, the night is fast approaching."

They nodded with a, "Yes, Alpha," before going back to their duties.

Aiden placed his hand on my back, leading us inside.

"Those were some funny looks we got, how did they take it?" I asked, eyebrows pinched together.

"Better than I expected," He rubbed my back. "While shocked, they're happy to be deceived seeing as you are alive. Although, I'm sure by the time we make it to the meeting room, everyone will be aware that you're alive."

"They're not hurt by us keeping it from them?"

"I'm sure some will be, but we'll explain everything and I'm sure they'll understand. They will, once we tell them the good news," He comforted me by tucking me under his arm.

Once we were settled into the ballroom, which was used as the meeting room given that it was large enough, I felt a sinking in my stomach at everyone's expressions.

They varied from happiness to surprise to shock to confusion to a multitude of angry eyes.

Aiden kept my hand gripped in his, though, which I was thankful for.

"I know you have many questions," Aiden began, voice strong, "and we will answer them all, but I want everyone here to know these secrets were kept not because I lacked trust in my pack. Instead I was worried about my own ability to keep everyone safe because I had nothing to protect you. No answers, no theories and no possible idea what I was going to do."

The tension which plagued the room like a city filled with smog began to slowly dissipate.

I took over then, forcing the strength of the Alpha blood that ran in my veins to give the courage I needed.

"Your main concern must be why I'm alive, and to put it simply... Jenny's blood was my cure," I let that news settle among them as hushed whispers grew to questions being thrown at me.

"So, you're saying mermaid blood works? You're cured from your illness?" A member of the pack asked.

"Yes, mermaid blood does indeed work as a cure and I no longer suffer with my heart. Despite us not knowing exactly how and why it worked that day compared to our attempt before, Kai and Matt found our answers for us," I waved them both forward.

"Weren't they kicked out?" Someone else shouted in question.

Aiden shook his head, "Not quite. Due to the traitor, Dylan, causing chaos, I took it as an opportunity to let both Kai and Matt go find us a solution. You see I started to distrust Dylan a few months back after he began insisting I wage a war against another pack to find us a Luna. Given our situation, it wasn't exactly something a Gamma should be advising, even if he said it was a joke. If I'd let him in on their mission, there wasn't a doubt in my mind he'd have the vampires kill them. So, under the disguise of kicking them both out of the pack, I sent them to find a possible lead I've had for a while."

"And this lead had the answer?" Someone asked.

I nod for Kai to explain to the pack what he found.

"Matt and I spent the last month or so tracking down someone that can help us, and while we swore secrecy on their identity and location, we were given the answer. The blood of the merfolk can cure any ailment, but they must be willing to give up their blood to you," He explained.

I watched the embarrassed expressions on the faces of the merfolk who tried to give me blood back when Dr. Nazra tried blood infusion to cure me. I smiled to myself recalling their unwillingness to participate that day.

On the other hand, the rest of the merfolk looked terrified.

"That means the vampires were right," I heard one merman say with a tremble in his voice. "We're going to be hunted until they suck us dry."

"No," Kai interrupted them. "That's not exactly right. According to our source, merfolk blood cures in the most extreme sense. Therefore, instead of becoming immune to the sun's effect, they'll be cured from vampirism. They'll age until their actual biological age."

More chatter erupted until someone else asked, "Are you sure about this? Can we trust it?"

"It's our only chance," Aiden stated. "Our source is trusted, but it's the only answer we've gotten since this fight started. We've all lost someone we've loved," His voice cracked with emotion at the words before he cleared his throat and went on. "If we don't use this opportunity, then we'll never get a day of peace for the rest of our lives. No guarantee of a tomorrow for either us or our children."

Rick grinned at us then, stepping up, "Then what do you propose we do Alpha?"

Aiden smirked, "A blood drive."

He went on to explain his devious plan with Dr. Nazra's help and the merfolk were quick to agree with us, all willing participants.

By the time our pack meeting was over, there was a buzz of energy as everyone began preparing for tomorrow, the start of our forever.

Luckily there was no more animosity among our pack as I was hugged and warmly welcomed back by pack members as they filtered out of the ballroom.

By the time the last merfolk and werewolf left, only Rick, Calypso, Dr. Nazra, Jenny, Matt, Kai, Aiden and I remain.

"How exactly are we going to get the vampires to meet with us?" Calypso asked then.

The first flaw in our plan.

"How about a parley?" Jenny suggested and I raised a brow at her. "What? I've seen Pirates of the Caribbean and it is something us merfolk do when we need to meet with the sirens."

"It's not a bad idea," Aiden said. "I did some background checks on the leader of the vampires, Jean Marcel Antoine. He was a captain during the transatlatic slave trade in the Caribbean back in the 1700's. Quite famous before disappearing one night. Then there were records of him being spotted as a pirate out on sea during the dead of night, stopping British ships under the French crown until their abolition. I speculate he stopped those ships to feast on those aboard, which would explain many of the missing passengers and the folklore which began spreading among the islands once the boat arrived at their destinations."

Calypso nodded, "Soucouyant. It's a popular folklore in the Caribbean brought over from French myth. I remember my grandmother scaring us with stories about an old woman in our village shedding her skin and shifting into a ball of fire before going to houses and sucking on the blood of her prey."

I felt the cold trickle of sweat running down my spine at the haunting tale both real and fictional. If my grandma told me that story when I was younger, I don't think I'd be able to sleep at night.

"I'll have a letter typed up and left on the beach with a sign," Aiden decided. "Hopefully they get the message and this will go as smoothly as we plan."

"I'm sure they'll only agree to meet us at night, though. On their territory, nonetheless," I said.

Rick agreed, "If that's the case then I'll round up our best and strongest fighters. Not all, in case they try to infiltrate the castle while we're gone."

"We should have them taken to the city," Kai said. "Whoever can't fight, including the mermaids, should be taken to a hotel in the city the morning before we meet up. They won't be able to follow them during that time or find them while we have our meeting."

"That's a great idea," I piped up. "I'll get a shuttle service to pick them up for that morning."

Now that the details were all worked out, everyone went back to their rooms, but Aiden stopped Kai and Matt from leaving.

"Hey, Kai," Aiden said, placing an arm on his shoulder. "There's actually something we've been wanting to ask you."

He raised a brow, "Okay, ask away."

"Would you accept the position of Gamma to the Oaks Pack?"

Matt and Kai exchanged a look which had me nervous at his possible denial.

"I mean, I don't know-"

Aiden shook his head, "The pack needs you, Kai."

That caused him to grin, "If would let me finish, I was going to say 'I don't know how I can possible reject that offer.'"

"So you'll do it?"

"Of course," His smile faltered before he said, "but we should probably talk about why I accepted Dylan's challenge all those years ago."

"I had been wondering."

Kai reached out and took Matt's hand as recounted what happened.

"At the time Matt and I didn't know we were mates yet, but I knew I was gay. Of course I came to that realization after watching Power Rangers as a kid. But when I'm surrounded by hetero couples all finding their one true mate, I assumed maybe I was mistaken about my identity. I was already in love with Matt, but what if he wasn't my mate?

Every day I wondered what if my mate was a woman, what if the pack doesn't accept me and Matt? If we were shunned or kicked out then we would have nothing. No home or family."

I watched as the colour drained from Aiden's face, now understanding the struggle his friends faced through their lives.

"If I'd known-" Aiden began but Kai shook his head.

"I know big guy, you would have assured us we have a place here in the pack before any bigoted idiot. But we were young, still are, and I just wasn't ready to face that. Matt wasn't ready to come out to his parents either. But, when Dylan joined the pack, he caught Matt and I making out. I begged him to keep it quiet, but he blackmailed us. I had to accept the challenge and give up my title or he'd tell everyone about us. I had to protect Matt, I couldn't have given him up for that."

"Oh God," Aiden's eyes held anguish. "I should have known. I should have put an end to him sooner."

"It's all in the past, Aiden. When others in the pack started coming out and we realized we were mates, everything fell into place for us."

Aiden shook his head, "I'm still sorry. Matt and Kai, I'm truly sorry for not knowing sooner. For not making you feel as welcome and comfortable in the pack as I should have."

"We wanted to tell you sooner, but despite Dylan being an absolute asshole most days, he was clever. So, we just decided to leave well enough alone," Kai said.

Matt shrugged, "Sometimes life takes us down a dark path to ensure we get to where we are today. If Dylan hadn't done all that he did we probably wouldn't have gone out to find the Mélusine when we did and Tate wouldn't have gotten Jenny's help to heal her heart."

Matt was right. Despite the pain we've all been through, somehow we've made it out with each other. We're here today to see a better tomorrow, and that's what mattered the most.

CHAPTER 37

The blood-suckers' response came the night after we dropped the message in a bottle on the beach. The old-fashion cursive of the letters on the expensive note left my stomach tightening in unease. There was something almost eerily sinister about the lightness of the words on the letter, as if we were planning a cheerful get-together instead of deadly encounter where one side would be leaving and the others would be left lifeless.

Dear Furry Friends,

I have been waiting for this delightful invite for ages, and while I do wish I could travel to your enchanted castle, I possibly could not make the trip in my rather old age. But do not be perturbed my dear friends, we can still have a beautiful soiree at my private residence. Do dress in your finest gowns, because I simply could not peel my eyes away from dearest Tate last time she was running from us in the castle. The scent of her blood still tantalizes me, but it's rather unfortunate she's close to death if not already dead after Dylan was kind enough to send us an invite to his party. I simply cannot wait to see of the outcome at our party and don't worry, my caterers have prepared your dog chow. We wish to receive your presence two nights from now.

P.S. Parlay will be only upheld if the Mermaid Child is brought to us.

Kindest Regards,

Jean Marcel Antoine.

The sign-off at the end confirmed Aiden's theory on the name of the vampire leader, but that wasn't what further churned my stomach, it was the fact that the vampire's name was written in red. No scent of ink, but rather a scentless trail which I knew was mermaid blood.

From Jenny's white-faced expression when she saw the letter, I knew the mermaid blood belonged to Anvi, Jenny's mate who was kidnapped after Tourmaline was born.

Jenny's silent horror was matched with Aiden's roar of anger as the glass bottle which carried the message splintered in his fist when he read my name on the letter. Drops of blood splattered the sand as he swore under his breath, vowing vengeance and questioning if taking me along was a good idea.

After pulling the shards of glass out of his palm, it didn't take much convincing to get him to agree to my going these as well. I had my own bone to pick with the dead.

Lucky for us, the rendezvous point was not far. The address which was scribbled on the back of the letter was at an old hotel about a twenty-minute drive away from the castle, in an abandoned part of the beach which was closed many years ago after a failed resort was shut down and nature took over. Or rather the vampires.

Our set time to meet was at one in the morning, sufficient time for those blood suckers to set up their established defenses and feed, I imagine. But also enough time to hunt us down in the dark of night if we have to run.

D-2

"Are you ready?" Aiden asked as he led me down the steps to his bedroom.

I felt a flutter of nerves in my stomach as my eyes travelled across the flickering candle flames in the dim room. Nothing but a few burning candles, which were carefully placed around the room, and the glow of the moonlight brightened the room.

"I am," I answered on a whispered breath, my palms clammy from anticipation.

Aiden squeezed my hand in his as he gently tugged me away from the awaiting bed and towards the sofa near his mini library.

"I think I prefer the bed," I mumbled looking anxiously at the king-size mattress.

My mate chuckled as he held my chin and turned my eyes back to him, "I'm sure you do, but let's talk first."

"Talk?" My eyes widened.

"Do you not want to?"

I shook my head vehemently, "No! No, we can talk."

Aiden's eyebrowed furrowed as pulled his hands back to himself, "Tate... I know you said you wanted this, but if you're not ready-"

"I am," I assured him but my quick response had him shaking his head.

"I feel as if you aren't and that's okay. I don't want to rush you into this, I swear."

Aiden kept stepping back as he put space between us, unsurety written across his face.

"Aiden?" I asked as I shook the natural nerves out of my shoulder, "Do you not want to?"

His eyes widened at my suggestion as his words tripped into each out and he blubbered out a, "Of course I want to. Tate, goddammit, I've wanted you for a long time."

That had the corners of my lips tipping into a smile as I asked, "How good at you catch?"

With quirked eyebrows and a worried expression he asked, "Why?"

My response came in the form of running and launching myself into my mate's arms, his large sturdy frame not moving an inch as he wrapped his arms around me and I folded my legs around his waist.

"I want you Aiden Oaks, since I laid my eyes on you, I've wanted you. So don't you think for a second you're denying me the right to becoming Luna tonight."

A sparkle of mischief lit his eyes aflame as his hold tightened on me, "Well if you want me this badly, Mate, then I have no choice but to oblige."

"Finally," I jokingly sighed with exasperation. "In the grand scheme of werewolf culture, we're definitely behind."

He nodded as his eyes trailed over my lips and I took my cue to press my lips against his.

After a round of breathy sighs and tangled tongues, he pulled away and drew those intoxicating kisses to my neck and collarbone, "Then let's officially make you the Luna of the Oaks Pack."

"Once you continue kissing me, I have no objections."

Aiden's laughter reverberated through me as he walked us towards the bed.

D-1

"Good morning my Luna," Aiden mind linked me as he woke me with a kiss.

Slowly peeling my eyes open, I was stricken by his handsome features which were accentuated by his dirty blonde hair framing his face.

"It feels like a crime against womanhood for his hair to be that perfectly mused right after waking up."

"Oh, does it?" He grinned down at my slip of thought.

My face flushed with heat at the realization that our mind links were now connected and I pulled the sheet over my head with a groan.

"If I'd known the thoughts running through your head were this good for my ego, well I would've done this a while ago," Aiden said as he tugged the covers away from my eyes.

"Your boosted ego is at the expense of my mortification," I sulked. "I don't think I'll ever live that down."

Aiden simply wrapped his arms around me and pulled me in so that my head was tucked under his chin, "It's a good thing I love you then so you'll get to find out how equally embarrassing I can be."

I tilted my head back and peeked up at him, "Have you really ever let a thought slip?"

He grinned, which I found to have a new appreciation and addiction for, "Never."

With a groan, I slid my head back into the warmth of his chest, not feeling embarrassed by my errant thoughts anymore, but rather enjoying this new feeling that's blossoming in my chest. The warmth of love and the mate bond. A feeling that when tomorrow reaches us, we'll be ready to conquer the world.

Together, Aiden and I.

But we had one more thing left to do before we could begin our fight against the vamps.

"Are you ready to send Tourmaline off?" I asked Aiden and felt his body stiffen before relaxing under my touch.

After a minute of silence, I felt him take a deep breath before answering, "It's not that I don't believe we won't be successful tomorrow, but there's a big possibility that we won't. We don't know their numbers or the layout of their location. It leaves a lot of room for things to go bad very quickly if they decide to attack us without listening first and giving us a chance to scope out the area. And sending Tourmaline away is the best option we have, if not the only one... I just don't her to think this is goodbye for us. She's lost a lot you know and packing her up with a strong possibility that we may never see each other again has to be one of the cruelest things I can do to her."

I cupped his cheeks, bringing his eyes to mine, "Tourmaline knows what's about to happen, she's a smart kid and a brave one. I know that no matter what happens, she would never blame you, Aiden. You're her dad, her protector. She knows you only have her best interest at heart."

His eyes got misty from my words as he whispered a thank you to me.

"For what?" I asked.

"No one has really ever called me her dad."

"You are in all sense of word, her father, Aiden. Don't ever make yourself of her feel otherwise."

Through the shiny new mate bond I felt a sense of ease as the anxiety, I did not realize Aiden held, dissipated.

After Aiden thanked me in more ways that one, we were rushing to meet the others in the foyer, a hopeful temporary goodbye to Rick, Calypso, Tourmaline, most of the mermaids and a few other pack members.

Aiden had a private jet ready for Tourmaline, Rick and Calypso along with a couple more wolves which was headed to my brother, Thane's, pack. Thane and Emery agreed to keep Tourmaline safe while we handled our situation, ensuring they are not followed by any stray vampires. If things didn't go as planned, Rick and Calypso had a well mapped out plan of where to head next to keep everyone safe, especially Tourmaline.

Svalbard archipelago in Norway would be their home in the summer for the midnight sun while they'll keep travelling on a constant basis for the other parts of the year. The other wolves would remain with Thane's pack as naturally integrate if they come without an Alpha.

As for the other mermaids, they are headed to France to meet the Mélusine who found safe passage and accommodations for them in their community.

At the front door, I watched from a distance as Aiden bent down to Tourmaline's height as she faced him with a smile before she got into the car, but I could see the worry expression in her eyes.

"Promise we'll see each other again?" Her small voice asked him, not asking for a specific date.

"I'll try my best Tourm, I promise you that," Aiden's voice cracked, not promising something he can't guarantee.

"Then I hope we get to see each other again, Dad." She flung her arms around his neck, hugging him for a long time, tears welling in her eyes but never falling as she kept her grin when she released him.

Aiden simply nodded and I felt how choked up he was, not able to speak.

Tourmaline turned her gaze to me as she ran up to me and I lowered to pick her up. She wrapped her tiny arms around me, giving me a big hug.

"I can't wait for you to get married to my dad," She whispered in my ear conspiratorially. "I hope you get to be my mom soon."

Before I could really gather my thoughts at what she said, she was wiggling out of my arms, bounding towards the car where Rick and Calypso were waiting for her.

"Bye, Tourmaline," I was able to call out to her as the cars all peeled out of the driveway.

Aiden approached me with tears on his cheeks but a smile on his lips, "Did she just imply that you're going to be her mom?"

"I think she did."

"And how do you feel about that?" He seemed nervous as he asked.

"Like we should get married today," I answered honestly as Aiden pulled me into his arms, understanding that I was not scared of the idea of being Tourmaline's mom if that's what she wants.

CHAPTER 38

"Do I get one of those?" Jenny pointed to the open crate guns loaded with wooden bullets as fire brewed in her eyes.

I grimaced, unsure about handing her a deadly weapon.

"I don't know-"

"Just," She held up her hand to stop me, "show me how to load and fire and I'll be okay. You're not my target anymore, Tate, whether you believe me or not."

The thing was, I did believe her. The vampires stole as much from her as any of the werewolves. But Jenny has also been constantly tortured with the memory of having her mate kidnapped by the vampires and is reminded of it every time she played spy. She's been a puppet on a string with the promise of her mate being returned while knowing Anvi was as good as dead at the hands of their enemies.

"Okay," I said watching as her mouth gapped open for a split second before snapping close.

She cleared her throat, nodding, "Yes, that was a good choice."

I couldn't help the small smile on my lips as I pulled one of the large custom made shotguns out of the crate along with the wooden bullets that have been carved to ensure the tip was deadly sharp.

While the crowd of werewolves moved around us, trying to get every last detail sorted before we leave the castle, for hopefully not the last time, I demonstrated to Jenny how to put the safety on the gun on, ensure she kept the barrel away from herself or anyone on our side before loading.

The green haired mermaid, who I once considered being my biggest enemy when it came to winning my mate's heart, was now standing here with me as I taught her the safety and practically of the gun. A paradoxical reality to where we began and the absurd situations we have been in, both as enemies and now allies.

In a seemingly absurd twist of fate, she was my savior and I somehow became her... friend?

Maybe it was my good teacher or her laser focus, but either way after a few minutes, Jenny quickly caught on to the mechanics of operating such a lethal force.

I, myself, had to learn to operate the weapon for this fight. It wasn't the modus operandi of werewolves, not when we have claws and sharp canine teeth. However, it was an efficient method for what we plan to do tonight, especially since we'll be in human form for the most part.

When it was finally midnight, marking the hour countdown to our meeting with the vampires, everyone began filing out of the castle, climbing into a fleet of trucks and buses which carried our precious cargo; blood filled syringes packed in coolers of ice. The largest blood drive I'd ever witnessed.

Two buses of werewolves were going to follow Aiden's vehicle, the other were going to wait about a mile away, not unknown to the vampires, but close enough to reach us when we revealed the secrets of the blood.

As the last pack member walked out the front doors, I stood back as I saw Aiden looking around the castle from his stance in the center of the foyer.

A wistful glance at his home and the laughter that filled the walls.

When he finally turned and spotted me staring at him, a small smile on his lips.

"Ready to go?" I asked.

He nodded as he stride towards me, "Not quite." Aiden brushed my hair back, his hands smoothing the strays until he caressed my neck, "If we're ambushed-"

"We won't be-" I tried to sooth him, but he shook his head.

"If we are... leave me, okay? Run as fast and as far as you can, I'll hold back whatever danger it is, I just need you to run," His somber tone created fissures in the shield I wore tonight to protect my brave façade. I'd be ignorant to believe tonight didn't come without danger.

I shook my head vehemently, not willing to make a promise I can't keep, "No, I can't do that, Aiden. Don't ask that of me, please."

Pressing his forehead to mine, I felt the tension in his body. Practically heard the desperation in his head. "If something happens I'll be the only one there to hold them off and I need you to leave me and go to Tourmaline. If our plan goes awry then I need you to take my place and lead the pack. I need you to raise her for me. It's the only way one of us would survive."

"I don't-"

"Please, Cupcake. Please." He begged.

My resolve faded as I nodded, now fully understanding the severity of this situation on him. The crushing weight of the what-ifs and the lack of surety he's able to give to the people who depended on him the most. That included a little five-year old who already lost her parents before she knew them.

"Okay," I promised, grasping his hand where it held my cheek before sealing the sincerity with a kiss.

Describing the kiss as a good-bye wouldn't be right, rather it felt like a desperate attempt to keep the other safe with a shared silent promise. An exchange made to ensure that when we walked out of that abandoned resort, we'd be walking out with our other half.

Pulling away, I plastered on an easy smile, "Now, let's go kick some vampire ass."

Aiden definitely saw through me as he grabbed my hand, giving in a squeeze as we exited the castle.

On the drive towards the vampires' lair, I felt my hackles rise as if we were being watched.

'We are,' Aiden responded to me through mind link, mildly scaring me as he answered my errant thought. 'They've been tailing us since we exited the castle grounds, their leader must have sent them to ensure we were en-route.'

'That's creepy,' I wrapped my arms around myself, the darkness of night not helping one bit. To add to my creeping apprehension, I spotted the tell-tale signs of oncoming rain as the dark sky was coloured grey from storm clouds.

By the time we were pulling up to the gates of the massive resort, lightning began dancing in the sky as thunder rumbled beyond the dark clouds. It resembled ancient war drums beating as warriors prepared themselves for battle by performing a ceremonial dance. In an uncanny way, I had a comforting sense of ease as if the Moon Goddess herself were sending us these signs for good fortune instead of appearing as traditional bad omens.

In the blink of an eye, two vampires flanked the front of our vehicle entourage, guiding us to a massive circular building at the center of the resort which overlooked the dark sea. The gentle crashing of the waves against the shore a stark comparison to the sky's anger.

As we filled out of the vehicles, a few more vampires filed out the main entrance of the resort, a mix of smirks and sneers thrown our way as two big vamps told us to leave our wooden stakes behind. They seized our weapons as we pulled out coolers of blood syringes.

"What's in there?" One of the vampires asked as he sniffed.

"Mermaid blood," Aiden answered with a gravelly tone which caused the blood suckers to share a widen-eyed exchange.

"Follow me."

Without much preamble we were lead through the dilapidated lobby where the overhead light fixtures flickered onto the water-damaged flooring. Broken glass crunched under our boots as we walked, the broken windows boarded up and lined with tarp. Not an ounce of sunlight could reach inside, leaving the cold sea-breeze carried in by the storm to rush through the front door. The usual sea-salt air compromised by the stench of rotting flesh which was the signature fragrance of these nocturnal creatures.

There was silence among our mind-link, the usual quiet chatter now replaced with our focused attention on strategic exits, hidden traps and secret weapons.

From the lobby, we were lead down a long hallway on the left, the sound of loud whispers and boisterous laughter growing louder as we approached large double doors, the deadly stench maximizing with it.

Aiden's hand reached over and took mine, interlocking our fingers and giving my hand a gentle squeeze we entered the dimly lit room. His protective nature in full force.

Silence befell us as the sea of vampires parted and made a way for us. The room was similar to the castle's grand ballroom, except where the castle glittered gold, this cave was carved bare. The paint was peeling until the building's structure was bare, the carpet was ripped out and the panels of wood were broken, scuffed and grimed, the lopsided chandelier above was missing half its crystals and holding on by a link of chain.

As we approached the front of the room, the French vampire that Aiden and I had met in the human town months ago was now sat on a polished throne elevated on a dais.

However, it wasn't the shiny throne that Jean Marcel Antoine sat on, nor was it the eerie smile he held as he brought a wine glass filled with blood to his lips which caught my attention. It was the blue-haired mermaid at his feet who's leashed around her neck my a thick chain. Her blue hair was cut short, looking as if someone took a blade and jaggedly sliced it off. The scrap of dress she wore was tattered and blackened. She appeared weak as bruises lined her brown skin, an unhealthy dullness washed her out as if she hadn't seen sunlight for years. But she seemed nourished and fed. The thought of why that was the only positive thing turned my stomach. Keeping her full and alive was their only way to access her blood.

A loud gasp echoed behind me as Jenny finally came into the view of her mate.

Anvi's head snapped up with renewed life, her bewildered eyes immediately latching onto her mate's, a look of horror I had witnessed in my life filled her eyes.

"Run!" She screamed, but her voice faltered as she began coughing in fits. Trying to use her gravelly voice, but failing to control her gasps for air, as if she hasn't spoken in years.

Jean, the head vampire, tugged on the chain around Anvi's neck, causing the poor girl to tumble back. Jenny moved to step towards her mate, but I quickly grabbed her arm and pulled her to my side as a few vampires jerked closer at her movements. I subtly shook my head her at, warning her to stay still.

"Now, now Mon Chéri, you know the rules," Jean tutted as Anvi began shaking violently on stage, wrapping her arms around herself as tears poured out of her eyes.

I heard a familiar snicker before I smelt him. Dylan walked up onto the stage, taking his place at the right side of the vampire 'king.'

"Welcome, friends," Dylan grinned brightly, but his smile faltered as he spotted me. "You're-"

"Alive? Obviously." I answered with a smile of my own.

Jean look between us, clarity washing his features as if he just remembered who I am, "The sick one, from that day on the beach." Turning to Dylan he said, "I thought you said she was as good as dead."

Dylan eyed me suspiciously, "She was supposed to be... I don't understand."

"We have the answer to your questions," Aiden simply stated. "But it comes at a price, which is why we're here."

"Yes, yes," Jean agreed as he swirled the liquid in his glass around nonchalantly, but I could tell from his posture that we piqued his curiosity. "But do be aware little pups, if I'm not satisfied with your answer then I'm afraid you won't be leaving here... alive. Although, I might keep those two, one because I've always wanted a pet dog and one because this little blue hair minx is running my patience thin."

His jeweled fingers lazily pointed at Jenny and I which caused Aiden to release a feral growl, stepping in front of me to block

Jean's line of sight. I can't deny that I wasn't apprecivative for that as my blood turned to ice from the threat.

"If you want what we have to offer, you better watch your god-damn mouth," Aiden snarled, anger pulsing through him.

"Or what? You'll bite me, Fido?"

Aiden opened the cooler next to him and took out a syringe of blood before dropping it to the ground and crushing it under his boot, "One cure less, you blood sucker. Keep talking shit and I'll die along with the answers you desperately need."

Jean immediately sat up at the sight of the red liquid, inhaling deeply as the non-scented blood created a sparkle in his eyes, "Is that-?"

"The blood of the merfolk, yes."

"And aside from my obvious skepticism that this works as opposed to my own tries, why might I ask that you bring this to us?"

"As a bargaining chip."

Jean's brow lifted, "And what exactly do you want to bargain for? This thing?" He pointed to Anvi.

"Among other things," Aiden agreed. "All this blood is yours, if you promise to leave my pack and the mermaids alone. You get your cure, we get our lives back."

Dylan rolled his eyes and scoffed, "What? We're supposed to believe after hundreds of years of trying, you found the cure? That you miraculously saved Tate after I've witnessed first-hand your attempts of saving her with mer-blood?"

"Never question the determination of a father," Kai spoke up, facing his opponent.

"Well, I see you came crawling back after they kicked you out."

Kai smirked, "At least my Alpha doesn't called me a dog."

Dylan bared his canines but Jean help his hand up at him, forcing him to calm down.

"Fine," Jean settled. "You can have your world peace or whatever, but I how do I know this works? How do you expect me to believe you were able to pull this off with only her to show it? For all I know you just stitched her up and gave her regular blood."

"Sniff me," I challenged.

Aiden made a sound of disagreement at the back of his throat, not liking where I was going with this. We hadn't exactly discussed it before.

"You're forgetting who's the dog breed among us," Jean scoffed.

"You did it when we met in the human town, remember? You said you smelt my dying heart which didn't have a cure."

"And you found your cure?"

"The merfolk blood."

Jean was still weary but pointed to one of minions closest to us, "Sniff her."

Aiden stepped between the approaching vampire and myself, holding up my wrist for her to smell.

The vampire's expression held confusion as she started to inhale deeply, and encroach future in our space until Aiden pushed her back, causing both of our sides to tense up in defense.

"Well, anything?" Jean snapped.

The vamp backed off, shaking her head, "Nothing, she smells like a regular healthy wolf."

"Impossible," Jean stared at me in amazement, a real grin marring his porcelain skin.

"How about we test it out?" Aiden asked, putting our plan into action.

"By all means," He agreed snapping his fingers to the same vampire who smelt me.

"I don't think this is a good idea," Dylan butted in, still suspicious of us. Can't blame him, he spent enough time in the pack to know they're a lot smarter than bringing sun cures to a den of vampires.

"Quiet, boy," Jean snapped, making Dylan's protest immediately cut off. "Go on, show me."

As the first pitter patter of the rain began, Aiden pulled another syringe from the cooler as the rest of us inched closer to the other coolers, prepared to begin pulling them out as Kai mind-linked the rest of the pack to start making their way to us.

Everyone watching with bated breaths as Aiden uncapped the needle, holding the vampire's arm and injecting the blood of a free willing merfolk.

Seconds grew to a minute as we watched the vampire slowly begin to gray. Her smooth young skin became ashy and wrinkled as he back arched and her knees gave out from beneath her. Within minutes, the immortal vampire returned to her true age and crumpled to a heap of human skin before us.

Angry gasps and yells surrounded us as we quickly armed ourselves with syringes and pulled out wooden bullet guns from the hidden compartment in the cooler.

Jean's fiery eyes met Aiden's as he stood from his throne, tugging on Anvi's chains, "What is the meaning of this?!"

It was Aiden's turn to smirk, "I guess you haven't figured it out yet, huh? The merfolk blood, when given of free will, cures everything."

"But," I continued Aiden's sentence, "it cures to the most extreme. Meaning your vampirism or immortality or whatever you want to call it, is cured. You return to your real age, and well if you're as old as you are, then I guess you're as good as dead."

He was basically foaming at the mouth by the time I was done, "Kill them!"

CHAPTER 39

Chaos erupted as the storm rolled in. Heavy droplets of rain splattered onto the roof while thunder clashed with the blares of the firing guns we aimed.

I picked up a syringe and rolled it towards Anvi on the dais. She grabbed and uncapped it, but before she could inject Jean, he grabbed it out of her hand and moved behind Dylan, the leash still in his hands.

Before I could run towards her, I was swallowed into the sea of angered vamps.

The circled us with vicious snares, hundreds of them running around and jumping from rafters so high up as if they were bats in a cave.

With Aiden at my back, I kept my arms raised, one with the gun aimed at their chests and another with a syringe. Daring them to step close enough for me to inject.

And dared some of them did as Jean hysterically yelled orders out in his native tongue. None of which I understand, but imagined the words were along the line of kill us all.

Too bad for him, the vampires quick reflexes were matched by our own agility and we stuck needle after needle into the porcelain skin of the blood suckers.

What I hadn't expected was most of those who approached us didn't age more than a few years, if any at all.

"They're new..." I whispered in realization to myself.

Distracted by my errant thoughts, another vampire leaped at me from above, but Aiden was quick to shot him down, but the cold body knocked me back, sending me into the hard grip of another.

I didn't waste time in stabbing another syringe into this one's leg, feeling as they woman who seemed to be in her early twenties turn warm against me, her grip lightening considerably.

From the corner of the eyes, I spotted Aiden raise his gun for her and shouted at him to stop.

"No!" I yelled, blocking his line of fire. "She's human, some of them must have recently turned. We can't hurt them, just let them get out of here."

He nodded, turning his focus on others as I gripped the girl's arm and told her to run.

But it wasn't so simple.

She made it a few feet away from me before another vampire snapped her snack. Horror curled in stomach as the lifeless body dropped to the floor, the scent of blood wafting into the air.

The murderous vampire grinned sinisterly which I matched with a smoking gun, feeling numb as the nightmare around me unfolded.

There were too many of them, and the more we injected, the more came filtering into the room from side doors and rafters.

One by one, they started picking us off like pesky ticks.

The warmth of blood from fellow pack members splashed on my arms, cooling too quickly. The feeling of loss accompanied the drying blood as I felt their passing disconnecting them from the pack's mind link.

I couldn't see them in the crowd. I couldn't even look down to offer them comfort in their dying moments.

We were out numbered.

I shot rounds of bullet until I was out of ammunition which didn't go unnoticed by the vamps.

'Get down, I'll cover you,' Aiden mind linked.

With steady hands, but a shaky mind, I searched for a cooler of mermaid blood syringes where extra bullets were stored, but they were coming up empty.

Just as I looked towards my mate, who appeared to be out of wooden bullets himself, I heard the pounding of hundreds of wolves before they came barreling into the once fancy ballroom.

The pack had arrived, and the real fight was just beginning. And honestly, I couldn't be more relieved despite the pandemonium around me.

In wolf form, the pack easily threw the vampires around and made their way into the room, monopolizing the already tightening space.

Laying the gun down, I picked up several syringes as a fellow pack member in wolf form approached, bringing vampires to me between their teeth so that I can inject them.

Soon we were synchronization as wolves assisted those in human form to inject while the others tore apart the remaining vampires who targeted the coolers of blood, buying us time.

"Help me reach Anvi?" Jenny asked as she came up behind me, counting her remaining bullets.

"I'm a little pre-occupied here," Came my response as I injected yet another, watching age devour the cold blooded man.

"But they'll escape with her," Jenny's hysterical voice caught my attention as I looked towards the stage, noticing that Jean and Dylan was now dragging the mermaid down and heading to an exit.

"Shit," I searched the crowd for Aiden then, noticing that in the midst of the mayhem we got separated.

'Jean is leaving,' I mind-linked him.

Aiden's eyes found mine as he nodded, 'Stay put, I'll handle this.'

"As if," I scoffed under my breath as I looked to Jenny. "Let's go."

Determination like no other schooled her expression but it was only a mask for the fright in her trembling hands as she loaded her gun, dropping a bullet in the process.

My hand came over hers, giving it a gentle pat of reassurance before I started moving. The pack helped us move across the floor, dodging flying bullets and blood-craved bats.

But just as we were about to reach the dais, I felt a searing pain shoot across my arm as a vampire's teeth scratched my skin. Another wolf grabbed the legs of the vamp and dragged them back before the entire fang had the chance of penetrating my flesh.

The skin of my arm turned a nasty shade of blue as the poison tried to penetrate my system. But as quickly as the attack had occurred, I began healing. A relieved sight since it was the first time I've gotten hurt since Jenny's blood healed my body.

Curiously, though, the regeneration of my skin transpired alarmingly fast. As a werewolf I was accustomed to rapid healing, but not to this degree.

I looked up with a mystified expression to Jenny whose mouth was agape as she witnessed my arm heal.

But we were both shaken from our momentary stumper as yet another vamp pounced our way, this time from the rafters above.

The red-eyed creature aimed for me, fangs bared and avoidant of Jenny's healing properties. I prepared myself for an attack, syringe at the ready.

However, the vampire never made it to the tip of my needle as Jenny shot him through the chest. A total green haired bad-ass if I've ever seen one considering she learned how to shoot mere hours ago.

With new found adrenaline, we picked up our paces. Ducking beneath leaping wolves and rushing through vampire dust, we were about a meter away from Jean, Dylan and Anvi as their backs faced an exit door.

But as the view cleared, the horrifying picture came into focus.

Dylan, the backstabber, held Aiden at gun point. And if my gut was right, the firearm held silver bullets. To add to the daunting scene, Jean held Anvi's chain collar so tightly I feared for the girl's life as the ancient vampire swung another gun around.

Before I could stop Jenny from approaching them, she moved into their line of vision. Jean's attention immediately snapped to her as he dragged Anvi to her feet and held up the gun to her head.

"Uhh, uhh, uhh," Jean shook his head with a deadly grin. "Neither of you move, or else."

Jenny's shaking hands steadied as she held her gun up, "Let her go and I won't shoot."

"Oh, how adorable, you think you can bargain with us."

Chuckling Dylan added, "If you let us leave, without following us, we'll leave her a few miles from here."

"If not, then I'm afraid we're going to have to shoot you both," Jean finished.

I turned around in the crowd, trying to find Kai or someone else that could help me, but every werewolf in sight had their own problem to handle in this room.

'Kai,' I sent a mind link.

'Luna?'

'Where are you?'

'Close to the entryway, about five meters away.'

I mentally ran through the interior of the building when we walked through, trying to sort my thoughts.

'I need to take the main exit and find a door on the right hallway which leads inside the ballroom. Dylan and Jean are there... with guns. I'll try to buy us some time, but you need to be quiet as you approach.'

'Where's Aiden?'

'Being held at gun point.'

'I'm on it,' I could hear the panic in his voice as he began to move.

'Kai? Please be careful.'

'You too, Luna.'

During my brief conversation, things became heated between Aiden and Dylan as my mate was laughing (with his hands up in surrender) while Dylan was practically foaming at the mouth with anger.

"Shout the hell up!" He screamed at Aiden. "Or I will shoot you."

"Try me," Aiden retorted. "You were too weak from the beginning. Barging into my pack and blackmailing my Delta. You never had the loyalty to be a part of any pack, Pup. And you never had the ability to challenge any of us head on, yet you expect me to believe you could shoot me?"

Aiden fell into another fit of laughter, riling the rough wolf up. What was my mate thinking?

Dylan fired off the gun this time, basically aiming at my heart. But Aiden's quick reflexes dodged the bullet as if he were filming the matrix. The bullet landed in a vampire near me before Dylan shot off another.

This time, the bullet came dangerously close to me as it wisped past my ear.

My eyes found Dylan's as he smirked at me, "Think you can miss a next one, Luna?"

Aiden's spine went ramrod straight as he spun around, no longer considering his safety as he looked at me.

I held up my hands, walking closer as I tried to pacify the situation.

"Let's talk this out, no need for guns or bullets."

"Tell her to drop the gun," Jean said nodding to Jenny.

I was within the reach of Aiden's tense body, my eyes focused on Dylan as I spoke to Jenny, "Jen, put the gun down. We can work this out."

"No!" She screamed. "Give me Anvi first and then I'll drop it."

Jean scoffed, "No deal."

Jenny fired off a shot, sending the bullet towards Jean, but he was quick to move away before he whispered to Dylan, "Shoot them, for God's sake."

As if the next events took place in slow motion, I watched as Dylan's finger twitched on the trigger as I launched myself against Aiden. Hard.

The sudden impact of my weight knocked him back just as Dylan's gun fired. The streak of silver catching the light as Aiden's body fell to the ground but the metal zipped towards me, embedding itself into my right shoulder.

Pain that I could only describe as hell burst through my arm and chest, seizing my breath and suffocating my lungs.

Aiden's hands were holding me so tight, I'm sure I would've bruised, but I barely felt him as the growing pain singed my flesh as it buried deeper within my shoulder.

All at once, Aiden began yelling as he tried to assure me, or himself, that I was going to be okay as the exit door flew open and Kai's wolf burst through. He successfully took Dylan and Jean by surprise as his wolf moved towards his enemy.

When Aiden gently rolled me off of him and onto the floor, I felt tears dripping onto cheeks and my shirt became damp from blood. Aiden was weeping as he screamed for Dr. Nazra into the room.

Silver bullet was fatal to werewolves after all.

Trying to mind-link in this condition felt impossible as my head swam from the loss of blood. It was easier to catch my breath as I stuttered, "Dig the bullet out."

My mate didn't question me, but his own breathing laboured as he pulled my shirt down enough so he could see my wound, letting out curses when he did.

As Aiden took his own shirt off to wipe my blood from his view, my head lolled to the side as the pain sent waves of exhaustion running through me.

Dylan was firing bullets at Kai, who easily out maneuvered him, quickly making the man drop the gun which was empty.

I screamed when Aiden's fingers dug into my wound just as Dylan shifted, Jean tried hiding, Jenny yelled and another wolf I faintly recognized as Matt joined the fight.

The torturous anguish knocked me out as Aiden dug into my flesh deeper until he touched the bullet and I heard him wince in pain.

When I came to, the fire in my shoulder was gone with only a slight burning and ache as the skin began healing. Dylan's wolf was now on the ground with claw marks on his sides and Kai standing above him. The former Delta was panting on the ground as death approached him on four legs.

With a swift baring of wolf canines, Kai grabbed Dylan's jugular and ripped him apart. Sealing the fate of the wolf who once betrayed and stole his place.

On the other hand, Aiden had me wrapped up in his arms, bloody fingers and all as he whispered prayers to the Moon Goddess and held me tighter with every version of please he said.

"Aiden," I soothed as I moved my good hand to touch his wet cheeks.

Lifting his face from where he buried it in my hair, he looked at my alive body with awe and wonder.

"But how?"

I shook my head, not really knowing how I'm alive either. No werewolf has ever survived a silver bullet. Not even when it was dug out of their chest.

"I think it was the..." My eyes went to Jenny's spot where Matt and Kai were standing next to her as Jean held his gun up, looking lost at who to aim for.

Aiden's eyes went to Jenny, a thankful expression on his face before turning to me, "God, Tate. What the hell am I going to do with you."

But it was a rhetoric question as he held my face between his palms and kissed me so deeply and fiercely, I almost lost track of where we were and what we had yet to do.

"Never do that again, you hear me?" He urged as his fingers rubbed my cheeks and I felt blisters of the index and thumb of his right hand.

Instead of answering him, I pulled his hand to my sights, rubbing at the dried blood and seeing the wounded skin of his fingers.

They were severely blistered from touching the silver bullet, ruining the skin and fingerprints of his fingers permanently.

"Aiden..." I sad sadly.

"I'm fine," He assured me. "We're fine."

I nodded as Kai sent us a mind link to get a syringe of mer-blood ready for Jean.

Breaking our spell, we got off the floor and I noticed the war died down considerably. There were a few vampires left, most running out the doors as wolves chased after them while the others faced their demise through the cure they sought.

Among the bodies in the room, there were a few werewolves from our pack, squeezing my heart as I reached for a syringe. I began feeling survivor's guilt as touched my healed shoulder where a bullet sized cavity just sat.

When I turned back to head of the coven, Aiden had shifted into his wolf while he and Kai raced towards Jean, knocking the gun out of his hand and pulling him away from Anvi.

I passed the syringe to Jenny before she went to her mate, understanding and gratefulness returned through a nod as she dropped her own gun and moved towards Jean.

Before Jenny could deliver the final blow, Aiden took his time in ripping the vampire apart, limb from limb. Allowing him to re-heal before doing it again while Kai helped subdue him. Getting his divine revenge on the cause of his brother's and sister-in-law's deaths among countless merfolk and pack members. Finding peace for his niece, himself and his family who stood with him today.

As Aiden ripped the vampire apart one last time, he grabbed the head of the still-living man and held him up for Jenny as she stuck the needle into him.

In seconds, the once powerful blood sucker who lived beyond his time turned into a gray haired human before he crumpled into dust, returning to nothing.

It was finally over.

Jenny was finally able to go to her mate and hold her in her arms for the first time in five years. Anvi appeared timid and mentally far-away from the moment, but she recognized her mate. Allowing her to wrap her in her arms and whisper in her ear as sobs echoed through the room from Jenny. The first time I've seen her cry.

Matt and Jenny helped Anvi out of her prison as the rest of us began moving the few casualties from our pack so that they can receive a proper burial.

As the last of our pack exit the doors of the resort and the storm finally blew away with only a drizzle left behind, Aiden set the place on fire, ensuring all the vampires were permanently eradicated.

The merfolk were now free.

CHAPTER 40

The day after our fight was filled with mournful goodbyes to the ones we lost and tearful hellos to those who returned.

Once the storm had subsided, the glorious glistening sunrise met us as we made our way back to the castle. The sky painted a beautiful welcome home backdrop as the castle dazzled in all its glory, as if the rain washed away the years it remained hidden on the coast. It was a welcome sight after the last few hours, but as Alpha and Luna, Aiden and I had much more to do before we could breathe a sigh of relief.

Beta Rick and Calypso was our first phone call made as we announced our winnings. Tourmaline, being only a mere five years old, finally broke out in tears as she was handed the phone and was comforted by her Uncle Aiden. Reassuring her that her only blood-relative was safe.

While we awaited their return to the pack territory along with the other wolves and mermaids who went into hiding, we faced the number of deaths from our side. Almost fifty wolves had met their fates in that derelict ballroom by the cold hands of our enemies.

Forgoing sleep, my mate and I entwined our fingers in a knuckle-white grip as we went from pack member to pack member to offer our gratitude, condolences, sorrows and comfort. Mourning alongside them as they prepared the burials for their loved ones. Everyone's emotions had taken the brunt force of the night as the castle settled in a sombre silence for the entirety the day.

We hadn't a moment to properly discuss what happened back in that resort.

As night approached, Aiden and I found ourselves outside. Not in the protected courtyard, but rather outside the gates of the castle as we awaited everyone's arrival. An area that just yesterday we hadn't dared to venture out to under the darkness of the night sky.

Looking up at the moon, I smiled for the first time that day, "I miss howling at the moon."

"Whatever my Luna wants, she will get," Aiden wrapped an arm around my shoulder and pulled me closer into his side. "I'm sorry I brought you here only to lock you inside a tower, but we're free now. We can run along the coast in the night, sneak into the lighthouse when you're feeling mischievous. You just have to say the word, Cupcake."

"Mmm... that sounds like the perfect life," I leaned my weight into him, welcoming the warmth of his body against the chill of the night air. "But, just to be clear, I never blamed you for this and you have nothing to be sorry for. I'm actually glade that you found me when you did, or else I imagine our lives would be a lot different that it is now. Me still sick, or dead, and you still trying to protect your pack. It all turned out for the best, didn't it?"

"As if the Moon Goddess herself planned it," He nodded. "A wolf with a heart disease just so ends up in a pack with mermaids who have healing blood. I honestly couldn't have written that myself."

I really looked up at the moon this time, squinting at the silver planet as if I could see the ancient Goddess herself. Was she truly real? Connecting Aiden and I with a thread of fate that surpassed the usual mate bond. Placing us together to save the other.

Pulling me out of my reverie, I heard the crunching of tires before I saw the line of vehicles making their way to us.

The first car barely came to a stop before the door pushed open and Calypso was helping Tourmaline out of the car.

"Dad!" Tourmaline yelled, racing towards us.

Aiden pulled me along with him as we met Tourm in the middle, bending to scoop her up in his arms and holding her tightly to his chest. As if they both shared the same thought, they turned their heads towards me as they each reached a hand out to pull me into their hug.

Tourmaline's glistening eyes, filled with excitement and merriment, had my heart bursting with emotions, causing tears of joy to run down my cheeks as I hugged them both. My little family.

My shoulders finally relaxed in relief as I had my world in my arms, safe from harm and together again.

Over the next few days, the castle began bustling back to life after the funerals were held and the mermaids returned, freely going back to the sea.

A week after our victory, we held a vigil on the beach as the sun began to set over the horizon. We lit candles for all who have been lost from vampire attacks. From Tourmaline's parents to countless mermaids and wolves who all fought to protect each other. A found family filled with differences but connected by a shared sense of preservation and will for life.

Today also marked the day the mermaids would be taking their leave from the castle walls, finally returning to the ocean they once called home. Some were heading towards the Mélusine for guidance, others would take up post in foreign waters to protect the ocean while a few were staying back to help their little Queen as she grows up to be their leader.

A now familiar green-haired mermaid, who I - since recent event - called a friend, approached with her mate by her side, eyes still cautious and wild.

Anvi had a long way to go in recovering from her years in captivity under the torture of the blood-suckers. Too frequently, the castle was awoken by her screams that were a result of her nightmare plagued sleeps, causing her to be an insomniac unable to shut her eyes.

"I think it's time we take our leave," Jenny said as she stopped before me, Anvi wondering over to the other mermaids.

"How is she?" I asked.

"Not good," Her voice cracked as she answered. "I never imagined death would be a better alternative, but after what she's been through... I question if my decision in begging the vampires to keep her alive was the right choice."

I gathered the mermaid's hands in my own, "She's your mate Jenny, never doubt your choices on that. You once asked me what I would choose, remember? And I would have done the same thing because no matter what, they kept her alive for a reason. I don't think there was any changing that."

Unshed tears threatened to spill over as she nodded, "Thank you, Tate, for helping me. For helping us. I don't think I could ever express how sorry I am for what I did."

"You saved me, in more ways than one," I reminded her, hinting at the silver bullet accident. Without Jenny's merfolk blood in my veins, I would be dead a long time ago. "We're even."

"We are," Aiden agreed as he stepped up from behind me. "You and Anvi are welcome back in the castle at any time."

"Thank you, I really mean it. Right now, though, I think the sea is best for Anvi's recovery. I also heard the Mélusine may have some ancient remedies for our kind, which may help speed up her healing."

"Then, when you're ready, we'll be happy to have you both back. Whether it's just a visit or to stay with your Queen, there is always a place in the pack for both of you. I mean it," I promised, pulling her into a hug.

Not long after, the mermaids all lined up on the coast, their Queen Tourmaline before them as she took her first steps in the ocean since the night of the fight.

I could feel Aiden tense up next to me as she approached the vast expanse of water, seeing her go in alone a very unfamiliar sight to him. Rubbing his back, I tried to comfort him as his niece took her steps towards the ocean.

And, like a scene out of a Disney movie, the waves almost shimmers to life as she enters. The waves slowly lapping at her feet while the sun rays danced across the glistening surface. The ocean was welcoming back their Queen.

One by one, the mermaids followed, taking their leave as Aiden ensured them that they were all welcome back at any time.

"I can't believe she's growing up so quickly," Aiden whispered to me as Tourmaline splashed around in her mermaid form. Sea-creatures were quick to find her, swimming around as if they were ready to play.

"We still have her for a few years," I grinned as she waved at me. "And we have the whole world to explore with her now."

"You are right, but when she turns eighteen, I'm afraid I'll have to let her go off to do her duty in the sea below."

"Then let's make the most out of the time we have her for."

Aiden responded with a watery smile before he quickly grabbed me at the waist and ran towards the ocean.

It was only later than night, long after everyone retired back into castle, did Aiden and I finally broach the subject of my 'super' healing.

We sat snuggled on a blanket in the sand, a bonfire blazing away as the waves quietly ebbed and flowed at the shore.

"About what happened that day in the resort, with the silver bullet-" I started.

"Will be kept between us," Aiden made no room for argument. "The only ones who witnessed what happened was you, Jenny, Kai, Matt and myself. I already consulted the others about it and they swore secrecy. No one else would know about it."

I nodded, "If the world found out about a silver bullet cure, history would just repeat itself. Instead of the vampires, the werewolves and the rogues would go after the merfolk to exploit them for their blood. It would be a complete massacre if a pack becomes invincible."

"History we do not want to relive," Aiden agreed.

"Then let this be the last time we ever speak of it," I stated.

Aiden and I promised each other, holding the other tighter as we sat in the comfort that this knowledge that held power was in safe hands.

"Although, I would say that after you've put me through hell and back - a few times - I feel as if I don't need to worry about you getting hurt anymore," Aiden chuckled.

"Oh, I have a feeling you're still going to worry," I teased.

With a heavy sigh, he pulled me in with a kiss on my forehead, "I will, for as long as we both shall live."

EPILOGUE

2 0 Years Later

"Mom? Where's the chocolate?" Tourmaline called to me from the pantry.

I popped my head through the doorway, unable to wipe the huge grin on my face, "top-shelf, far left." Hearing Tourmaline call me 'mom' never gets old. Not even when she's been calling me by that title since she was eight, a whole seventeen years ago.

Going back to the kitchen counter, I began measuring out the ingredients to Aiden's famous chocolate cake recipe. He was usually the one baking this cake, since neither Tourmaline nor I could reach his standard. However, it was my mate's birthday and Tourm has since started the tradition of making her dad's cake for him.

At first we nearly killed him on his birthday with how god awful the cake tasted, but I can safely say with nearly twenty years of practice, we've nailed it... mostly. Honestly, I think Tourm enjoys spending this time with just me. We usually gossip about the mermaid world and I fill her in on all things in the pack life.

Tourmaline turned into a better adult than Aiden and I could ever hope for. At sixteen, we discovered that she inherited the wolf gene from her father as strongly as the mermaid gene from her mother. When she shifted, her wolf was large and coated with a pink shade of fur which matched the colour of her hair perfectly. Strong alpha blood ran in her veins as she easily commanded attention. At eighteen she began spending more time out at sea. Something Aiden was particularly unfound of given the dangers that once lurked in those waters.

At first she hardly returned to us, helping her fellow merfolk reclaim the ocean and saving the coral reefs. Queen Tourmaline quickly assisted in rebuilding their colony as she made peace with the sirens and brought the Mélusine back to the ocean, uniting the races and expanding their population to take care of the ocean together.

She was an exemplary leader and Aiden already informed her that, when she's ready and if she's willing to accept, the Alpha title was hers. While she had the position of mermaid Queen to deal with, we had a feeling she was still up for the challenge in reuniting the two groups. This was also driven by the surprising number of mate bonds forming between mermaids and werewolves, taking all of us by surprise yet signaled the new era of leaders.

Now at twenty-five, I gazed at Tourmaline as if she were my own. Just like the two kids which Aiden and I welcomed over the years. Gregory, our only boy who was named after Aiden's dad, was fourteen while our youngest girl, Addy, was eight. Tourmaline was eleven when Gregory was born, and she were happy to see her excitement in becoming a big sister and expanding our family.

When she returned from the pantry, armed with a myriad of chocolate ingredients, I laughed at her silly expression as began whisking away. Finally sliding the cakes into the over, I turned to her, "Have you thought about taking over the pack yet?"

Her snapped to me quickly, eyes wide, "Did you just read my thoughts?"

"No," I said wrapping an arm around her shoulder. "But, does that mean you've been thinking about it?"

"I have... but I don't know if I'm ready," She chewed on her lips, a habit she had when she was nervous.

"And why do you think you're not ready?"

"The most obvious reason."

"Which is?" I asked, truly confused.

Turning to me, I saw a sadness in her eyes I hadn't noticed before.

"I don't have a mate. I'm twenty-five and neither the merfolk nor werewolves have my soulmate. Dad found you when things were so difficult back then and because of that the pack became strong enough to fight," Dragging her hand through her pink locks, she sighed. "I just... I don't know if I'm strong enough or smart enough to handle something like that alone."

"Ahh, but you forget that you're not alone," I stated simply. "You have your dad, me, your siblings. Sweetheart, you have so much more on your side than we did back then with the merfolk, sirens and Mélusine. If Aiden didn't think you had it in you, then he wouldn't have offered."

"You think so?"

"Trust me, I've spent an insane amount of time with the man. I know exactly what he was thinking when he chose you as his successor."

I felt her shoulders sag under my arm, "As happy as I am about that, I still... Mom, I'm scared I don't find my mate, but I'm also scared that I do. What if I can't protect my people alone? Or worst yet, what if we end up like my parents?"

Squeezing her in my arms, I comforted her, "You have so much time. So much to do and see. I promise when you find your match, it will come at the perfect time. And you just have to trust me when I say Aiden and I will never allow anything to happen to you."

I couldn't help but feel a bit teary-eyed at Tourmaline's confession. All these years after and the weight of her parents' death still terrorize her like a ghost clung to her back.

"Ohhh, I smell cake," The voice of my son, Gregory, came as he walked into the kitchen rubbing his palms together. "Share a slice?"

"Gregory, out!" Tourm quickly recovered as she shooed her brother out of the kitchen, knowing that he was as bad as Aiden when it came to chocolate cake. He'd probably steal a piece from the oven if it wasn't so hot and under-baked.

I couldn't help the smile on my face as she chased him around the kitchen island. Their little sister, Addy found us in the kitchen as she walked around with a mermaid doll which was created in Tourmaline's image. Addy adored her sister and wished she was able to be a mermaid just like her.

After the kids shenanigans almost resulted with the cake on the floor, we quickly ushered everyone into the large dinning room, Aiden acting surprise by our gesture of cake and balloons.

He gave Tourm a hug, having not seen her since a month ago when she visited.

I looked around the room then, as everyone sand happy birthday for their Alpha, noticing how so much time has passed yet it felt like very little.

Calypso and Rick had kids of their own now. Two boys, a blessing to them after Calypso's infertility journey. On the other hand, Kai and Matt adopted three kids, one mermaid and two wolves. Dr. Nazra also found her mate, but skipped the kids part. Even Jenny and Anvi was here to celebrate, paying us visits at least twice yearly.

Jenny and I have grown close over the years, understanding each other better as we aged. Her mate, Anvi, was also doing much better, but never the same as before. The trauma she experienced left deep scars, causing her to avoid speaking, physical contact and looking into anyone's eyes.

Now in our forties, Aiden and I were able to build the pack into something we were proud of. A home filled with love and family, protected from all evils.

The vampires were long gone. Never to be seen around our castle again, despite the rumors that a few still lurked in this world. Despite that possibility, they never showed up near our territory, which I believed had more to do with their new found fear of merfolk blood.

Later that evening, while the kids played in the beach, the mermaids summoning dolphins and turtles for Addy while Kai taught Gregory how to surf, I turned to Aiden.

"How do you see our future from here?"

He smiled easily, crows feet cornering his eyes, "Maybe another kid... and some much need rest when Tourmaline takes over."

"Tourmaline's taking over?" I asked surprised.

"She told me before we came down to the beach," He brushed my hair back from where the wind was blowing it into my face. "Said that you helped her make up her mind."

I shook my head, "I didn't do much."

"Doesn't matter," He said kissing me. "You're the best mom to them, so they value whatever input you have."

Hearing that warmed my heart, but I quickly broke out of the spell when I fully processed all that Aiden said.

"Did you just say another kid? Because I swear to the Moon Goddess, Aiden, I am not-"

Before I could finish that thought, my phone buzzed on the blanket.

The familiar name of my niece popping onto the screen.

"Evy! How are you, my munchkin?" I answered, happy to hear from my brother, Thane's, daughter.

"Aunt Tate? I need your help..." Everette stated.

www.ingramcontent.com/pod-product-compliance
Lightning Source LLC
Chambersburg PA
CBHW071423190726

48292CB00001B/89